DESCENT

S.M. WRIGHT

ISBN: 978-1-7341554-3-3 (E-book)
ISBN: 978-1-7341554-2-6 (Paperback)

This is a work of fiction. Names, characters, businesses, places, events, and incidents are either the products of the author's imagination or used in a fictitious manner. Any resemblance to actual persons, living or dead, or actual events is purely coincidental.

Cover illustration and design by Maria Freed, aka MissChibiArtist.

S.M. Wright/Far-Flung Press
smwrightauthor.com

To my Dad,
The grand weaver of tall tales.
You taught me to appreciate a good story.
And if it's not so great, to embellish the details.
I'm not as gullible,
thanks to you!

CAST OF CHARACTERS

Akakios Sarris [Ak-Ak-ee-os | saer-rihs]: The Oneiroi captain of the *Boreas*, he seeks to unite with his nephew, Sotiris, the son of his deceased brother, **Amyntas [ah-MEN-tas]**, and sister-in-law, **Kallistrate [kal-eh-STRA-tah]**.

Aleksandr Lomonosov [ah-lehk-SAHN-dər | luh-muh-naw-suhf]: A reclusive Mramorian scientist, he might be Sotiris's best hope for a long-term normal life.

Ambrosios Carras [am-BRO-ios | cah-RAS]: The Oneiroi first lieutenant of the *Boreas*, he serves as its pilot and lead interrogator. He is Chrysanthos's spouse.

Anaïs Cassius [A-NA-EES | KAS-see-oos]: Katya's adoptive sister, she owns a fashion brand on her native Trides. She and Katya are close.

Bodil [BOH-deel]: One of Hedda Strom's subordinates, she is completely loyal to Plasovern, even enrolling in a Magistrate military academy to gather intelligence for the terrorist organization.

Charis Velis [CARE-iss | Vel-is]: The Oneiroi commander of the *Boreas*, she is the second command after Akakios, prized for her levelheaded nature.

Chrysanthos Carras [Chreh-san-thos | cah-RAS]: The mechanic of the Oneiroi vessel *Boreas*, he holds the rank of master chief petty officer. He is Ambrosios's spouse.

Elpis Moros [el-PEACE | m-OR-os]: The medical officer on the Oneiroi vessel *Boreas*; she holds the rank of lieutenant commander.

Faustus Cassius [FOWS-toos | KAS-see-oos]: Katya's adoptive father, who works as an archeologist. He descends from a prominent Magistrate family, with his brother **Pontius [PON-tee-oos]**, holding a mystery position within its government.

Garbi [GAR-bee]: A human lab assistant employed by Usha, Garbi has been crucial to the success of Plasovern's drug to treat Sotiris's defect.

Hedda Strom [HEHD-dah | STRUM]: A woman of legend and myth, she is one of the several heads of Plasovern, known for her brutality in the struggle for planet sovereignty.

Isla [EYE-la]: A Csek lab technician employed by Usha, Isla has been crucial to the success of Plasovern's drug to treat Sotiris's defect.

Izem [ee-ZUM]: The opposite side of the coin to Strom in Plasovern, he is a well-respected terrorist leader from Tizzet. His methods are more controlled compared to Strom's.

Jekaterina Mikhailovna Menshikova [Jeka-te-rina | Mikha-ilov-na | Men-shiko-va]: A former Moscanov princess before the empire collapsed, her family's expulsion of her saved her from the purge. She now works closely with Zakhar Kozlov.

Kahina [Kahi-na]: Kahina works closely under Izem, who is like a father figure to her. She credits him with saving her life.

Katya Cassius [kAH-tih-uh | KAS-see-oos]: A Mramorian orphan, she has served in the Magistrate's military since she was eighteen. Now, she tries to keep her children safe in a galaxy coming undone.

Krasimir [kreh-Seh-mir]: A subordinate under Strom, he maintains an icy exterior that hides a brutal storm underneath.

Kyrillos Rallis [kyril-los | r-ah-l-ihs]: The second lieutenant on the *Boreas*, he oversees communications.

Matfey Sobol [mut-FAY | So-bəl]: A Mramorian pirate, known for serving under General Volkov during the war, he now serves as a prominent figure in a movement to liberate Mramor.

Militsa Belova [mIH-lih-tsah | BEE-Luv-ah]: A protégé of Zakhar Kozlov's, she is employed at a scientific institute on Mramor.

Mina [MEE-nə]: A seventeen-year-old Reznic girl, she came under Katya's care when she was stationed on the planet. Over months with Plasovern, their relationship has grown strained.

Pelagia [peh-LA-gya] and Pelagius Tocci [peh-LA-geoos | to-Chee]: Fraternal Oneiroi twins, they serve as ensigns on the *Boreas*; they are the youngest crew members.

Rein [RAYN]: A Reznic native and former crew member of Katya's *The Maelstrom*, he is deceased after the events of *Heritage Lost*.

Sotiris Sarris [saw-tEE-rees | saer-rihs]: An Oneiroi toddler, he was born with a genetic mutation that makes him a danger to himself and others. Following drug trials, a normal life seems within his reach.

Usha [oo-sha]: A Filitre, she is known for her drug empire. She also maintains a strong relationship with Plasovern and Hedda Strom.

Valens Ulpius [vey-luhnz | al-PI-oos]: Formerly a colonel, now deceased, who'd overseen day-to-day operations in a sector on Reznic. He and Katya were involved.

Yakov Kuznetsov [YA-kəf | kuz-NET-sov]: A violent Mramorian revolutionary, he might not be entirely removed from his past even as he works with others to liberate Mramor.

Zakhar Kozlov [zu-KHAR | kuz-LOF]: A lawyer from Katya's homeworld, Mramor, with a strong interest in planet sovereignty. Aleksandr Lomonosov employs him.

Zhihao Cassius [CHEE-Khow | KAS-see-oos]: Katya's adoptive sister, she has a close relationship with their Uncle Pontius, who holds a secretive position in Magistrate government.

Zinon [zin-on]: An Oneiroi teenager born with the defect; the crew of the *Boreas* liberated him from a Jar'rask ship in *Heritage Lost*. He continues to struggle with his genetic mutation, and his time with the Jar'rasks has made him volatile.

CHAPTER ONE

Accusations, so clear in small, almost iris-less milky blue eyes, bore into Katya through the synth glass. Even removed from the medical procedures on the glass's other side, her skin itched. It wasn't her body plastered with devices to monitor every bodily function. But that made it worse. Every time.

A steady blip shot across one monitor, a perfect mirror of Sotiris's heartbeat. His limbs thrummed with energy, legs kicking back and forth over the examination table's ledge. His arms lifted him an inch or two off the table before settling again, a feat impossible only three months ago. A knot formed in Katya's throat. Strom had promised normalcy, but it almost seemed she—no, Usha—had delivered a miracle. Though not without a cost.

While the body proved an incredible mechanism, capable of great resiliency, even when poked, prodded, and introduced to foreign substances, it had its limits. Katya's fingernails curled into her palms. And Sotiris's had reached its. Angry red splotches and peeling skin, barely healed, glared at her. The damage stretched from his right shoulder, down his back, and disappeared beneath his underwear. She knew it continued, had caused fits at bedtime, made sitting difficult, particularly the stretch along his legs.

As the drugs warred with the mutation, they'd struck unintended systems. His fragile Oneiroi skin often became collateral damage. Nothing had been worse than the seizure invoked by the second drug configuration.

Rubbing the back of her neck, Katya swallowed against a knot. The seizure remained seared in her mind. In that moment, she'd been inept, powerless. She'd failed her role as guardian. Even though she'd been rendered unconscious by the mutation, she refused to allow it to assuage her guilt.

On cue, Sotiris slipped from the table, his toddler-size patience done. Two sessions of being poked and prodded in one day—this last running close to two hours—was more than most adults could handle.

His yelp penetrated the glass as one so-called doctor—Garbi—caught his arm, further bruising skin. Sotiris didn't stop, putting his weight into his desired escape. The scene twisted Katya's heart. She should be in the lab, but—

"This one's working much better," Usha's gravelly voice intoned next to her. The pale Filitre took a drag from her electric pipe and exhaled, its earthy, cinnamon-laced blend clashing against the stringent antiseptic that consumed the clinic.

The drug manufacturer had graced Jomsborg, the station Strom and her terrorist cell called their temporary home, about two months after Katya, Mina, and Sotiris had arrived. Bedecked in her immaculate finery, she carried not a trace of Esh's conflict. She'd commandeered Sotiris's treatment plan, though Katya had long assumed she had been orchestrating it from afar all along. An expert in drugs and chemicals, it made sense. Katya had known there was some tether between her and Plasovern. Given Strom's warm welcome, she decided it ran deep.

"No allergic reaction," Usha continued, with no intonation. "He's remained awake and alert all day without heart palpitations or seizures. And now it's been in his system for more than forty-eight hours. He should ease naturally into sleep." She pressed her index finger against her chin. "It should require fewer doses."

The reddish light in the observation area, perfect for Usha and Sotiris, brought a glimmer to the cascading metallic fabric of her sleeveless top, a purple to match her stained lips. She almost looked as reptilian as her arm wrap: two snakes, with gleaming, jeweled eyes, intertwined in an elaborate dance, or one in the process of devouring the other. The Filitre exhaled, smoke twisting in the light.

Standing next to Usha, Strom's lips curled. "The trial's progressing marvelously. As always"—she leaned into Usha's space—"you're most thorough."

Despite the words' playfulness, the recipient's only response was to flip a strand of white-silverish hair over her shoulder. Still, Katya swore she spotted the faint outline of a smile.

Yes, Katya belonged on the other side of the glass with Sotiris, providing comfort, but where she stood now, beside these titans, was essential. As much as Strom frustrated her, enjoyed finding and poking every button, Katya needed to be involved in the conversations between her and Usha ... if only to glean what information she could and try to be Sotiris's advocate.

Clearing her throat, Katya asked, "Can this formula be turned into an oral drug?"

Despite the glass and poor lighting, the previous injection sites contrasted with Sotiris's pale skin. Garbi and the Csek technician, Isla, had returned him to the table and tinkered with the monitors surrounding him.

Katya's frown grew more pronounced. "It should be prioritized."

Usha waved her hand, and a Csek attendant, who'd been lurking in the shadows, stepped forward and took her pipe.

"It's a process, Ms. Cassius." A slow blink. "I've dabbled in many formulas for various purposes—medicines, pleasure inducers, ritual components, and so on—over much of my life. You may not believe it, but my efforts span eight decades. If I've learned anything, it is patience. If we get hasty, the consequence can be … disastrous." She toyed with her wrap. "I believe you recall what happened when my disciples failed to heed that lesson."

The image stirred again, Sotiris convulsing on the table, drool escaping his mouth. Katya's mouth dried. But she couldn't hold it against either Garbi or Isla, who'd been under duress. The defect had uncoiled and threatened to strangle the station. The incident, as everyone labeled, had dictated the erosion of safety measures.

"Once the formula's fully tested, the method of administration will follow," Usha said, reclaiming her pipe as though it were an appendage.

Katya shifted her weight, once again left to take Usha at her word. She could work all manner of codes and sort out the bowels of most smaller vessels, but she knew nothing about medicine. So she tried to narrow that knowledge gap. She read basic humanoid medical books and articles in the downtimes between sessions at the clinic, but that only got her so far, especially with Sotiris's Oneiroi physiology. So she listened to everything: the doctors' comments, often too heavy in medical verbiage, and the moments where Usha and Strom conversed in the outer room.

She touched the smooth glass despite herself. She'd brought him here. That never left her mind. She had to work harder to know what they were doing to him.

"It's an excellent step," Strom drawled. "Within five months, we've made incredible progress. It's almost unbelievable that we've potentially found a winning combination. Anywhere else, it would have taken years."

Tingles spread up Katya's arms. "I suppose we should be grateful Sotiris is receiving so much of your attention."

Beaming, Strom stepped around Usha to invade Katya's space. She wore a floral perfume with woody undertones and a scarlet blouse that fit her frame tightly. As was her custom, she'd left the first three buttons undone. "I've been nothing but to the point with you. I know that's how you like it." She rested a hand on her hip. "There's too much to be gained by providing his people with a treatment. It only makes sense for us to perfect this drug quickly and safely." She faced the window. "That boy's safety is our priority. We can't approach his people without him, can we?"

Inside, Sotiris yanked off one device and tossed it across the room before lurching to get off the table. Garbi halted his momentum, catching him with one arm in a partial hug. Her other prevented him from plucking off more devices.

"And it looks like we're done here." Strom chuckled.

Usha sighed, a long stream of smoke cascading over her curled lips. "So it would seem."

Katya brushed by the two women and pawed open the door, which slid into the wall to admit her. Behind her, Strom and Usha struck up a conversation, something about the components, corsaline ... darme—

Sotiris, who'd slipped from the table, flung himself at her, his little fingers pinching skin when he tried to ascend her leg like a kitten.

"Go?" He peered at her with his owlish eyes. Then another tug on her pant leg and the flesh beneath. "Go."

She cupped his chin with one hand. "One minute."

He blinked, and when she didn't move to take him through the door, it morphed into a scowl. She ruffled his hair with her free hand, a momentary distraction.

Garbi approached them. "Please hold still a little longer, and we'll get everything off." Then, directly addressing Katya, she said, "We'll need to leave the neural device on for the night. I know he's eager to get them all off, but this one will give us a better idea of how the corsaline's affecting his neural patterns."

Isla, an opal-hued Csek, whom Katya had long labeled a drug manufacturer, rattled vials about on a roller cart. Her four hands worked in tandem as she sorted and examined the contents of each one. She had yet to speak during their encounters, delegating interactions to Garbi. Katya would love to know what she said when they were absent.

Garbi peeled away the devices from Sotiris's arms and legs, which bore patches of paler skin and lingering splotches of an adhesive. As she worked, the woman gabbed about little, innocuous things: special delicacies freshly arrived from the Medzeci Empire, favorite spots on the station to view space, and mostly about her pet coocerroo, a bright orange bird. Sotiris understood none of it except for tone, and hers landed in the spectrum of animated. It distracted her patient, even as, she plied Katya with questions about his eating habits, activity levels, all leading to the ultimate one.

"Have you felt him prying since the treatments began?" Garbi tapped against her own temple.

Katya straightened, having been lulled by her tales about her pet. "No ..." She brushed Sotiris's black bangs from his face. "I've felt nothing." Not since the switch in formulas during the second month following the incident.

Sotiris pinched her calf, eliciting a hiss. And perhaps that fueled his growing frustration. Stripped of his people's manner of communication, he wielded grunts, screams, and other vocal expressions to express his needs and desires. Gestures filled in the gaps somewhat, but that barrier in communication hadn't been fully bridged. He did grasp a few words here and there, primarily ones he deemed most beneficial: "no," "yes," and "go."

Garbi eyed her, almost as if trying to see through her skull. "Given the extent of the mutation, it's probably for the best he's not exercising all of his abilities." She pulled the last device from his back with care not to irritate already damaged skin. "It's a shame we don't even fully know how a healthy Oneiroi operates, let alone one with the mutation. It'll be hard to determine which drug components are having the greatest impact, but the corsaline seems most promising."

"Trial and error." Katya squeezed Sotiris's hand, noting the absence of whatever darme was. Was that even its full name? She hated it, wished there were other avenues, even if it would be the same story anywhere else, except maybe on Demos Oneiroi or Meracus Domus. The teenager from the Jar'rask vessel filtered to the forefront of her mind. She shivered with the phantom touch of blood trickling from her nose.

"Unfortunately, it's a part of the process, especially given so many unknowns." Garbi nudged the neural device on Sotiris's forehead to test its hold. "We'll examine the data tomorrow and see if he's sleeping properly. That'll tell us for sure if the corsaline is working. Please try to keep it on."

"I'll try my best, but no guarantees." Sotiris tugged on her arm, putting all his weight into it as he leaned toward the door. Katya actually stumbled a bit when he did so. "If that's all, we'll take our leave."

"Bring him by again tomorrow at nine, and we will administer another dose." She smiled, one belonging to a healer, and gave Sotiris a little wave. "We have a good feeling about this formula."

"Thank you," Katya said before allowing Sotiris to drag her from the room.

Strom and Usha still conversed in the observation room, their posture loose as they stood close together. Only now they spoke in an unfamiliar language, possibly Filitrish. Usha lowered her pipe upon breaking into a chuckle; a plume of smoke arched its way to the ceiling. The moment dispersed when Katya and Sotiris entered.

"I'll be here for the morning dose so we can talk." Strom smiled. "We really haven't had a chance to since you joined us, and I feel bad about leaving you hanging. I want to see how you're adjusting."

Katya stood straighter, her hand tightening around Sotiris's. The inevitable words she'd been expecting and dreading.

She shrugged and ignored the invitation. "It's an adjustment, to say the least. But one has to do what one has to."

A deep chuckle from Strom greeted her answer. "Ah, don't we all? I look forward to our little chat. For now, it appears you're in a bit of a hurry." The woman waved at Sotiris. "Have a good evening. Don't get up to anything … too naughty." Her grin only grew larger after Katya's lips dipped further.

"Usha." Katya inclined her head to the other woman.

The Filitre only exhaled more smoke, while her eyes — golden and akin to freshly stirred embers — stayed partially lidded.

Without interruption, Katya guided Sotiris to a table near the door. There she helped him change into his pants and a long-sleeved shirt, which protected his fragile skin from Jomsborg's artificial sun. The soft, light cotton-like fabric slid on to his body, though its collar caught the device on his head. He bristled and threatened to flop to the ground. Still, she worked the fabric until the shirt slipped into place. Batting his hands away from the device, Katya reached for his sunglasses but relinquished them so he could put them on himself. It'd become a new insistence of his. As he played with the frames, she blotted what skin remained exposed with a specialized sunscreen.

Behind them, Strom and Usha carried their conversation down the red-soaked hallway, eventually holing up behind a set of doors.

She had yet to enter the space beyond. She suspected it housed more equipment, labs, and, likely, Usha's quarters. Straightening Sotiris's shirt, she muttered, "There. All set."

With his hand in hers, they left the private medical wing and entered the exterior hallway, which was bathed in bright artificial light. Gurneys dotted the way, empty and waiting. Besides the gurneys, the hallway remained barren until they entered a triage station, where nurses and doctors shared charts and discussed supplies. The number of medical professionals had surprised Katya at first, but many had been displaced by wars and Magistrate occupation. Rather than stay, they'd chosen to make their home with Plasovern, at least until their homeworlds were returned. That mindset permeated the station. It, despite all its tech, security, and comforts, was only a temporary home.

A counter separated the medical professionals from Jomsborg's occupants. When Katya and Sotiris crossed that threshold, they found themselves among those waiting for medical care in the lobby. All of them came from Strom's native Varraganar System. They shared fair skin, light hair color, and dominant blue eyes. They had hardened eyes and callused hands, many likely self-described freedom fighters. Currently, there were more women with their young children—refugees who'd fled the three sister planets. Katya scanned them out of the corner of her eyes as she passed, noting how they pulled their children closer, away from Sotiris.

It'd been a surprise at first, the number of families. She had expected splinter cells dispersed across the galaxy, not a mini-society. But families existed no matter the cause. Why leave them on contested worlds?

Katya directed Sotiris across the space, her grip like steel. Their eyes set her on edge. Had they lost someone during the incident? Jomsborg, from a cursory glance, was a close-knit community. If not directly related, they probably knew the names and faces. Sotiris craned backward, enthralled by the other children. They, however, shied from him, hiding against their parents. She kept him moving forward, crossing the threshold into a common space filled with chatter.

A handful of the station's inhabitants lingered outside a commissary, collecting allotted supplies and trading tales, all of which were shared in the tongues of the Varraganar System. Across the way, a childcare center reverberated with laughter and high-pitched voices. Sotiris stumbled next to her while craning his head toward it. In another universe, he might have been able to join them, actually socializing with age peers. Without the defect, he might have been on Demos Oneiroi at this very moment, not hobbled by a language barrier or experimentation.

Sotiris lurched backward.

"I know, I know." She squeezed his hand. But that universe could never be a reality.

They retraced the same steps they'd taken for five months to a large doorway that led to a curved connector. The first month had been dedicated to surgeries, hers and Mina's, and recovery, racking up an incalculable debt. She didn't doubt for a moment that Strom wouldn't call for repayment. Weakened and in pain, she'd had no choice but to leave Sotiris in the care of Strom's people so research could begin. His pernicious abilities had necessitated it.

The air was slightly cooler in the connector, but it would still become too warm for the young Oneiroi. However, he rebuffed her attempts to carry him and instead guided her through the long connector. Based on a circular layout, Jomsborg amounted to a series of such connectors, pods, and expansive common areas, which formed the station's main body. This particular one connected two pod systems and one common area.

The number of Varraganar citizens walking past them could almost convince her they comprised the station's entire population, but that wasn't true. Other Plasovern loyalists had moved in as well—to Strom's domain, built with Medzeci Empire bones. Everything about the station, excluding its name, screamed Medzeci—its materials, the construction, and the language plastered around it. And it wasn't even the highest quality of bones. From what Katya had seen, the Medzeci had cobbled the station together using the excesses of the Fringe Campaigns, the conflict that had seen it and the Magistrate tear into each other over space.

She fell short as they came across the viewing area, a good length of extra-thick synth glass, curved to match the connector's contour. Medzeci stars. Her heart quickened. Her entire life, she'd hoped to never see these stars. For if she did, it would mean the treaty had failed. That war had rekindled. She could almost laugh at the surreal twist of fate.

The stars gleamed while mining skiffs came and went from the gas giant, which hid Jomsborg in its bosom. While in Medzeci space, it was within striking distance by the Magistrate. A targeted attack would eliminate one of the greatest threats to its hold on the Fringe, but it would also draw in Medzeci, breathing life back into a conflict that had actually strained the Magistrate and its immense resources.

"Ma! Ma! Ma!" a toddler shouted, jumping up and down on a bench. His fingers traced the stars, leaving smudges on the extra-thick synth glass. Katya winced when he banged against the glass with his fist, even knowing he couldn't break it.

A group of teenagers played with their electronic devices, projecting holograms, which they hit until the images cracked and dispelled. Sotiris dug his feet in and attempted to get a better look at the game. No one had noticed them yet, and Katya wanted to get out before they did.

"Come on," Katya said, tugging on Sotiris's arm.

A fine sweat glistened on his brow, and they hadn't reached the common area with its artificial sun. Garbi and Isla had determined the Oneiroi had inefficient sweat glands. The species' evolutionary history had never developed such glands in the same fashion as their human brethren. She brought Sotiris into her arms and carried on despite his grunts of protest.

She shifted him from her bum left shoulder, the window, and the shrine established on the corridor's far end. Faces peered at her from print photographs, building pressure in her chest. Four faces. All too young. They'd once graced the station, then slipped into space, never to be found. All because a toddler could not control an ability he'd been born with. There were plenty of observation points in Jomsborg, but its inhabitants had chosen this one. A rebuke, a message, a pointed reminder, not to Sotiris, who was too young to understand, but to her. She was the Magistrate woman. The one who had brought this great blessing and curse to them.

Her breaths came more freely after stepping through a giant arch to be met with blinding light and all its warmth. Katya inhaled deeply, lifting her face. An illusion, but a damn good one. Still, she longed for an actual sun. Months … it had been months since she'd felt any sun on her face. Images of her father and siblings emerged from dormancy. They were in the hilly countryside roaming through the tall grass, rolling down hills, chasing each other, undeterred by the thought of insects. The odds of her ever seeing them again—

"Go!"

Katya sighed but smiled despite herself. "Yes, go." Leave the faces so far behind.

His warm hand tugged at her cotton top, now stirred by the excess heat, which propagated the plants and trees that filled the spaces.

While he disliked the common spaces, the station's other occupants gathered there like ants to a mound. They sunbathed, jogged, played games, among other activities. A group gathered fruit and vegetables from a plot. From Katya's limited understanding, it was only one prong of Jomsborg's agricultural enterprise, which also relied on extensive hydroponics and aquaponics bays.

"Ha!" many voices shouted, unified.

Katya straightened when Sotiris's head hit her jaw. A man shouted again as his young charges fell into another pose, once again giving a unified vocal response to him. *Copre an*. A form of martial arts that had found disciples on and off its homeworld of Re'alle. After the conflict on the world, the Magistrate had rolled the form into the hand-to-hand combat instructions received by officers. The group before her were little more than children, yet they moved through the forms with ease, never faltering, even as they transitioned to the more intricate steps, which had taken her at least a year to master as a young woman.

Sotiris wiggled against her, flaring her old shoulder injury and forcing his way to the ground. Before she could grab his hand, he darted along the pathway leading to the dormitory pod they called home. He gave a wide berth to the group of young martial artists, especially when their instructor fell into a cascade of short, clipped words. Once clear, Sotiris returned to his path, never once stopping.

"Sotiris!"

He barreled on. Months ago, she had believed he would never walk. Now, she marveled at how quickly muscles could form with proper nourishment, regular sleep patterns, and therapy. Though she preferred him being a little slower. Katya groaned as he raced up the ramp to the lifts.

"Sotir—" He gave no heed to her voice.

She closed the gap between them and caught his shirt's collar, halting his momentum. "You don't take off like that!"

He blinked at her tone shift, but then his frown morphed into a smile.

Little imp.

She hefted him back into her arms and entered one lift, allowing it to rocket them through the station. The doors slid open to a mixed-purpose common space. There was some greenery, but unlike the area they'd left, very little recreation occurred here. It had a small café space managed by a reptilian Dradorian, who had established the business at Plasovern's invitation.

Beyond the café and its two levels of seating, there were little enclaves filled with small tables and benches. Screens canvassed the walls. Some contained information for operations in Medeza, the only recognized language of the Medzeci Empire, though others had existed at one time. She recognized it by its flourishes. A few characters still held meaning from language classes required of officers. From those remnants and the information's distribution, she determined it relayed arrival and departure times. The destinations shared the same characters. Likely redacted.

She paused in front of one screen, which was broadcasting a Medzeci news feed. She didn't understand a word coming out of the talking heads' mouths as they bantered back and forth, with different infographics appearing and disappearing from the screen. The show cut to a hiccup of black before the Medzeci flag spilled across the screen, followed by the imperial anthem blaring. A new presenter garbed in deep purple robes sat behind a desk. The light glinted off her gem-encrusted gold headband and golden horns, twisted into sharp points. Katya couldn't tell if the horns were real or not. There'd been rumors that the dominant Luzepan species forced others in their domain to don horns, but with all stories traded at the heated conflict's height, she questioned their authenticity.

The woman spoke at a fevered pace, her voice fluctuating at extremes. Within a nearby secondary screen, an impressive hover-coach, decked out in jewels, passed through floral-lined streets. The camera zoomed in to its interior and the horned forms of two Luzepans.

The imperial family. When the vehicle stopped next to an expansive palace with gold embellishments and intricate architectural sculptures, the occupants stepped out. Their robes flowed around them in all their grandeur, weighed down with gems. Katya wondered how they could even move while wearing them.

The entire display, including the soldiers that lined their path, bespoke power. It'd been a matter of propaganda during the Fringe Campaign: Our leaders do not hide. A dig at the magistrates, who clung to shadows, hidden from the general populace and even high-ranking politicians. Speakers handled all public affairs. This approach had saved the Magistrate from infighting, which had festered throughout its incarnations.

The imperial Luzepans disappeared into their opulent palace, and Katya resumed walking with Sotiris in front of the other screens, her ears perking when one spoke in Magistrate. A commerce report from the Fringe. Plasovern had set most screens to the Medzeci space; however, a pair of screens relayed news from two independent systems: Morodon and Perspheene.

Her head pounding, Katya glanced away from the bleeding colors of the screens and faced the café. Her eyes landed on bubblegum pink and traces of teal. Mina. The girl lounged on furniture just outside the café. With her were four other teens, three boys and a girl, all with wildly colored hair. They were in line with Mina's age, though one boy was likely in his early twenties. They were all from the Varraganar System. Strom's people.

Her chest tightened as Mina laughed, a full gut-buster. The others joined her. As they did, one of the younger boys clambered on to a chair and gestured enthusiastically while regaling his friends with some tale.

Mina had never had much of an opportunity to socialize with her own age group. Sure, there'd been the base's small school on Reznic, but the teen had never developed lasting friendships. On *The Maelstrom*, all opportunities dwindled to nil. Katya shifted Sotiris to her other hip. She should be happy. Mina had been a ghost of herself that first month, after the Jar'rasks, the surgery. Yet all Katya felt was trepidation.

Katya changed course, heading over to Mina and the others. She didn't know these friends well. They'd appeared thirteen weeks into their stay, just after Mina's seventeenth birthday, and grafted themselves into the teen's life. She'd gone from never leaving their designated apartment to disappearing for long swathes of time. Mina and the group had clicked like lost, disenchanted teens often did when stuck on a station. When she was in the apartment, she wore new styles of clothing that exposed more skin and had spouted innocuous Plasovern propaganda.

Katya's fingers curled against Sotiris, bringing him closer while resisting the urge to retreat.

The teens straightened upon her approach. Mina shifted closer to one of the younger boys, likely eighteen or nineteen, their hands almost touching. Ah, there was something there. Katya could understand. He—Dag, if she recalled correctly—was handsome and muscular, his tight shirt revealing his abs' every curve beneath. He'd dyed his hair a platinum hue; when he'd first been introduced, it had been an electric blue. He carried himself with an air of surety lined with mystery. Yes, there was plenty to be infatuated with. No wonder the girl had so quickly embraced Plasovern. Dag's well-callused hands, undoubtedly from hours spent handling firearms, caused her stomach to churn. These kids had callused hands, and it would only be a matter of time before …

"Katya!" Mina grinned. She waved her gloved left hand. She'd taken to wearing long gloves to conceal the off-colored skin tone of her right cybernetic limb. Despite advances in technology, such a simple thing as skin tone eluded the mechanics. "How's our little Elite?" She ruffled Sotiris's hair, earning a squeal that ended as a raspberry, flecks of spit hitting Katya's neck.

"Going strong," Katya replied. She noted the distance the Varraganarians gave him while avoiding eye contact. "So, what are you and your friends up to today?"

"Just hangin'."

"Should I expect you late again?"

Mina's current infatuation cleared his throat. "Don't worry. We won't be out too late. Just going to watch ships come in, maybe check out the latest shipments."

"Shipments?"

He shrugged his shoulders. "Food and stuff."

"Stay out of the workers' way." Katya turned, a frown threatening to form when Dag's hand rested on Mina's lower back. Three months. How fast was it going?

Instead of further comment, Katya buried the gripping dread and waved goodbye, departing for another ramp with Sotiris. It took them to a mezzanine.

She mentally begged the girl to stay out of Plasovern's affairs. She knew how peers could be. Then throw in a teen romance. Ships were always leaving Jomsborg to go to some Plasovern-fueled conflict. If she got on one …

Katya inhaled fully, holding it for several seconds before releasing it. She repeated the step two more times to combat the spiraling sensation blossoming in her mind that threw off her heartbeat. A direct confrontation wouldn't work, especially not in front of peers. Her father had shown her that in his parenting of Seneca. It only stoked rebellion and reckless behavior. But there was a conversation waiting to be had, caution to be sowed, but yet cowardice stalled it from happening.

Continuing to the lifts, she plugged in their quarter's level and sank against the metal back of the first one that opened. She held Sotiris close as it moved. Katya had never been one to avoid conflict. She ignored the voice, achingly similar to her father's, that protested. *"When dealing with emotions, dear daughter, you evade like a pro."* She knocked the back of her head against the lift. That she couldn't deny.

The door to the lift opened, but she remained rooted too long for Sotiris, who dug his chin into her shoulder, his favored method of hurrying her. It aggravated her injury and always ensured her utmost attention.

"Yeah, yeah," she muttered and stepped out.

Despite the surgeries to repair the damage, it still flared occasionally. She'd been lucky. Its angle, the fact there'd been chest seal on the ship they'd commandeered, had likely saved her life. If it'd been an old-fashioned bullet hitting her, her cards would have fallen differently.

They reached the proper connector to their vacant dormitory pod. If they had neighbors, she'd yet to see them or hear them. She reached around Sotiris into her front pocket and freed the keycard, which she tapped against the reader. The door shushed open, a burst of cold air knocking against her face. Despite herself, she sucked in air.

Sotiris wiggled against her, using his weight to bring himself closer to the ground. As soon as Katya let him go, he darted into the cramped common room and dived into the small pile of toys they'd scrounged up: a few stuffed animals, a circular puzzle with knobs and swiveling parts, and a few worn spaceships with dents and chipped paint.

Katya left him to play while she increased the light intensity by a notch and pulled on a sweater she'd left draped over the small sofa. Then, in the small kitchenette, she set a kettle to boil and grabbed a can of instant kanabean, the Medzeci version of coffee. It may have also been created from a bean, but it was bitter, far bitterer than the blackest coffee she'd ever tasted. Over the island, she witnessed Sotiris reaching for a tube of molding clay.

After the kettle whistled, she stirred her cup before setting it on the island's top and lifting Sotiris and his clay, placing him in his seat. She slipped into the one next to him. Splitting the clay into two balls, she gave him one and kept the other. Sotiris set into his clump, a smile plastered to his face. He banged his fist into the ball, flattening it before pulling pieces off.

She lifted her cup and skewed her face as its bitter brew connected with her tongue. What she wouldn't give for coffee, just coffee, even decaf. Setting aside the kanabean, she picked up her own ball of clay and rolled it in her palms.

Its smell stirred memories of introductory art courses, the joy she'd found in them. Joy stowed away for ambitions. She reshaped her hands, pushing the clay into an oval shape. From there, she pinched and pulled. Sotiris pressed against her arm as she worked, enraptured as a bird took form. With the body done, she molded wings—then the spell broke. Sotiris lurched forward, taking the clay bird from her hands.

His expression morphed from wide-eyed wonder to scrunched confusion as he opened his hands. The bird was no more.

Tears formed in Sotiris's eyes, and Katya rubbed his back. "You have to be more careful."

He blinked at her, tears creeping down his cheeks. The lesson, for now, went unabsorbed, but she hoped one day it would take root. It had to. For all their sakes.

After a meal, she settled him, and like clockwork, the drugs made his eyelids heavy and his head bob, though he resisted. Like always. It was almost comical that he should be the one resisting sleeping. A burst of energy would not arrive until the morning when the cycle resumed … over and over again.

"I never saw my life ending up like this." She ran her hand through her mid-length hair and yawned. An action the boy reciprocated.

She lifted him, cuddling him against her body, even as he refused to lower his head. Walking into the shared space, she rocked him, which elicited moaned complaints. She didn't let up.

"Shhh, shhh—" Katya cleared her throat. "Shush, little one, night is upon us; the field mice have gone home, cuddled together …"

She lumbered to his room, made off-kilter by Sotiris's dangling legs, which he swung about. "There they slumber—no cat, no fox"—she gritted her teeth together—"to worry o'er."

While suspending him off the ground, she pawed open the door to his room, the smallest of the three bedrooms, where only a bed fitted inside. Its temperature was colder than even the common space, and its lights were always off.

"Sleep, sleep till—morning's li-ght."

She rested him on the bed—"Oh no, you don't!"—she caught his feet before they could reach the floor. His eyelids grew heavier, the fight dying as the drugs regulating his system forced him to rest. Swinging his feet on to the bed, Katya tilted him so his head rested on the pillows. By the time she had pulled the light blanket over him, he was out.

She brushed his cheek with a finger. "Let's skip the scavenger hunt in the morning, aye?"

No response. She kissed his forehead and left, shutting the door behind her. After prepping another cup of kanabean, she perched in front of a long-outdated console. It was no slate; however, it had a connection to the Net, for all the good it had done. She'd yet to trace the special ops team. She gulped the bitter, unsweetened drink and returned to beating her head against the proverbial brick wall: her hunt for ghosts who obviously didn't want to be found, or perhaps the Magistrate wanted to ensure they weren't. She frowned, taking another sip.

She was a glutton for punishment. But what else was there to do? Rudderless, stuck in routine: doctor appointments and searches. Without this ritual, she imagined she would flounder worse than she already was. A former major on Reznic, dismissed for reasons unknown, flitted to her mind. A bottle in hand, stumbling from odd job to odd job. Others shared that fate, unable to adjust to civilian life. This frustrating, dead-end search kept her sane while, conversely, driving her insane. But she needed to gather answers for Sotiris, return him to his family ... no matter how much she'd sacrificed, no matter how much he'd wormed his way into her heart. And so she tried to trace the uncle until words blurred on the screen.

CHAPTER TWO

Chirp! Chirp! Chirp! Flailing, Katya smacked at the wall, the incessant alarm galling her with each miss of the console. It reminded her of crickets—albeit mechanical. It drudged up memories of a pesky cricket that had wandered into the Cassius home and serenaded them until its death, twenty agonizing days later. Her hand collided with thick synth glass. There. She retargeted her attempts and basked in the ensuing silence.

With her arm over her eyes, she lounged. She hadn't thought of that episode in years. There'd been a lot about Meracus Domus seeping forward through the ethers of her mind. A hollowness settled into her chest. She didn't want to delve into them. She'd been away for years with only spurts of homesickness. Those moments? Primarily reserved to Valens's sofa on Reznic, where his painting of Meracus Domus's river country had enraptured her. And even that simple remembrance threatened to stir other ghosts she had no desire to face.

Krezk!

She launched from the bed—her shoulder moaning its complaints—and rushed to Sotiris's room. Her sleep-addled brain had failed to connect why there'd been an alarm to begin with.

She winced as her bare feet met cold tile outside her door. It'd become a game of sorts, at least for one of them. Though that was unfair. He only wanted to avoid discomfort, as any normal humanoid would.

His door opened to a vacant bed. Krezk. He'd beaten her to the punch. She got on her knees and checked the cubbies under the bed. Empty. So he'd decided the common area would be his best bet.

Sofa? No, only an empty cavity. She blew the bangs from her eyes. Apparently, he'd learned she could easily pry him from there. The various nooks and crannies in the living area brought similar results, leaving … Katya pinched the bridge of her nose and entered the kitchenette.

Cabinet door after cabinet door, until pressed against the metal back of one, trying to blend with the mixing bowls, was Sotiris. She reached in after him, only for her hand to collide with a bowl.

"Oh, no, no, no—" Katya pried the bowl from his grip and placed it behind her. "I'm not after them." She pushed aside another and caught his arm. In retaliation, he shoved his back against the metal, contorting his body to make his removal akin to forcing a dog from its kennel.

"Come on now." She got him halfway out, Sotiris hissing at her, particularly when she pulled harder. He twisted, exploiting the weakened grip in her right hand; however, her left held. "You can fight all you want, but we're going. No matter how much we hate it." She nudged his leg up, dislodging the foot pressing against the cabinet edge. Katya stumbled backward at the sudden give, but as she did, she held Sotiris, who squirmed and wiggled like a feral cat.

Groaning, she eased herself back on to her feet, her shoulder aflame. "Do we really need to do this every morning?" She deposited him in his chair before latching him in place. At least he hadn't learned how to break past the security codes. If she ever had to hunt for him through the station…

"Here." She set a cool mush in front of him, along with an imported milk from some Medzeci mammal Katya didn't know, but it agreed with Sotiris's stomach, and that was all that mattered.

As he munched on it, Katya ate one of the ration bars they'd received about a week ago. She followed it with a cup of instant kanabean. From there, she dressed before readying Sotiris, being sure to grab his favorite stuffed animal, a Skogarld forest cat. Its speckled and patterned body pressed into Sotiris's chest when she lifted him.

She stopped in front of Mina's door but fought the urge to rouse the teen. There was little point to it. Not unless she wanted to be surrounded by a grump for the rest of the day—if the girl had even returned. Sotiris dug his chin into her shoulder. Besides—she gritted teeth—dealing with one grump was enough.

"Yeah, yeah."

Vacating their quarters, the pair retraced their steps from the previous day and all the ones before it. Sotiris rested his head on her shoulder, being as limp as possible so he settled like an anchor against her arms and hip. His second favorite game: fatigue her arms and then make a break for it. While he'd developed some speed, endurance had yet to be built. In the moments when he had broken free from her, his limbs always gave given time, with the station's heat leaving him panting.

Their trip proved routine until they exited the lift. Katya frowned and tightened her hold on Sotiris after the doors opened to a mass congregation crowding the railing and craning their heads for better views of the shared space below. More stretched the length of the ramp down to said space. A ruckus reverberated through the area. Almost chant-like, the shouts' rhythm quickened Katya's pulse.

Creeping forward, she peeked through the small gaps formed as she snaked her way through the masses. Below, people bumped shoulders, maneuvering to get better views while clearing a path. Brightly colored hair amidst the chaos caused her breath to catch. Mina and her friends wormed their way through the crowd. Their hair allowed Katya to track them until newcomers to the mezzanine jostled her and Sotiris farther from the railing.

Halfway down the ramp, Katya paused at a slight gap. Bedraggled people exited the far connector, holding on to each other. Their clothing had been singed. More poured out, hunched, emitting fatigue only the battle-hardened could. They carried little in belongings, and Katya assumed they'd fled rapidly. A tall, well-built man with a ragged scar running across his dark face stepped from the connector, and the atmosphere shifted to pure electricity.

"Izem!" someone shouted and, in turn, broke a dam Katya hadn't known existed.

Chants of "Izem" rose from the floor, often accompanied by fist pumps into the air. A cornucopia of odd cheers followed. Katya didn't understand them, but she knew their gist. She glanced at those beside her, caught in the fervor and its calls for the Magistrate's destruction. Tingles passed along her spine, and she pressed her way down the ramp. A coldness settled on her face.

Izem, the Lion of Tizzet. The second head of Plasovern, as some had nicknamed him. The flip side of the coin. With the name, Katya pieced together that something must have dislodged him from his homeworld. But what?

A woman bumped Katya, causing her to hiss. No apology. Her companion also rushed past her, her wake brushing against Katya. They chattered before also diving into the chant.

She shifted closer to the wall and away from the scene. Sweat collected at the back of her neck. While no one had noticed her, she feared that heightened energy being turned against her and Sotiris. She was, after all, the Magistrate woman. Sotiris's hand smacked Katya's face, and the spell broke. Katya raced down the ramp and took an alternative connector from the normal one. Along the way, they passed a couple.

"He doesn't come very often," a man said in proper Magistrate as he walked, occasionally bursting into a slight jog. "I wonder what's going on."

A woman, who fast-walked to keep up with him, shrugged. "Hard to say. Nothing good."

Katya felt the woman's gaze catch on them. The Plasovern agent said something, but Katya did not slow her rapid pace away from the swelling chorus behind her.

Because of the alternative route, they arrived late to the clinic, with the heat having deteriorated Sotiris's mood. She had to work around his wiggling frame as she plugged in her personal entry code. Then he offered no aid when Katya struggled to undress him for the session, clinging hard to his stuffed wild cat. Even when she pried it from his hands, he stiffened his arms. It made it almost impossible to remove his shirt, especially with Katya striving not to irritate his skin. She frowned, finding the back fabric already stained. The wound had begun to ooze again.

She folded and placed the shirt on the table before doing likewise with his pants. Then she returned the stuffed animal. As she faced the viewing area, she realized Strom's absence. There was no trace of Usha, even. They weren't late enough to have missed them if they'd been. But with Izem's arrival …

Garbi poked her head through the doorway. "Oh, there you two are. I was worried we might have to send a rescue party to find you."

"Our path was a bit crowded."

She smiled, a sterile thing. "So I hear." She waved Sotiris forward, but he didn't budge, forcing her to swoop down and hoist him up, toy and all. She ignored his complaints and took him straight into the examination room, where she settled him on the table. "Izem's arrival has set Jomsborg ablaze."

"And sent Strom elsewhere."

"Indeed." Garbi brushed Sotiris's bangs away from the neural device. "At least he left it on. We'll run the data today while we complete some basic tests." Brushing a loose strand of hair from her face, she straightened and addressed Katya. "We'd also like to run a few neural tests on you. Just to make sure everything is in order."

In order? Barbs spread across the base of her skull. "Is there a reason things might not be … in order?"

An eyebrow rose. "Not likely with this new treatment — so far, that is. But Mistress Usha wants us to be thorough. There can be no mistakes, and we must be sure his system isn't developing a workaround. Your brain, so far, has been his favorite to interact with." Garbi messed with settings on a slate, likely linking it to the neural device. "It's for safety purposes. We don't want the mutation out of control. We've seen what that can do."

Katya ran a finger under her nose, chasing phantom blood. They truly had.

Garbi skimmed over whatever was being relayed on the screen before listening to Sotiris's heartbeat and checking his eyes. In the background, Isla remained ever present, only this time consumed by her displays rather than the various drugs being crafted.

"Does Izem come to Jomsborg often?" Katya asked.

That caused the Csek to break from her work momentarily and bear her deep purple gaze solely on to Katya. She, however, did not say a word. Had she taken a vow of silence?

"Infrequently," Garbi supplied, not pausing in her work, rubbing some green salve on Sotiris's damaged skin. "It's hard for him and others to come and go from Tizzet. He has to choose his opportunities wisely, or he'll end up dead or in the Magistrate's care."

Katya hummed. And conversely, Strom, who'd left her homeworld, would be temerarious to step foot on its soil now. Still, she wondered what had stirred the lion to retreat from his homeworld. Something had to have changed. More importantly, she weighed what impact his presence on Jomsborg might be. He was popular. His presence could harm them, but Strom herself was mercurial at best. Friend for today, but what would tomorrow bring? Katya loosened her jaw, which had become vice-like. For now, observe. Attempt to gauge this recent addition to Jomsborg and determine the dynamic between him and Strom.

"Oh, look" — Garbi extended her slate toward her — "a message from Mistress Strom, sending her regrets for missing your conversation. She requests your presence tomorrow morning after dropping Sotiris off. It'll be in her private quarters, pod three."

Katya's stomach tightened. "Where is pod three?"

"Toward the official 'top' of Jomsborg." She cast aside the slate, stripped the neural device for its place, and hefted Sotiris on to the MRI's sliding bed. "I'll give you a mobile minder before you go. It'll get you where you need to be tomorrow."

Sotiris, quite forlorn, hugged his critter close to his chest, and the bed crept into the heart of the machine.

"I figured you haven't been into the command section of the station."

"Haven't been invited before," Katya returned. She'd been limited in her exploration of Jomsborg, but now, this invitation presented the opportunity. Her heart fluttered in her chest. But it also held risk. She would still be stuck talking with Strom, and who knew what the Plasovern leader had in mind.

"Just mind your business when you go," Garbi continued as she moved to the MRI's controls.

"I aim to."

Garbi grinned while Isla's fingers echoed on synth glass in the background. "Good."

Katya settled on a spare chair and did the only thing she could: listen and wait.

The minder, proffered as promised at the end of Sotiris's session, weighed heavily in Katya's pocket even as she settled in her chair for the evening. The Oneiroi toddler had already succumbed to slumber and been placed in his bed. Left alone, she stewed and dreaded. Garbi could have given her the device in the morning; instead, she'd made a deliberate choice not to. Wrapping her hands around the warm metal mug of kanabean swill, Katya inhaled its robust scent—its only redeeming quality.

After freeing one hand, she turned on the ancient console, built into their quarters. Dated. In a way, it reminded her so much of *The Maelstrom* with its antiquate features. Though, even the austere Magistrate had updated consoles on the vessel, whereas Plasovern had left this one untouched. At least it still worked.

She ran her fingers across the flat board in front of her, spelling out *Gershna*, the name of the Jar'rask ship. Nothing. She sipped from the mug before skewing her lips. She pried further into the Net but found nothing, not even hearsay. No rumors of a mishap, no posted repair orders. These would be the only telltale signs the Magistrate would allow to slip. Elites turning on Elites could not leak. More hints might exist on *Intortus*, the dark corner of the Net, but there was no tapping into that from this console.

The *Boreas* brought matching results of nothingness. Being a special ops ship, that was not surprising. Upper Brass would typically scrub such vessels from dispatches. As with each nightly session, she was left to wonder: Had they escaped the *Gershna* or been captured?

Amid her search, she rolled her shoulder. The cooler temperatures stirred aches, something that would likely plague her for the rest of her life. Maybe further work could be done, but that would have to wait.

Grimacing, she plugged in "Oneiroi." She would prefer connecting with the uncle, who had a familiar tie, rather than some random Oneiroi who would likely give Sotiris into Magistrate care. The uncle, if he'd followed her instruction, would know the result of such trust.

She glanced at the clock in the screen's corner. Eleven crept ever closer, and Mina remained MIA. If she had returned the night before, she hadn't left a trace, which wasn't out of the norm. It didn't make her any less nervous or guilty. Setting aside her mug, she rubbed her jaw. She'd made that girl so many promises for the future: education, training to become a pilot … And now, she was letting them all slip through her fingers, replaced by a dangerous cocktail that she'd brought Mina into. Being on the cusp of adulthood, though some cultures would argue Mina already was one, her time for influence was ending.

She paused over one entry — a small nugget buried in an article. Seven months earlier, the *Paralus*, an Oneiroi peacekeeping vessel, had been removed from Tizzet — Izem's homeworld. Their replacement had been Breks. Katya rubbed her face before taking another sip of kanabean. The article cited increased guerrilla warfare as a reason for the transition. Cross-referencing with other sites and articles, she gathered the *Paralus* had been recalled to

Sergrey after a five-year tour above and on Tizzet. It marked the last in a series of Oneiroi peacekeeping missions on the world.

A sickening feeling spread through her gut—yet she couldn't pinpoint why. She digested this information and paired it with Izem's emergence on the station.

Had the Breks really proved more of a challenge?

She lifted her mug and imbibed air. While on her second cup, she didn't feel it. She was unsure what kanabean's exact caffeine count was, but it had to be less than the average cup of Magistrate coffee.

"Tsk." She set it aside. "They're not making this …" Her finger returned to the board: *Maelstro*—she jerked when the door opened, the word unfinished.

"You didn't have to wait up for me."

Shaking her head, Katya cursed under her breath before saying, "I wasn't."

Mina increased the lighting and temperature. "You're really falling into old habits," the teen said as she entered the kitchenette and rummaged for something. She settled on one of the sugary beverages she'd scrounged up somewhere.

"Isn't it a bit late for that?" Katya asked, swinging her chair around.

"Says the person who's been guzzling … how many cups of kanabean?" Mina rattled the instant mix can, which Katya had left out.

"It has no kick."

"Maybe you've developed a caffeine immunity." Mina quirked a smile at her and slid on to the countertop. There she popped open her can, a hiss punctuating the space. "Still finding nothing?"

Katya brushed aside her bangs and sighed. "I doubt I'll ever find anything."

Mina lowered her drink and belched. "Maybe it's a sign." Then when Katya raised an eyebrow, she shrugged.

"Maybe we shouldn't be trying to find them. They weren't exactly above nixing us when they were hunting us down. Who's to say they'd give us the chance to speak. They're too ingrained."

Katya's brow creased. "He was worried about his nephew. He seemed to genuinely love Sotiris."

Mina snorted and chugged more of the drink. "Yet he would've turned him over to become a weapon."

"He didn't know what the Magistrate had been doing."

Mina rolled her eyes dramatically. "Swell parents, huh?"

"Desperate parents."

"Who have destroyed other desperate parents' homeworlds."

Rocking to her feet, Katya returned her mug to the kitchenette, squeezing Mina's shoulder as she passed. "They are Sotiris's species, and that man is Sotiris's family, someone who will understand him in ways we never will. He deserves that."

The girl made no response, and Katya washed her mug before replacing it in the cabinet. Mina remained hunched over, her feet swinging, hitting the cabinet doors on their return. While the can was pressed to her lips, she didn't seem to be imbibing its contents.

Sighing, Katya took another approach. "So, what was in the latest shipment?"

Mina shrugged. "Random stuff: slates, a few parts, some books and magazines. Only a couple of crates had food supplies. Then there was a lot of wiring, some devices I'd never seen before—probably Medzeci tech—and something called octa-thingamajig, or oxy-something-or-other. Dag said it was a cleaning agent they use on ships or something."

Katya hummed in response and stretched while crossing over and shutting off the console. Out of the corner of her eye, she watched Mina as she finished her drink. Exhaling, she faced her.

"Mina …" She hesitated.

The teen grunted and hopped down. She started a new search, possibly for a late-night snack.

"Be careful." The girl stiffened and swung around, but before she could speak, Katya added, "I'm glad you've made friends here, and that you're … more yourself again. I'm just saying to tread carefully. Don't get in the way. Let's leave it at that."

"I'm careful."

"Good." Katya opened the door to her own room. "Turn down the lights and temperature when you're done. And don't stay up too late."

"Yes, *mom*." Mina rolled her eyes.

She grinned. "Night."

The teen muttered a similar farewell around a granola bar. Shaking her head, Katya entered her warmer room and slumped on her bed. When she did, the minder pressed into her leg through the pocket. Impossible to forget.

CHAPTER THREE

The minder proved straightforward in use. Pebble-sized, it fit in Katya's palm with a very narrow screen that only showed her direct path. Deprived of a slate or earpieces, Katya had no choice but to squint at it. The gadget guided her through another pod and several connectors to a common space with its lifts. The minder vibrated, and the dots formed the number two. She pressed the appropriate button as others around her entered their own destinations. A pair pointed at her minder, one giggling at. Katya ducked her head, her face warmer than it had been.

Stops went by until she was the only one left in the lift. Not that she found herself overjoyed to be nearing her destination.

Stark, unadorned metal walls, with angled beams crossing over them, greeted her when she stepped off, conjuring thoughts of a warship, or, more aptly, a prison station. It lacked the polish edge of Magistrate designs, not a surprise: Most Medzeci constructs did. Instead, its architects favored raw strokes in their designs that bespoke strength. Straightening, she trudged on.

This—her eyes traveled to the sharp, angled ceiling—had been the original station before engineers had added the pods and connectors on to an old goat. Even those additions were surplus from the Fringe Campaigns some forty years ago.

Katya moved closer to the wall when two official-looking Plasovern agents passed her. Her minder vibrated, berating her for stepping far enough off its predetermined path. Touchy thing. She grimaced and shook it while carrying on. Along the way, she met more people, some in uniforms of sorts, each varied to a degree, probably reflecting the different planets they hailed from. Varraganarians outnumbered them and seemed to prefer street clothes rather than anything resembling a uniform, a look Strom had embraced herself. Pass under the radar.

Her eyebrows lifted upon discovering a Sarchin—notable for their fur, a brownish-gray, and the furless red skin around their eyes, just above their noses—among their number. As far as she'd be aware, the Sarchins had approached the Magistrate after voting to join the conglomeration of planets and systems. The group glanced her way but did not impede her or try to speak with her. The Sarchin played with their mustache.

The minder sent her through a rudely cut arch, which had a connector welded to it in the coarsest manner. Unlike the station's other connectors, it surrounded its occupants with cold, unmoving metal, a deep gray that toed the line with black. There were no expansive windows. The ceiling was not rounded either, maintaining the pitched, angled appearance.

Ahead, a set of five people milled in what amounted to a circular conservatory. One a Varraganarian. The other four Tizzets. Around them, four doors dotted the area's periphery. The minder pointed to the door straight ahead; however, when she stepped toward it, a member of the Tizzet delegation broke from their group and blocked her path.

Katya stumbled back when the Tizzet woman bore into her space as if to push her from the pod entirely. The other woman, whose deep amber-toned skin formed tight lines around her mouth, stood fractionally taller and had a lither frame than Katya. Even so, she had an imposing presence, particularly with her jumpsuit. Even through the woman's sunglasses, anger radiated from her eyes.

So Strom already had business. And apparently, it hadn't wrapped up.

"No one past here." The woman's tongue stumbled over the Magistrate language, deeply accenting it. She pointed to the hall Katya had come from. "Leave."

Katya held up her minder. "Strom requested me."

Her interrogator balled her fists, an action reciprocated by Katya.

"It's all right." The Varraganarian woman wedged her way between them. Her platinum blonde bob, cut shy of her jawline, barely concealed a blemish that resembled a chemical burn. "She's expected by Mistress Strom."

Izem's subordinate bristled. "Izem is not. We were promised—"

The dark makeup lines that flared into points deepened when Varraganarian agent closed her icy eyes. "They've been in discussions for hours now. Perhaps a break is warranted to speed negotiations to an amicable conclusion."

The Tizzet delegate snarled but allowed Strom's aide to depart through the door into Strom's quarters. When she disappeared, the Tizzet woman paced, running her hand against a series of tight braids interwoven into intricate patterns, which cascaded between her shoulders.

"Who are you?" She rounded on Katya, her lips pressing together.

"Katya Cassius."

A Tizzet man who'd been off to the side muttered something in a language that flowed from word to word with only the briefest breaks for breath. To Katya's ears, there was almost a melodic, chant-like quality to it.

"The Magistrate woman, huh?" The woman settled her hands on her hips.

The description brought heat to Katya's face, her skin crawling. A reminder of her status so precariously dependent on Strom's good graces. Should the terrorist leader rescind them, the station inhabitants would tear Katya apart.

"At one time."

The woman snorted. "So … now?"

So now … Katya blinked. "I don't know."

Before the woman could say anything further, Strom's aide waved her toward the room. Katya bypassed her welcome party, tracking the taller Tizzet woman out of the corner of her eye until a suitable distance lay between them. Then her full attention diverted to the one in front of her. A kid. The Varraganarian had to be in her early twenties.

"You'll have to forgive Kahina; she's merely performing her duty." She pushed her hair behind her ear, showing the burn reached from her jaw to her cheek. Knowing what she did of Plasovern, Katya wondered if it'd been gained in the manufacturing of bombs. "They've just wrapped up. Allow me …" She popped the door open before allowing Katya entry first.

She stepped in, then stopped. Serettiley lace and its earthy, elevating aroma struck her senses, sickness brewing in her chest. At the same time, her stomach felt like it'd taken a gut punch. So many flashes of memory overwhelmed her. Shared drinks, staring into the river country painting, hands exploring her body, loss—these memories released a concoction of potent emotions, the type she couldn't untangle or sort. Her chest tightened to the point of pain, and all she could do was inhale the fragrance and stifle tears.

Would you still think I'm gold, Valens? Standing here in Hedda Strom's lair?

Her lips quivered even as she quashed the display. She couldn't afford visible cracks. Her Varraganarian escort, who now stood in front of her, gave no signs of having noticed her rattled state, but Katya didn't know how she couldn't have.

Focus. She pressed through the haze and stepped closer to the other woman.

The space was expansive, with a large sectional sofa, several rugged pine chairs, a copious amount of furs, and a variety of paintings, wood carvings, and tapestries. A few preserved birds peeked out from odd points in the room. Ferocious-looking raptors positioned on high cabinets; their polished talons glinted. Then on a credenza pushed against one wall, Katya spotted the cone of Serettiley lace incense housed in an abalone shell, likely from Strom's homeworld.

All inspection shattered with the crash of a fist. Izem leaned heavily over a large pine table while Strom stood serenely at its other end. The man had changed from his battle-touched clothing to a colorful red geometric tunic and plain black pants. It suited the moment as he almost appeared to be spitting fire in Strom's direction, some deal appearing unmet. Strom, meanwhile, remained as placid as an iced-over lake.

"We cannot wait any longer," Izem hissed. He pounded his fist into the table a second time. "My people—"

Strom sipped from a stein, taking her time before returning it to the table. "I understand. But I need your patience. I promise you, it will be rewarded. But for now, you've had a long journey, and I"—she extended her right hand to Katya—"have a guest that I must attend to."

Izem's dark brown eyes landed on Katya, tracing every inch before rounding on Strom, a finger in her face. "I won't wait much longer."

Strom chuckled under her breath when Izem stormed from the room, the door latching behind him. She returned to her drink. Her morning drink at that. Though in space, perhaps that qualifier was irrelevant.

"I could've come back later," Katya said. "I don't want to cause any more headaches." She nodded to the incense. "That's why you're burning it, isn't it?"

Strom beamed, but neither confirmed nor denied Katya's statement. Instead, she smoothed her loose silk shirt, a deep plum. Lace traced its deep v-neckline, which dipped further with her action, revealing more of her assets. "No frets about that." She lifted the stein toward Katya before downing the rest of its contents and setting it aside. "Headaches are temporary things. If treated right."

Katya's throat tightened. If only that were true. It hadn't mattered how many cones or joints Valens had burned. The headaches only worsened with the other symptoms.

"Let me confer with Bodil here, and then we can chat. It's been a while since we've talked one-on-one." Strom crossed over to Bodil while gesturing in the air with her right hand. "Make yourself at home, pour yourself a drink. I won't be long."

Katya remained rooted as the two women retreated into a connected room. She stood, hands clenched behind her lower back, for several moments, head torn between memories and a giddiness so removed from herself. Shifting, she sought out cameras. She was paranoid enough to consider the possibility that Strom and Bodil were presently watching her in the next room, judging her actions. Strom would likely laugh at her inactivity. Predictable. Rigid. The Magistrate soldier waiting for orders.

Inhaling through her nose, Katya took comfort in the Serettiley lace, its tendrils prying stress from her. It almost made her homesick for Reznic, though the only draw to the planet was long gone. She meandered over to the credenza, sweeping over a stuffed white bird with talons fit to rip an arm off to, instead, settle on the framed photos, all print, that lined its back.

Faces of stoic Varraganarians stared back at her in various shades of color and black and white. In one photo, a group of three worked on crude bombs. In others, people merely stood by landmarks on what Katya assumed to be Skogarld. One particular black-and-white photo featured a young girl, perhaps eight, wearing a long white cotton dress and braided pigtails. She stood in front of an iron fence with flowers concealing much of its bars. Was it Strom? She struggled to gauge the photo's age. The Varraganar System had developed at a different pace than the Core, but her best guess placed it at forty or so. Strom was probably only in her mid- to late-fifties. It could be her.

The photos beside it were older, stained, and torn. The fashions featured more fur — Katya stood transfixed. Despite herself, she picked up a wide horizontal frame. Across its length, bodies hung suspended by ropes on a massive platform, a capital punishment the Magistrate had relegated to its past some ninety years ago. Written in a rough white instrument were "Vestporten bombers" and a series of names. One: Hedda Strom.

Tingles rippled along her spine. There was no way.

"Horrible, isn't it?" Strom asked. At some point, she'd rejoined her, though she was a distance away, straightening the chairs surrounding the table. Bodil, in the background, slipped from the quarters altogether.

Katya had no words. She set the frame down, its metal scraping across the wood credenza. She stepped away as if burned. Strom moved to a bar cart and picked up one bottle after another before mixing a pair of liquors into two long-stemmed glasses. Twisting her hands behind her back, Katya traced each movement.

The older woman chuckled as she lifted both glasses between her long fingers. "You look as if you've seen a ghost."

"Magistrate intelligence was right: There have been multiple Hedda Stroms."

Strom clucked at the statement but, like the mention of headaches, left it untouched. Instead, she came beside Katya and extended one glass to her, then upon her inaction, added in a matter-of-a-fact way, "It's medicinal."

"It's too early," Katya returned.

Rolling her eyes, lips upturned, her host set the glass on the credenza. She imbibed from her own while lifting the execution photo with her free hand. "This was taken within the first year of the occupation. The Hedda Strom pictured was only nineteen … the daughter she left behind, only five months. They'd both been failed by their government, which had let their murderers in."

"Did you take her name to vanquish her foes, or was it given?"

Strom returned the frame to its place, then sauntered over to an overstuffed chair. "That unfortunate woman was my great-grandmother. Even as a child, she had more sense than our leaders. Old fools. They wrecked our system's economy, allowed our resources to be plundered, and our people to be devastated in a haze of drugs." She slung a fur from the chair around her shoulders and sat down. "She understood the interlopers, drunk on our resources, would have to be forced off-world. What better way than with bombs?" She drank from her glass. "Inelegant devices then—her downfall—but I must admit decades later, they work marvelously."

Indeed, they were. Plasovern had only grown more efficient in their use, getting them places that should be impossible. Docked ships, Magistrate buildings along the Fringe. Locked down Ereago. They just slipped through.

But it'd all started in the Varraganar System. Ironically, it'd been the system's acts of rebellion that had severed the Magistrate's use of capital punishment. Officials had witnessed in horror how it bred more intense violence that consumed its soldiers and those standing too close—before following them home. A sour taste seeped into Katya's mouth. She couldn't move past the photo, tracing the ropes with her eyes. Pro-Magistrate residents of the Sister Planets had to have this image seared in their minds, an ever-present inkling that should the tides change, it would be them.

Katya shifted her weight between her feet. She had to resist the urge to scratch an itch that had materialized along her scalp. The Varraganar System had been a cursory blip in her education, portrayed critically as a backslide into more imperial tendencies, which had transformed into a quagmire that, ninety-eight years later, the Magistrate seemed unwilling or incapable of extracting itself from. The reason, according to her teacher? Those pro-Magistrate citizens they were serving. With age, Katya now believed a healthy mix of pride and a developed reliance on resources—valuable ore, elements needed for space travel, among other luxuries—kept the Magistrate entrenched.

Strom gestured to the sofa. "Have a seat."

Katya lingered as if tethered by some invisible string to the credenza. Every muscle was tense, prepping for a fight. Why was she even mentally preparing an argument for

Strom? After the past few months, why did that urge keep bubbling to the surface?

She took the drink meant for her and plodded to the sofa, where she settled on the middle cushion, a distance from Strom, who eyed her over her drink's brim. Katya tried to read her, but as always, found her as opaque as the darkest sea.

"You really should have a sip," Strom said, sinking into her chair. "It's rather good."

In the spirit of moving the meeting along, she did so, not breaking eye contact with the terrorist. Orange, with a bit of heat, it warmed her throat and chest.

Thankfully, smirk in tow, Strom obliged. "How are you finding Jomsborg? I hope it exceeds your Magistrate expectations."

"It does."

Strom rolled her eyes. "I've noticed your protégé is really fitting in. She and her new friends have been accommodating, moving crates and the like."

It bristled Katya, but she wouldn't bite. "I'm glad she's made friends."

Strom tilted her head, likely mentally calling Katya on her bullshit. "You've been more of a recluse, but I suppose that boy requires quite a bit of care, particularly with all his appointments." She passed her glass to her left hand to set it on a side table. "How have your searches been faring around those?"

Katya stiffened, knuckles whitening around the glass's stem, though she loosened her grip to avoid snapping the fragile glass.

Why are you surprised? She chided herself. Of course, Plasovern monitored everything she did on that console. "Unfortunately, I've been at a standstill on that front." She leaned forward. "Have you had better luck?" With measured control, she took another sip.

"They've managed to vanish. Whether by their own means or by the Magistrate's ... that remains unknown." She shrugged. "A shame, really. They would've had no option but to listen to our offerings. There was no going back for them."

"But this isn't why you wanted to chat."

Strom rested her elbow on the chair's arm. "Not the only reason. But it was one subject that needed broaching. The other is your future."

Her scalp's itch migrated to the back of her neck, but she maintained her grip on the glass.

Nothing is free.

The smug expression on Strom's face left a salty taste in Katya's mouth. She was the last person she wanted to have this conversation with, but she held no power here.

"Don't look so shocked," Strom said. "You're so driven, task-oriented. You've been in the Magistrate's forces for how long? Fifteen, sixteen years? To suddenly lose that rigid lifestyle must have been incredibly jarring. Sure, you had the run to distract you, but I'm sure it's been catching up with you on the station now. The itch. Or maybe it's more of a drowning sensation."

"I wouldn't know what you're talking about." Katya sipped from the drink.

"You do. You're just deluding yourself with routine." Strom folded her fingers together and rested her hands on her lap. "But, you know, and I know, through that distraction, you can feel it under your skin."

Valens flashed to her mind, one of the few people who pushed her buttons in such a way — called out her dogged pursuits, questioned her goals, and pressed her forward even when she didn't want to. It had rankled her, but not as much as this. To have this woman, who feigned familiarity and understanding for manipulation ... and who hadn't missed the mark yet.

"What do you want now, Cassius? You should really think about that. Your life can't revolve around this child. He can be a part of it, yes, but you need a drive that is your own. You could never be happy without some grand challenge. Eventually, you're going to tire of treading water."

"I'll worry about that once everything's settled."

"Life never settles." Strom threw back the fur and slid on to the end of the sofa, still giving Katya space but barely. "One can only hope for patches of calm waters to catch a breath. I'm afraid the calms don't stretch too long."

The muscles in Katya's legs tightened, and her eyes darted to the door despite herself.

Strom and her honeyed voice leaned closer. "There are some here who believe I've brought a Magistrate spy back with me."

"Surely, your people will follow *your* lead."

"Here's the thing, though." Her face now stood inches from Katya's, close enough to feel her breath. "I don't know what I brought back with me." Strom toyed with the fur lining the sofa, her eyes never drifting from Katya. "I do, however, know loyalties can pull us in bizarre ways. Sometimes, against our own best interests. I can only imagine what thirty-four years can imbue, especially when the only family you have ever known remains behind."

Katya downed the remnants of her drink and cast aside the glass, not caring if it stained the fur. "Cut the false care. What do you want from me?"

The terrorist leader laughed, her hot breath berating Katya's skin. "Always to the point. But to answer you: a display of good faith. Something to show my people there isn't a Magistrate agent in our midst—partaking in our rations and offering nothing to the cause—while we take a colossal risk."

Strom pointed to the ceiling, and for the first time, Katya noticed a patch of burns and divots. Her lips parted, a sinking sensation traveled along her spine into her gut.

"One of my men had an adverse reaction during the incident," Strom confirmed. "No one was harmed, but it understandably stoked fear. You can understand, I know."

The phantom drip of blood stirred, as it often did when she considered the Oneiroi defect's power. No commanding officer would be blamed for eliminating such a threat, the type that had crippled more than half the station. Lost life. But such was the value Sotiris held ... for now.

"You are here because of the boy. He's truly latched on to you like a *vermond* piglet." Strom remained transfixed by the splatter pattern now etched on her ceiling. "And I don't want to get on his wrong side."

Katya couldn't blame her there. What Sotiris could do couldn't be dismissed.

"Because of your own displaced background, I was also willing to show some leniency." Her breath burned. "Maybe guide one of Mramor's lost daughters home."

Leniency. The word curled Katya's toes. Like she was a child. But it was also a hint of what Strom would have done if not for Sotiris.

"Your display of good faith?" Katya asked.

"We need a pilot."

She swallowed. "For what?"

"Nothing directly against the Magistrate, I promise." Strom pressed a piece of hair behind her ear, drawing a flinch from Katya.

Katya's throat tightened. "Just piloting, huh?"

"You would be a courier, nothing more." Strom withdrew her touch and stood. "I'll admit you have a certain skill in the cockpit ... pulling escapes out of thin air."

The pit in Katya's stomach hardened. That did not bode well.

"Breaking through a barricade might be necessary."

A burning sensation spread in Katya's chest while an acidic taste plagued her mouth, the alcohol combining with stress—she needed an antacid. "Just a barricade?"

"It's hard to say if it's in place yet." Strom shrugged. "Our communications have been spotty lately. Interference and all."

"So you're sending me blind to ..."

"Ereago. You'd be delivering supplies, including food and medicine for civilians trapped by Magistrate aggression."

Bombed-out storefronts, people who shuffled through the streets as if they thought the sky would fall on them, boots crunching on stone. A cold sweat laced her forehead. Rein beside her.

"No." The word escaped before she could stop herself. "No, I can't go back there," she clarified.

"You won't even leave the ship, just stay in the cockpit," Strom said. "No need to even look at the planet itself."

"What about Sotiris and Mina?"

"We'll make sure they're properly supervised and cared for." Strom waved her hand as if to brush aside Katya's concerns. "We'll pause the trial runs while you are away. Usha and I believe we're at a good point to simply observe this current medicine and dosage. Mina will remain on the station, per our original agreement. She has proven to be adept at watching him, no?"

Katya forced a genial smile on her face. "She won't enjoy her social life being curbed."

Strom snorted. "Youth seldom do."

A knock at the door interrupted their conversation, and Strom called, "Open door!"

She then beamed when a man with platinum blond hair stepped into the room. His face—Katya sat straighter—was smooth, unblemished as if formed from marble, not a crease in it betraying any emotion. His eyes, a slate-like blue, met hers and held them as if daring her to blink.

Katya stood as Strom beckoned him over. In the background, Bodil returned but lingered near the door, straight-backed, arms at her side. Waiting for orders, Katya realized.

"This is Krasimir," Strom said. "He'll be overseeing the mission."

He gave her nothing, no nod of the head, no hand to shake, no smile to garner a sense of camaraderie. Katya, likewise, did not acknowledge him, though a muscle in her back spasmed. The automaton-like stare unsettled her. This was not a commanding officer she wanted.

Swallowing, Katya extended her hand as the silence stretched. "I suppose we'll be serving together." The gesture went unreciprocated, almost a relief. Her palm had become a sweaty mess, but she resisted the urge to wipe it against her pant leg when she lowered it.

"So I hear." His deep bass harbored no intonation.

"Krasimir does not do *touching*." As if to prove her point, Strom used one finger to move a strand of the man's jaw-length hair, an action that drew a scowl. "So you'll have to forgive him. But don't worry, you'll find him an apt officer. His success rates speak for themselves."

"I run my ship tight. My orders are ultimate. I do not take questions or backtalk." As he spoke, he straightened until he towered over her. "Am I clear?"

"You've made yourself very clear," Strom said before Katya could respond. "The mission will launch at six hundred tomorrow. You should have plenty of time to prepare your girl and boy for your departure. If all goes as planned, you should be back in a matter of two weeks."

A lot could happen in that time. She clasped her hands together behind her back while Krasimir looped over to Strom's stock and poured a drink. Katya's jaw ached. What choice was there? Something swelled in her, something she couldn't put her finger on ... just dread. As she lowered her hands, she wiped them against her pants.

"I'll let you make those arrangements," Strom continued. She gestured Katya forward and brought her hand along her back to guide her toward the door.

Katya stiffened at the gesture, but allowed it. What choice did she have when her future rested in this woman's hands?

At the door, Strom's fingers pressed in beside her spine, not hard enough to hurt but to garner her attention. "I highly recommend approaching this mission with an open mind. See what we're doing for people who simply want their homes back." The pressure increased. "Remove the Magistrate lenses. They have an insidious way of clouding complexities."

"I'll do my best."

Strom clapped her back. "I'm sure you will." But as Katya stepped through the door, the other woman cleared her throat. "It was Krasimir who had the adverse reaction. I'd remember that."

The door shut, separating them. Except for a couple of guards, she stood alone. Izem's entourage had probably left the moment he had. Wiping her hands on her pant legs again, Katya set off, stiff-legged and unsteady. Her mind raced in a nebulous, frantic manner, tearing apart every second of the interaction. In the main connector, she froze. Usha, an open umbrella clasped in hand, passed her without acknowledgment. The click of her heels marked her progress toward Strom's quarters.

Once she traversed the corner, Katya spurred forward, retracing her steps. As she walked, she narrowed thoughts to the present: get Sotiris, pick up supplies from the commissary — the points of her life she could control.

Once in the lift, she hit her destination and sank into its cool metal wall. Ereago. She rubbed her lower face as the lift swooped down its track. Run a blockade. Tremors overtook her hand, and she dropped it, clutching it with her other. They only spread to her legs. Lowering her head, she caught the phantom trace of Serettiley lace interwoven in her shirt's fabric. What would you say, Valens? What would you think? Even with him in a grave, she wondered, perhaps because she didn't even know what to think. While he would disagree with turning to Plasovern, her father would have understood on some parental level.

She calmed the vice in her chest with steady breaths. There was always a price, and now she had to pay it. Even if it tarnished her.

By the time Katya had gathered Sotiris and their allotted food items for the month, Mina had risen to create a small omelet despite her preponderance for late mornings that bled into afternoons. Now, she ate while nestled in a cocoon of blankets in front of their small holoscreen. She grunted a greeting, but her eyes never left the screen.

Sotiris let go of her hand and joined Mina on the sofa to watch the talking heads as images of people flashed on the screen. From their glamorous poses, devoid of the trappings of the empire, Katya assumed they were celebrities. However, she didn't understand a single word being spoken.

Katya brought the bulging bag to the kitchenette and sorted through it, stowing everything in its proper place. Most of the items were nonperishable, though a few leafy greens from Jomsborg's gardens had been provided. It would be up to Mina to eat them before they spoiled.

Her gaze lifted to the girl as she pointed to the screen and said something to Sotiris. The vice returned.

Clearing her throat, Katya fought to keep a level voice. "We need to talk."

"Oh?" Mina lowered the blankets from her head.

"I'm leaving on a mission."

Mina's face lit up. "That's—that's fantastic!"

Running a blockade was anything but fantastic. Katya faced away and poured herself a glass of water, ignoring how Mina bristled at her silence.

"It shows trust."

Cold water splashed against her hand as she overfilled the glass. So naïve. Trust. She could have laughed. Strom did not trust her. But then again, she also didn't trust the other woman either. She swallowed the liquid, bits escaping from the corners of her mouth. Mina's naivety could be so easily exploited. She set aside the glass and stared into the drain. What tests would Strom lay out for her?

"It'll be good for you," Mina tried again.

Katya faced her then, and her expression prompted Mina to continue.

"I'm worried about you." The girl puckered her lips, almost in a pout. "Ever since … since our escape and coming here, all you do is stay here." Mina gestured to their quarters. "You do nothing but take Sotiris to his appointments, then come straight back here and dive into the Net. You don't work out anymore, don't tinker around with things anymore, and beyond Sotiris and me, you don't socialize with anyone anymore."

Katya lifted a box of rice from the island and hoisted it into its place, doing likewise with the other remaining boxes. It drew a sigh from Mina.

"You never said what all happened." Mina left the sofa and joined her in putting things away. "Something happened, or maybe it's just the sudden change. This mission could help with the transition. Give you a cause."

It wasn't her cause. She doubted it could ever be. She didn't say it aloud; the Plasovern cause had become Mina's. Even now, the girl's posture tightened, brewing for a fight. She was too young to rationalize that she and her mentor could have differing opinions. But then again, this was perhaps the first cause, a belief she had formed independently. So she was more than prepared to defend tooth and nail. It was a battle Katya would put off for now.

"It'll be something new to do." The tension building in Mina's frame dissipated.

"Can I come? It'd—"

"I need you here." Katya squeezed Mina's upper arm. "Sotiris will be done with clinic visits until I get back; however, you'll need to keep up with his doses and watch him."

In the other room, Sotiris chortled, having abandoned the sofa to clatter two die-cast toys together.

"That means I'll be stuck in here."

Katya handed the commissary bag to the girl to put away. "It'll only be for about two weeks. I need you to look out for his well-being. Protect him. That'll be your mission. Are you up to it?"

Mina frowned. "You know I will."

"Good." Katya ruffled Sotiris's curls on her way to her room. "I'll be getting things around. It'll be an early morning tomorrow." She fell short, a sensation of creeping coldness striking her neck. "Mina. If things go topside on this mission ... try and do right by him."

"Nothing's going to happen."

Katya faced her fully. "I mean it. Do I have your word?"

Mina blinked at her, folded bag in hand, face scrunched in uncertainty. "Yes."

Even with that word, her stomach didn't settle from the knot it'd spun itself into. Mina was too young, too enraptured ... her experience so different from Sotiris's own. But there was little to be done. Strom called, and she had little choice but to answer. She palmed open her door and started packing.

CHAPTER FOUR

Blood thrummed through Katya's veins, the ETA now a matter of minutes. In the cockpit, she'd pulled in Magistrate news signals. "Cease-fires fail one after another … the interference of Plasovern and Medzeci … the situation here has deteriorated." The feed bled in and out, either because of their distance from Ereago or interference on the planet itself. "Insurgents have knocked out … Magistrate forces are regrouping."

Katya closed her eyes as the feed became a garbled mess of static and barely recognizable words. The conflict on Ereago had been destructive—she knew that firsthand—but now what would she be flying into? An inferno. In past conflicts, Magistrate forces had seldom had to regroup.

Even with Magistrate lenses, as Strom called them, she was not so blind to its missteps. Ereago would stand as a testament, perhaps as a headstone, to the Magistrate's interventionism and hubris. It had laid bare the republic's overstretched position while serving as a beacon to enemies, broadcasting that it, like a snake, had eaten too big a prey. The planet's factions had not been understood by the Magistrate, and they would never be ruled by it. The Magistrate should have never taken the Mertis's petition at face value.

The static grated on her nerves, leading her to switch feeds. She stayed on the more comfortable Magistrate frequencies, which played music, random news—albeit nothing about Ereago—and sports; they were comforting.

Behind her, the door opened. "They've sent the landing site," Krasimir said.

He crossed to the navigation panel, his motions fluid but with an edge. There, he entered the information, unnervingly emotionless. Just as if they weren't about to storm through a blockade with a freighter. She'd seen people like him before, could pull it off herself in times of crisis, yet … his face never seemed to crease. Unable to read him, Katya barred emotion from her own face when near him.

He had popped into the cockpit sporadically during the journey. Katya suspected he was trying to keep her on edge. His silence in those encounters had achieved it.

The destination appeared on her screen. It was very close to Esh. She pressed the seam of her sleeve against her wrist. The Magistrate had lost serious ground.

As if expecting her concerns, Krasimir said, "I've been assured you can manage a rocky landing."

She swallowed before answering in a steady tone. "We'll be fine." She then pressed her luck. "Any reason we're landing so close to the capital?"

"That's where we are needed."

Out of the corner of her eye, she followed Krasimir when he turned on his heels and strode from the freighter's cockpit, probably to wrap up the remaining prep work. Orders, contingency plans, and, of course, there were the crates they had loaded—Katya could only assume their cargo was weapons. She rubbed her neck with her free hand, prying the collar away from her skin.

There was no return from this. A pinched laugh followed the thought, knowing she'd long passed the point of no return. Running her hand through her hair, she focused on the data being relayed. Focus on the mission. Ignore the weapons in the hold, the torrent of mixed emotions, and the thoughts of her father and how disappointed he would be.

Katya slapped her own hand. Focus. Mina and Sotiris need you.

The navigation screen lit up along its edge with a line of Magistrate blue. The blockade. How long had it been in place? It had to have been shortly after their excursion on-world. Holes existed in its formation, likely from Plasovern picking off vessels with well-timed attacks. However, it remained formidable.

She launched the freighter's advanced firewall and accelerated. They had to be a bright purple dot on their screen. Sure enough, fighters streamed from the two nearest destroyers. Gritting her teeth, she took complete control of the freighter. She couldn't outmaneuver them, but she could outrun them. She kept straight to maintain speed. Elsewhere in the freighter, the weapons system breathed to life. Katya hissed. She needed to compensate for the bursts that rocked the freighter off course, slowed them.

"Krezk."

Lurching to the side, Katya avoided the stream of shots that arched toward them. Her fingers found the acceleration section of the console. Punch it! The images blurred on a small segment of the viewscreen while the other, which relayed data, flashed all kinds of red at her.

The freighter launched several bolts, sending some of the Magistrate fighters spiraling out of control. Keep it steady, Katya repeated, even as everything around her shook. A coppery flavor touched her tongue. Had she bitten the lining of her mouth? Pressing on the helm, Katya stayed in front of a stream of fire. Atmosphere would be their savior. She strained the freighter, now pulling out in front of their chasers.

"Come on, come on," Katya said under her breath.

Stay ahead of it. Her sensor emitted loud warnings as fighters pursued. Inching up their speed, Katya could feel the freighter groaning, warning her of its limit. She glanced at the blue dots. They weren't keeping up. Their smaller engines couldn't manage it—just like their shielding and small frames couldn't bust through the atmosphere like the bulkier, better-shielded freighter.

Even with that shielding, Katya rocked in her seat when the freighter hit what felt like a brick wall. Still, they slipped through the mesosphere, out of the fighters' reach. The ride smoothed. She cut the engines and brought the gravitational thrusters online.

Her navigations console relayed their path toward solid plumes of thick black smoke, through which a toppled city poked out. Far more destroyed than during Katya's last visit. Structures lay in hovels or stood as tattered monuments, mourning a city that had once prospered. The damage crowded the ring around the spaceport now. Large Magistrate tanks and other armaments of war waited inside the port's walls. Miles to the north of Esh, more Magistrate forces stretched to their second stronghold, Lort. And that city gave all the appearance of becoming the last major foothold on the planet.

Katya clicked on the intercom. "We'll be touching down in ten."

No response. Exhaling, she focused on her task. The skies remained clear of planetary fighters; perhaps their supplies had been depleted over the months of fighting. Any ground support also appeared to have been neutralized. The navigation console beeped at her, and she slowed their pace and began the descent. Much lower now, makeshift camp contrasted against the rugged brown terrain dotted with clumps of brown grass and torn trees. Across its proximity, rudimentary tanks and heavy vehicles guarded it. As the freighter started its final pass over, the camp's occupants, a collection of heavily armored insurgents, came into view. They comprised both native Gatas by their clothes and a hodgepodge of Plasovern fighters. There were others nearby, more Gatas and other native species, but they were all civilians.

After landing the ship, Katya kept the engines warm. She expected a hurried departure. An orange light flared on one console, signaling the opening of the cargo ramp.

Pressing her lips together, she drummed against the console, one leg fidgeting. Damn it. Katya rose from her seat and headed to the freighter's hold, where her new team members and faction soldiers from Ereago unloaded crates in quick succession. She stayed out of their way, passing along the edge of the hold. Some of the faction soldiers barked orders and made wild gestures for those who couldn't understand.

Katya crept to the ramp to get a clearer view of the camp. A hot air struck her face as she did. Heavily armed soldiers secured a path for the crates, keeping the civilians at bay. In the windows created by them, twisted faces stained in tears poked through. Their eyes seemed much larger than their cavernous faces, the skin pulled tight against their skulls. They all wore tattered clothing, which hung from their slight frames.

One woman jumped around, seeking the openings while cycling through languages. "Passage!" she screeched, landing on the Magistrate language. "Passage!"

Other garbled cries and shouts, some in the native tongue, penetrated the cargo hold. Even over the cacophony of humanoid voices, Katya caught the distant roar of the big guns.

A woman screamed above it all and wove her way under the arm of one insurgent, stumbling into the cleared path. Her bright orange and red floral headscarf stood out as she pleaded with the crate haulers, who did their best to ignore her. Katya wondered when the woman had last eaten. She was gaunt, her grayish skin hanging around her eyes. Her broken steps brought her closer to the freighter until a gun butt struck her head with a crack. Katya flinched, heat burning her cheeks. Two men hefted her before tossing her into the crowd.

Krasimir shouted at them, the first cracks in his facade forming. He relied on the Magistrate tongue: "Stand back! Stand back! No one will board. The next person who crosses the barrier is getting shot!"

A Gata man echoed in one of Ereago's native tongues, likely translating Krasimir's message.

Some backed away, faces crestfallen and soaked in tears. Most, however, clung to the hope of refuge. From their clothing and the patterns on their headscarves, the majority were from a minor sect called the Hetrosy. Viewed as something less, something other, by most of the other inhabitants of Ereago, the Hetrosy had found themselves pushed around throughout the planet's history. And now, with all-out war—Katya bowed her head—they'd found themselves exposed, no haven remaining. Flight had become their only option. And fear was a powerful motivator to bold action.

Another woman, three children behind her, grabbed hold of Krasimir's coat as he walked past. She dropped to her knees and sputtered out a chorus of words in her dialect, tears streaming down her cheeks. Krasimir backhanded her, freeing himself from her grasp.

Katya's jaw tightened painfully, and she clambered down the ramp.

"Back! Stay back!" Krasimir shouted again. Another, a Gata, added to his calls in their language.

As Katya reached the bottom of the ramp, she estimated the crowd at about twenty. While most were Hetrosy, a few groups were not. The majority, however, were families simply seeking escape from a wrecked planet. The Plasovern crew could easily take them off-world, but the operation would bear risks: Those lingering on the fringes could swamp the freighter.

She hesitated when her feet met Ereago's soil. The crunching sound of her foot made her cringe. She hated this world; she hated what it threatened to trigger in some cobwebbed corner of her mind. But its people hadn't asked for conflagration. Most hadn't even taken part in this strife.

Krasimir's voice grew in fervor and pitch. The crowd surged as the crates going down became fewer, only to be pushed back.

Katya approached him. "There's got to be something—"

"Get back on the ship!" he screamed at her. His eyes bulged while he brandished his firearm and fired a shot into the air.

Katya flinched and stepped back.

"Move back!" he roared at the crowd, firing another warning. The weapon then leveled with a woman who kept pushing.

"Stop!" The word ripped from Katya's mouth, which contorted when the weapon swung to point at her own chest.

"Get back in the cockpit!" The marble of his face cracked, twisting to resemble a theatre masked, elongated and inhuman. "I won't ask you again."

Blood drained from her face. The barrel stirred images of a reversal, her and Rein on the Jar'rask ship. Her face contorting, she mentally begged the woman to turn back. Her own throat couldn't even voice the thought. The gun never wavered, and in Krasimir's eyes, she saw a count. His finger minutely moved on the trigger.

… Mina, Sotiris.

Raising her hands, she took a step back. Then another. The barrel passed over her, drawing a shiver.

Something shifted, shouts becoming louder — she couldn't understand them. Perhaps sensing their window closing, the refugees rammed into the insurgents. A few Gata drove the butts of their rifles into them or used their muscles to throw them back.

Against her better judgment, Katya exposed her back to Krasimir and bolted up the ramp.

She reached the cargo hold when a series of pops issued. Stumbling over her feet, Katya latched on to one of the hold's arm rails.

Outside, mass screams and cries curdled her blood. She flinched when more pops echoed against the metal. Her knees threatened to buckle. White-knuckled, Katya put more weight against the rail. Get it together. She forced her breaths to slow, relying on training.

Sensing eyes on her, Katya straightened and staggered forward, climbing her way to the next level. In a daze, she reached the cockpit, where she collapsed in the pilot's chair. The muscles in her arm and legs trembled, and her shoulder raged.

What was wrong with her?

As if detached from her body, her hands rubbed her face, trying to return feeling to her cheeks and lips. She was better than this. How many firefights had she been through? She'd never cracked like this. Katya rolled the heel of her palm against her eyes. Only that one. The trafficking ring. It'd resulted in too many casualties — kids, members of her team. But anger had followed that mission. This … She clenched her shaking hand.

These people had just wanted out.

She just wanted out.

Rein had just wanted out.

Biting her lower lip, she buried her face in her hands. Her body shuddered.

If she didn't get it together, she was dead. Krasimir wouldn't hesitate to kill a cracked pilot. Her breaths poured out of her frame. Strom's throwaway line about the man caught in her mind. He'd still been moving when Sotiris had wrenched the station's population into his dreamscape. Cold, calculated, he would have no care what Sotiris's reaction might be to her disappearance, and with the drug well on its way, there would be no reprisal. Swallowing down the acid in her throat, she willed her hands on the console, forcing a check with slow breaths. She leaned into every ounce of training, divorced the fear, the panic.

Stay alive for Mina and Sotiris. Katya couldn't give him cause. She couldn't have helped these people. She bit at the quiver in her lower lip. Mission before all else. The kids were it.

The surrounding systems went red, serving as stimuli to force her from the episode. Planetary fighters were being scrambled by Mertis, or perhaps by the Magistrate itself. It was impossible to tell, but she watched their approach on the console. They'd found them.

The com system came alive. "Return to base."

"Copy." She didn't recognize the voice, but she didn't question it. She revved the engines while waiting for the cargo ramp to close.

Distance would be critical. If they couldn't keep it, the fighters would tear them apart. Outclassed in the atmosphere. The hatch sealed, and Katya ripped upward, the freighter trembling around her at the force. Stay out of reach. A blockade was waiting for them, this time with fighters on alert, arriving already damaged to that party was not an option.

Her console blinked warnings of impending approaches. Ten minutes. By then, the first wave of planetary fighters would reach them.

"Report." The same voice asked over the intercom.

"Incoming planetary fighters. Trying to clear them."

Katya focused on their pursuers—Boita LF-650s. They were sleeker than what the Ereagonian military would have on hand and had only entered the Magistrate Air Force a year and a half ago. Apparently, the Ereagonian conflict had moved up the Magistrate's list.

Barreling to the side, Katya avoided the line of enemy fire. Like a wolf pack, the fighters tried to corral the freighter. She banked to avoid clipping one fighter and, in doing so, broke through. The engines warmed, eager for space; she pushed them until the viewscreen displayed stars.

Over the intercom, she said, "Blockade coming up."

Steeling herself, she transitioned from the planetary thrusters and punched it. This time the blockade waited, prepped with fighters swarming from the warships like hornets. She ramped up their speed. It would be their only savior.

Behind her, the door opened, and her handler entered. His mere presence was akin to a bucket of cold water being dumped on her. The tightness in her throat and chest grew. If she made a mistake … She tensed when he moved in behind her.

He stood there like a sentential, observing every action she took to break through the blockade. Her skin itched, threatening her focus. She tracked the fighters and timed their approach while also factoring in when the warships would have them in range. But with Krasimir's looming presence, she couldn't dismiss how easy it would be for Krasimir to cap her, push her corpse aside, and take the helm.

She spiraled from the fighters and warships. She breathed through her clenched teeth.

"Is this within your means?"

Cold sweat trickled down her neck. "It'd be a challenge for any pilot." She swallowed against the tightness. "We'll get through."

"When we do, jump to these coordinates." A light tapping emitted from the navigation console when he entered them. "We'll then make a third jump before returning to Jomsborg."

Katya pulled up hard on the helm—forcing Krasimir to take a step back—to pass over one destroyer, fighters now biting at their back. They were coming from all angles. Plasovern was insane to send a single ship, one target for the blockade to target. But perhaps the return was never necessary.

One destroyer's front cannons roared to life as they passed over. Her console shouted warnings and instructions at her. They became more distracting than helpful.

"Krezk!" she shouted when a fighter—struck by its own destroyer—clipped their freighter.

The impact jarred her bones and sent the freighter corkscrewing. Emergency thrusters activated without instruction to right their dangerous path toward a destroyer. *Errshh!* Metal rubbed against metal. Katya fought to stay at the helm while her environment tossed. The awful sound dissipated after the thrusters pushed them off the other ship.

The near-disastrous accident offered one perk: the fighters had backed off. Katya revved the FTL drive, readying it for the right moment. Weave. Bank. Get out of range. One destroyer broke from formation to pursue. The freighter would never outpace it.

"I'm activating now."

"Be prepared for it to follow," Krasimir said before alerting his crew to cease firing.

Three. Tw—the destroyer bore into them, its guns peppering the surrounding space. Katya punched it. The damaged freighter shuddered as it made the jump to Krasimir's coordinates, which were in the sticks. The viewscreen flashed, alerting to a tagalong.

"Next coordinates," Krasimir said after sending them to the helm.

"On it."

The destroyer broke out a few minutes later. Katya bit into her cheek. There would be a fifteen-minute gap before they could make the second jump once the drive had recycled.

Apparently, the Magistrate was furious enough about the war on Ereago that it would waste fuel and energy to chase after one insignificant freighter. Increasing their speed, Katya created a sizeable head start, well out of reach of the larger vessel's weapons.

Krasimir leaned in beside her. "This next jump will lose them. They followed us once, but they won't waste fuel on a second."

She knew she wouldn't have. One freighter wasn't worth it, no matter any hatred a commanding officer might have for Plasovern.

She monitored the distance between, pushing the engines as the FTL system recycled. Down to ten minutes. The destroyer gained on them. Eight minutes. She brought up the second set of coordinates, and the computer launched its calculations. But then the destroyer jumped.

"No matter what, when that drive comes online, punch it."

A tingled passed up her spine. Five minutes. The radar picked another ship: Magistrate blue. Four minutes. Smaller, more nimble ... an interceptor. It would be more challenging to evade than the destroyer. She caught the start of its name, and her heart seemed to skip a beat. *Bo—*

She banked hard and ran in the opposite direction of the faster ship, and as she did, its full name, *Boorten*, registered. It wasn't the Oneiroi ship. It was just the same make and class.

Three minutes. It pursued, cutting the distance between them. In a dogfight, it'd rip them apart. Two minutes. Her finger hovered over the FTL controls. One.

She punched it. This time the jump was longer, moving them closer to Medzeci space. It'd be a dangerous gamble to see if the interceptor would follow them and enter enemy territory. It violated already-tattered treaties, little more than pieces of paper without bite beyond preventing full-out war. But for the longest time, that was the only incentive needed by the Magistrate and Medzeci.

When they broke out, her eyes widened. An asteroid field. Her fingers dug into the console, already knowing what was to come.

"Move into it," Krasimir said.

"Already on it." She guided them in, using the field's interference to erase their presence. As an extra measurement, she killed the FTL drive and powered down everything she could within reason. It then became a game of keeping pace with the chunks of rock and ice.

The interceptor broke into the sector—barely a ping on their now-malfunctioning radar. Now would be the most dangerous part of their cat-and-mouse game. Would the interceptor enter the field, try to wait them out, or give up? Their blue dot wavered on the screen, its location shifting—not that it meant anything with a faulty reading. The interceptor could be sitting still for all their equipment could tell.

Katya skirted around an asteroid that sensors had barely alerted her to in time. The boulders needed to be her primary focus. At least, the minerals and metal in the asteroids put the interceptor at the same level of disadvantage as them. Practically flying blind, surviving off luck.

"Get to the other side. But bring up the FTL drive before we're completely cleared. I want to jump immediately after exiting. Am I clear?"

"Very." With luck, they'd be able to make a clean jump. She dipped the freighter below an asteroid near the field's edge. Her hand rested on the FTL controls and fired it back up as they inched out.

On the other side, the radar was still not picking up the interceptor. Was it in the field, or had it not even bothered to chase them into it? She gave it no further thought as she brought the FTL into gear, launching them away from Magistrate space. It left a hollow sensation in her gut.

Krasimir worked the navigation console. "I've inputted two additional jumps. You will follow them."

"Understood."

Out of the corner of her eye, she watched him stalk from the cockpit, going who knew where. But with his departure, her tightly spun muscles uncoiled. She rested her head on her chair's back while not removing her eyes from the screen. She didn't expect the interceptor to follow, but she wasn't taking chances either. A tremble passed through her left hand, and she grabbed it with her other.

When it ceased shaking, she flipped on the com system and shuffled through its frequencies. Magistrate stations wobbled in and out of existence as Medzeci ones solidified. Two more jumps. That was all that separated her from them. Just two more. But then what? She ran a hand over her left cheek. Up against a wall, she'd picked the first solution available, or at least what her blood-loss-addled brain could grasp: Plasovern. She couldn't act so rashly again. It would be fatal.

The drive refreshed, and she continued to the next destination. All stations flickered into oblivion.

CHAPTER FIVE

Jomsborg reflected light from the distant star, Mezizi, as it orbited around the gas giant, Gorlone. Due to its size and liquid metallic hydrogen supply, the location proved perfect for concealing Plasovern's stronghold should treaties fail to stop the Magistrate from entering Medzeci space and dismantling it.

"Bringing us in," Katya said over the intercom as she piloted them closer to the station. Then over the long-range system: "Freighter *Dargo* requesting permission to come aboard."

"*Dargo*, we read you. How was the run?" a woman asked.

Katya's fingers stiffened on the controls. "Cargo delivered."

"Glad to hear it. Return to your home bay."

After affirming the instructions, she brought them up to level twenty. The shielding—something borrowed from Medzeci—allowed them to pass through, and Katya set the freighter in its designated space. She stretched while initiating the cooling sequence and bringing all systems offline for a well-earned rest. A muscle in her arm refused to stop twitching as she completed the routine. She'd been sleeping in the cockpit too long, but the thought of sharing quarters with unknowns after Ereago was not palatable. Her legs uttered their own complaints through their length. The last task complete, Katya grabbed her light bag and abandoned the cockpit.

She passed several crew members. None of them spoke to her as they gathered their own gear and chatted amongst them. In the cargo hold, a few cleaned up loose ends. Katya nodded to one who lifted his head when she strode by. He, after a pause, returned the gesture.

Down the ramp, she came face-to-face with Krasimir. Her frame tightened as she froze.

Gone was the wild expression of rage he'd worn on Ereago, replaced by his regular unperturbed expression. Now, as she stood at the ramp's end, his eyes latched on to her. He swiped his hand to the side as he swiveled to a less-crowded segment of the bay, away from the loud work occurring elsewhere. Katya clutched her bag's strap, twisting it, and hesitated to follow him. Despite the chill in the hangar bay, her face grew overheated.

Don't trigger him. Loosening her grip, she trudged after him, unease clawing at her chest.

Little knobs appeared when the man clenched his jaw and breathed in sharply through his nose. He had a good five inches on Katya, extremely visual as he entered her space.

"Your lapse in judgment will be noted to the proper channels." Some of the heat from Ereago billowed to life in his eyes and raised tone, though the marble facade remained flawless. "You jeopardized the mission. I would reflect on that."

The tremor in her arm reared its head, and Katya slipped it partially behind her back.

Krasimir did not back down. "In the future, you'll remain in the cockpit unless instructed otherwise." His gaze traveled up and down her contour — she didn't balk, even as her innards contorted. "I leave any reprisals to Mistress Strom's digression. But mark my words, if we work together again, I will not hesitate to shoot you next time. And do not think the mistress will be so forgiving for long. Her patience is not infinite, and her wrath is swift. Remember that."

She did not doubt that. Strom was the backbone of this wing of Plasovern, all tactics likely shaped by her. Still, Katya couldn't stop herself. "All they wanted was to get their families out."

Krasimir lifted an eyebrow. "Our tactics and decisions are not for you to judge."

"So putting bullets in civilians amounts to 'tactics.'"

He paused. "Forcibly boarding our freighter was not a practical or advisable solution for their situation. They were forewarned but chose to be hostile."

"None of them had weapons." Katya compressed her hands into fists. "What options did you, the Gata, the Mertis, or the Magistrate give them? The fighting's made Ereago unlivable. You're only dousing it in more flame. What are you going to leave them? Why not give aid to refugees?"

He shrugged, face blank. "Allow Ereago to deal with Ereago. We're not the Magistrate; we've no desire to dictate how they govern themselves."

"So you're abandoning the Hetrosy to be torn apart."

His tone morphed into one of patronization. "The Magistrate threw off a fragile balance so carefully laid by the native Ereagonians with its forced governance. You might wish to educate yourself before so haughtily throwing around accusations, one *adopted* by Meracus Domus."

"There are still refugees dead by your hand. What are their children going to do? Or did you kill them as well?"

No response. He swiveled, posture unchanged, and walked back to his team. Katya shoved her trembling left hand into her pocket before going in the opposite direction. She kept her steps measured, the only part of her she could control. Her erratic heart left her chest sore.

Part of her expected a blast in her back as she retreated, becoming lost among the bay's chaotic activity. Her guard didn't loosen until she felt engulfed by ships.

The bay hosted numerous varieties, from freighters of different makes to personal pleasure crafts—whatever Plasovern needed to complete its missions. Pressure sensors had been built into the floor under them, which could prevent theft. Katya shifted her bag to her good shoulder, using the moment to further inspect the sensors. They would probably trigger some response if a ship lifted without authorization. Bag straightened, she continued.

Multiple persons of varying species worked in the area, none paying her mind, undoubtedly used to people walking by. Katya wondered if the bay had a graveyard shift, a prime opportunity to unleash the plan percolating in her mind.

Like a prospective buyer, she inventoried each ship, noting strengths and weaknesses. A Kureynoone interceptor—what amounted to a Medzeci knock-off of a Boita—hummed to life to her right, lifting off and navigating toward the shielding, which would slow unauthorized travel. From a distance, the interceptor could be mistaken for a Boita, allowing it to dole out more than a few black eyes. She swallowed against the dryness still plaguing her mouth and throat. It didn't compare to the damage the Boita interceptor she'd placed in Plasovern's hands could deal. While quick enough, the Kureynoone had been built from a conglomeration of hackney components. They were temperamental at best, a potential deathtrap at worst. She pinched her lips between her teeth when the ship jumped after gaining distance from the station. Despite its foibles, it offered possibilities.

She resumed walking, outlining camera placements overhead, which were spaced enough to catch almost everything. One camera had been knocked at one point, throwing off its position to leave a blind spot. Odds favored other cameras, having become similarly skewed.

Her cursory inspection complete, she picked up her pace, reaching a waiting area of sorts, bathed in artificial sunlight. Large planters filled the circular space's center, their broad-leafed plants basking in the light. Katya followed the plants' example and lifted her face. It wasn't a real sun, but it was a lie she could stand. Around the room's periphery, crate-laden carts and random parts waited as Plasovern agents pored over inventory lists on slates.

Like those in the bay, they didn't seem to notice her. Exterior forces had never infiltrated the station. Its reputation as a haven smoothed the edge many of these agents would carry in the field. Her jaw set. That was ripe for exploitation.

Katya trudged into one of the station's central promenades, where a group of women chattered. Their children played a game, using their hands to clap patterns. Their shrill laughter caused Katya to flinch. One kid, about four, took off running, with another in pursuit. She thought of the starved Hetrosy children, and her ears pounded.

"Katya!"

She jerked toward the voice and stepped back when Mina barreled toward her. "What ..."

The question never fully formed as Mina doubled over in front of her. Mina. Alone.

"Where's Sotiris?" Her throat tightened while her eyes darted about, but didn't catch sight of the child.

"He—They, they needed to check him over."

Katya's brow furrowed. "Did something happen?"

"No, no," Mina breathed. "He's fine; they just had to check his—"

Face flushed, Katya ran through the promenade. Strom and her ilk had expected more time. The Plasovern leader wouldn't have made the promise she had to Katya before she'd left otherwise. What was their game? Her blood boiled in her veins as she tore up the ramp to the lifts. Mina's feet clattered behind her. She sputtered something, but Katya wasn't in the mood to listen.

The girl squeezed in the lift beside her.

"I saw nothing wrong—"

"Of course you—" Katya bit her tongue. Redirect the anger. "I had guarantees they would pause the trials until I got back." Her jaw popped. Never trust someone consumed by a mission. Of course, Strom wouldn't wait.

"They just wanted to check him out. They thought something was off with the formula. It couldn't wait." The girl's mouth formed a thin line. She rested her hand on her hip and looked at Katya with a raised eyebrow. "Why are you acting—"

"Not now." Katya exited the lift, sidestepping a group of people waiting to embark. "Go back to our quarters or to your friends."

"What are you going to do?" Mina remained in her wake. Her face became more pinched.

"Have a chat with Strom. Now do as you're told."

Mina balked. "You need to cool down!"

What she needed was a stiff drink. Katya ran her fingers through her short hair, her nails scraping against her scalp. The garbled emotions from the freighter crept up on her. Not here, not now. She'd have to untangle them, purge them. She wrenched her bag's strap with her left hand, which trembled.

Mina, meanwhile, balled her fists, staring at Katya as if she'd lost all reason. The teen had no idea. Enraptured in a cause, unaware of its cost. Had she been any better? A knuckle popped. She'd never killed children, never.

Around them, a few people had stopped to watch their exchange. The last thing she needed was attention.

"Later, Mina."

The girl's mouth opened only to close, and Katya resumed her path to the medical center. Her heartbeat rose as she neared it. She needed to calm down, at least enough to make rational decisions. A muscle in her upper leg trembled. The barrel of a gun flashed into her mind. She couldn't afford to play her cards wrong. However, all she could picture was Sotiris hooked to various machines and a dead Hetrosy on a distant planet.

When she arrived, a group of nurses intercepted her at the door to the private corridor.

"This is restrict—" one started to say.

"Let me through." She squared herself against them and pushed through. "That's my kid in there. I'm not leaving without him."

Hands grabbed her clothes, stretching them. Her bag slipped from her shoulder, and she let it drop to the floor rather than be anchored by it. She grunted when one nurse dug their nails into her arm. Shifting her weight, Katya prepped to backhand them. Only the intercom came to life.

"Now, now, now," Strom drawled. "There's no need for that. Let her in."

Katya brushed their hands off of her, reclaimed her bag, and proceeded into the secluded wing. There, Strom waited, her red shirt unbuttoned at the top, allowing her bra to peek through. Usha stood in the background, arms folded over each other.

"We had a deal," Katya shouted. "I played my role for you, but you exploited it to do"—her index finger shot toward the expansive window exposing the examination room—"whatever you're doing to him." Tremors overtook her frame. "You gave your word, but given your subordinates' actions, I can't say I'm surprised they're meaningless!"

Strom didn't recoil from her vitriol. In fact, she smiled smugly. "I take it the mission didn't go smoothly."

"If you consider the slaughter of civilians not smoothly, then no, it didn't go *smoothly*." She crossed the space between them.

Through the window, she caught Sotiris's curly hair against the white cloth his head rested on. Devices were fastened to his skin.

Her pulse spiked. Katya wanted out. She wanted them out. She wanted to scream that sentiment, but she hadn't abandoned sense.

This situation required a carefully played hand. Strom wouldn't let them go, not when she needed Sotiris, the codex to a mutation that had to be unraveled. While Strom wanted the Oneiroi off the Magistrate's roster, Katya didn't doubt there was more lurking beneath the surface. But for now, Strom had to remain in her corner. A temporary wall. She swallowed hot words and sputtered to backtrack, but Strom spoke first.

"Do you feel better?" When Katya stood dumbly, Strom smiled in a manner anything but comforting. "Good. Follow me."

The blonde waltzed farther down the corridor to the section of rooms previously barred. Katya's throat tightened. She glanced into the examination room, where Sotiris remained stationary on the table, likely sedated.

Next to her, Usha inhaled from her pipe before expelling puffs of smoke. Her gold-hued eyes popped through the haze of red light and smoke, almost glowing like embers. She cleared her throat and pointed her pipe in the direction Strom had gone. Grimacing, Katya did as instructed.

Tingles coursed through her limbs as she crossed over into the restricted space. Like the main corridor, red light bathed it. Katya suspected Usha stayed within these rooms. A whistle drew Katya to a room with an open door. She hesitated to enter, a sense of dread washing over her, akin to a noose tightening around her neck.

"The room isn't rigged," Strom called.

The woman patted a dark purple—or at least it registered as purple under the red lights—velvet seat cushion on a sofa. It served as the tamest piece of furniture in the space, which featured a series of other odd-shaped seats spread throughout the room, some sparking wild thoughts regarding their intended purposes. But they fit Usha's aesthetic.

Katya entered but remained on her feet.

Strom nestled into the corner of the sofa, arms draped along its back and arm. "So, the boy or the mission first?"

Silence hung, and Katya shifted her weight upon realizing Strom had dropped the ball in her court. She needed to choose her words carefully. As the moment stretched, the terrorist leader rapped her fingers against the arm, and Katya hoped her face wasn't twitching with each tap.

"You'd assured me there'd be no treatments while I was gone."

"That had been my intent." Her tone afforded nothing but candor. "But the formula wasn't holding. There'd been slips."

Katya's face chilled, thoughts redirecting to Mina, left all alone with Sotiris.

"Just slips," Strom continued. "Not like before. Mina doesn't recall it happening, but that's expected given the ability in question. Others in the near vicinity of your quarters, however, felt sleep disruptions and the inability to focus. Others missed their shifts. Given what had happened last time, I think, with your military background, you can appreciate my command decision."

Framed like that, she couldn't damn Strom. If it'd been her command, she would have done likewise. But it didn't sit right. The coincidence that the drug's degradation would occur while she was gone. Over the course of two weeks? She folded her hands behind her back. It was too convenient.

"And now?"

Strom's lips pinched as she shifted her gaze to the floor before reverting it to Katya. "There's work to be done on it. It's disappointing, but we knew it'd be a process."

It spelled more time spent in the clinic, more trials, and more red peeling skin. The base of her head itched. There would be more decisions she felt unprepared to make—and the entirely wrong person to make them. It really should be his uncle.

"What's been done so far?" Katya twisted her hands together behind her. "Why was I barred from entering?"

"A simple misunderstanding. The majority were new rotations and were unaware of procedures." Strom propped her head up with one hand. "As for where we stand, a small tweak to the formula and a lot of brain scans to judge effectiveness."

That would explain why they'd had to sedate him since he rarely held still in the machine. She shifted her weight again. But she could find no trust in her.

"Satisfied?" Strom shifted on the sofa. "Should we address your other concern? The innocent civilians who were trying to force their way on to one of our ships?" Strom definitely witnessed her eyebrows raise. "What? Krasimir keeps me well informed. Did he not give them warning?"

Heat berated Katya's face. "They were desperate. Desperate people will do anything to save their families."

Strom laughed. "This I'm well aware of. Desperation can make one a hero or a villain. Simply because one is desperate doesn't entitle them to one of our ships. Would the Magistrate freely give away one of theirs?"

"They have taken refuges before." Her entrance into her father's care was a testament to that.

Strom waved her statement away. "Our mission is to supply materiel, food, and training. What occurs on-world falls into the decision-making purview of those native to the world. The Gata are the true natives, and they have asked us to leave all matters to them."

"They were starved and unarmed."

"It was not our call."

Pain coursed up Katya's arms as her hands clenched. "Krasimir had me fooled then."

"You still have Magistrate lenses on." Strom pulled her legs on to the sofa. "Everything is the Gata's call. You've arrived at conclusions based on your assumptions. Did you witness the entire incident? No. Krasimir gave warning shots. The Gata moved beyond warning shots."

She hadn't witnessed it. She couldn't deny that sequence of events. Doubt it, yes, but little else. Her knees ached; she'd locked them too long. The hypocrisy burned her throat because Jomsborg did house refugees. Of Plasovern's own heart or with some value.

"Some might say you have an obligation to help them." Plasovern had escalated the conflict, brought in weaponry. Had placed the Hetrosy in a losing position.

"That is so Magistrate." Strom entwined her fingers as she sat up. "To insert oneself into a situation and impose moral superiority. Let me share a story I was told not too long ago. Like countless times in its millennium-long history, the Magistrate set itself up as a benevolent observer in a global conflict. After all, they were space-faring. This pitiful world had only ever been able to purchase hand-me-downs they had no hope to understand." She rolled her eyes. "They watched in horror as the conflict escalated to new brutal levels. When one group tried to enact change by toppling a government that the Magistrate, with its longings for empire, had grown enraptured by, it couldn't resist but impose its right.

"You can slough the word 'empire' off like a skin, but is what lies beneath really that different? No. Only the words change. Intervention. Peacekeeping. Security measures. Border protection. But really, it's still aggression, exploitation, manipulation … assimilation. All packaged with pretty words."

Strom's painted lips skewed, and she leaned even further. "And sure, its *intervention* painted a rosy picture: Mass slaughter averted!" She lurched to her feet and invaded Katya's space in a manner stirring memories of drill sergeants. "But beneath the propaganda, so many missteps were made. The magistrates and their servants couldn't fully grasp the politics, let alone navigate them."

Katya swallowed against the sour taste in her mouth but held firm, refusing to budge no matter how close Strom's mouth grew, her breath heating her face.

"They stumbled from one blunder to another: leaned on a faction that should have never received power, then ignored their transgressions. And amid the chaos of war, revolution, and disease, they transported over a thousand children off-world to be dispersed among loyal Magistrate families."

An ache shot along Katya's jaw, now clenched.

"Yes, there were orphans in the mix, but were they all?" A gleam entered Strom's eyes. "The Magistrate had neither the resources nor the desire to answer that question. Just shipped them all." Strom walked to a table and picked up an electric pipe. With the flip of a button, she activated it and took a drag. "A sizeable loss for a planet already reeling from massive fatalities. But children always suffer in conflicts."

Katya clenched her clammy hands. She still had no desire to scratch below the surface, to explore what Sotiris had uncovered. Though standing there, back screaming of tension, she caught the trace of gunpowder.

"It could be countless planets, but you know which one I'm talking about, don't you?"

"It doesn't justify what happened on Ereago," Katya gritted out, dodging the implication. Though she knew. Of course, it was Mramor.

"I will let the inhabitants of Ereago decide that."

Katya brought her hands to her side and loosened her shoulders. "Planet sovereignty over everything."

"Yes," Strom took a deep inhale of the pipe. "If you were a true Mramorian, you'd appreciate that cause. But alas, all you know is your Magistrate parent."

"My father is a great man."

"Oh, I don't doubt that. But do you ever wonder about your biological parents? How you came into your father's care?"

"That doesn't matter."

Strom quirked one of her eyebrows. "Doesn't it?"

Katya met the question with silence. *It's only natural. Truthfully, I'm surprised you haven't asked before now.* It didn't matter. What happened now stood thirty-some years in the past.

"Run then if you must, but the truth will always remain." Strom blew out a stream of smoke before deactivating the pipe and dropping it to the table. "Still, there's the question of future missions."

"I won't work with him again."

A smile stretched across Strom's face. "But you would work again? Just not with Krasimir."

Katya's stomach quivered, but she answered, "Yes." The more she could be in the hangar bay without rousing suspicions, the better. Mobility was key to extraction, so she would sacrifice this battle to Strom.

"I'll pair you with Bodil. You'll find her more to your liking. Like you, she is by the books."

Her tongue clicked against her mouth's roof. Bodil was in Strom's inner circle as much as Krasimir was. It was not an ideal situation. "I look forward to working with her."

Strom rolled her head from side to side as she moved around the room. "I'll keep the missions easier. That should give you time to work out the trauma you are experiencing."

Katya wanted to deny it, but her tremors were as apparent to Strom as they were to her.

"I should've known better than to send you with Krasimir, given your experience with—what was his name?" Strom leaned against a curved furniture piece that resembled a hoverbike. "Whatever happened to him?"

She gritted her teeth before answering. "Who knows."

Katya held Strom's gaze, her shoulder straight, showing none of the tremors that had passed through them.

"As you say. Now let's get you and your boy on your way." Strom tapped the com in her ear. "Garbi, finish up with Sotiris. Katya will pick him up in a few minutes."

Following that call, Strom escorted her from the set of rooms.

"Beyond the nerves, how are you feeling?" Strom asked, her steps fluid as they approached Usha outside the examination room. "No headaches?"

Had the medicine failed that badly? Katya shrugged. "It's only been an hour and a half since I've been back. There's been nothing like that."

"Tell Garbi if you feel anything. With the latest changes, we have to be hyper-vigilant."

Katya straightened her jacket's collar. If there was a crack for Sotiris's ability to slip through, she would be the first to know. Not that it'd helped last time. Sotiris's reach had spread well beyond her and quickly.

"I will."

A potent herbal concoction curled Katya's toes and scattered her thoughts. She clawed at them, tried to order them, but in the haze pouring out of Usha's mouth, it was futile.

"It'll just be headaches," Usha intoned, holding her pipe to the side. "That should be the extent."

Inside the examination room, Garbi dressed a drowsy Sotiris, whose head dipped and had to be supported by Isla. A dark sensation gnawed on Katya's subconscious, suggesting she'd become a test subject too. Her lungs clenched as Usha took another drag.

Removing her pipe from her mouth, Usha released a stream of smoke. Only when it evaporated into nothingness, she spoke. "Given a few weeks, we should have a potential alternative developed. Our problem solved."

Once again, Katya could only take her at her word. "I'll collect Sotiris then." She paused before entering the other room and faced Strom. "I await the next mission."

Strom tilted her head, and Katya was unsure if it was in surprise or dark humor. "It will come before you know it."

Nodding in acknowledgment, Katya slipped from the corridor into the examination room. There, Garbi finished dressing Sotiris. She smiled broadly at Katya, but there was a layer of fakeness, much like with her cheery chitchat, which she now started. She used the same tone that she adopted with Sotiris, setting off warning signals in Katya's hazed brain.

Carefully, Katya took Sotiris into her arms, his weight threatening to throw her compromised balance. She dreaded walking back through the corridor while the part of her brain that still worked fretted over what Usha's pipe would do to the toddler. Adjusting him, so his head rested on her shoulder, Katya nodded at whatever Garbi was yammering about before leaving.

Her concerns for the pipe proved unwarranted. Strom and Usha had vanished, likely in the set of rooms Strom had taken her to. Without the electric pipe, the clinic's filtration system had cleared whatever Usha had been smoking.

Casting a lingering glance at the private wing's closed door, Katya's grip tightened around Sotiris. She could only tread the line with Strom so long before the Varraganarian would make a command decision. She should have never been so direct with her, but it might play in her favor. Strom would expect it. She had proved to be predictable, which had probably saved her life. Resting her cheek against Sotiris's warm head, she allowed the recycled air to clear her mind a bit more before setting off. No matter what missions came her way, she would complete them, lull Strom's suspicions.

She adjusted Sotiris's weight again before departing. Sotiris slumbered as they went, and she half expected the phantom tendrils to return, but they never came.

She took a beeline to their quarters, actually relishing its chill when she entered. Inside, she rested Sotiris on the sofa and wrapped a lightweight blanket around him.

She shuffled to the kitchenette and prepped a meal that was more than the ration bars she'd been eating for the past few days. Since the clattering pans failed to summon Mina, Katya figured she had sought comfort from her new friends after their interaction. She added oil to a skillet and heated it as she chopped vegetables that, in her absence, had wrinkled. With a knife, she pushed them off the cutting board into the skillet, sizzles following. She added a variety of herbs and spices before she moved to the next skillet, which she used to brown the remaining sausage. Her stomach churned as the aroma hit her nose.

Despite her ravenous hunger, she tried to focus on the next moves. Her thoughts kept returning to Mina. A potential wrinkle. Plasovern had given her something more than a prosthetic hand. In much the same way, the Magistrate had given Katya more than a home. Her hand shook on the meat skillet's handle. She strengthened her grip and picked up her stirring, the pink gradually vanishing. Friends, a new understanding of the galaxy, a mission she was raring to take on. She would not leave easily.

Katya combined the two skillets and cooked it longer after adding a Medzeci sauce Mina had procured. It added a nice tangy flavor, though she'd never found out what its components were.

She then ate the finished product in silence on the kitchenette's small island, where she had a clear view of Sotiris. He hadn't budged since she set him down. Would he even sleep tonight?

She cleared all but a quarter of her plate when Mina trudged through the door, her eyes darting around until they landed on Katya.

Katya didn't speak. She would allow Mina to set the terms. It was passive, more passive than she preferred, but it was pointless to escalate things. Not until plans were further underway. When there was no other choice. Her stomach threatened to revolt against her meal. She had entrusted so much in Mina … during their time on the run. She couldn't do that here. Mina could not be her partner in this.

Mina settled on the stool next to her. "What are you eating?"

"A skillet with what's left." Katya shrugged. "If you get a chance, pick up some more supplies." She smiled. "Apparently, a two-week supply doesn't hold us over for long."

Mina hummed in response. She made no acknowledgment of what had transpired earlier.

Katya took another bite. "So, your new beau. How are things going with him?"

Mina's head shot up. "He's not my *beau*."

Katya raised an eyebrow before standing to take her empty plate to the sink.

Pressing her lips together, Mina ducked her head, perhaps to conceal the growing blush as it spread across her copper-hued skin. "He … He's sweet." Her tongue darted over her lips. "I don't know. He makes me feel special. Really special. Like I can do things."

Katya's chest constricted. "Of course you can do things. You've always shone brightly. You're intelligent and kind. You've more than shown you can handle yourself in the most adverse situations, and I still believe you could be an incredible pilot."

Mina didn't respond, and it constricted Katya's chest.

"Never doubt your worth, Mina."

The teen rolled her eyes. "I don't. It's still nice to hear, though." More rose seeped into her cheeks.

A small smile tugged at Katya's lips, but she didn't razz the girl any further, crossing instead over to Sotiris. His eyelids remained serenely still. She wondered how long it would take him to work the sedatives out of his system.

Behind her, Mina ran water into a kettle. It surprised Katya. She'd expected the girl to check-in, see order restored, and return to her friends for whatever they did during the day.

Straightening, Katya moved to the console. "If you're making instant kanabean, please pour me a cup," she called. "I could use a pickup."

Mina grunted in acknowledgment and grabbed a second cup. A clattering followed as she rummaged for a spoon. "So," the teen stretched the word. "Did you lay into Strom?"

Katya peeked. Mina leaned against the island, eyes fixed on her. The kettle and kanabean mix forgotten. The teen pressed her lips together while she'd folded her hands together in front of her on the counter. She was practically begging Katya to allay her worries.

"There was a robust discussion."

Mina's eyes narrowed.

"Nothing irreversible," Katya assured. "So don't look at me like that."

The girl didn't stop, but she at least held her tongue. It came as a relief. She didn't want to dive into the details with Mina, even as her mind threatened to become stuck in a loop of dissecting her meeting with Strom. Katya rubbed her face as she launched a distraction, but not the ghost hunt she'd been engaging in since things had quieted. To a point, at least. Instead, she moved to something lighter: a serial, *The Bog Cat Chronicles*.

"So you are at it again, huh?" Mina set a mug next to her. Her tone held a definite whine to it, maybe even a coating of derision.

"At what again?"

The teen lowered her head and didn't answer; she probably couldn't through her clenched teeth.

Katya rolled her eyes. "No, for your information, I'm catching up on a serial. I need to unwind and couldn't think of a better way to do so. And" —she gave a dramatic sigh— "I'm over twenty issues behind."

She launched the edition of *The Bog Cat Chronicles* she'd left off on. Each story was self-contained, following a gumshoe on various cases from murder to pilfered artifacts. It'd suited her on Reznic, where reading time had been sporadic. What she'd ended up reading most of the time had been the latest reports on drugs, syndicate movements, and hacking incursions. *The Maelstrom* should've offered more time, but she'd dropped off, perhaps no longer needing the escapism as much. Though she'd also found herself immersed more in keeping the Boita freighter operating.

With a raised eyebrow, Mina appraised the screen, almost as if she didn't believe Katya.

"So the mission was a hard one?"

"It was on Ereago."

Mina shifted next to her. "Oh."

"Oh," Katya echoed.

Mina hadn't left the ship when they'd been on the planet. She hadn't seen the blown-out storefronts or its populace racked with fear. The teen would only remember the lockdown and then their miraculous escape.

"There's a blockade now," she shared. "And matters have deteriorated on-world."

Mina bristled. "Deteriorated for who? The Magistrate?"

She faced the teen fully, setting her gray eyes on her in an unwavering fashion. "For everyone."

Looking at her feet, Mina seemingly mulled over the response before shuffling to the kitchenette for her own mug of kanabean. Her back remained turned to Katya as she leaned against the island and sipped, the liquid too hot to inhale as Mina had grown accustomed to doing. Lifting her own mug, Katya allowed it to warm her palms. Through the steam, she watched Mina brood, likely pulling apart her words and contrasting them with what her new friends were telling her.

Sipping her own drink, Katya tasted nothing but regret in its bitter structure. She set it aside and cleared her throat.

"Conflicts have high costs, Mina."

The teen jerked at the sudden address, her head lulling to the side toward Katya but not fully facing her.

"For all involved," Katya pressed. "Combatants and noncombatants." The desperate women loomed like a beacon in her memory, fresh and raw. "No one wins in a case like Ereago."

Mina lifted her mug but paused before drinking. "But in the long run, they'll be free."

Or tossed into a shallow grave if not left for scavengers to pick apart and scatter their bones.

"They will be," Mina reiterated, pushing off the island. When she didn't receive a response, her jaw jutted forward in defiance.

Katya resisted the urge to engage, her throat going parched, the lingering kanabean aftertaste turning sour. She met Mina's challenging brown eyes. She could not be a confidante. Anything said would be verified with her new friends, who would take it up the chain. Her hands slipped beneath her legs, the tremor in the left more pronounced.

She struggled on words, any, as Mina waited. The need to lay seeds without setting off alarms burned her tongue. In the end, she was saved when the teen abandoned her mug and the room. Rubbing her fists into her face, Katya kicked herself.

Failure.

As always, she mentally turned to her father, who had never seemed at a loss for words, no matter how thorny the subject. What would he have done? The chair cut into her lower back. No answers came. No matter the turns Seneca had taken, her father had never faced a situation like this. She was left to thread the needle of keeping Mina out of Plasovern's web alone.

CHAPTER SIX

Sweat tethered Katya's loose t-shirt to her frame as she tore through the corridor on her own accord. Her heart hammered in her ears, almost deafening her footfalls.

So far, she'd been a lone figure, most of Jomsborg in the residential sections still slumbering. Wiping sweat from her eyes, she ignored the ache brewing in her side. Out of shape. Unacceptable. She huffed, upping her pace on the fourth day of her new jogging routine.

She entered a major artery and deviated from her past route, turning left instead of right into another connector. Katya hoped Strom would decide she was getting mission ready because she didn't doubt her shift in habit had been noted. Pushing her bangs aside, she regretted not having a headband. An annoyance and distraction while trying to commit every inch of Jomsborg to memory.

Slight alterations here and there gave her a larger view of the station while not arousing her monitors' suspicions. So far, she uncovered no restricted areas, and even if she had, she would have avoided them. It would draw too much attention to be caught in their vicinity. Too soon, and any plans she might develop would be for nothing.

Avoiding such spaces and keeping the jogs short were all aimed at going under the radar.

Taking another corridor, Katya slowed upon entering another common area with its grass and artificial sun. She had the space to herself. Unfastening the hip flask, she imbibed the cold water, droplets escaping the corners of her mouth. She returned the flask and settled on a bench. With her feet sprawled before her, Katya basked in the light.

Despite Plasovern resourcefulness and self-sufficiency in food production, this common area, with its light perfect for agriculture, remained untapped or relegated to recreation. It was peaceful. The only missing piece was a slight breeze. She missed Meracus Domus in a manner she hadn't before, even in the worst bouts of homesickness on Reznic or the other bases she'd been stationed on. Its sun. Its breezes, shifting tall grasses. The smell of the Viridico River. The sweet fragrance of water hyacinth.

Her reverie ended when loud voices drew nearer. She rose from the bench and walked. Security officers on patrol entered and continued in the opposite direction, their conversation never breaking.

After stretching her limbs a bit, Katya transitioned back to jogging upon reaching another connector. She followed its curved walls. Small cameras, almost indiscernible against the dark metal walls, dotted its upper corners, effectively covering all activity. She had noticed none in the common spaces. Probably too well hidden.

She passed two people sitting on a bench, both clutching pastries and thermoses. They paid her little mind. A major benefit to jogging. It made her presence innocuous.

She entered a more residential area with a smaller public space devoid of artificial solar lights. It housed tables, where several people dined on breakfast, conversing amongst each other. They shared darker skin tones and wore bright clothing, which marked them as belonging to Izem's party. The scent of cooking food hung heavily, and her empty stomach stirred. Katya skirted around them. They quieted and watched every move. A distinct sense of being an intruder almost turned her around, but curiosity spurred her forward.

Whatever the group said was lost to her ears, but the harshness suggested she shouldn't outstay her welcome. She continued into a corridor of residential doors and sidestepped one as it opened. In its doorframe, she caught the figure of Izem's disciple, Kahina. The woman still wore her sunglasses, obscuring much of her emotions, but the way her lips parted suggested surprise at Katya invading their territory.

Katya didn't interact with her, remembering how the other woman had invaded her space just weeks ago. And the way she stepped into the hall behind her, arms crossed, hinted she'd like nothing more than to tear into her again. Still, she didn't obstruct Katya or shout anything at her back.

She kept running and worked her way toward familiar terrain. At least now she knew where Izem's Tizzet delegation lodged. She dawdled in a commissary area, where Plasovern agents pried open newly arrived boxes for shelving and distribution. It was the first time she'd stumbled upon a shipment being unpacked, and she imagined it would take more visits to establish any delivery patterns—if any existed. They could be completely random, based solely on when Medzeci deigned to send them or Plasovern had "liberated" them.

Leaning over, Katya clasped her hands behind her knees and stretched her muscles. The movement enabled a prolonged view of today's catch, a series of instruments used for welding ship exteriors. As they removed them from the crates, lumps of straw fell to the ground. A rustic touch. It suggested a backwater source. Her muscles pulled taut as she held the position for a few more moments. Raising, she stretched her arms and resumed walking. The new vantage point enabled her to see more contents, including slates, chips of some variety —

Katya jerked to the side to avoid running into a worker. Now having garnered some attention, she proceeded from the space, stretching as she went and allowing her heart to calm. She welcomed the next connector, which she had to herself. It lacked the windows that others had, but it was almost comforting to be surrounded by impenetrable metal. At its end, she entered the common space she and Sotiris regularly passed through. Here, she trudged while still making some display of cooling down.

The commissary, while undoubtedly containing useful tools, would present a challenge if she sought to lift anything. Too many people and, she suspected, cameras. While future jogs might reveal chinks in security, she decided other commissaries and storage areas on the station would present the same challenge. The safest route was to misappropriate bits of cargo, one at a time, while seeking opportunities on-station. A device left unattended here or there — anything prone to go unnoticed. Her back creaked as she reached upward. It would be a long game, perhaps longer than she wanted, especially with Mina growing so enamored. The length also increased the risk. Especially as missing items piled up. Of course, they would zero in on her. The outsider with mixed allegiances.

Katya picked up her pace into a brisk walk. One step at a time, and right now, she needed to get a quick bite and a cup of bitter kanabean before escorting Sotiris to his appointment.

As always, she reentered their quarters before the toddler had woken. She discarded the flask in the sink, where she filled a glass with fresh water to guzzle. The liquid's chill burned in her chest, but damn, it hit the spot. Her eyes, as she stood next to the island, rested on Mina's door. Had she come back? She was more ghost than not nowadays.

Katya pressed her lips together as she set aside the glass. They'd gotten too close to a truth. They both knew it and feared what lingered under the surface ... that they could believe in different things. And as someone bereft of support as a child on Reznic, Mina gave the chasm a wide berth. If it wasn't seen, did it really exist? It was best not to scratch beneath the surface and discover her mentor wouldn't or couldn't follow her — that, if she pursued her new cause, it would be on her own.

Swallowing down the knot in her throat, Katya shifted, her legs restless. She'd be damned if she removed that support without a fight.

She placed the empty glass in the sink and walked past Mina's room, burying the desire to peek into the room. She also wanted to avoid the looming chasm a little longer, to conceal her intentions. Use Mina's fear to deter her from uncovering her intentions, her actions. She adjusted her sweat-covered shirt.

Before entering her own room, she peeked into Sotiris's, where the boy snoozed. In the dim light, his eyelids twitched, caught in REM sleep. She crept into the cramped space, trepidation brewing in her stomach, the phantom trace of blood under her nose erupting as her hair stood on end. She touched him. Nothing. She gave a firmer nudge. It took moments for his eyes to groggily open. There was a distorted quality to them when they did, with his pupils more visible than usual. With a shudder, he moaned, scrunching his face. Then, with a struggle, he focused on her.

Katya smiled and combed his hair with her fingers, even as horror burgeoned along her spine.

What were they playing at?

Sotiris rolled his shoulders as he rotated in his bed toward her, a yawn escaping. Katya forced herself to release her grip on the bed's edge. Smoothing the sheet, she maintained the smile. "Ready to start the day?"

An indiscernible noise, something between a whine and hiss, emitted from him, and he tried to roll away from her, eyes closing. She half-expected the tendrils to pull at her mind, dragging her to sleep as if she were a marionette. They never came, and the pounding in her ears lessened. Change, shower, dress, and come back, though her mind screamed that would be akin to turning her back on a cobra. Enough.

She rose to her feet and left. In her own room, she stripped and tossed the sweaty clothes into a pile. Her fingers lingered on her right shoulder's rough patch of skin, where the blast had hit her. Sighing, she sat on the bed, fingers still pressed against the exit wound's scar. She avoided thinking of that day, all of it. And she couldn't dabble in it now. She grabbed new clothes and suppressed the strangling sensation that threatened to throttle her; instead, she buried it under routine.

Katya waved Sotiris's cat-like toy through the air, keeping his eyes on it and off the gadgets being fixed to his skin. It mostly worked. However, from time to time, he would bat at Garbi's hand or try to dislodge a sensor, but the adhesive held true. Strom and Usha remained absent throughout the process, their normal position outside the window empty. They could be tuning in via cameras, likely with mimosas in hand.

"We'll leave these on through the day and night." Garbi pored over the information being relayed to her slate.

Katya nodded. It had become a standard practice with all formula changes. Everything had to be monitored. She weighed whether to mention what she'd witnessed just hours beforehand. It could help, but … there was something she couldn't put her finger on that held her tongue.

Off to the side, Isla flipped through files with her upper set of hands near one data center while one of her lower hands typed into a console; she didn't even look at the screen as she put in her notes. The Csek mind was a marvel like that, multitasking to a level most species were incapable of. Katya had marveled at her older brother Harsha's skills, which included playing two instruments simultaneously. But unlike the pale opal-hued Csek before her, Harsha was a talker. Isla, like during all the previous sessions, outsourced interactions to her more sociable partner.

Katya leaned marginally to get a better view of Isla's work. What did those files hold?

"… We'd like to run a few scans on you in a couple of days," Garbi said, startling Katya. At some point, the other woman had discarded her slate and begun slipping Sotiris's shirt over his head.

Katya blinked. "Scans?" Why now? She didn't vocalize the last question, though she hadn't bothered to conceal her confusion on her face.

Garbi guided the boy's arm through the sleeves. "Lucky you, you seem to be his favorite. So, we'd just like to take a quick peek to be sure everything is good. We'll be able to compare scans taken when you first arrived … not too long after he and the other Oneiroi child had been most active in your mind." Her smile was so sincere, with a sliver of apology. "They won't take long."

Sotiris slipped from the cot, his forest cat clutched in hand. Garbi rolled her eyes and shook her head, but let him go. His battery of tests was complete. He hovered near the door and cast glances from it to Katya and back again. The message was clear: Let's go!

"That'll be it for today."

Katya hesitated at the examination table. There'd been no shot. With gnawing unease, she watched Isla power down the console, sealing her work. Katya needed to know what was in those folders.

Returning Garbi's smile, Katya left with Sotiris, carting him back to their quarters. The doors opened to a chilled room. Katya set Sotiris on the floor so he could play, then retrieved her sweater from the sofa, working her arms through its baggy sleeves. The temperature hinted Mina was either still asleep or had never returned. Toeing her way to Mina's rooms, she thumbed open the door.

The teen lay sprawled on her bed, arms stretched in front of her, the left still grasping a slate, which emitted a dim light, probably nearing the limit of its battery. Likely a gift from one of her friends, a sign of trust. Mina's back gently rose as she dozed. The wide-neck tee dipped down, revealing red marks along her shoulder, the result of a late-night make-out session.

How far had it gone? She trusted Mina's judgment but still worried. The teen's UID remained in place, so there would be no unexpected pregnancy; however, it didn't protect against STDs. Perhaps another chat was in order to ensure safety was being observed.

Katya closed the door and entered the kitchenette, where she started brunch by raiding their replenished vegetable supply intent on making a stir-fry. Her precise cuts with the knife distracted her from the worries that poked at her like gnats. The action stirred memories of the times her father had given their chef evenings off so he could cook for his family. He relished the act and made sure each child had some culinary skill. She smiled ruefully. Not that she'd used hers very often. Nope, she usually took whatever slop was dished out at the mess or hit up restaurants. Then on *The Maelstrom*, there'd been Mina, who loved cooking.

Something brushed against her elbow, and Katya stilled the knife. Sotiris craned his neck next to her, having abandoned his toys. He stood, fixated on her pile of minced vegetables. He remained a fixture as Katya continued to create the stir-fry while setting aside plain noodles for him. She had yet to find a vegetable he would eat and decided the Oneiroi, given their frozen planet, had never had them in their diet. Stirring all her ingredients together and layering on the sauce, she reveled in the pleasing aroma wafting through the air.

She bent down and offered the spoon to her shadow. The boy licked it and scrunched his face before wiping his tongue with his hand. Katya rolled her eyes. "And your hand tastes better, huh?"

He tilted his head. "No?"

The door to Mina's room opened, and Katya's response to Sotiris evaporated. She smiled at the teen. "I'll have an early lunch ready soon."

Mina stood in her quarter's doorframe, one shoulder exposed. Her hand reached up and sought to smooth some of her turquoise waves. "You're back early."

She gestured to the nodules on Sotiris's head. "Just monitoring."

Mina skewed her lips. "That's it?"

With concerns about another incident, Katya agreed with the girl. It didn't sit well with her. That they also expected her to be examined ... there was more beneath the surface.

"That's it."

Silence fell between them, which Katya filled with the wooden spoon clanking against the skillet as she dished out equal portions for her and Mina. She handed the plate to her and then plated the plain noodles for Sotiris, pouring some plain bone broth over them.

"Get something warmer on and join us," Katya told Mina while helping Sotiris into his chair. The boy slurped up the noodles, using his fingers, even as she pushed in his chair. She batted his fingers when they dove into the noodles again. "Fork." She pressed the utensil into his hand.

His milky blue eyes met hers; he sputtered, dropping the fork.

"Use it."

A few more corrections followed before Katya could dip into her own rapidly cooling plate. Throughout this ordeal, Mina ate her stir-fry with vigor.

The girl had put on a hoodie, concealing her neckline, but Katya couldn't resist.

"You and Dag seem to be getting on."

The teenager sputtered around her fork, a warm blush spreading across both cheeks, even stretching to her neck. "I don't know what you're talking about."

"I hope you remember past conversations."

The blush deepened. "Wh-when's your next mission?"

The vice returned to Katya's chest. Despite how her meeting with Strom had ended, nothing had followed—no missions, no further meetings. Instead, Strom had withdrawn herself, not even attending Sotiris's sessions in person. Katya rolled her shoulder. Strom was playing a psychological game, never allowing her to know exactly where she stood. It reminded her of the first two months on Jomsborg, when they'd dangled in the wind.

And now, this situation with Sotiris …

Katya shoveled stir-fry into her mouth. Likely, Strom had this very room tapped and was as eagerly awaiting her response as Mina. Swallowing, Katya drank from her water glass before answering. "I think Sotiris's situation is of greater concern to Plasovern than the use of a pilot." She toyed with the remnants on her plate. "Do you remember being pulled under?"

Scratching at her neck, Mina dropped her gaze. She spun the noodles around her fork, not stopping even when the ends were little nubs.

"I don't even remember the first time." It came out like a wisp, a hint of more.

Her own experience had been … less than pleasant. Tiny fragments, details dissipating to a persistent itch of memory. "They'll get it sorted."

Mina stopped twirling her fork. "Everyone will be relieved."

"Do your friends say much?"

"They largely ask things." Her index finger ran up and down the fork's smooth handle. "About him. What he's like, what he eats, and whether I'm afraid to be around him or not."

"Are you?"

Her eyes lifted. "Sometimes. Not so much now that there's a cure, even if it's a work in progress. But you have to admit, despite how adorable he is" — she flicked a finger at Sotiris, who'd gone back to eating noodles with his fingers — "what he's capable of is frightening. His species is frightening." She ate some of the probably chilled noodles before settling the fork next to her plate. "I love him. He's my favorite little Elite. But the Magistrate should have never brought the Oneiroi out into the galaxy."

It was a sentiment most beings would agree with, not only regarding the Oneiroi but all the other species that made up the Magistrate's Elite forces. And perhaps the Elites themselves would agree. She dipped her hand into her lap. The Jar'rask interrogator had readily shared his people's aversion to the cooperative endeavor forced on them by the Magistrate. Like any species, the Oneiroi had to prefer their own homeworld. Yet, an insidious quality lined the statement.

"Perhaps. But the galaxy is as much theirs as ours." Katya stood and took her plate to the sink. "They just shouldn't have been compelled into the roles they were given." A role ensuring they'd only ever be the galaxy's bogeyman. "Help me clean up, and then why don't you pick something for us to watch? That's unless you have places to be … such as with a certain young man?"

The girl blushed thoroughly while her head lowered, as if tethered to an invisible weight. She did eventually slip from her seat and help with the dishes after muttering, "I'll find something."

After tidying the kitchenette some, Mina launched the entertainment console. Snippets of stations floated into the kitchenette as she surfed through what was available at Jomsborg—a limited number of Medzeci channels. By the time Katya wrapped up cleaning Sotiris, Mina had landed on a drama station, where a zealous girl waved her arms about while screaming at another girl. The language belonged to Medzeci, but Mina ad-libbed over it, often distorting her voice for each character. Sometimes, she even added grandiose motions with her hands. Katya blurted out in laughter as she took on the airs of an old man with complaints of rheumatism, gout, and eye crust.

"No, no," she berated the console as the scene switched. "I was just getting to my bowels. They don't work!"

In between, she'd break down some of the actual words being spoken. Katya blinked. In five months, the teen had picked up so many words and phrases.

"You could be a linguist," she said.

"Unlikely." Mina then resumed her act, this time as one of the younger girls in the cast, bemoaning that her purse was not the prettiest of them all.

Sotiris had joined them on the sofa amid the drama. Between his arms, he clutched his beloved stuffed Skogarld forest cat, resting its plush head under his chin. He'd cuddled against Katya, warming her side. And at some point, his eyes slid shut, and his breathing leveled out. Katya nudged him, but he didn't stir, nor did his ability.

What was Strom playing at?

Life on Jomsborg kept its rhythm of appointments and listlessness. With no piloting needed, jogs became Katya's lifeline to sanity. She rose early and took off, allowing the physical activity to erase her nerves. The waiting, the frustration as Sotiris's sleep habits shifted from what had become the norm. While he might nap during the day, there'd been no further incidents. Still, the sight only inspired dread, especially following her conversation with Mina.

Her footfalls resounded off the metal, changing tenor when she entered a connector. If he became only an item of fear not only for Mina but for the entire station ...

She left the thought unfinished, focusing instead on her path, the pull of her muscles, her breath, the sound of her feet. Passing through the connector, she came across the greatest deviation from the ordinary: an unexpected jogging buddy, the Tizzet woman, Kahina.

The why escaped her. But because Katya stuck to a set route, only expanding it, Kahina always found her and usually fell into step with her by the first common area. From there, it didn't matter where Katya dragged Kahina on the station; she followed, sometimes practically side by side or a step behind.

And sure enough, Kahina waited, stretching her legs. The woman wore a full-body suit made of stretchy material. It had to have some breathing qualities too, or else she would have overheated during their longer jogs together. Slim-fitting gloves covered the Tizzet woman's hands; they lacked cutaways. She always had sunglasses on, an athletic variety that conformed to the curves of her face.

She never discouraged the other woman, nor had she tried to lose her. What point was there? Other than to raise red flags. So they carried on together, not a word uttered, just their footfalls communicating dogged determination forward.

Perhaps the language barrier prevented Kahina from talking. She hadn't seemed apt with the Magistrate's prime language. Katya pursed her lips, and sweat, with its salty flavor, reached her tongue. The other woman would have to make the first move. She refused to budge on that one guiding rule, which she'd formed when this occurrence became routine. She would not chance letting even the most mundane statement balloon into dangerous speech. Like with Mina, whatever she said wouldn't remain solely with Kahina. It would pass to other ears, probably being twisted with each set.

The Tizzet woman's continual presence prompted another question: Why had Izem remained? The widespread assumption on Jomsborg had been that he would pass through as he'd done in the past. Yet the visit stretched. Why?

Katya glanced at the other woman from the corner of her eye. Much like her, sweat dotted Kahina's brow, only finer, not as profuse. She could always ask, but she never did.

Instead, she took her fellow jogger along an alternative route—a different connector and set of ramps. When this intrusion into her routine had first occurred, Katya had scaled back before becoming emboldened again. Time's passage had only spurred her to test boundaries. She needed a mental map of Jomsborg to find any potential advantage she could. She avoided the docking bays, however. No sane jogger would view them as prime candidates for the sport. Further inspections of them would have to wait until the next mission … Whenever it came.

Bright light greeted them as they left a connector and ran into a green, lower-level common space. Katya shifted to the space's edge, feeling very much like an intruder. The Sarchins, who'd joined Plasovern in what amounted to an exile, had claimed it. The majority on their Fringe-positioned planet, Shirenoi, had voted to join the Magistrate, a rare example of unity across species lines. Rather than cave, the *Urshlakh*, or wayward clans, had dedicated their skills to Plasovern, yet conversely had no genuine desire to displace the Magistrate from their homeworld. No, they simply saw themselves on a pilgrimage to preserve the old ways. Let the others fold, bend themselves to Magistrate culture, but never them.

She struggled to tell them apart with their uniform coats of fur, a brownish gray. Those in the common space paused in their tasks to peer at the interlopers, the red, furless skin framing their large, coal-like eyes. A few twisted their flowing mustaches, perhaps a nervous twitch or maybe annoyance. Males and females shared the feature, and their clothing choices did not say male or female in a way Katya was used to. Though a few had children clutching to their backs and shoulders. Potentially mothers? On-station, male and female alike wore elaborate brocades, with motifs resembling forests and the native fauna of their world. Beneath these robe-like items, their tails, with flashy bushes of white at their ends, poked out, curling in on themselves.

Very few were in the space currently. Most, because of their small statures and silent fighting methods, were out on assignment. Since so many Sarchins had embraced admission into the republic, they would pass effortlessly on those missions until it was too late for their targets.

Within this common space, they had set up weathered wood carvings. Splintered cracks had formed into some of their iconographies. Despite herself, Katya slowed to better gawk at the images embedded by a carver's hand: a Sarchin holding a spear, a child, some item, and an engraving that'd been so blackened by moisture its subject had grown indiscernible. Potted trees dotted the area, and little shops, staffed by and for Sarchins, waited.

In the center, a makeshift garden, which amounted to more than a foot of dirt on the metal floor, had green shoots supported by poles and lines of twine. Many of the plants harbored blooms, which promised fruit in the future. Two Sarchins walked through its rows. Their black eyes briefly followed the two joggers, but lost interest.

Katya picked up her pace, heading to a ramp, which connected to the overhead promenade. Near it, a shrine big enough to hold at least ten Sarchins, maybe four regular humanoids, had been erected from a red wood. It had no windows and had a dome shape. Its roof was impressive, with branches woven into delicate patterns but tightly to block the station's light from the interior.

If she was alone, she might have paused on the promenade to marvel at the intricate designs, a fine art her father would have appreciated, but since she was not, she pressed on. Her lungs burned by the time they reached the upper common spaces again, and Katya slowed to a walk and took time to stretch her arms and neck. This shared space held the bakery Mina adored. The aroma of freshly baked bread and pastries sent her mouth into overdrive and hit her stomach hard. She fully entered cool down, circling the area, bringing her heart rate down while furthering her stretches.

Kahina followed her example, forever her silent sentry.

When Katya reached a table away from other early risers, who milled with their ration cards, she launched into her stretch routine. Sweat trickled down her frame and neck, and she regretted not having a towel.

"Why do you run?"

Katya jerked her head toward Kahina and abandoned her hamstring stretch.

The other woman leaned against the nearby wall, watching her as if with a microscope. Her lower lip jaunted out.

Straightening, Katya mulled over the question. It was so unexpected she didn't know what to say, so she bought time. "Pardon?"

Kahina crossed her arms and repeated the question in her thick accent. "Why do you run?"

"For my health." Katya shrugged and returned to her stretches. "Something to pass time."

A derisive snort was her answer. "No, you do not." She didn't look at Katya, choosing instead to eye the people waiting for fresh bread. "Your steps have purpose."

"Don't everyone's?"

Bowing her head, the rough exterior she projected broke. Kahina actually smiled, enough to even reveal the white of her teeth. "To different levels." She flicked a finger to the others lined up. "For food, basic necessities. Some just from one point to the second. Others? It is more. There is drive."

She nudged her head up to the space's promenade, where someone rushed to the lift. "That one has greater purpose."

"I think you underestimate the importance of fresh bread."

Kahina chuckled a bit before pushing herself from the wall. "Important, but not enough." She came to tower over Katya while she held a lunge, further stretching muscles. "I wanted to know you, Magistrate woman. Know why you have done as you have done. How you have come here. My people are runners. Times and technology have changed, but not that. No. It is a spiritual matter: you and nature alone. It is freeing." She moved her tight coils over her shoulder. "I know that look you carry. You do not run without purpose."

"It is, as you say, a freeing activity for the mind."

The other woman clucked at her. "But there is more."

Her jaw tightened. Why was she prying? What did she hope to uncover, and for whom? Katya pulled herself up from the lunge and weighed her words, ultimately settling on, "Perhaps I run for those in my care."

"The boy and the girl."

"Sotiris and Mina."

The other woman tapped at her chin before her voice lowered. "There is one like your Saw-tEE-rees at our home. Brought by Magistrate."

A piece clicked into place: Izem remained only because he had no other choice. She thought back to the news articles, specifically the troop movements. The Oneiroi had been removed from Tizzet, a world where they'd been fixtures since its enrollment. Meanwhile, Breks had moved in with a child possessing the defect ... something the Magistrate could not risk the Oneiroi discovering. Her mind shifted gears. The recent changes in Sotiris's care rankled her. The timing followed so closely with Izem's arrival on Jomsborg. They were trying to get something from Sotiris.

Katya schooled her face into the perfect reflection of serenity and tested the theory. "When the *Paralus* left, right?"

"Precisely when." Through her sunglasses, Katya felt her shrewd gaze. "How did you know?"

"I caught an article." After wiping the sweat from her face with the lip of her shirt, Katya added, "I've seen what they've done to Oneiroi children like Sotiris. It then only takes a while to connect the dots: your arrival, the departure of the Oneiroi vessel." The shift in Sotiris's treatment went unsaid. She recalled the snippet of Strom's and Izem's exchange she'd overheard. What had Strom promised Izem?

Kahina exhaled loudly and then rolled her head from side to side. "Our world was occupied by the Magistrate long ago. Before my birth. Though is it called occupation? No." She drew back, returning to her previous pose against the flat metal wall. Her one gloved hand toyed with a nearby rivet. "The shadows have been among those interlopers since that time. But this child they have now ... we are lucky to be here, to be alive. Our compatriots remain, but for how long? We cannot say."

"What do you intend to do?"

"What must be done. What is there but to do?" Kahina shrugged. "We will have our home. One day."

Katya shuddered as she straightened, sweat tracing her spine. "And Sotiris is the key."

"Maybe." She pinched her lips together and glanced at the ceiling, its artificial light casting odd shadows on her face. "If there even is a key to be found. I have my misgivings. But fret not, we have no ill will to your child."

Heat boiled in Katya's chest. No ill will? Yet, Sotiris was being poked and prodded for a solution to be used against another born with the mutation. A weapon that in Plasovern's hands could be turned on an entire species. The twitch set into her left hand.

Kahina pushed off from the wall and came next to her. "You should not trust Strom." It was the barest of whispers, made more clandestine by the other woman's steady retreat.

"Understatement of the century," Katya muttered under her breath.

Left alone, she freed her ration card from her shirt's small pocket and joined the throng of people, hoping to score the sticky buns so beloved by Mina and Sotiris. And as she waited, her mind tore apart the newly gleaned information. She needed to speed her process.

CHAPTER SEVEN

Sliding into their quarters, Katya left the sticky rolls on the kitchenette's countertop. They'd cost her time, and Sotiris would be up and hidden by the time she got out of the shower, but it was a necessity given the stern glares people in the line had shot her. She gathered fresh clothes—a bland stormy-gray long-sleeved shirt and basic jeans. And sure enough, by the time she'd bathed and dressed, Sotiris had left his room and evanesced himself somewhere in the common room.

She returned to the kitchenette and rattled the bag as she removed two of the rolls. "I guess I'll have to eat these by myself."

The words summoned Sotiris from his hiding spot by the console, rushing forward upon spotting the sugary delicacy. He allowed her to lift him into his chair before tearing the roll to bits, which he stuffed into his mouth. She'd have to wash his hands and face before taking him to the clinic. As genial as Garbi had been, she doubted it would please the woman if her instruments became coated in a sticky glaze.

Katya ate her own as she went and knocked on Mina's door. "Hey, I brought a treat. You'll want to get yours before Sotiris does."

She returned to the kitchenette, still munching on her own roll. With her free hand, she liberated the kanabean container and a mug before turning on the stovetop, kettle already in place. The gap stretched, and Katya suspected Mina was elsewhere, but then the door opened.

The smile on Katya's face dissipated when she turned to the teen. Red, puffy eyes peered back at her, lips pressing inward as if to stave the slight tremor. Katya's chest tightened.

"What happened?"

Mina's mouth clenched as she wrapped her arms around herself. "Dag's gone."

A tingle flared along the back of Katya's neck. Gone had so many connotations with Plasovern involved.

"On a mission," Mina ground out.

Oh.

Mina jerked away, her stormy brown eyes glaring holes into the kitchenette cabinets. "I wanted to go. But mission command wouldn't let me."

"You're too young."

A noisy inhale and exhale, and then those tumultuous brown orbs returned to Katya. "They aren't much older than I am." Mina moderated her tone, but it came out pitched. "They are allowed to help. They're given responsibilities. I'm"—she shoved her hands into her hoody's pocket—"I'm left watching. I don't want to watch."

"And what would you prefer to do, Mina?" Katya discarded the sliver of sticky roll remaining and wiped her gummy fingers against her pants.

The teen glanced at her sock-clad feet, just for a moment, then: "Join the fight. They are cracking in the Fringe, just a bit more of a push, and they'll have no choice but to concede."

"Is that what Dag says?"

"Everyone does."

Sotiris stirred in his chair, the sticky roll no longer there to occupy him. His head swiveled between Mina and her. To remove him from the conversation, Katya set him free to play with his toys, which he did while still glancing at them, something in their tones catching his notice.

"Ereago for sure," Katya said. Even months ago, while delivering grain to Usha, she would have conceded that ... but having witnessed its further degradation, she knew without a doubt, the Magistrate would have to withdraw. "The entire Fringe? Unlikely."

Mina bristled and asked hollowly, "Then you still favor the Magistrate?"

Katya froze as if doused by icy water. Knowledge crept into her brain: This room was bugged. Strom was going to have a field day.

"I didn't say that." The words flowed from her tongue. "I'm being realistic."

Even concealed in the pocket, Katya caught the whine of Mina's prosthetic tightening to the point of complaint.

"But you're still loyal to them."

Katya ran her fingers through her long bangs, grimacing as they stuck a bit. Moving to the sink, she washed the residue from her hands and measured a response to satisfy two audiences—Mina and Strom. Like her, Strom was a realist; she knew underneath Katya's facade laid conflicted allegiances. So far, the Plasovern leader had been testing how deep those allegiances' fault lines went—how far Katya would go. The water burned, and she removed her reddened hands.

Across the way, Mina shifted her weight as Katya dried her hands on a kitchen towel and faced her. The girl's toes curled against the tile flooring.

"To an extent, some remains." There would be no lies, not on this to Mina. "My father rescued me … that doesn't just evaporate." There were also still some wearing the blue who she considered friends. Then there were the ghosts who'd died wearing it and tugged reproachfully at her. She returned the towel to its place and shrugged. "Call me too old, but I prefer to be cautious." Seeing the girl's jaw tighten, she added, "You're young, passionate. I can see why you are so enthralled. If I were younger, I would likely be the same. But there is wisdom in patience and learning exactly what you're signing up for."

Mina grunted. "Like you did with the Magistrate?"

Her breath hitched, and as heat flooded her chest and face, she forgot her second audience. "That's enough."

Mina bit into her lower lip, her hands hammering against the sides of her legs. "Look what the Magistrate did to us! Plasovern's standing up to them. They're trying to take back what the Magistrate stole from so many people!" The cybernetic arm groaned, the glove pulling taut.

"But at what expense?" The words rushed from Katya's mouth, pitched too sharp.

"At what expense did the Magistrate conquer those worlds?! It's weaseled its way in and sucked them dry, taking, taking—always taking!" The seams stretched and gaps formed between the stitches. "They cut off Dag's people from their most valuable resource and kept it for themselves to conquer more planets. They overhauled Skogarld's government, stripped its people of their liberties, imposed curfews—"

"Did Dag tell you why the regulations went into place?"

"That doesn't matter!"

"Because people were being blown apart," Katya pressed. "The rebels were bleeding Skogarld, pro-occupation, anti-occupation—it didn't matter. Plasovern's precursor knocked out a city corridor with bombs." The photo on Strom's credenza loomed with its dangling corpses. "The Magistrate isn't faultless; it traded brutality for brutality." She swallowed. "Blame belongs to so many. Ultimately, the Magistrate should've never been on Skogarld, but by the time it'd been established on-world, extraction wasn't simple. There are people on-world who would be massacred if the troops did. It's not just Skogarld. It's Ereago. It's countless others. The path forward isn't simple. Plasovern is falling into the same pit the Magistrate did: thinking it knows best."

"Yet only Plasovern is being damned for it, and the Magistrate gets to continue in its *rightness*?"

"A sledgehammer is not a solution."

"But they won't let go without one." Mina's lips formed a thin line, her hardening expression daring Katya to deny it.

And she couldn't. Because for varying reasons, the Magistrate would not dislodge itself from contested worlds without a massive force demanding it. Despite what the cynic might say, it wasn't always resource-driven. That sledgehammer would not only remove the republic but crack fragile peace accords, established by its stabilizing presence, particularly on fractured worlds, where factions vied for supremacy.

Deeper creases formed along Mina's brow with her silence. "So you see why Plasovern has to act as they do."

"Oh yes, shooting unarmed civilians is justified."

"Magistrate propaganda—"

"No," Katya's voice cracked. "I saw it with my own eyes."

A crack formed in Mina's expression. Her lips parted, and doubt slipped into her eyes—soon smothered by a certainty born from youthful passion and the assuredness that goes hand in hand with it. "There had to be more."

"They wanted to leave."

Mina shook her head, her nostrils flaring. "They had to have done something. Plasovern is about liberation." The seams popped. "You know nothing." Tears prickled in the teen's eyes. "You're too ingrained!" Mina shouted, damning her with the same pronouncement she'd brandied against the Oneiroi.

She then tore out of their quarters, not even bothering with shoes.

Katya shoved her hands into her pant pockets, where the left vibrated against her leg as if palsy plagued it. Her breathing came in waves, and she wanted to melt into the floor. Padding to the bathroom, she splashed cool water against her face. Red eyes greeted her in the mirror, water still running along her face's contours. Because she was looking, the slight mark left by the Jar'rask's tongue glared at her, contrasting marginally against her rather pale complexion.

Get a grip.

She loosened her hold on the sink and turned from the mirror. She'd left Mina alone too much. Allowed her to be swept away. She wiped her hand against her face, displacing moisture. She tugged a towel from its ring and dried herself while taking an extra moment to massage its coarseness against her skin and compose herself. Damn it. She'd allowed herself to get rattled and said far more than she should have.

Gritting her teeth, she gave the wall behind her a sharp kick. A pinched-off scream smothered in her throat. Carelessness would get her killed.

Then her brows shot up. They were late. The appointment.

She dashed into the shared space and grabbed Sotiris, sticky fingers, grunting complaints, and all, before rushing from the room. Once again, Mina had to wait. But for how long would she?

Out of breath, Katya stumbled through the clinic's doors and froze. The lobby, usually awash with patients, laid bare of people and chairs. The low tables lined the edges while large boxes filled the cleared space. Smaller ones lined the counter at the reception area. Past them, nurses sorted through paper files, stuffing them into boxes before moving on to the next. One nurse held a slate inches from her nose as if she were rather near-sighted. Despite not understanding the words, Katya assumed the nurse was questioning if specific things had been filed yet from her tone.

Yesterday, there had been no signs of a sudden move. Katya's stomach clenched as she stepped forward, shifted Sotiris to one side, and tapped with her free hand on the reception area's glass.

"Excuse me. What's going on?"

The nurse with the slate jumped and dropped the device, though she caught it before it hit the ground. Flustered, she held it to her chest and stared, blue eyes wide. After muttering under her breath, she cleared her throat. "A new space opened up that is more advantageous." She pointed the slate to their usual point of entry. "Ms. Usha's drug studies will continue here." Moving to a panel, she undoubtedly signaled Garbi to their arrival. "Please proceed."

Katya did as instructed, even as unease settled on her like a cloak weighing down her shoulders. As she was prone to do with most occurrences on Jomsborg, she looked for layers and potential underlining reasons. For over five months, this clinic had been a fixture. Why change it now?

In the list of needs before breaking with Plasovern, the clinic ranked highly. She could not leave without the medicine. She would even place it above transportation. If Sotiris lost control … Plasovern would easily reclaim them. Or the Magistrate would capture them since she favored a return to its space where she had an edge. Those were best cases versus being splattered across space after hitting debris or slowly starving in a blissful, sleepless dream. He was a danger, and no matter how sweet he was, it was a fact that she couldn't dismiss without dire consequences.

In the hall, she removed Sotiris's clothing per normal but kept her attention on the door behind him. Metal, likely steel. If they locked her code out during the off-hours, it would require either explosives or a stolen keycard. Both would tip off someone to her plans rapidly—one a lot quicker. She folded Sotiris's shirt with one hand while holding him in place with the other. There was time to work it out. Of all the items she needed, the drug must come last.

Garbi, wearing her regular white lab coat, entered the hallway and greeted them with a warm smile. "I was worried I'd have to send the rescue party when you guys weren't coming!" She wagged a finger at Sotiris. "It looks like someone didn't want to come this morning. But don't worry! Only a few tests today, and then you'll be free."

Katya slid off Sotiris's pants, and Garbi surged in, hoisting him up and carrying him into the examination room.

By the time Katya caught up, Garbi had already seated Sotiris on the examination table and hooked the devices to his forehead.

"If you don't mind, Isla will set up a scan for you and some other tests," Garbi said. "We can't put it off." The last bit hovered toward apologetic.

"For science," Katya muttered before following Isla behind a separate curtain. Sotiris made an "oof" sound when she vanished.

On the other side, Isla sorted through various larger nodules on a rolling desk, not acknowledging Katya, who stood inches away, shifting her weight while waiting for instructions. When they came, it was with Isla's minimal hand gestures, pointing to a backless stool. Katya slipped on to it, having to use the balls of her feet to do so. There, Isla braided and pinned up Katya's hair. The action sparked unwelcomed memories of home, even if not in the style she'd worn. Once the obstacle was removed, Isla plastered nodules on Katya's forehead, temples, and the base of her skull. Smaller ones were placed along the back of her head, drawing tears as Isla forcibly pried hair apart to place them.

The Csek then peered at her slate. The nodules warmed against Katya's skin, but not so much to burn. With a stylus, Isla scribbled notes between scrolling through whatever data and imagery were being produced.

Setting aside the slate, the woman retrieved a finger device that she cuffed on one of Katya's fingers. The other device suctioned itself to her upper arm. Isla added more notes to the slate before taking a pin light to Katya's eyes. She lingered too long on each one, so when Katya closed them, the perfect hollowed circle remained for minutes afterward.

The session concluded in under a half-hour. Isla striped the nodules from her, taking some hair as well; however, before releasing her, the Csek brought over a needle.

"What's the blood for?" Katya asked while unpinning her hair and rubbing the affronted sections of her scalp.

From across the cloth curtain, Garbi saved Isla from answering. "It's routine, I'm afraid. We like to check Jomsborg residents periodically to make sure they haven't brought anything back with them. We really should've checked you after your last mission. Given your emotional state, Mistress Strom requested a reprieve on policy."

The Csek grabbed Katya's arm, pushed up the sleeve, and fastened a latex hose. It was a wise policy, but something still left her unsettled as the needle penetrated her skin and crimson filled its canister. After halting the blood flow and applying a cotton ball and medical tape, Isla took her haul and retreated to the desk.

Rolling down her sleeve, Katya eyed the Csek until she walked off with the vial and slate to her primary station. Katya pressed the cotton into the needle site, hissing a bit when she applied more pressure. The Magistrate had been keen on regular examinations. While immunizations could safeguard against many diseases, one didn't chance infections, especially given the Magistrate's expansive territory. But there was something more here. She popped off the stool and cleared the cloth barrier.

Sotiris swiveled to her instantly, and across the way, Garbi, who had removed a syringe from a locked medicine dispenser using a code, implored him to stay seated. Katya rushed to hold him until the other woman could administer the drug.

The dispenser could be a problem for Katya's plans. She wondered how often Garbi and Isla updated their pin numbers.

"There!" Garbi beamed. "All done!"

The last words apparently clicked in Sotiris's head, and he lurched further into Katya's arms, clinging ferociously.

Garbi discarded the spent needle in a medical waste receptacle and picked up her slate and a bandage, which she applied over the burning mark of the injection site. Once placed, she scrolled her finger against the slate's screen.

"Your blood pressure and heart rate are elevated," Garbi said, erasing any question if it was Sotiris's data or hers. "Was it particularly stressful this morning?"

Stressful barely touched it. "A bit," Katya agreed. "I've also never done well with examinations, particularly when etched with silence."

"Oh," Garbi mouthed. "I'm sorry about that, but Isla can't speak. She had her tongue cut out to make her more pliant. Mistress Usha offered a vocal box, but she declined."

Katya blinked and tightened her grip on Sotiris. "My apologies, I didn't know."

Garbi shrugged, most of her attention back on the slate. "It's not something we discuss, nor does Isla care to share it." She added, "Bring him by tomorrow morning. We won't run any more tests for a while."

"What about the drug's administration?"

That apologetic smile returned, curdling Katya's gut. "It's a process. Safety's our top priority, I promise you that." Garbi tapped at her slate screen. "Everything's looking promising, though. So I'm sure it won't be too much longer. Mistress Usha is quite pleased with the progress we're sending her."

So, Usha was off-station but still heavily involved. Not that it mattered. The promise always remained that an oral version would be completed any moment. It never was, and she wondered if it ever would be.

Katya carted Sotiris to the door, Garbi following with idle conversation and hollow promises of progress. Katya smiled during it and nodded her head. The facade momentarily slipped when she met Strom's waiting form in the hallway. Clad in form-fitting leggings, heavy boots, and a long, fitted dark-hued duster, the woman resembled a soldier, particularly with her blonde waves tamed in a bun, save for a few flyaways.

"Ah, Mistress Strom!" Garbi greeted her with a shallow bow.

"I trust all is well?" Strom asked.

"All's good." Garbi pinched Sotiris's cheek before waving. "I'll see you tomorrow." Then she swiveled and reentered the lab.

Like a carpet being ripped out from under her, Katya stood off-footed before Strom, suddenly very alone, even with Sotiris still resting on her hip.

"Don't stop on my account," Strom said. "Get the boy dressed."

Katya stepped around Strom to the table and helped Sotiris. Strom's eyes bore into her back as she worked, assisted by the Oneiroi boy. Sotiris was all too eager to go, sometimes slowing the process when he tried to take over, particularly with his pants. The attention behind her only flustered her fingers more, and the shake threatened to emerge in front of the last person she wanted to know. Even if she likely already knew.

Strom's duster rustled. "The joys of youth," the woman said. "Always so eager to carry forward. That girl of yours isn't so different, is she?"

Katya turned when Strom chuckled.

"It's good to see such passion in the young, don't you agree?"

Seizing Sotiris's shirt, Katya buried herself in the task to avoid answering. Her mind rifled through her conversation with Mina, gauging the damage it had done should Strom have been eavesdropping. Plenty. Sweat lined her palms as she batted away one of Sotiris's hands to tug on the shirt. Or had Mina said something? She dismissed the thought almost immediately. Despite their recent differences, Katya couldn't bring herself to believe the teen would knowingly betray her … but she was young, confused, and perhaps eager for a sympathetic ear. She swallowed against a bitter flavor in her mouth.

"Youth has its benefits," Katya returned.

"And its flaws." Strom approached the side of the table until she was in Katya's line of sight. "Do you know where she is currently?"

Her heart faltered in her chest, her fingers gripping the shirt's fabric too tightly. Had she left the station?

Strom's dyed lips, which the red overhead light turned into a macabre black, perked. "She's up on Level 19 pouting." Her tone light, almost singsongy, rubbed salt into a gaping wound. She knew something Katya didn't, and she basked in it. "Young love and the heartbreak of being left behind. Of course, it won't always be like that, but at … how old is she again?"

Katya swallowed and, through her teeth, replied, "Seventeen."

"Of course." Strom leaned forward. Her perfume, a floral mix with cedar, taunted Katya's nose. "It's the end of the world at that age. Though, I hope it's not something more." The bridge of her nose crinkled. "She looked rather despondent, and now that I think about it, it's the first I've ever seen her without gloves on since the surgery."

The busted seams leaped to Katya's mind. She could picture Mina tossing the damaged glove in frustration. "There was an accident this morning with the gloves."

"Ah," Strom breathed. "I'll see another pair is delivered. But there's another matter that I needed to speak with you about."

Releasing her hold on the shirt, which was already in place, Katya rose until her face was in line with Strom. The roiling within her body remained concealed under a tepid expression.

"You said you would still work."

Her heart leaped in a complex mix of anticipation and dread. She needed this. An opportunity—the word, much like an intense citrus, wilted her tongue—to be in the hangar bays without raising suspicions. There was a timetable, and she needed to settle on a mark. Something to blend into the Fringe. Decent maneuverability and speed. To outrun anything that might follow them.

"Yes."

Strom's eyes curved this time as she smiled, baring her teeth, which took a pinkish hue under the light. "Good. I have a courier mission. It'll be a day trip to a nearby station to pick up supplies."

"When do I leave?"

"In a couple of days." She adjusted her duster. "After Bodil returns. Her command should be more to your liking. You two strike me as kindred spirits in command styles, though, I suppose, sometimes that causes its own problems. But let's keep that to a minimum this time."

An edge underlined that last statement, cementing the need to keep her head down. Her chances with Plasovern were running out. She coiled her fingers around Sotiris's hot hand. And she suspected the Oneiroi toddler's fondness for her might no longer save her. Not now when the drug sealed his ability.

"There will be no problems."

"Good." Strom finished smoothing the wrinkles along her duster's front. "I suggest smoothing things over with young Mina. I'm sure the new gloves will make a decent peace offering."

"I'm sure."

Strom then waltzed down the hall to the private rooms. Katya clenched her hands into trembling fists when the door closed. That woman.

"Go?" Sotiris had grabbed his sunglasses at some point, smudging up the lenses.

"Yeah, go."

Before she opened their exit, she smothered on the protective goo and hefted him up. His endurance wasn't there yet, and she had another stop to make.

The boy dug his chin into her shoulder, grating skin against bone, when she diverted from routine and the path home to go to Level 19. Having left it unexplored, she continued blindly, following its connectors and hoping to uncover Mina's location. In one, a pallid Varraganarian couple sprawled over each other on a bench. The edge lighting on the synth glass window gave gauntness to their faces. The dark color inked beneath their eyes only added a corpse-like quality.

Katya gave them a wide berth as she passed but still heard the man mutter something under his breath, drawing a one-word response from the woman, who rested her head against his shoulder. She made to lift it but never did. Her face, as if tethered to some greater weight, sank further into the crevice between his arm and torso.

Were they on drugs? She considered finding someone in case the pair required help, but tossed the instinct to the side after footsteps approached her from the rear. Let them handle it. Still—she glanced back as she strolled forward—something unsettled her.

After stalking the connector's entire length, she arrived at a common space unlike those in the newer lower levels. For one, there was no bright artificial sun, just harsh light that lacked warmth and, conversely, almost wasn't enough for the space with its black metal. If not for the glint bouncing off the space's walls, she would have believed she'd stumbled into a cavern. A cavern with industrial walkways, not designed with civilians in mind. A slender figure sat on the far one, which ran parallel with a wall of paned synth glass—hopefully guarded by reliable shielding.

Mina.

The teen sat on the walkway, legs dangling over the ledge as she faced the expansive window, lost in the stars. Her arms rested on one of the lower rails and stretched outward. As she approached, Katya realized Mina's attention was not devoted to the station's exterior but to her mismatched hand and its unnatural sheen. The girl moved one finger after the next, her expression caught between revulsion and despondency. A heaviness settled in Katya's limbs when she approached.

They had never really addressed the psychological fallout from the Jar'rask vessel, not even by a mile. Routine had allowed that painful process to be back-burnered, and here, she was prepared to do it again, just until they crossed into the Fringe again. In her mind, she caught smatterings of Valens teasing about emotional avoidance. But what room did he have to talk, really? They'd all trained to partition off disruptive emotions. But Mina wasn't a soldier. She was a girl hurting so rawly.

Katya's throat constrained as she crossed into Mina's space and lowered herself and Sotiris until they sat next to the girl. The motion and Sotiris's muttered "Ooo" broke the trance, and Mina started, glancing at the two with wide eyes.

"What ..." Mina trailed off.

"I didn't like how our conversation ended."

Retracting her hands from the rail, Mina muttered, "Neither did I."

The following silence stretched, with Katya fidgeting and struggling for words to convey what she wanted to say. There was so much she wanted to say, but it all felt so flat, inadequate. Instead, she took in the young woman next to her. How much Mina had grown struck her hard. Especially when caught in a moment that dredged up a night now years in the past. They'd still been strangers, then. Two people, adrift in grief, on a small observation deck, seeking Reznic's long-extinct constellations.

The present-day Medzeci stars blurred when Katya faced them, and she blinked to clear her vision. It had been the night after Sotiris's former namesake, Aquila, had been killed on a mission. That death still weighed heavily on her, never failing to conjure what-if scenarios, which couldn't breathe life into the dead.

"I ..." Katya swallowed and started again. "I was young once too. So eager to cut my teeth. So sure of everything—convinced of rightness and wrongness." She'd set off running along the soldiering path, despite her father's lukewarmness for the profession. Something had called, and she'd answered. And she hadn't been alone. "I think most of us felt the same. I know, beyond the shadow of a doubt, quite a few people I served with cared deeply for the worlds we were on, wanted to serve their people and improve their circumstances. A few died for them."

Mina's head dipped, likely also thinking about Sergeant Aquila Salvius, who'd stolen from the mess hall for her, the kind soul he'd been.

"But the Magistrate has its blunders." She pressed Sotiris to her side when he tried to scoot closer to the edge. "It's so easy to become clouded in rightness, which can lead to doing things that are decidedly not. It's an alluring trap: to think you alone know best. That line of thought is the Magistrate's foible, maybe its hemlock. Landed it in inadvisable conflicts, noble and ignoble. On Reznic, we gave those trying to loosen the syndicates' grasp a fighting chance. Ereago? Intervention only stoked divisions and attracted Plasovern. Now the planet's burning." Katya frowned at her knees. "I see the missteps now. But when I was young, no … it never occurred to me." And even if she had … "Life is seldom clear-cut. Though perhaps you're right. The Oneiroi should've been left to be swallowed by a naturally occurring mutation."

A sharp inhale issued next to her.

"It's nature," Katya continued. "Let it take its course."

"But they're weapons."

"Yes." Katya shook Sotiris's hand as it tried to tug at her shirt. His lips mouthed "go." "But the species continues. With how little technology they had, they likely wouldn't have been able to save themselves."

Mina didn't respond, only pressed her forehead against the railing, lips turned downward.

"Adulthood isn't easy. And sometimes, what is done is done. We all try to do our best—for better or worse." Katya squeezed the girl's shoulder with her free hand. "It's tough for me to cast aside decades of my life for Plasovern."

"I understand that." Mina didn't meet her eyes. "But with how things are … you could try harder."

She couldn't. Exhaling through her nose, Katya peered out the window. A skiff passed by rather close to the station. It tipped in a wave, likely to someone on the station. Below, someone giggled shrilly. She could understand Plasovern's aims, couldn't fault them for wanting an existence removed from the Magistrate, but she could never accept Strom's tactics to achieve those aims, which reaped death. Ereago loomed in her mind. There were so many factions on-world, and Plasovern had effectively disregarded all but the Gata's desires. No different from the Magistrate.

She pulled Sotiris away from the ledge as he leaned forward, eyes wide. Now, however, was not the time for debate, as it would not bridge the gap between her and Mina. She would have to trust it would heal with time.

After clearing her throat, Katya said, "And I am."

Mina instantly straightened and faced her. The hard lines on her face smoothed out, though the slight raise of one eyebrow suggested a great deal of doubt.

"I'm piloting again."

The teen's face hardened again, and she almost erased all emotion from it. Only the flame in her brown eyes remained. "That's why you came. Not to check on me, but get your babysitter."

"Of course not. You're always more than a babysitter to me." She curled her fingers against Sotiris's wiggling torso. "But I see why you might doubt that. I've been very absent. I know that." Katya didn't shy away from the girl's narrowed gaze. "But you mean a lot to me. I want you to be happy. I want you to be cared for. I want you to be safe. It may seem like I'm holding you back, but I'm trying to protect you."

Mina bit her lower lip. "But I don't want to be protected." She nudged her head at the stars. "I want to be out there. So badly. I want to be there with you."

"Trust me. I miss having my copilot. One day" — if Mina ever forgave her — "it'll happen. I promise. But right now, someone needs to be with Sotiris, and I need to earn my keep here." As Mina bit her lower lip, Katya added, "It won't be forever."

"It had better not be," Mina mumbled.

Katya rose to her feet while holding Sotiris in place before hoisting him up. "Adulthood swallows us all in time." She smiled, even though Mina scowled at her. "You'll see." She freed a hand from around Sotiris and extended it to Mina. "You coming?"

The teen shot one more glance at the window, undoubtedly thinking of Dag and her other friends, before accepting it with her biological hand. Mina did much of the raising herself but still held on to Katya's hand.

"Maybe we can get some more sticky rolls," Katya said as they walked.

"That'd be great."

The chasm, camouflaged for now, still waited, ready to swallow them the moment they could no longer ignore their differences. But for now, it would work to Katya's plans.

The courier mission had transformed into a series of quick courier missions, all based in Medzeci's outer region. Most had been to Fringe Campaign-era stations converted to forward sentinels and storage depots. Their stocks of materiel suggested a state of constant preparedness, simply waiting for the order to resume the fight. The sweeping supplies could expunge life on numerous Fringe worlds. It chilled her to see such armaments in Medzeci hands, but only a fool would not expect their existence after the Fringe Campaigns and the cooled border skirmishes that had followed. Katya supposed the galaxy had always been teetering on the edge of full descent.

If the right match was lit …

She forced the thought away and focused instead on her more immediate concerns: running preflight checks as ordered by Bodil. While doing that task, she ran through her mental list of essentials needed for extraction from Plasovern.

The courier missions had opened doors like she'd hoped they would. She'd started small, liberating pocket-size tools and scraps of wire. Missing items that wouldn't draw notice or that someone might chalk up to an absent mind. During the last mission, she'd nicked a pocket knife, which she now kept in the crudely sewn inner pocket she'd added to her jacket. Her sister Anaïs would be so proud, if not helpfully constructive.

Katya settled into the freighter's dumpy chair, kicking her relatively light duffle bag as she did. Around her, the systems completed their diagnostics. Even without knowing their destination, she deduced it would be another Medzeci mission; this piece of scrap metal couldn't endure a trip beyond it. The *Frezzte*, the fifth freighter she'd piloted for Plasovern, was a bulky, outdated Kureynoone. Its design was hideous, and she suspected it would handle like a rock. Despite the diagnostics' glowing results, this would not be the ship for her to steal.

She shifted in the seat, sputtering when metal poked her through the cushion. Whatever vessel she selected, it would be her last theft. Running her hand against her forehead, she fought the wall of dread encircling her. Yes, she'd been collecting little things here and there, but they were negligible when compared to the bigger, more noticeable items she needed ... those things could sink everything.

A slate might be easy enough, but one's sudden disappearance could draw more attention than she wanted. As an outsider, she would garner it first. A chip capable of housing a virus devious enough to grind Jomsborg's operations to a halt would likely be easier to swipe. Chips were abundant. She moved it up in her ordering. A weapon beyond a pocket knife would be ideal, but, like the drugs, they were highly monitored. It would take the right moment.

Running fingers through her bangs, she sighed. And the moment she got her hands on a weapon, the plan would quicken. There would be no choice. She lowered her hand as the trembles returned.

While she had access to a few of Jomsborg's hangar bays, it had only revealed a hiccup in her plans. The environments and their contents shifted frequently. Particular vessels weren't guaranteed to return, and many didn't. Ultimately, she might have to take a model based on specs alone. Dangerous, but with little choice, she would make it work.

Bodil entered the cockpit and marked their destination on the navigation computer. A space station, two days away. Unsurprising ... but its name reeked of familiarity. E-92-A. The station had served as an advance outpost during the Fringe Campaigns. The Magistrate had tried to destroy it, as it'd been a devastating advance position. Despite those efforts, it'd stood with stalwart defiance throughout the conflict's entirety. It'd even defeated the C-Class destroyer *Aeneas* in what had been a propaganda coup for Medzeci.

"It's a warehouse now," Bodil said, some expression having been conveyed by Katya's face. "We'll be ready to embark in a few minutes." Without issuing further instruction, the other woman left.

Strom had been right about Bodil: Her command, while often brusque, was acceptable to her, even reminded her of past Magistrate commanders. Though there was an edge to the younger woman, which reminded Katya that Bodil was Strom's woman through and through. Katya never let herself slip into a false sense of security around her. Bodil breathed the cause, and she would not tolerate deviations from it.

At least, it would be a short mission. A console beeped. The engine readings were within optimal perimeters. The door reopened, and Katya spun from the data. Her lips parted to find someone unexpected.

Kahina stepped in, a duffle bag strapped across her chest. As per usual, she wore a jumpsuit, but this one had a softer edge, with looser material and a skirt overlay that contrasted the black fabric with bright geometric shapes. It exposed little skin thanks to its long-sleeves and halter neckline.

Swiveling in her chair, Katya fully faced the other woman. "I didn't think you worked for Strom."

The woman smiled, revealing her teeth, and dropped her duffle bag next to the communications console. "I don't. I am ... bored."

"No one else to run with?"

Kahina shrugged and sat at the communications console. "They talk too much."

Another voice—Bodil—intruded. "We're ready."

Katya focused on the task at hand and lifted the freighter from the hangar bay. As she pulled away from the station, her chest tightened. It always did. Normalcy had settled between her and Mina, yet she was losing her. She pulled farther away from Jomsborg and activated the FTL.

Kahina had sprawled in her seat, mouth skewed as she read the data on the screen through her sunglasses. "No space?" She pointed at it.

"The data says it all."

She whistled. "But it's not nearly as pretty."

Katya glanced at her, but was unsure how to respond. The silence that had become ubiquitous between them during runs settled. Only now, it hovered uncomfortably, the sliver of familiarity and lightness prodding Katya to speak. Mostly she wanted to probe why Izem's right-hand woman was here, traveling to E-92-A. Kahina's smooth face gave no hint. However, one finger tapped against the opposite wrist at an insistent pace.

This station would be different. "What can I expect?"

The tapping ceased, and Kahina sat straighter. "Basic station courtesy, like the rest. Heightened security. Don't misstep."

"Any clue what type of cargo we're taking on?"

"Odds and ends," Kahina responded. "Parts."

Katya raised an eyebrow. It didn't mesh with the station.

Leveling a finger at her, Kahina grunted. "You'll see. They do not loosen their hands."

Not loosen their hands? Ah, stingy, she deciphered.

"You will see," Kahina intoned again, rocking to her feet, bag strap in her hand. "Don't sleep on toes."

She then left Katya to her vigil and a lumpy chair that would be her bed.

The next evening, or early morning, Katya trailed after Kahina to the cargo hold, where at least fifteen Plasovern agents readied hovercarts for loading whatever cargo waited. Katya stifled a yawn. While the freighter had shifted its cycles to ease its occupants to their impending destination, her body had refused to leave Jomsborg time behind. Sleeping—more like closed-eye shifting—in the cockpit hadn't helped. She'd maybe nodded off for half-hour increments in the chair. After two nights in the torture device, her body groaned with each step, with a constant stabbing in her lower back. Turning her head to any degree to the left also proved to be inadvisable. She should've found a bunk.

The team worked efficiently to load cargo straps to the carts despite the gross hour not breaking a stride. Amid the flurry, Bodil gave instructions in a Varraganarian tongue and organized efforts with sharp hand gestures. Her icy blue eyes seemed to calculate the number of carts needed, but that effort lapsed when Katya and Kahina approached.

"We have this handled." The words left her mouth terse.

Kahina squared her posture. "You know why I am going." While Katya remained rooted, Kahina sauntered to the connector tube, the station old enough to warrant its use. "I serve Izem, not you. I will speak with this Tachta myself."

Bodil bowed her head, her bob a shimmering curtain obscuring her emotions. Then she jabbed her finger toward the cockpit. "Remain at your post."

So while Kahina disembarked, Katya climbed the ladder to the overhead catwalk, where she lingered to witness a good portion of the Plasovern delegation push the carts into the connector tube. Only five stayed behind, preparing gravity clamps that would keep all cargo in place.

When a set of eyes landed on her, Katya shifted farther down the catwalk to a more secluded spot. She rested her arms on the rail and waited. It had to have been a good thirty minutes before the first three carts returned, loaded with fiberglass containers and sealed metal crates. A few had small panels with refrigeration readings. Even without their conductor present, the crew hoisted the boxes from the carts to designated points in the hold. Katya pressed her lips together when agents moved two metal crates to a newly emptied cart and took them to an unknown location.

A worker popped open a fiberglass container, now rooted in place against a far wall. Parts. Likely for ships. Pushing off the rail, Katya crept back down the catwalk as more containers were popped open and a woman with a slate appeared to make notes on content. Pushing logic and hoping station protocols would waylay Bodil, she slipped her way back into the cargo hold, where she kept a moving distance from the agents. Used to the swell of motion around them, her presence went unnoted.

One man sorted through gears, more checking for discrepancies than actually counting the crate's contents. Katya wondered if Medzeci had shorted Plasovern before, hence the caution. Good on top, concealing defective product on the bottom.

A shout caused her to step backward, but she soon realized it came from a cart operator beckoning the rest to lumber down the tube again. Those left behind continued their haphazard inventories.

When a second detail returned with equally full carts, Katya waded into the shadows of the hold. There, she freed her hair tie and slipped it on to her wrist. She moved around the fringe of the activity as, like the first team, they unloaded and departed again.

A teenage boy settled a smaller plastic box on top of one of the larger fiberglass crates. He popped the box's lid, said something in his tongue, and moved on to the next.

Data cards ... encased in portable plastic cases ... prime for the taking.

The boy couldn't have done more than a cursory scan of the contents. Katya leaned closer but couldn't discern the cards' storage sizes. The virus she had in mind would require a decent amount of space. She wiped her sweaty palms against her pant legs and steadied her breath.

If the size wasn't large enough...

But if they were, and she didn't swipe one, she would miss an opportunity that might not come again.

Around Katya, the others had their heads buried in crates, occasionally calling out information to the woman with the slate. She appeared to be taking detailed notes.

An ache bloomed in her shoulder. The moment the chips entered the commissary, they would be out of her reach.

She plunged her shaking left hand into her jacket's pocket and then used her other to snag a chip from the back of the box, where several had gone loose from the slots, making a jumbled pile. As she stepped back, she nudged the chip, still encased in its plastic container, under the elastic of her hair tie with her fingers. In a fluid motion, she backtracked, staying along the edge. No one stopped her, pointed out the theft. Heartbeat rattling in her ears, Katya worked toward the ladder, where she stationed herself.

Another load returned, and with it, Katya progressed up the ladder. On the catwalk, she witnessed the teenager retrace his steps, closing the crates. Katya's hands grew clammy when he reached for the data card box, which he closed before moving on to the next. Breath hissed through Katya's teeth. Theft unnoticed. Without a sound, she sequestered herself in the cockpit, falling into the chair while her heart pattered quickly on.

Secluded, she pried the chip from the band and held it up. A terabyte. That would more than do. She concealed it in her bra. When she returned to the station, she could begin programming the virus. She already had a base in her mind, similar to one a drug-dealing syndicate on Reznic had used. It'd hobbled a Magistrate outpost on the world plagued by its criminal organizations. The virus would start small, a slight nuisance targeting small systems before ballooning and assaulting more, consuming attention. She only hoped Jomsborg's life support systems and gravity had suitable firewalls. She wanted confusion, not a high death toll.

The pressure in her chest disappeared, and Katya returned to her feet. She had time before either Bodil or Kahina returned. Kahina had seemed intent on something, and Katya wagered whatever the task was, it would devour time. As for Bodil, she would probably remain on the station to monitor her compatriot.

Kneeling, Katya popped the main navigation panel's hatch off, exposing miles of clumped wiring. She weaved her fingers through it, seeking any nodules, not unlike those used by commercial freighter companies to monitor pilot flight behaviors and routes. There. She probed her finger around the metal device's edges and tested its connection to the console wall.

Like the previous ones she'd uncovered in past Plasovern vessels, it would be an easy fix ... unless they'd jury-rigged it to explode. But given the number of unwarranted situations that might trigger such a program, she doubted it. She closed the console and stood, not disturbing anything else. Stretching out her back, she rotated, examining the upper ceiling and its corners. No cameras, but there were other ways to bug a cockpit. Strom could be on Jomsborg, listening to her breathe and shuffle about. Likely, she would picture her as some caged animal.

As for the panels popping off, the woman would hopefully assume Katya was being thorough, particularly after inspections showed no tampering.

When the door opened, Katya resumed her monitoring position at the helm, mild relief following when she realized it was Kahina who had returned.

With rigid posture, the Tizzet woman approached the communications console and messed with its settings, perhaps sending a message back to Izem.

Clearing her throat, Katya asked, "How did your business go?"

Kahina gave no response beyond abandoning the console when Bodil entered the cockpit. "There will be a detour, ladies." Her steely eyes pierced Kahina. "I hope you used proper protocol for that message."

Kahina sneered. "Of course."

"Where am I piloting us to?" Katya edged in, hoping to defuse the tension sparking between the others, even as the sudden diversion from routine left her unsettled. Mina would not be pleased …

"W'yrea." Bodil's jaw tightened, turning its chemical burn white. "You will find the planet in the navigation console, along with the dock. It's reserved solely for Plasovern." Then to Kahina, she added, "There will be no more communications."

"Of course."

Bodil's fist tightened, her weight shifting back, but she never struck the Tizzet woman. Instead, she left, issuing Katya one last order before the door closed. "Once fueled, get us underway."

"Yes, ma'am."

Katya launched the navigation program and found a pre-programmed route, probably used by Plasovern agents often. It added an extra two weeks to what had been a four-day mission. She'd have to wash her clothes on board; despite packing extra, it wasn't enough. She would also need a room. There was no way she was camping in the cockpit for that long.

Next to her, Kahina grunted and seated herself. "My business is lukewarm." She shrugged. "Strom holds their ears, though she shows very little."

"And how does she do that?"

Kahina crossed her arms and jutted her lower lip out. "She knows their language. No, not Medeza. This is not what I mean." She pounded her fist into the palm of her other hand. "The methods. The wideness. This, they agree with. We are too small-minded, they say." She snorted. "They care not for Tizzet."

"Then why bother with Medzeci?"

"Money. Supplies. Medicines. Weapons." She brushed her hand against her braided coils. "Begging for scraps around Strom. But where else is there to go? Will independent systems give to us? No. They do not move around giants. What if those giants move toward them?"

Such a betrayal as funding rebels would draw a response from said giants. The independent systems had been wise to strengthen their borders and avoid poking either the Magistrate or Medzeci Empire.

"There is no other," Kahina said, practically in a sigh. "Even if they do not see value in what we do, we must beg. There is no other way forward." She wove her fingers together in her lap. "Their way is not long lasting. It will not create stability."

Katya struggled to imagine what would create stability. There were so many factions within the Fringe, not even counting the waiting presence of the Medzeci.

"A planet must handle its own," Kahina plowed on. "Strom does not differ from the Magistrate: a foreign influence." She smiled. "Strom and Izem are like oil and water. Never truly meeting. She is like the darkest oil that even light can't pass through. Izem, like water, is life. He does not conceal his hunt."

The irony didn't escape Katya. While oil poisoned and obscured, water could be just as deadly, capable of clearing much in its wake. It was an apt metaphor from what she could gauge. Izem did not operate like Strom did with obfuscation, but he was no less brutal to his foes.

Katya mused, "Two sides of a coin for sure."

Her companion quirked an eyebrow. "As you say?"

"Just a saying, we had in the Magistrate for Strom and Izem," she responded. "Are there other leaders or factions? I'm only familiar with Strom's and yours, though there was always speculation about several splinter cells."

"Many, but scattered. Most fall in line behind Strom or Izem," Kahina said. "Matter of taste."

But with Izem's reduced access to resources, most had to align themselves with Strom. It was tactically savvy to do so. Yet …

"Why Izem?" His name reverberating among the masses on Jomsborg rose to her mind. The cries had come from foreigners to Tizzet. What drew them to him? "I thought he only cared for Tizzet."

"Tizzet is our fight, but we help those who also seek liberation. Yes, we are resource poor, but Izem has planned great attacks for other's homes. Much without Medzeci." Kahina waved her hand in the air as if chasing away a noxious odor. "Others favor Strom's tactics."

"Hitting the Magistrate wherever they can. Like a sledgehammer."

She nodded. "Others still come and go." Leaning toward her, Kahina cupped one hand to her own mouth. "Strom has lost the Fuusi Arm planets. Its representatives came and left. They saw the ultimate fruits of Strom's approach."

Katya sat straighter, and the portly Mramorian freighter captain who'd given their crippled vessel a tow to Barsaa sprung to mind. *"Don't think too hard of Zakhar."* Strom's voice breathed in her ears like a phantom. He'd been the representative, along with his crew. How soon after he'd surrendered their whereabouts had he cut ties? Her throat tightened. Had he used her—no, Sotiris—in negotiations? For a retreat ... or did he hope to secure some other promise from Strom.

Mramor ...

It did number among the Fuusi Arm planets. The Magistrate had welcomed them all into its fold over the years, her former homeworld a little over thirty years now. Most still did not meet the Magistrate's commonwealth status requirements to form their own senates. Instead, they relied on an appointed governor and that individual's council.

To go from sovereignty to guardianship ... That would breed unrest.

Katya considered pressing for more information, but what was the point? It had nothing to do with her. Instead, she said, "You so freely voice your distaste for Strom. Aren't you worried she's listening to our conversation?"

Kahina's lips withdrew from her white teeth, humor bursting in her eyes. "My feelings are well known, but I still live."

Katya rested her head against the seat's back as the fuel reading crept upward. The Magistrate was fracturing, but it wasn't alone. Medzeci and its funds had glued together Plasovern. And it was a fragile glue. Katya recalled the tension between Izem and Strom when her presence had interrupted their meeting. The way his muscles had tightened as he, an equal, was dismissed. No, not just him. Strom had discounted his people's needs, all for a woman not so removed from his enemies.

It would be possible to play the factions against each other during her departure from Jomsborg, but—Katya toyed with her jacket's fabric—it would be like playing in a landmine field. Best avoided. She wasn't politically savvy. She lacked the knowledge to do so effectively.

The fueling light flickered green, signaling completion. Then the central console showed the fueling line unclamp and withdraw. As instructed, Katya wasted no time departing. After achieving a safe distance from the station, she brought them into FTL, their course set on the pre-programmed destination.

Kahina, who'd settled in her seat, tapped a random beat against her leg while Katya performed routine monitoring. As time passed, the rhythm sped up before the other woman clapped her hands against her upper thighs and stood up. "There is no point to stay here. You can room with me."

Katya cast a backward glance at the console. All its automatic warnings were set, so there was little reason to linger. Still, she reached over to the intercom. "Destination set. Warnings in place. Leaving cockpit."

It took only seconds for Bodil's voice to emit from the speakers. "Understood."

Hoisting her duffle bag on to her good shoulder, Katya fell into rank behind Kahina, who led the way to the crew quarters. She brought them to narrow shared quarters that harbored a staleness as if the recycled air wasn't being adequately circulated through it. A chill had settled there too. The dark metal walls didn't deter the prison vibe.

"Take bottom," Kahina said, referring to the bunk bed setup. The Tizzet woman bent over a bag already in the space. Unzipping it, she rummaged until she removed a toiletry bag. "I'm R-and-Ring."

A long, hot shower would likely relieve her body's stiffness, but Katya flopped her duffle bag beside the lower bunk. "I'll wait for the morning."

Kahina shrugged. "Your choice to sleep in filth." She then slipped from the metaphorical shoe box.

Taking the folded, scratchy brown blanket, Katya unfurled it and made the bed. She didn't bother undressing before crawling under it. The material would only scratch her skin if exposed to it. She twisted in the bed, more like a mat placed over a metal slab. Even basic Magistrate cots afforded more comfort. She grimaced and shifted sides as the metal beneath aggravated her hip and bad shoulder.

After finding some measure of comfortability, Katya evened out her breaths. Eventually, she hovered in the restful silence between sleep and alertness. Time blurred, and her mind grew clouded. Still, the opening door jarred her. Through heavy eyelashes, she witnessed a dark figure cross the barely lit space, stopping at the other duffle bag. Kahina. She recognized her lithe form.

The other woman paid her no mind. Somewhere in her mind, Katya realized she was only wearing a towel. Having served in close quarters before, this didn't alarm her. Katya started to turn away to give her privacy but froze, eyes opening further when the towel dipped along Kahina's spine. From her neck down, pale splotches mottled her dark skin. A knot formed in Katya's stomach. The connection of the Oneiroi to Tizzet paired with Kahina's skin, jumpsuits and sunglasses revved her mind into overdrive, speculations weaving in and out.

Kahina slipped on a nightgown before removing a necklace crafted from an array of colorful wood beads and aged metal ones, which caught the minimal light. She fingered them, muttering something in her native tongue.

Throat tightening, a sensation of trespass overtook Katya, and she adjusted herself toward the wall, causing Kahina to pause for a fraction. The new position sent sweltering agony through her shoulder, but Katya held it, feigning sleep.

Behind her, the bag rustled, and a few minutes later, the upper bunk bed released air as someone crawled on top of it. The feeling she'd intruded on an act of incredible intimacy didn't abate, even as Kahina began to snore.

CHAPTER EIGHT

Weaving between lines of air traffic, memory consumed Katya. W'yrea carried a remarkable resemblance to Reznic, engulfed in towering buildings with the natural world banished to curated arboretums, gardens, and parks. The Medzeci world favored architecture with bold, angular lines. Reznic's style, meanwhile, proved decidedly eclectic—architecture shoved into a blender and then spat out. Both planets cherished their bright billboards that flashed in the night, neon colors beckoning viewers to indulge. The gilded touches on W'yrea's dark metal buildings caught the hues, embracing them as if they were their own.

Polished. Uniformed. Stomach-churning. Those words sprung to Katya's mind as she followed the navigation console's directions to the Plasovern rendezvous. Yes, Reznic, excluding its wealthier corridors, had many collections of beaten-down, mismatched structures, but they at least had personality. Reznic's buildings had been characters with their own stories, often entailing dirty business deals, unfinished staircases, bodies in the walls, and ample libations.

These? Sanitized.

Though she would take W'yrea's traffic over Reznic's. It had rhyme and reason, less taking life into one's own hands.

Hot breath touched her cheek, and Katya fought the urge to cringe. Bodil had been a fixture at her shoulder since they'd broken out of FTL. She keyed some passcode into the console, enabling their passage through W'yrea's violet sensory field. It reminded Katya of her sister Anaïs's homeworld, which was encased in a similar field. Only it was one of healing, not of security.

That field, though. Nothing could pass through it without notice. It mocked the Magistrate's relay system, which merely tracked vessels within its space. However, compared to what the Medzeci Empire had developed, it was a sieve to be exploited.

Another quiet exhale left Bodil, almost as a sigh.

Grinding her teeth, Katya buried herself in the helm, though she wanted to snap at the other woman: Step back!

Instead, she slowed their pace and redirected them to a section of the city that was decidedly more industrial, with heavy equipment moving giant grates on to ferry ships. Smoke rushed up against the washed-out night sky from lofty smokestacks. Airports designated for freight dominated the sector, and their port—112—wasn't far. Katya strained to recall what the Medeza characters alongside the destination meant. Familiar, but lost to the years.

Arriving, Katya lined the freighter up with an overhanging docking platform, clamps securing it.

Bodil activated her com. "Get the hovercarts. Be prepared to move a lot of equipment." She clicked it off.

"Is there anything I can help with?"

Bodil stiffened like she'd forgotten she was still hovering in Katya's space in what had been an awkward silence. Even Kahina had ditched the cockpit.

The Varraganarian's face resembled a ceramic mask devoid of lines. "Help?"

"I like to stay occupied."

Blue eyes lingered on Katya, partially lidded in disinterest. Then the corners of Bodil's unpainted lips tilted. "I'm well aware. Straight to Respectus from intermediary. Ranked one hundred and one that first semester, then hit a brick wall at thirty-two. Probably that language requirement, or more likely, someone stymied you. But no matter, you pressed on. There was that Magistrate shipping yard in the Mezzo, then served with the military police on Cantus. Then, Reznic. I'm very sure you stayed occupied there."

Katya forced her hands to remain flat against her pant legs. "It was the career."

"It never rewarded you." Bodil cocked her head in a patronizing manner.

A heated response rushed to Katya's tongue, only to meet her teeth. With it came a swell of warmth in her face, and she hoped there wasn't color to match. Balling her fists against her thighs, the conversation's sense of déjà vu scoured her ego. To have her entire career constantly laid out as if it had all been worthless. Every effort pointless. She ground her teeth together. But what had it awarded her? Dead-end appointments and this last twist: cast out of even the Fringe to the Medzeci's version of it. Her knuckles pressed into flesh while her heart sped and chest constricted. A void hovered over her and threatened to swallow her, mocking the time invested, lost.

Still, memories of her and Valens sequestered in a dark bar, her peering at him over the rim of her glass, followed by recollections of other equally idle moments spent amongst friends, the work that had mattered, the children saved from unspeakable fates—these were moments she would never trade. No matter the end, she couldn't throw every moment out with the wash.

"Maybe not in prestige." Katya loosened the vise in her chest. "But it wasn't devoid of its rewards." It had made her, molded her into the person she was, introduced her to people who had profoundly impacted her. "It held value to me."

Bodil smirked. "You should hold yourself to a higher worth."

The woman sent more transmissions from the communications console before clearing her throat. "Five hundred and one. That was my wall with the Magistrate."

Katya's brows rose. "You don't strike me as the type to join a Magistrate academy."

Bodil's smile warped disconcertingly. "Everyone has their history." She shrugged. "I learned what I needed. And I learned it well."

A chill coursed through Katya's body.

"Stay oc-cu-pied, Ms. Cassius. We will put you to work," Bodil said, tone lined with rancid honey. "But remember, I will personally extract the price should you betray us." Bodil brushed past her to the door. "Also, tread carefully. The Medzeci do not suffer slights, no matter how inconsequential."

Bodil left her, though Katya didn't remain behind for long after locking the navigation console and initiating the cooling sequence. She kept a distance behind the woman. The chip sewn into her bra's constant poke made it impossible to forget her betrayal, especially with Bodil's threat looping in her brain. Katya had no doubts the Varraganarian was talented in combat and espionage; she was too close to Strom to not be. Now a new layer formed: She was Magistrate trained. Her constant military posture took a new meaning.

Had she been an honest recruit or a Plasovern plant dedicated to learning inner workings, and who knew what else?

But in the end, Bodil's history didn't matter. No, Katya had joined a group of dangerous individuals. And, she'd done so despite all she'd heard and seen. In her darkest moment—bleeding out, Mina with a missing limb, and Sotiris still capable of sinking them all into oblivion—she'd ignored the danger. Of course, such a rash decision would hold consequences. And she would be a fool not to look over her shoulder constantly when she broke free.

The burn radiating at the center of her shoulder swelled, and she tucked her trembling hand into her pocket. Elites had hunted her yet she'd survived, partially from dumb luck, but her own quick thinking had aided her. She would pit her Magistrate training against Bodil's any day. Steadying her breaths, Katya clenched her hand, throttling the tremors.

Down in the hold, the crew readied carts to retrieve the supplies. Katya joined them but hung back. Unease welled in her core. She stiffened at the abrupt presence off to her side.

Kahina, sunglasses on despite the time of night, inclined her head. She'd washed the outfit she'd worn at E-92-A, the jumpsuit with a skirt overlay. Apparently, there was someone on W'yrea she wanted to impress.

The Tizzet woman gestured to the ramp with one hand. "Shall we?"

A genuine smile flitted across Katya's face, and she followed the other woman to the metal platform outside. Despite herself and her eventual goal, Katya found a camaraderie forming. She would almost call Kahina a friend—if not for allegiances.

Kahina snapped her fingers and pointed to the sky. It shifted to a deep purple almost indistinguishable from the faded night sky if not for its movement shooting across the expanse. A faint metallic sheen caught the neon lights until the towering buildings concealed whatever the device was. Like on Reznic, the city's torrent of bright lights choked its stars. Another glint passed overhead. Was it from the impressive sensor array? No, she discounted that. A third pass.

Kahina chuckled. "So much control, they defy nature."

Ah, it clicked in her mind. The Magistrate had performed a similar feat on her sister's original homeworld, Trides. Formerly called the Magistrate's backbone, Trides had a heavily industrial past, which led its environment to suffer. Extraordinary corrections had to be implemented to heal the damage. Magistrate scientists had spared no expense to curb the destructive weather that threatened one of the Republic's gems.

"They modify their weather."

"Yes," Kahina said. "They know no seasons here. Only comfort."

"Fascinating."

Katya's head remained craned toward the sky, taken in by the ceaseless movement of air traffic and lighted displays. In the distance, small drones grouped together to form advertisements, though nearby structures blocked all but their effort's top.

Bodil called something out in her native tongue, and the others with their carts followed. One woman pointed to a spare cart, and Katya gripped its handle. She had asked to help, after all. From the caravan's rear, she followed the others as they snaked through a small alleyway flanked by industrial buildings.

Bodil brought them to a central pathway, much wider than the one attached to the dock. Warehouses made up this district. While duller than the buildings blocks away, these structures were equally lit. Medeza characters and numbers adorned their fronts, designating their addresses. F-25 proved to be their ticket, with Bodil opening a side entrance.

Katya shielded her eyes when she stepped into the structure to protect them from the many overhead fluorescents. Boxes upon boxes filled the space, sorted into neat clusters, sealed away by shielding units. Some crates displayed Medzeci imperial red ropes, while others stood unadorned.

A clack, followed by a steady stream of one after another, disrupted her focus. Her head shifted to meet a hoofed Luzepan ambling toward them, draped in a black fabric that flowed around its frame. Its knotted hair formed a crisscross pattern that cascaded down and around its looping bone outgrowth. These horns, much like the city, had been dipped in gold. As it walked, its long, dangling ears bobbed back and forth. Ember-hued eyes traveled over them, the flat irises adjusting as they went. The being settled on Katya, long enough to send a chill down her back.

How much had Strom relayed to her Medzeci contacts? Across Jomsborg, they knew her as the "Magistrate woman." Had it traveled farther? Her stomach churned. How could it not have? She could not imagine Medzeci turning a blind eye to its terrorists. No, it would know everything. How else would it avoid any knives being thrust into its own back? Her mind flickered to Sotiris. Would Medzeci not scoop up an Oneiroi child if the opportunity presented itself? She balled her clammy hands. If it did, she could do nothing.

Clack, clack, clack. Her gaze lifted to the Luzepan. In its wake was a more reptilian being, wearing equally voluminous robes. Lacking horns, it wore a stylized band featuring golden, curled facsimiles. He kept two paces back from the obviously higher ranking Luzepan.

The official rolled his head before clearing his throat. Smooth Medeza poured from his mouth when he reached

Bodil. She returned it, a slight accent coating her words. The Luzepan gestured to some twenty-odd crates behind a shield. Still speaking, he guided Bodil closer to it and lifted his wrist to a sensor—the shielding dissipated.

Common Magistrate soldiers had spread a rumor that the Luzepan chipped their own, at least anyone with political ambitions. The gossip had ballooned amidst the Fringe Campaigns' fearmongering, further stoked by the post-conflict environment. But now, she wondered if it'd been leaked intelligence.

Bodil brought two fingers forward, and two crew members cracked open a crate.

Kahina bumped the cart Katya had been manning and got her to push forward a bit. Close enough to see a hoard of small firearms, all packaged in carrier cases with clear tops over the lip. Packed wall to wall, a thick foam buffered the weapons, preventing any shifting during the transportation process. Their maker proved unfamiliar—their thin, elegant shape excluded them from the lineups of the major Magistrate arms manufacturers. She imagined they would feel awkward in a large hand, but they would be ideal for sneaking into high-security locations. The firearms, however, also didn't scream Medzeci. They'd treaded a fine line of not overtly supporting Plasovern ... but usually, waylaid Magistrate firearms had been the go-to. Katya pressed her lips together. There'd been a recent shift.

"You," Kahina said, drawing Katya's attention. "You and the Oneiroi crew."

Blinking, Katya shot the Tizzet woman a quizzical look.

"The Magistrate," Kahina whispered as she gestured about with her fingers, lips moving like she was seeking the right words. "They have changed their weapons. Placed a kill switch in the codings."

Raising an eyebrow, Katya could not fathom the logistics required to introduce such a feature to the sprawling Magistrate military force. In a matter of months, at that. Impossible.

"Not all, yes," Kahina continued. "But the sources used by Plasovern and Medzeci have been affected. Too costly and too easy to wreck the entire gun when removing. Sourcing has moved to Renmark firearms."

Renmark was a Fringe manufacturer that had billed itself as the elegant weapon for wild space. They had never really caught on, nor were they known for reliability. Side-eyeing the open crate, Katya decided they'd ramped up production. Its operators had probably thrown all their chips in with Plasovern because the Magistrate would stomp down the business once the uptick was noticed. What was happening in the Fringe?

"The Oneiroi betrayal spooked them." Kahina folded her arms across her chest. "If more do as the others … they must bake in protections."

And there was her long-awaited answer: The Oneiroi special ops team had likely done something more than forcibly board the Jar'rask warship. Austerity guided the Magistrate. To ditch it and unroll what amounted to a frivolous add-on suggested an incendiary act, or …

"Are they still at liberty?" Katya asked.

"Free?" Then, upon receiving a nod, Kahina expounded, "Word is yes."

A massive loose end, the Magistrate had lost confidence in tying up. Why else would they order a retrofit of this magnitude? Katya covered her mouth with her hand as her brain tore apart this information. The upper echelons were preparing for the eventuality that this wayward crew would relay what information they'd gathered on the Jar'rask ship back to their people.

The lid clicked shut, snapping Katya out of her reverie. The two men then hefted the crate on to their cart. Others collected their own loads before pushing their carts back to the freighter. Caught in the action, Katya and Kahina retrieved their own and followed the line out. As they did, Katya noted Bodil and the Luzepan conferring near a metal box about the size of a sofa. The being patted its top while he spoke. Then he led Bodil to an enclosed office.

Katya glanced at Kahina, half expecting her to follow them to advocate for her cell's needs, but she never did. Instead, they took a position at the rear of the caravan. A reasonable distance settled between them and the others.

"You don't want to speak with the Medzeci representative?" Katya asked, no longer able to resist the bubbling curiosity.

Kahina shrugged. "No point." Her jaw clenched. "We are not big picture. And I speak enough Medeza to know my intrusion would be unwelcome. Besides, Izem only wants to know what is coming in. He will get what he can out of Strom. The rest"—she snorted—"we will find elsewhere."

"Izem means a lot to you."

Kahina pressed her lips together and folded her hands behind her back as she peered up at the bleached-out sky. "I owe him my life." Then, over her shoulder, she said, "I think you appreciate that, no?"

Her father drifted into her mind. She imagined his distress when the months dragged on with no word from her. Guilt bubbled in her gut, so she displaced it.

"You're part Oneiroi." The words were out before she could stop them.

Kahina smiled. "I have all their weakness, none of the strength." She stared ahead, never pausing in her. "My skin burns, I run too hot, my joints ache. My eyes … don't start me on my eyes."

Katya warred with her inquisitive desires. The Oneiroi, to her knowledge, followed isolationist tendencies, but to ask would entail walking into an active minefield given Tizzet's history of occupation. She'd never been on a planet under the Oneiroi's jurisdiction. She didn't know what it entailed.

They turned back into the narrow alleyway, which led to the dock.

"Does it matter?" Kahina said, unprompted. "I was other. Hated. Part of our oppressors. My skin, not dark enough. My mother struggled and succumbed. Always trying to be good enough." The corners of her lips turned downward. "So she sacrificed herself."

She batted a finger back at Katya. "Don't feel sorry for me." She faced the sky again. "Izem cared nothing for that part of me; he saw me as I was. He protected me, cared for me when others didn't. I know how you see him. But to me, he is the greatest man. Through him, I gained acceptance. Until I could stand on my own two feet and demand it. Now my actions speak for me, and they cannot say I am other."

"Are there others like you on Tizzet?"

"No." The leather gloves around her hands pulled tautly. "No."

Once at the ship, the two unloaded the cart and retraced their steps. Both nodded to the others when they passed. Politeness never went out of style, especially when most of their travel companions didn't find them endearing. The process repeated until the designated supplies had been cleared from the warehouse. Task completed, Katya and Kahina rested in the cockpit, away from the other Plasovern agents.

There, Katya checked settings and prepped the engines for the impending takeoff order. Kahina stayed with her, sitting in the communications console's seat and fidgeting with a slate. One item that remained on Katya's list.

Katya shifted in her own seat, a cold sweat collecting along her back, made worse by the cooler air surrounding her. Below her, another needed item waited. But taking one pistol would speed up her exit plan to a new level. Was she prepared to do that?

She adjusted a variance in one of the atmospheric thrusters. One missing pistol would catch notice, and suspicion would land on her. Too soon. She moistened her lips, a headache forming. But when would another opportunity present itself? There would be no opportunities on Jomsborg. One chip, one firearm, one Magistrate woman on the ship. She flattened her hand on the console to prevent her fingers from running through her hair. But she was running out of time. Mina … Mina was going her own way. Strom would use her as a pawn. Katya? With the drug in place, her usefulness was fragile.

The twitch presented itself, and she dropped her hand from sight. One case. Her eyes widened at the thought, grasping it, tugging at its angles and possibilities. It could work. Throw Strom and her investigators off. Broaden their pool of suspects. The move might buy her more time, but only so much.

Settling in her chair, Katya contemplated every potential mishap. She would have to reduce the chance they would discover the missing case before they arrived at Jomsborg. She needed a sizeable time gap before they uncovered it and realized only one pistol was actually missing, narrowing the suspect pool to her.

Yet the Magistrate registration chip remained. The thought doused the blooming adrenaline in her veins. Even if all other elements aligned, she couldn't take a Medzeci-chipped ship into Magistrate space.

"Dark thoughts?" Kahina asked.

"Just tired from moving crates and the mission that never ends."

"Uh-huh." Her white teeth flashed, and she said something in her native tongue. "It is something we say before we do things naughty."

Katya's limbs stiffened. "I know nothing of such things."

The smile widened, but Bodil's arrival stalled any further prodding. The blonde's expression soured at the sight of them.

"Take us home. I will relieve you at twenty-three-hundred."

"Understood."

"Excellent." Bodil faced Kahina. "There will be strict radio silence until we are on Jomsborg." She then stomped from the cockpit, her heels clicking against the metal.

"She has sand up her ass," Kahina said.

"Indeed."

Despite herself, Katya's lips curled. Underneath it all, her heart thundered.

Play this right, Cassius. Bide your time, finish this shift, and then act. If successful, she would narrow her need to stay in Bodil's and Strom's good graces to another week or two. Mina's smiling face shot to life before her. She wouldn't understand, not for a long time. But maybe one day.

Detaching from the dock, Katya launched them back into space and directed them toward Jomsborg.

Katya bided her time; she couldn't risk the gun case being noticed as missing during the long journey back to Jomsborg. Yet she was skirting the line where the opportunity would pass. Monitoring the readings before her, Katya inhaled through her nose, held it, and released it. Almost twenty-three hundred. Like clockwork, Bodil would appear, freeing Katya. The cycle ended tomorrow with their return to Jomsborg. The freighter's time cycle had already shifted to match the station's so most crew members currently slumbered.

She pictured the crates' location in the cargo hold and mapped the best places to obscure herself from view. No matter the hour, stragglers always stirred. Clenching her left hand in her right, she forced herself through the breathing exercise. It had to be tonight. The plan would adapt. She could manage the shortened time window. The virus construction loomed in her mind, but she soothed it. It would get done. There was plenty of time. The Magistrate registration chip, however … It was a major stumbling block.

When the door opened, her breath hitched.

Showtime.

Straightening her jacket, she greeted Bodil, sharing the active system scan. Bodil had little interest in it or Katya, settling in the main chair with a slate she'd brought with her. Not needing to be told, Katya slipped from the cockpit and traversed the upper catwalk, scanning the cargo hold below. No one. Her heart sped up, the adrenaline now raging through her veins. Now or never.

She descended into the dimly lit hold. Keeping her back straight, she walked with purpose. Confidence could be a potent weapon, opening doors. Walk like you belong, nice even steps, no looking about. Straight and steady.

On Reznic, there'd been a drug dealer who'd simply crossed the detainment center's yard like a walk in the park and then circumvented the fence. No one had stopped him, too taken aback to believe what was happening in front of their eyes. In some cases, their minds had simply accepted it. The man had then evaded capture for a day, while the on-duty guards had cleaned latrines for weeks. Magistrate officers chuckled about the event around mess tables for weeks, but there was wisdom in the drug dealer's methods.

She rounded a crate from E-92-A and grabbed a stray crowbar beside it. Her targets were feet away. To her knowledge, no cameras guarded the hold. Her precursory checks over the past few days hadn't turned up any. She crossed the empty space between the two clusters and snaked to the new one's far side, placing the crates between her and the catwalk. She peered up and found it vacant. Without hesitation, she drove the crowbar into the box's seam and put her weight into triggering the locking mechanism and hopefully not an alarm.

Errr-err, the mechanical bits groaned. She cringed and stopped the action, waiting. No footsteps came, and she resumed working along the ledge for the perfect pressure point.

Movement. All efforts ceased, and she hunkered down. Seconds ticked by. Nothing followed. Once again, she jabbed the tool into the crate's cavity and pulled. The angle proved right as the lid popped open.

Katya's breaths wanted to exit in huffs, but she regulated them as she grappled with one case. It rattled. Wincing, Katya berated herself. She might as well have been her father's dog, Pollux, rustling through the trash. She almost yelped when the carrying case gave, the sudden lack of resistance sending her stumbling backward. Her shoulder flared, dragging moisture to her eyes.

Shit.

Balancing herself, she set the case on the floor and gripped her shoulder, massaging it and its pin prickles. A vent kicked on, startling her. In an instant, she pushed past the pain and dipped closer to the floor. The half-expected shouting never materialized. Steeling herself, Katya spurred herself back into action by closing the lid. The mechanism latched, and Katya hoped her tampering would go unnoticed when unloaded on Jomsborg.

Reaching down, she picked up both the firearm case and the crowbar. She deposited the latter where she'd found it and toted the other past the ladder, which led to the freighter's upper levels. She slid between odd bits of equipment, which reeked of oil, and slumped next to a small maintenance hatch. It opened to a small cavity containing variously colored wiring. The cobwebs dangling in the corners and excess dust suggested no one regularly inspected it. She tested its dimensions and found the case holding twelve Renmark pistols fit, albeit more snugly than she would have liked. If she slid it back far enough against the hull, anyone opening the hatch likely wouldn't spy it right away. She had no choice but to take this wager.

Settling against the wall, she popped the carrier case's metal latches. Around her, every mechanical hum and click transformed from harmless ambient noise to potential discovery. Katya ground her teeth. *Get it together.* She rubbed her sweaty, shaky hands against her pants and cracked the case open. A burning sensation coursed from her fingertips to her shoulder, nettling the old wound, the moment they touched the slick metal grip of a dainty Renmark pistol. It was the first firearm she'd touched since the Jar'rask vessel, since she'd shot—pressure built in her ears—him.

Footsteps.

Pressing against the metal wall, Katya tried to minimize her presence while also stilling herself. Her breath caught in her throat. Above her, someone shuffled about the catwalk. *Clack, Clack, Clack.* Their footsteps on the grated metal suggested they were heading to the ladder.

Krezk.

Katya freed the pistol from the padding and waited. The person on the catwalk spoke when a new set of feet approached them. They carried on a conversation in one of the Varraganarian tongues. Laughter. A rivet pressed into the back of Katya's head after she scooted further behind a spare parts bin.

The fabric of the pair's clothes rustled. Through the slits in the catwalk, Katya caught one punch the other's shoulder before kissing them soundly on the lips. When they pulled apart, the one beckoned the other to follow ... into one of the crew quarter clusters.

Katya released her left wrist, which she had apparently clasped to prevent its shake. Frowning at the pistol in her hand, she exhaled slowly. After ensuring the safety was on, she slid it along her side—shuddering as the metal touched her warm skin—and nestled it under her bra's band. She tested the hold and decided without sudden movement, it would stay in place. Next, she adjusted her shoulders and ran her right hand along her back to gauge if the outline was too obvious. Impossible to tell. But at least, with the lights synced to Jomsborg, she would have the darkness on her side.

Wiping sweat from her brow, Katya pushed the case fully into the hatch, maneuvering it as far back as possible while avoiding dislodging any wiring. When satisfied, she sealed the hatch.

She waited. Then, not hearing any further noise above, she ascended and proceeded to the communal bathroom, its lights flickering on the moment she crossed the threshold. Exposing her back to the mirror, she moved the pistol farther to the side, where her arm would better conceal it. Add in her duffle bag, and it should be indistinguishable. That done, she splashed cold water on to her face to banish the fine layer of sweat.

Her hands trembled as she pressed them into the metal countertop. Dark rings glared back at her from under her eyes. What a mess ... She even resembled a specter, so pallid. Katya shoved off from the counter and trudged to her shared quarters. Her mind reeled, grappling with what she'd done. May the storm wait until they reached Jomsborg.

Rather than lessen her strain, the return to Jomsborg brought a constant thrum to Katya's body. The question of when they would notice the missing gun case hung over her head. Another thought chased it: How soon until they discovered the case with its one missing pistol? The microscope would land on her the moment Plasovern realized they were only hunting one person.

Katya shifted her duffle bag as she crossed the swamped hangar bay. It shielded her illicit gain, secured under her bra's band, which also looped through the trigger guard. Past noon, the hangar hummed with energy that had been lacking when they'd left in the early hours some days ago. Beneath the activity, an odd vibe reverberated. Workers kept a faster pace. There appeared to have been an influx of supplies. Something else—anticipation?—hung in the air, prickling at Katya's scalp. Something more lurked under the surface. A massive mission?

Her chest tightened. Would she be able to nick a ship in this atmosphere?

The pistol rubbed against her as she walked. She would have to. Glancing back at the freighter, she watched the Plasovern team organize their load. Bodil had dismissed her from the task. So far, the crew's movements proved routine, with no alarms set off. Katya banked on the missing case escaping notice until the supplies reached the armory. Then she hoped the case remained buried until their extraction.

Katya bent down off to the side to retie her shoelaces. As she finished the left, Bodil and the glass case containing the freighter's Medzeci registration chip passed her. Even if she liberated a ship, not having a chip would hinder them. Tightening the laces, she rose and followed from a distance. She was heading back to her apartment; that was all. Not stalking a superior, not caging the site where they locked the chips. However, her ability to tail her target fell apart quickly as Bodil met with the ever marble-faced Krasimir. Katya veered off, not willing to be noticed.

Perhaps leave the ship unchipped. That prospect didn't ease the knot in her throat. She had no money to her name, making purchasing one impossible, especially since she would have to pursue seedier avenues. Stealing one carried its own risks. The only remaining option, docking on a backwater world and eking out a living, proved unpalatable. Given black market prices, it would take years to earn enough. Years they didn't have. She couldn't calculate Plasovern's surplus of Sotiris's medicine, but likely it wouldn't cover such a time span.

She had to grab the gun, she thought, kicking herself. She never doubted Strom monitored her quarters or had them periodically searched. Discovery was inevitable; keeping it hidden on her person only delayed it.

Feet rushed toward her, causing Katya's muscles to tighten.

"Run with me," Kahina's voice prodded. "We have been too cooped up."

Katya lifted an eyebrow at Kahina. "Oh?"

A smirk was her answer before Kahina took off and then, jogging in place, waved for Katya to follow. Their conversation in the cockpit flitted to mind. The Tizzet woman suspected something, and Katya couldn't help but speculate that she wanted to test her or attempt to uncover her mischief.

"Come!" Kahina commanded.

And after some hesitation, she did. Her face reddened with the juvenile action. Kahina didn't take off, but she also didn't slow her pace. Katya wondered how much the act of running cost the Tizzet woman. How badly the concussive falls of her feet impacted her weakened joints, the result of warring genetics. Her exterior countenance betrayed no pain or any other hint of strain. Just as before knowing her genes, Katya saw nothing amiss, except maybe she didn't sweat like most humans.

"Where are we going?" Katya asked after catching up.

"You'll see," came her sing-song answer.

Katya moved from the path of an empty hovercart being pushed into the cargo bay. What was she? Four? "Maybe I'd rather know beforehand," Katya drawled. "I have kids to get back to. Mina will want to be relieved from her tribulations as a babysitter."

"Tri-bu-so-ion?"

"Troubles, suffering."

"Ah, I know these." She shook her head. "And that girl only thinks she does."

"They are more than passing acquaintances—companions," Katya finished when the other woman's brow rose.

"So many new Magistrate words. I won't keep them long. A hundred languages on my world, and I know fifty-eight. There is no room up here." She tapped her index finger against her head. "Once the Magistrate leaves, the need will pass. Then too, I will let go of Medeza."

"You're ignoring my question."

Kahina wagged a finger at her over her shoulder. "Trust me."

Having no reason not to, Katya complied. They passed up several levels, the inclines testing their lungs. When they reached the Tizzet's level, Katya stiffened, but curiosity kept her from retreating. Since their initial arrival, socializing Tizzet people had dotted the hallways, likely monitoring those who passed through. Now, their absence screamed. What had happened while they'd been gone? A crawling sensation begged her to rush to Mina and Sotiris to ensure their safety. To hear what news and gossip Mina had collected.

Kahina slowed and began her stretches, her chest lifting and compressing. She muttered something in her native tongue as she rolled her back and stretched one arm. While Katya didn't know the words, the tone bled with relief, perhaps gratitude at being home.

Katya's chest rose rapidly from the exertion, but she didn't fall into post-exercise routines, the rub of the firearm a constant reminder to limit her movements. Running had already been a poor choice. "So we've arrived, I take it," she said around her breaths.

Kahina nodded. "Izem will see you."

Stiffening, Katya blinked at the other woman. However, when a door to the side opened, her attention jerked away. A man with a dark complexion stepped out and spoke to Kahina in their shared tongue.

He stepped into the hall fully, clearing entry into the room, but Kahina didn't budge. Instead, she turned to Katya with her hand outstretched.

"Your gun," she said. "No harm will come to you. Izem wants a good meeting, with no unfortunate concerns." She flicked her fingers to the pistol concealed by Katya's arm.

Glancing around the hall, Katya could only assume Strom's cameras would—

"Our tech makes them useless. Strom has accepted this one blind spot; she has no choice. The pistol. I will return it."

The man had widened his stance as if preparing for a fight.

Against her screaming in her brain, Katya unfastened the back of her bra and freed the pistol, sliding it out from under her shirt. She held it tight for a moment before pressing it into Kahina's open hand.

"Good." Kahina then batted at the other man, berating him in their language until he sheepishly—cheeks reddening—put his back to them.

Katya's own face warmed, realizing it was to give her the chance to refasten her bra. Reaching behind her, Katya fought with the hooks, settling for only one snapping into place. As her hands lowered, Kahina nodded her head and ushered Katya into the room.

The interior, gray with no personal effects, had been set to a withering temperature, mirroring one of Tizzet's climate zones. The furniture resembled the same well-used pieces filling Katya's apartment—Strom had likely summoned them from storage upon Izem's arrival. While the room seemed impersonal, spices and the lingering aroma of cooking spoke of home. A whistle went off, drawing Katya's attention to the tiny kitchenette. There, a bulky man removed a kettle from the stove and placed it on a hot pad.

"Please sit," Izem said, his face smooth, much more peaceful, with Strom removed from the equation. "Kahina."

Said woman entered the kitchen and plated the food Izem had been preparing.

"Never start business on an empty stomach," he said, bringing two mugs to a metal coffee table. He pushed one—filled with a reddish tea—toward Katya as she lowered herself into the chair closest to the door. "We drink from the same pot; there is no need to worry."

"Mugs can be tainted." An unfortunate Reznic politician sprang to mind.

"It serves me nothing to kill you. I gain more from you alive than dead."

Still, she sat like a beam until her back and shoulders ached. A rustling sound drew her eyes to the shadows behind her. The man from the hallway had slipped into the room and now blended with them. He didn't appear to carry a weapon, but his body was primed for action even as he observed proceedings.

Kahina, balancing large serving plates on her two hands, exited the kitchen and knelt with a dancer's elegance to slip them on to the short table. The one plate featured a rice dish that cast off a bountiful aroma of various spices as it moved through the air. It had a golden hue, likely from one of the ingredients used. The cook had mixed little bits of vegetables into it. The other plate featured a type of flatbread. When Kahina returned, it was with a meat dish bathed in a deep brown sauce and a substance that had been patted into five little pasty-white mounds. The latter plate featured a chunky maroon sauce with bits of green mixed into it.

Izem took a bread loaf and broke it in half, extending one to Katya. Her father's ramblings on the action of breaking bread sprung to mind: an act so common among so many cultures some could almost deem it as universal. Faustus Cassius had written a detailed dissertation on this action, pooling oral and written references, art compiled across archaeological sites, any source he could uncover. These commonalities bolstered his overall theory that humanity had originated from a single world and its colonies—three, he postulated. Their distance and discordant exoduses had then allowed for a collective forgetfulness, aided by millennia and losses of tech in—

Across from her, Izem waved the bread. He cracked a smile, white teeth gleaming. "I promise there is no poison."

She accepted it. "No, I was … reminded of something." Her eyes stung. *"Don't disappear so far that you can't contact me."* Like salt in an old wound, those words returned to hound her. What must he think? That she'd been killed? Or had been so deeply imprisoned he would never find her again? But the danger was too much to contact him, especially from the Medzeci Jomsborg. Officials had to know it had been *The Maelstrom*—another name that burned—that day. Likewise, they had to know who'd been piloting it. They would monitor her father.

Izem dabbed his piece into the rice before adding some of the meat and its rich sauce. "Emm … business should never be conducted on an empty stomach," he repeated before taking a sizeable bite. "No good business, at least."

All her father's lessons on respect prodded her to copy her host's actions, so she did. The sweetness of the meat and sauce paired with the herbs in the rice caused her to close her eyes and savor. When was the last time she'd eaten something beyond basic rations? While not her familiar comfort food, that warm sensation carried over.

"A long journey also needs a good end." He swept his hand to Kahina, who responded by entering a side room. She returned with a small cloth satchel, which was placed in his open palm. With great care and a showman's flourish, he brushed away its flaps and removed—

Katya's heart pounded, deafening her ears. A registration chip. Her guard slammed into place, eyes narrowing as she crossed her arms and leaned into the chair. "What is this?"

He chuckled. "You know what it is. It's a continuation of whatever plan you have concocted. Only now, you don't have to worry about alerting Strom before you act."

"I know what it is"—she swept her hand toward Kahina, the food, and then Izem—"but this … What do you want for the registration chip?"

His lips quivered. "I am tired of begging for Strom's scraps, for any support to be given to my world, my people. That woman sits on a hoard of supplies like a Chachtet Beast." He pinched a bit of the white blob between his thumb and index finger, rolling it into a small orb. Then, he dipped it repeatedly in the maroon mixture. After popping it in his mouth, he chewed as if to stretch out the experience or perhaps to delight in making Katya wait. "Tsk-tsk. Haste is death in the endeavor you attempt. For now, eat."

Silence, except for the sounds of eating, hovered in the room. Kahina joined them in sharing the meal, moving to the floor like Izem and Katya had done. She folded her legs beneath her and partook. The man in the background remained statuesque among the room's umbra.

Dipping her own pastry into the sauce, Katya broadened her observations. Like her own rooms, this apartment featured three bedroom doors. Were they vacant, or was more muscle waiting in them? The quietness of the hallway flared, beckoning her to ask.

"Your corridor is quieter than normal."

"Hmm," he said between swallowing a morsel and drinking from his mug. "Many are prepping the ships. We linger too long while Tizzet cries for relief."

Katya sipped from her mug. "How long before you leave?"

"That depends on you." Izem dusted his fingers against his pant legs. "My people see this uneven partnership as at an impasse. Supplies once plentiful aren't there. Medzeci favors Strom's tactics, which are broader operations against an old foe. I do not know whether it is just to give the Magistrate a constant thorn or something more. I only know our fight is no longer seen as of use to them.

"But, you. You're a walking disaster when you please. Knowing what I know of you, I guessed it wouldn't be long—only the right shaking for a tidal bore. Strom could never be to your liking. Too much of your life has been guarding order. Strom is the antithesis of order." Izem drank deeply from his mug. "Kahina kept an eye out for signs."

The aforementioned intelligencer shrugged. "I saw the outline. When you got 'round in the mornings. You hid well, but I knew to watch."

"Kahina recommends you," Izem cut in. "I value her word greatly. So I propose a pact. You will move the Chachtet Beast from its proverbial cache."

"You aim to turn my escape into a distraction to lift arms."

"You are already doing it." He flashed the Magistrate registration chip. "I propose to make it easier, quicker. How long do you think you can hide that gun? Will they not notice one is missing?"

"I removed an entire case of them. It will take them a while to realize just one is missing."

"Clever, but … do you know where Strom'll come to find a missing case? *Here.*" Despite the implication, he applied no actual malice to his tone. "And she will find nothing, but it is still an inconvenience, for her, for us. From there, she will continue her hunt, and you can have no hope of hiding your weapon for so long. You are against a ticking clock."

The proffered registration chip in its see-through plastic carrier gleamed under the bright lights. She needed it. She couldn't deny it. While she might consider sneaking into Magistrate space with an unchipped ship, having that chip would make their travels easier, open more ports for them. None of her vessel considerations would pass as a grandfathered "obsolete, chipless" pleasure craft. Katya folded her hands in her lap, fixated by the chip before her.

He was right; Strom would eventually uncover her theft. This chip could get them out of her reach.

Her list of necessary supplies loomed over her, applying pressure to her chest. To cross off the crucial chip—their ticket to enter Magistrate space freely where they could blend in—was too tempting. She read nothing but honesty on Izem's and Kahina's faces. They truly wanted to use her escape as a cover to abscond with materiel. They trusted her methods would be disruptive, probably because they understood better than even she did the strategies required to leave Jomsborg.

But the Tizzet people had many advantages over her: their own ships vacant of Medzeci components, their own supply of registration chips, and a certain amount of freedom. Their methods might be different, but Strom respected Izem to a degree. She acknowledged his fight against the Magistrate, even if she deemed its confined nature a wasted effort.

But why stop at a registration chip?

She leaned toward Izem. "I need more." Yes, they wanted to use her, but she could make this work for her. "I need an open slate with no restrictions. I could steal one, but that would be another loose end for them to trace back to me. If it has an impressive firewall that I can modify, the better."

"A virus, huh?" Izem leaned back, scratching his chin. "How deadly?"

"More of a disruption. I'm not a mass murderer."

She returned to her drink, which was cooling. Noticing this, Kahina poured her some more from the warmed pot, to which she uttered gratitude.

The revitalized tea warmed her hands through the ceramic mug. "It will take down security in the hangar bay I've chosen to exit from. It'll also be like gum in the station's operations to keep them off-balance. Life support and power functions should be in alternative systems and have plenty of redundancies to prevent a complete collapse. The station team will still have their work cut out for them."

"Will it broaden out to attack more security systems?" Izem asked. "Beyond the hangar bay?"

Like the one guarding the armory. "It likely will. I am hoping for a broader loss of camera functionality."

"A brunt force attack could be beneficial to us all."

Katya's fingers curled into the ceramic.

"Hit harder," Izem continued. "As you say, redundancies are baked in. It will take it without mass casualties. If you don't hit hard with the virus, failure tips toward you." He folded his arms in front of his broad chest. "We will give you a slate. In turn, we will need to protect our own devices from your virus."

"I will share that information."

"Anything else?"

"Anything to help us pass while in Magistrate space. Given Sotiris's importance, the Magistrate has to still be actively searching for us. Additionally, I need the drug for Sotiris and a ship."

Scratching his chin, Izem reached with his other hand for more of the white substance, dipping it into the sauce before popping it into his mouth. "We have kits that can modify your face to a degree. The rest we cannot provide. Ships are too valuable; we cannot part with our own. You must proceed as you would have without us. As for the drug, what was given to us by Strom for our problem is already off-station. I believe you have more opportunity to get what you need than us."

"So, Strom came through on that."

"It seems as much."

So he would return home. "And what will you do to the child?"

"I feel no ill will to it." Lines spread across his forehead and around his mouth. "One cannot blame a viper for its nature, especially when it has been trained to bite. We will hopefully no longer harm each other."

"You don't hate it? The Oneiroi? They've left a mark on your world."

"Hate?" He shook his head. "I do not hate. That would give up too much of myself." He stood and paced. "Even the Magistrate. I sting them, but I do not hate." He sniffed. "It is a philosophical difference between Strom and me. The closest that I can get to what Strom feels is for the Frattet. They brought the Magistrate, the Oneiroi, to our world and allowed them to entrench themselves there with their sobs of mistreatment."

Kahina brought a slate from one room. "I've cleared it," she said before gifting it to Katya.

"Tell us the ship you intend to take," Izem said. "We will time our placement of the kit with your departure. We cannot be found to have aided you. Our own aims would be pressed if that became known ... at least too soon."

Still on her own, but on better footing. She powered on the slate and examined its capabilities. It would work. "I'm going for one of the faster freighter models, but ... there's been an uptick in activity."

"The number of Magistrate missions has been tripled. Strom is concentrating on dealing black eyes in the Fringe after a setback on Ereago. But I feel like something bigger is underway, and I want no part." He stroked his chin. "Medzeci is not so quiet anymore."

Izem passed the registration chip back to Kahina before reaching into his pocket. He removed an old-style com unit, so old any detection measures would likely fail to recognize it. He pressed it into Katya's hand.

"Keep us updated," Izem said. "Notice will be important, until then, Kahina will safeguard the chip. Now, I believe you have a young woman and small boy to meet with." He paused, his gaze narrowing on her. "Don't dawdle."

Oh, the double meaning behind that.

Kahina returned the firearm to her. Blushing, Katya shoved it under the band on her bra before hiding the chip and slate in her duffle bag.

Once her duffle bag was in place, Kahina escorted her outside.

"See?" Kahina crooned. "A favorable meeting."

Katya frowned. "You could have told me. It's not like I could refuse."

"Too many ears." The Tizzet woman clapped her on the shoulder. "Good luck. You will need it."

"Yes. Yes, I suppose I will."

She set off away from the Tizzet corridor. Several Tizzets were now out milling amongst themselves. No one looked at her as she passed. Her heavier bag batted against her hip while the gun poked and cut into her skin. Oh, she needed all the luck in the universe. If it proved to be a shot in the brown, she knew Strom wouldn't hesitate to eliminate her; she only hoped she would show mercy to Mina. Sotiris would be safe; he was far too valuable to be disposed of.

Like a Reznic drug dealer, Katya strolled Jomsborg's hallways as if she owned them, posture relaxed, face straight ahead, not a care to be found. With luck, those watching her would believe the lie.

CHAPTER NINE

gonizing hours stretched into days without a hint of anything being amiss on Jomsborg. Its cycles continued uninterrupted, as did Katya's routine with Sotiris and the clinic—spliced with the creation of a virus designed to grind the station to a near halt. She'd attempted to liberate a small portion of the drug during one visit, suggesting she could administer it while the drug trials paused. Garbi, however, wouldn't budge or loosen her grip on the supply, forcing Katya to bring an always-reticent Sotiris twice a day to the clinic. But her compliance brought a bonus: a chance to memorize Garbi's code to the refrigeration unit and monitor it for any changes.

Within those four days of schedule reclamation, a missing firearm case went unremarked, not to her directly or through overheard conversations. And as she and Sotiris carried on with their routine, Mina returned to being an apartment ghost, spending copious time with her friends. When their paths crossed, Mina presented her bubbly self, their differences apparently buried. If any rumblings happened behind the scenes, the teen hadn't caught wind.

Midday on the fifth day, the divergence sprung. Katya, fully clothed, was wrestling Sotiris in the compact shower when Strom summoned her. Vague as always. Dressing Sotiris, her heart beat in a frantic cadence. It had come. A case of guns missing, her off-grid meeting with Izem ... It was only a matter of time until Strom pried.

Sotiris batted at her hands as she finished dressing him and made a beeline to his toys, leaving her to strip off her wet clothes in her room. From there, she eavesdropped on his meaningless chatter and Mina's rattling in the kitchen. The teen had only been marginally distracted from her cooking when a drenched Katya had emerged from the bathroom.

A chill raced through her body as she pried off her clothes and tossed them in a soggy pile. Strom knew Mina was in their quarters. It never ceased to unnerve her, even though she knew they were being monitored. It was why she went to great lengths to keep the firearm and slate obscured, sometimes using Sotiris's storybooks or toys. That it was Mina—effectively a child—being so closely monitored frightened her. And Strom knew it, purposefully dug in, and rubbed it in her face.

Swallowing, Katya slipped on an altered bra, more devious than the previous one. She'd cut along the metal underwire, crafting a slot in the padding. The chip blended well and would require a more intensive investigation to uncover. She'd then stitched it in with a fragile thread so she'd be able to extract it easily.

She buttoned on a fitted shirt, picking it purposefully to discourage further probing. Strom liked mind games, so why not play some with her? Then, after tugging on black pants, Katya contemplated the gun. It would be suicide to bring it with her, but if she were Strom, she would tear apart every inch of the apartment in her absence, seeking any trace of the stolen firearms.

Bending over, she lifted the wet clothes and added them to the room's small built-in hamper. As she did, she removed the pistol concealed among her dirty clothes. With a fluid movement, she slipped it under her shirt, along her side. She resisted the urge to put on her jacket. There could be no jacket when she visited Strom, neither could there be a firearm. But where could she ditch it?

She stroked her jaw between her thumb and index finger. She'd devoted a lot of thought to it over the past few days. The apartment yielded no viable hiding places. Strom's team would ransack it, expose every nook and cranny. There were no room elements they wouldn't be aware of. And trusting dumb luck or sloppy methods was not a strategy for success.

The slate she would sacrifice to potential discovery. She'd erased every trace of her true purpose from it and had instead laid a trail of breadcrumbs for Strom: more Oneiroi searches, dives into Magistrate news … what Strom would expect on an ill-gained slate from Katya. Give a little dirt, and she might ignore any smoke. She left the thin slate in between the pages of a storybook. It was thick enough to stick out; however, the eye might pass over it given the innocuous setting. She did the same with the pocketknife, intermingling it with her sewing kit, which lacked scissors. Little things to validate Strom but lull her.

Straightening her shirt, Katya faced the door. The pistol would have to be hidden outside their quarters. Locations flitted to mind—some dismissed immediately, while others lingered but never truly stuck. She bit her mouth's interior as she stepped from her room. She should've had the location cemented before this moment.

Move with purpose, she intoned while trying to restore moisture in her mouth, which had become relatively arid. She would find a path forward.

Mina tilted toward her, a mixing bowl in hand, as she crossed the common space. The girl's face scrunched. "So what does Strom want?" she pried, leaning over the island.

She answered the cryptic call and undoubtedly had a swarm of building questions.

Katya shrugged. "Maybe a pilot."

"You've only just gotten back." The teen's shoulders slumped, lips pouting. Oh, the dread of babysitting.

"Missions don't care about personal comfort."

That earned a glower.

"Please watch him," Katya continued. "I can't say how long I'll be." Hanging in her mind was the ever-present knowledge she might never return. She swallowed against a tightening throat. "Keep him out of trouble."

"Yeah, yeah," Mina mumbled while forming a mouth with one hand to mimic the words. "Just keep it short. I was going to meet up with my friends."

Almost to the door, Katya paused. "I'll try, but with that woman, it's hard to say." She turned to see the calculations of time spent with her friends—her boyfriend—forming in Mina's mind. "But I'll try."

After waving to Sotiris, who returned the gesture, she disembarked. Keeping Strom waiting was unwise, yet she still had to find a place to conceal the firearm. The Tizzet people's blacked-out corridor screamed as the only viable location, but it risked her temporary allies and they might interpret it as a double-cross, especially when her theft had already placed suspicion on them. With her having recently visited the Tizzet people, Strom would be a fool to not investigate there too.

Think. She kept a steady pace as she walked through Jomsborg's major arteries, blocking the Renmark's outline with her arm. She tried to keep her arm's placement natural, not too stiff. The pistol's small design aided her, but she feared a trained eye would catch on.

She stuck to the typical path toward Strom's apartments at Jomsborg's peak. Cameras were everywhere, some visible, others more concealed. Katya was confident more existed than she'd spotted. Besides those mechanical eyes, people loitered everywhere.

Katya clenched her trembling hand into a fist and shoved it into her pant pocket. When she entered the first common space, she sidestepped a group of young men heading to parts unknown. She needed to decide her path, though anything but the direct route would catch notice. Her fist tightened.

Stop. Think. Calmly.

She roved through the common area, ditching the lifts for the ramp. Her legs needed a stretch. Strom hadn't said the meeting was time sensitive. She loosed her hand and placed it and the other behind her back, walking tall. As she climbed upward, she mentally combed through the levels between her and Strom. Most were too populated to hide the pistol. Not only would there be the risk of unwitting discovery, but there would be more cameras. She clicked her tongue against her teeth. The Sarchins' level.

Populated, yes, but it perhaps harbored the only blind spot on Jomsborg beside the Tizzet people's corridor: the shrine. Strom wouldn't put cameras in there, would she? No, it would be sacrilegious. No matter her thoughts on religion, the Varraganarian woman wouldn't nettle such a valuable resource as the Sarchins.

She headed upward. She passed a small mess area, which had every table full. All Varraganarians. Her stride almost broke when she spied a tall blond man along the serving line. Krasimir. His build fit perfectly, but then he turned, revealing a scarred face—as if exposed to exploding glass—and a bulbous nose. Her fingers curled against her hands, and she continued past.

She was being ridiculous. So what if it'd been Krasimir? He was getting food. Gawking, freezing … it only made her look guilty, like she had something to hide. But that man … his impassive face, his actions … they still chilled her.

Leaving the space, Katya sped up. She would be a sore thumb on the Sarchin's level, but if they once again preferred silent observation, she would have a window of time to find a solid hiding place for the pistol. But with her entering their shrine, there was no guarantee they wouldn't respond more directly.

When she entered the Sarchin's common area, her appearance garnered instant attention. A group of Sarchins sitting on a blanket with a teapot between them jerked their heads toward them while not jostling the handleless tea mugs in their hands. Their white mustaches rippled with the motion. Others who had been shopping ceased and chattered with clicks and grunts amongst themselves.

She didn't recall her first incursion drawing this much attention. But she'd been jogging then. A fast-moving interruption. Sheepishly, she strolled to the ramp, positioned next to the shrine. Its red wood and woven-branch domed roof served as a beckon. Her path remained directed at the ramp, but as she came closer, she paused and angled toward the shrine, drinking it in like a tourist. It wasn't a tough act. The carvings varied, some a language, while others were symbols or depictions of Sarchins.

She crept closer to the shrine, only to linger before its triangular doorway. Symbols had been carved deeply into the wood, and moss had been shoved into the crevices around its frame. A gold cloth dangled almost to the ground from the entry's top but did nothing to obstruct the entrance. She could easily pass through by bending a bit; however, she didn't. Eyes. She could feel them drilling into her back. Given their skill, Katya doubted she would outmatch one in a martial contest.

A clicking emitted behind her, and she turned to find one Sarchin, clothed in green brocade, clacking at her. When she didn't respond right away, the primate-like sentient waved its long-fingered hands in a sweeping gesture toward the shrine and trilled at her, its pointed teeth visible.

An invitation to look?

With a trace of hesitation, Katya bowed her head as she stepped in, pushing the gold fabric aside. No harassing shouts followed the action, so she decided it had indeed been an invitation. The domed structure had a small antechamber, which then opened to the main shrine. A gentle chiming greeted her. So soft. They had set it at an interval. She imagined it played a meditative role in the Sarchins' religious practices. She crossed into the shrine proper, inhaling its earthy fragrances, paired with a cedar. Its rustic wood stood in such contrast to the metal station she'd left. In her boots, her toes curled into the soft carpeting of moss and dirt. They, along with the ceiling's draped cloth banners, dampened all noise, even the endless hum of the station—leaving only the mellifluous chime. It was as if she'd been transported from the station and deposited into a forest.

Inches separated her head from the ceiling, from which a series of various-sized saplings dangled. Moss and string bound their roots in tight, contained balls. There were ten in total. She didn't know the significance, though she knew the Sarchins had come from a heavily forested world. A connection to trees would be expected.

Four wood columns supported the roof and had a leafy motif carved into them. At the space's center was a clothed table, with musky incense sticks burning. Several icons also lined the table, featuring stylized Sarchins in varied attire, some holding staff-like weapons.

Her basic understanding of the Sarchins' religion was they worshipped ancestors and even Sarchins who'd reached notoriety on their homeworld through performing feats beyond belief. Usually feats of the martial variety.

The Magistrate had held similar beliefs in its past, praying to ancestors for good fortunes and guidance. There'd been holidays dedicated to the care of graves. Of them, Parentalia survived, though it'd shrunk and shed some rituals. She eyed the Sarchins' carvings and the suspended saplings. Rather than icons, there'd been *lares*, or statuettes, on the Magistrate homeworld Meracus Domus, stolen from one of the first cultures devoured by it, according to her father. While family remained an essential element in Magistrate life, worship of it faded alongside the cult of emperors past.

She wiped her sweaty hands against her pant legs. This was wrong. A trespass. Blasphemy. But there was no choice.

Swiveling, she inventoried the room of its furniture — mostly simplistic benches set in a round. She noted a small pine cabinet with many drawers and a set of doors, tiny storage pots, and finally, the shrine table itself ... limited options. Her eyes trailed up the columns supporting the roof, but there were no nooks big enough for the pistol. She considered the hanging saplings, but they offered little concealment. Stepping over a little fence barrier, Katya knelt beside the table, lifted its skirt, made of a rough brown material, and peered beneath. There was a cavity with a shelf used for incense storage. Bending further, she cleared her view of where the tabletop met the body. The artisan had built a little ledge into its construction. She traced it with her fingers. Wide enough. A bit of a lip. Her two fingers hit a metal support, angled perfectly with a gap.

Around the table, the dirt and moss were undisturbed. The clawed table legs had sunken into the layer, likely unmoved since they'd deposited it into the wood structure.

Katya glanced behind her, then removed the pistol from its hiding spot against her ribs. Her other hand shook as she laid it against the floor for support as she craned under the shrine table. After ensuring the safety was on, she slid the pistol into the crevice created by the metal joint. Too much wiggle. If the table was so much as bumped, the weapon would tumble from its hiding place. She readjusted it, biting into her lip as she sought the right angle for a snug fit. Then in caught.

Nudging it, Katya found little give. It would hold. In fact, it was so firmly rooted she feared reclaiming it when the time came. She jostled the table and exhaled when no thud followed. It would have to—

Clacking reached her from beyond the shrine, and Katya put the display's covering into place before taking two sizeable steps from it and her sacrilege. Cloaking herself in the intrigue of a tourist, she gaped at the ceiling and its suspended saplings, not breaking even after fabric rustled behind her.

A Sarchin with an exceptionally long mustache came beside her, craning its head up. Its amber eyes peered around the structure as if to detect any disruptions. Her own drifted to the shrine table, its curtain. Just as it had been before she tampered.

"It's beautiful," Katya said aloud.

The amber orbs returned to her, but the Sarchin said nothing, perhaps stifled by a language gap.

It left Katya to stand awkwardly before thanking the elder Sarchin and beating a quick retreat. On the other side of the fabric barrier, she met with gazes of several Sarchins. She bowed to them, then snaked her way toward the ramp alongside the shrine. Her ears remained primed, seeking any sound coming from the shrine. But no disruption came from it, and she left the area, keen to not keep Strom waiting any longer.

Katya exhaled deeply when she entered the nearest lift. Her chest constricted as she activated it, shooting herself ever closer to Strom's level. Her divergence from habit would be remarked on. She ran over responses in her head while cursing herself for having been so predictable. What reasoning could she provide? At best, she hoped Strom would view her indirect route as a power play—something Strom could understand. The woman favored such strategies. But ... this diversion, following her dining with Izem, would be a red flag.

Weaving her fingers together behind her back, Katya closed her eyes while the lift hummed. She was being watched even now. She inhaled, stress draining from her body. What came would come. There was no dodging the shot if it happened.

She stepped off the lift as soon as its doors opened into the harsh darkened metal world of the old station, with its unforgiving angles. It even felt cooler than the rest of the station. Swallowing, she avoided two Plasovern agents working their way to the lift. Both paid Katya no mind. Nor did anyone else she came upon. She reached Strom's rooms with no trouble.

But when greeted by a new attendant who was not Bodil, her hackles rose. The woman before her was also Varraganarian, her skin fair and her hair blonde, albeit a warmer shade than Bodil's platinum. Her arms were bulky and well-muscled. She could probably overpower Katya in a fair fight.

"I'm surprised not to see Bodil."

The woman craned her neck toward Strom's shutoff room. "She carries her own."

Katya's raised brow sparked no further explanation. It left her mind to wander along several trains of thought all at once. Why was her warden suddenly absent? The threads of various possibilities wove in and out of her mind, from innocent to catastrophic. A vice tightened in her chest while she wrung her hands behind her back. If she'd picked up another mission, it could ease Katya's escape. The woman had promised to kill her if she betrayed Strom, after all. But she could be tearing apart Katya's apartment at this very moment.

Bodil's replacement opened the door to Strom's room, and the moment Katya stepped in, it closed behind her. Trapping her. She surveyed her settings, the raptors from Skogarld looming as they hadn't in her first visit. Their curved beaks and talons gleamed as if freshly polished. Her gaze leveled. Strom. She lounged on the sofa, laying on her back, legs propped up on one end. This time, no incense burned, though a muted remnant still clung to the space, the downside of prolonged use.

"You asked to see me." Katya ran her thumb across her clenched fingers, using the action to ground her, keep her voice level.

"I did." Strom stretched before lurching into a sitting position. "Come"—she patted the newly cleared space beside her—"sit with me."

Said the spider to the fly, Katya mentally added. She did as instructed, only favoring the plush chair away from Strom. It brought that smile to Strom's face.

"Refreshments?"

Before the other woman could get up, Katya replied, "No."

"You never change."

Katya's spine tingled. Her narrowness would get her killed. She simply shrugged. "I'm not hungry."

Strom snorted and pushed her low ponytail behind her shoulder. "So, what did you think of Medzeci?"

To the point, immediately touching the mission that had ended with a small crate of firearms vanishing.

"I can't say." Katya folded her hands in her lap. For once, her hand didn't shake. "We really didn't get to see much of the planet or its people for me to arrive at any conclusion one way or any other."

"That's a shame. But there are bound to be more opportunities for that in the future." Strom rolled her head against the sofa's back. "Though, I suspect, you'll arrive at some of the same conclusions I have about the Medzeci." She winked at Katya. "They make such odd bedfellows."

"One might suggest they are the antithesis to your cause," Katya supplied while forcing her posture to loosen against the fluff of her chair. "I can't believe the Magistrate propaganda is right: They chip their people."

Strom's fingers swirled against the fur draped on the sofa. "Hmm." It was almost melodic. "But they have ample other admirable traits. Dedication. Meticulous scheduling. A fine appreciation of art." Her lips curled. "Deep pockets."

Katya shifted in the chair. "Deep pockets indeed. Everything is gold with them."

That drew a chuckle. "Indeed. But without those deep pockets, we wouldn't be where we are now. No home. Just a handful of ill-trained, sectarian operatives, using weaponry little better than sticks. We would simply be throwing ourselves against the Magistrate ... at least now, we leave dents. Maybe one day ... something greater."

Strom fully kicked her feet off the sofa. "On that note, some of our young members are going on a retreat into Medzeci space. To train. I think you are acquainted with a few of them. Your young charge definitely is, and I rather think Mina would love to join them. I can hear your complaints bubbling, but I assure you, the training is perfectly safe. No combat involved."

Mina would push to go, especially if Dag was one of the junior members mentioned. The teen was coming into her own, and the day was fast approaching when she would strike out on her own. Katya pressed her lips together. Likely, this was a planned wedge. Strom knew how frayed their relationship was growing. This hill, if she chose to stand on it, would see Mina responding in a fashion she couldn't afford. Not now, as the escape plan careened forward.

"Mina would, but I really can't let her, not with Sotiris and his appointments, not if I get sent off again."

"It's not fair for the girl to be sidelined for him, though." Strom rested her chin on her hand. "She should be able to pursue the path she wants."

"When she's eighteen."

"An arbitrary number. One too many adults hide behind." Strom rose to her feet. "I have seen ten-year-olds serve as soldiers and twenty-some-year-olds so incompetent they might as well be toddlers." Something apparently caught her humor as she chuckled to herself. She didn't allow Katya in on the joke.

"Ten-year-olds shouldn't be soldiers."

"The galaxy isn't a perfect place, though, is it?" Strom sashayed into her small kitchenette and put a kettle on the stovetop. Her pace was languid as she readied a tray with cups and a kettle. "But you'd do well to heed my words on Mina. She deserves better than to be forced into a caretaker role. She needs to be allowed to explore herself."

"I'll consider it." She coated the words with sincerity, even as her mind raged that they would be gone long before the retreat. "Is this why you called me? To talk about Mina?"

Strom lingered in the kitchenette, rummaging around in cabinets, from which she removed a canister of biscuits. "You've gotten close to Izem's girl. Are sparks flying?"

"We're planning our wedding."

Strom burst into laughter. "You can be quite funny when you want to be. A shame it isn't more frequent."

"We've developed an acquaintanceship," Katya said over Strom's stifled giggles. "She's not the most talkative person, so we get along well enough."

"Well enough for her to present you to Izem."

And they had fully arrived. Katya made no comment. Allow Strom to lead the conversation at this point. The other woman's mind had often proven impregnable to her, and Katya would rather respond to her inquiries than misstep and give anything away by blundering forward. Never give an enemy a rope from which they could hang you, as an old Magistrate proverb intoned, stoking unwanted memories of the photo feet from her now.

Strom bit into a biscuit, sending crumbs to the countertop. As she chewed, she inspected Katya. Neither of them spoke. The Varraganarian probably expected her to crack under the weight and spill her guts. But she was made of a stiffer material than that, and it insulted Katya that Strom thought her so weak willed.

Crossing her legs, Katya cleared her throat. "I'll actually take a biscuit and maybe a cup of tea. If you're not adding alcohol to it, that is."

The Varraganarian blinked at her. Katya levied a thin smile at her.

As Strom filled the tray with the biscuits and readied the tea, Katya watched, her guard never slipping. Come on. Just ask.

Coyly, Strom set the tray on to the coffee table between the sofa and Katya's chair. The teapot and two cups joined it.

"It's a special tea, crafted to taste like wine. But don't fret; there's not a drop of alcohol in it. I enjoy the grape taste. It reminds me of home. They freeze grapes for a special wine, much like this tea."

"Of course." Katya took a biscuit from the tray and accepted a cup from Strom.

"What had Izem wanted?"

Strom's straight-to-the-point words were uncharacteristic. Apparently, she wasn't a fan of her own game being turned against her.

Heat seeped through the porcelain into Katya's hands. "It's hard to say."

Wrong answer. Strom's expression shifted to something predatory, the coy smile now fanged.

When the woman shifted forward, Katya hastened to add, "He asked about Sotiris."

Strom's lips narrowed, but she picked up her own cup, concealing whatever had been her intended action previously. Tingles coursed through Katya's upper legs, dread corseting her frame.

The spoon clattering against porcelain as Strom stirred in sugar punctuated the oppressive silence that smothered the room and Katya's thoughts. Like prey, she monitored Strom's posture, motions, calculating the potential for a strike. But as suddenly as it had descended, the palatable tension dissipated, with Strom leaning back into her chair and crossing her legs. Once more, the queen, no longer the terrorist with blood-drenched hands.

"Did he say what sparked his interest?"

"Not directly. I assume he has ongoing problems with the Oneiroi and was seeking an edge." Katya bit into the biscuit and allowed Strom to draw her own conclusions. The biscuit harbored a tart jam, and its tiny seeds broke against her teeth while she chewed.

Over the rim of her cup, Strom breathed, "Impatient man." She sipped. "So eager to go home to die. And he wonders why he doesn't garner the support of the Medzeci like I have. He can't see the bigger picture of a galaxy rid of the Magistrate."

"But is the Medzeci Empire better? They are, as you said, rather strange bedfellows. They are even less open to others' ways than the Magistrate."

Katya earnestly wanted to know Strom's thoughts on this. Surely, the similarities between the two cosmic titans didn't elude her. Both had conquered their cores before expanding outward until they collided with a giant equal in size and strength to themselves. After the initial skirmishes, a balance had followed in the galaxy that even independent systems benefited from. She didn't think Strom truly appreciated what she might unleash if her quest succeeded.

"Of course they aren't." Strom winked at her before pushing her bangs behind her ear. Her hand lingered by her com, which was nestled there. "But they aren't on my homeworld. So the enemy of my enemy"—she waved her free hand about—"you know how the saying goes. When my world is freed, we'll deal with the Medzeci as needed."

"They outgun you."

"So does the Magistrate."

"But not in the same way." Katya narrowed her eyes at the other woman, who didn't balk.

"It matters very little that Medzeci has armed us. It only matters that they *have* armed us. Those very weapons can turn in any direction. And there are other means." She took a long sip of tea before discarding the cup. "But that is irrelevant. I wouldn't get too close to Izem's group. It wouldn't surprise me if he aimed to use that boy of yours as a weapon."

Wasn't that what everyone wanted to do? Her chest clenched. He would likely spend his entire life with people trying to force that role on him. The ability to target a foe and disable them without so much as firing a volley was a tactical feat.

"I didn't tell him much. I take my role as guardian seriously. Too many people knowing about him isn't in his best interest."

"We think alike." Strom took a bite from a biscuit, chewing it slowly and deliberately before swallowing. "Should Izem question you further on this matter, send him to me."

Katya nodded, then set her cup and saucer on to the coffee table, rising to her feet afterward. "If that is all, I need to get back to Sotiris."

Strom's raised hand arrested further movement.

"You know," the terrorist drawled, "the same thing I said about that girl is true for you." Strom rocked to her feet, causing a muscle in Katya's neck to quiver. "What do you want now, Cassius? You should really think about that carefully. Your life can't revolve around this child. He can be a part of it, yes, but you need a drive that's your own. You're too driven, too task-oriented to be happy without some grand goal. You've just deluded yourself otherwise with routine."

Valens flashed to her mind, one of the few people to ever push her in such a way. It'd rankled her, but not as much as Strom, this woman who feigned familiarity ... and who had never missed the mark by far.

"I'll worry about that once everything else is settled."

"Life never settles." Strom invaded her space. "What will fill that hole for you, hmm?" She smiled and straightened the collar of Katya's purple button-down shirt. "When the routine fades and the haze is lost, what is found?" The fabric tightened against Katya's throat. "Underneath it all ... I can't help but wonder, Cassius. Do you still bleed blue?"

Katya started to speak when Strom's com chirped.

"Yes?" Strom asked; the predatory tone ditched for something more blasé. Something was said through the com, but the garbled sound was indecipherable, no matter how she strained. "Hmm." Strom hummed, her breath hot against Katya's skin. "Very interesting. Thank you, Albinsson. Yes, thank you for your diligence. Yes, yes. Very good. No, but thank you. We'll chat later."

She ended the call and dropped Katya's collar in order to gather the tray. "Think about what I've said, dear. For you and that girl. It's time to look toward the future and your place in it." She waved. "Go ahead. See to your boy."

Katya didn't hesitate, seizing the opportunity to put as much distance between her and Strom as possible. She'd avoided a noose.

While Sotiris played with his mound of toys, Katya surveyed the rooms, finding both the slate and even pocketknife where she'd concealed them in plain sight. In the background, the toddler squeaked and chortled nonsense sounds, banging two metal toys together. Mina had slipped out the moment she'd returned, saying something about a repair crew. Strom's words filtered to the forefront of Katya's mind. She couldn't force Mina on to a path, but she would try her best to dissuade her from the one Strom was offering. There was no way she was allowing the teen farther into Medzeci space to be swallowed by it.

Tomorrow evening.

Her heart fluttered at an uncontrolled pace. As her throat seized, she breathed deeply through her nose, held it, and then released it through her mouth. With several repetitions, the tightness suffocating her lifted. Through her bangs, her gaze settled on Sotiris, who carried on unaware of the panic attack.

He would survive. Plasovern needed Sotiris. Likely they'd take Mina alive too since she'd shown promise and favorable leanings. She wondered how Mina would respond to her execution. She banished the thought, her stomach turning.

Stretching as she straightened, Katya willed the vice from her chest. Then she gave Sotiris a noisemaker toy.

"Oh," Sotiris cooed as she guided his hands to produce a louder trill.

"Yeah," Katya whispered. "Just like that. Keep it up."

He jangled it; its cymbals clattered with each shake. Katya beamed and shook her hands up and down to encourage the motion. She then removed the com device Kahina had given her and activated it.

"Who calls?" Kahina asked.

"The idiot removing some sort of beast for you."

"Ah," she crooned. "I take you have news."

"Had a lovely conversation with Strom," Katya said, gesturing for Sotiris to continue. "I'm moving tomorrow night. Do you prefer I meet you before I go to the clinic or after?"

Kahina seemed to ponder this, falling silent. "Before. No point alarming them more if you are found at the clinic. I will give you the chip then. The face kit we will put on your ship, which is?"

Biting her lower lip, Katya considered the hangar bay its lines of ships, prioritizing speed. "*Kjære Vind*. Though if it's gone or has too much activity, the *Solar Storm*. The *Mezitzia* is the backup."

"You've planned well."

Katya ran her hand through her hair. It could all go wrong. While the odds favored that at least one mark would be untouched by missions, the possibility remained that all the ships would be in use.

"Have your people wait for my signal before moving. It'll lessen the chance of exposure or my supplies being taken." Swallowing hard, Katya pressed her luck. "Would you do a favor for me? It's about the gun."

When met only with silence, Katya elaborated, "I hid it in a shrine. Can you retrieve it? I'm concerned my return would bring too much interest."

"The Sarchins'?" Kahina asked.

"Yes."

Kahina sighed exaggeratedly. "I can grab your weapon. Where is it concealed?"

Katya rubbed her jawline, gaze shifting to Sotiris's play. She wondered how spiritual Kahina was. "The main offering table has a gap between its bottom and the floor. There's a slight edge in the wood; it's resting there."

"Such a trespass," the Tizzet woman clucked. "I can do this. Contact me when you begin. All will be in order by then."

The door slid open, and Katya killed the com device, shoving it into her bra.

She plastered a smile on her face to turn and greet Mina. "I wasn't expecting you back so soon."

"Just wanted to grab a hoodie. Going to hang out tonight," Mina said, not really paying attention to anything in the room, rushing instead to her room. On her return, she slid one arm through her zip-up hoodie before doing likewise with her other hand. Then, toying with the zipper, she muttered, "Dag's going to Paredetta."

Ah, a two-front assault. "Oh?"

"Yep. A few of the others too." She moistened her lips and continued to fuss with the zipper, her eyes fixating on it. "There's room for one more. The supervisor in charge, well, they're fine with me going. They actually … kinda think I'd do well."

"Strom had mentioned something about it."

Mina's head shot up, her mouth hanging open. "She did?" It was a mere whisper. Hope sprang to her eyes, and it crushed a part of Katya.

"When is this trip? She hadn't said."

"In a week? I think." Mina leaned toward her. "So you're considering letting me go?"

Katya glanced toward the wall and then back at the teen. Months ago, she would've been proud to see that light in her eyes, that passion. Mina had found a calling, much like she had at that age. The girl twisted her hands in the hoodie's pockets while she nibbled at her lower lip. She leaned in, barely perceptible. Katya swallowed, desperate to wet her dry throat.

"I am." The lie burned the moment it left her tongue. "Seriously considering it. I just need a bit more time." To get us out of here.

CHAPTER TEN

Katya's stomach roiled and rebelled against the thought of even attempting to eat breakfast. She had forced some stale crackers down last night. The word "premature" taunted her, and every loose piece of her plan glared at her. So many little ways it could all fall apart. The tumultuous sea of doubt and anxiety further churned with Mina's absence. When the time came, what would she do if she couldn't find Mina? What would she do if time ran out?

With trembling fingers, she fastened the buttons on her top. It would work out. She would force it to. She slipped on her jacket before exiting into the main living space. Sotiris leaped to his feet the moment she crossed the threshold and tried to dart.

"Not today," she growled, catching his arm. "We can't do this today."

There was too much at stake. Around his wiggling frame, she grabbed the Skogarld forest cat plush, her key.

"Here, here …" She pecked his cheek with its plastic nose, earning a glower. "We gotta go. Don't worry. We'll take him with." She prodded the boy with the cat. "Give it a good hold."

He scrunched his face, eyes lowering balefully. She half expected him to chuck the toy, but he held it so tight to his chest the fluff was redistributed in its torso.

Balancing on the balls of her feet, Katya brought herself to his level. "I promise" — she cupped his cheek, lifting his face — "things will change." It was the closest she could give him to an end. While he hadn't hammered down oral language, she still wasn't chancing loose lips.

Her hand left his face and took his hand. Like that, they headed to the clinic.

As she trudged Jomsborg's halls for one of the last times, her head pounded. Had Kahina moved yet? Could she even trust the Tizzets? How easy would it be for them to play both sides to garner the most favorable outcomes for themselves … but there was no time to doubt now. What she'd set into motion couldn't be stopped. She had no choice but to lean on them.

They arrived at the appointment to find Strom and Usha absent, which settled like a lead weight in Katya's stomach. Her gaze tracked the hallway to the private doorway at its end. Was Usha haunting her quarters, or was she even on the station?

"Our favorite patient." Garbi clapped as she leaned forward to be face level with Sotiris. "Let's get started, huh?"

His lower lip protruded, and he slunk into Katya's leg.

"Ah," Garbi cooed. "I know it's not fun, but it's something we need to do."

With the care of a nurse, she pried Sotiris from Katya and guided him into the separate examination room. Since nothing kept Katya in the hallway this time, she followed. She took the toy from him after Garbi hefted him on to the examination table. He squeaked at the action, hand reaching for the stuffed animal. Excellent.

Throughout the appointment, Katya kept the toy in the open, using it to distract Sotiris. She made sure that both Garbi and Isla observed it while never calling too much attention to it. It simply existed, and Sotiris loved it. That was all she needed to be established.

It left with them during the morning appointment and then returned with them for the evening visit.

Once again, Katya periodically waved it for Sotiris's benefit; however, not nearly as much as she had done before. It still existed in Garbi's and Isla's minds, but it was not as observed. So, while the pair poked and prodded Sotiris, Katya waited for the opportune moment to drop it when neither Garbi nor Isla were paying attention. Giving her a reason for returning to the clinic alone later in the evening.

Her moment arrived while helping Sotiris put on his shirt, something the boy resisted. His skin remained a little sensitive from the adhesives used in this round of tests. When the toy dropped during the shuffle, Katya toed it under a cabinet. Sotiris's flailing with the shirt, along with his shrieks, camouflaged the action.

Pinning his arm, she worked it through one sleeve before doing likewise with his right arm.

Then she willed Sotiris to not notice the sudden disappearance of his cat when they moseyed into the next room with its red light. Garbi followed, chitchatting while Katya slid the sunglasses on to Sotiris's face. Neither the nurse nor Sotiris had noticed the absence of the toy. Through the glass, Isla continued her repetitive task of data entry.

"We'll see you tomorrow morning as usual."

"No more spacing out appointments?" Katya asked.

"Not for now. We're ready to transition to a digestible form as you've asked for." She poked Sotiris's cheek and beamed when he scowled. "Isn't that great?"

Unfamiliar with such terms, she drew no response from the prickly Oneiroi child.

"It's great news." Katya smiled. With any luck, they'd left notes about such plans in their computer's database, allowing her to pilfer them after she broke into the system. She would then hand them over to the next doctor she enlisted in the cause of Sotiris. Her chest tightened. There would have to be a next doctor, always. "We'll see you tomorrow," she added, her tone light.

Her gaze flickered to Sotiris, who held her hand. She gave him a squeeze before starting their path to their quarters. He would go down in about three and a half hours to four. With him safely slumbering, she would steal into the hangar bay and place him in the freighter. He would be alone for five hours if even that … it would just depend on Mina. Her gut clenched, the shake in her hand drawing Sotiris's eyes to meet hers.

"Everything will be fine."

A blink was the only response she received.

It would be fine. She would get the drug and notes, would find Mina in time, Kahina would come through, the freighter theft would go off without a hitch, and they would break away cleanly.

In their quarters, Katya prepped a code-breaking software that the Tizzets had loaded on to the slate. She modified it using knowledge gleaned from Reznic syndicates—to speed things up. She gave the breaker more bite, especially since she expected a fight from any security system employed by Usha or Strom. If she could break through it …

Prioritize the medicine. She could bust her way to them, blowing whatever stealth she had. In a worst-case scenario where the breaker failed, she could leave the notes and data behind; the medicine, however, could not be. Sotiris had been without his powers for months now. Should they reappear, there was no telling how he would use them. What control he'd had over them might've eroded in that period of absence.

Her father's words that the defect would only get worse with time echoed in her mind.

Sotiris hovered in front of the screen and found its controls, summoning a nature program. He stood glued to the movements of some planet's charismatic megafauna as it snapped the limb of an elderly animal of a different species, careening it to the ground and kicking up dirt. Sotiris's lips parted.

A ticking time bomb. He'd been called that too many times to count. She even mentally thought of him as such.

She dabbed at her eyes and moved into the kitchenette, where she prepared a simple meal for them. Anything heavy would have only unsettled her stomach, but all the same, she needed to eat something, if only to strengthen her for what lay ahead. By the time she'd finished the broth soup, Sotiris had settled on the floor.

He protested when she brought him to the small table, but quieted when she placed the bowl in front of him. Eagerly, he shoveled the broth—his favorite—into his mouth. It increased her curiosity about what Oneiroi ate on their homeworld.

Mina didn't return during the meal, and she didn't answer Katya's calls. A rock settled at the base of her stomach with each ring, only for the call to cut out.

Damn it, Mina.

Like clockwork, Sotiris wore with each passing minute, lying on his side in front of the holoscreen. His enormous eyes closed, only to blink awake, his body stretching along the area rug. A yawn. Then his eyelids lifted a fraction before closing to sleep.

Katya waited a few more minutes before moving him to the sofa. She kissed his forehead. "Wish me luck."

Grabbing her slate, she slid it into the large interior pocket she'd sewn into her bulkier jacket, a cast-off donation from the quartermaster. It'd been far too big for Mina and not much better for Katya's frame, either. She then packed a bag for her and moved into Mina's room. It'd sprouted a personality with small Plasovern graffiti posters and other little decorative touches that spoke of home. Her throat burned as she took clothing items and basic hygiene items from the space. Mina had truly made it—Jomsborg, Plasovern—a home. She knew the cause had enraptured the teen, but she'd ignored or denied the extent.

She lifted Mina's gifted slate, a newer model. She slid it into her own bag. Until they reached a safe distance and the teen had cooled down, she couldn't chance her reaching out to someone in Plasovern. As she dropped the flap to her bag, she surveyed the room again for anything else she should take, but found nothing.

Turning to leave, she hoped the girl wouldn't freak if she returned during Katya's absence to find items missing from her room. She bit her lower lip. Mina would wait for an explanation from her. She wouldn't run off to someone else. Her grip tightened on the bags' straps as the statement rang hollow in her mind.

She positioned the bags by the sofa side farthest away from the door, where they would go unnoticed. She increased the sound of the holoscreen, though kept it at a reasonable range, before activating her illicit com.

"Kahina?"

"Now?" The other woman's voice reached her.

"Now or never."

"Meet me at the connector leading to the clinic. I will wait for you there. There is a security hole there, and I will have a blocker too."

"I don't suppose you have one I could borrow?"

"No. It would trace back to us. Izem is clear we cannot help too much. You understand?"

Katya nodded out of habit, rubbing her hand along her jaw, which ached. It had been too much to hope for. "I will see you there."

Shutting off the com, she cast one more glance at Sotiris before exiting the room. When she did, she made a show of searching the floor, the benches, and any other object along the way. Like one would do if they were hunting for a stuffed Skogarld forest cat.

The halls stood empty because of the late hour. Those who wandered them ignored her, even as she made a show of looking for something lost.

She eventually rendezvoused with Kahina, whose posture portrayed far greater ease than Katya felt.

"You look like your skeleton could jump from its skin." Kahina flashed her teeth at her. "Loosen up. Strom suspects nothing. Don't make her think she should."

"I could be dead in a few minutes."

"Or not." Kahina reached into her coat, removing the handgun. "I believe this is yours. I just hope some nature spirit didn't curse it given where it lodged."

Katya accepted it, slipping it in the pocket alongside the slate. "The chip?"

The other woman proffered it between two fingers. "Magistrate chip. You can make it work?"

"I'm a pro at it."

"Good." She shifted, keeping her eyes roaming. "We are not completely leaving you hanging. My people are monitoring the hangar. Option one is at home, and no activity around it. One will linger to give you an eye on situation. If you are caught, remember our kindness and that Magistrate training to keep your tongue sealed."

"They won't hear it from me."

Kahina extended her hand, which Katya accepted. She spoke in her native tongue. "It means 'smooth hunt.' I hope you find what you need."

They then departed each other's company, going in opposite directions. Katya still imitated a person seeking something as she closed in on the clinic.

Close to ten o'clock, its lights had been dimmed, the lobby cleared—though ever since the relocation of some operations, it had never been busy again. Beyond the glass, the nurses or doctors had cleared out. Favorable, but it didn't guarantee Garbi and Isla weren't burning the midnight oil. At the door to the main hallway, Katya inputted her own code, her heart quickening when it opened. If her suspicions were correct, her usage of it during an off-hour would send out a notification. She would have very little time.

Picking up her pace, she navigated the eerie red-lit hallway, a shade darker than normal. It conjured memories of Magistrate plays depicting an imagined underworld. She didn't linger on those productions as she entered the unlit examination room. She used the slider to brighten the space and freed her slate.

She connected it to one of Isla's computers, using a port. Turning the computer on, she launched the breaker and prepared to transfer as much data over as possible before introducing the virus. The breaker began its task, and she held her breath. It would work, or it wouldn't. She forced her gaze away to the medicine storage cabinet.

Approaching it, she pressed its numerical keypad to match Garbi's code. The cabinet opened, sending chilled air outward and exposing several glass medical bottles of various shapes and sizes. She ran a finger against them, stopping at the canisters she was familiar with. Her face chilled.

Two different labels ... Two different medicines. What—

She glanced over her shoulder at her slate, still running through different encryptions. Which was the one she needed? She lifted one bottle, carefully reading the label. *Zazperkanioc*. The other, *Izemic*. The first, injectable; the other—her face burned—delivered orally. So that was where the effort had been. To appease the Tizzets just enough. Likely, Izemic was something to protect them from the Oneiroi child present on their world, which targeted them.

She slipped as many canisters of Sotiris's drug into her coat as possible—fifteen. She frowned at the remaining five. Apparently, Usha and her aides preferred keeping a small supply. She wished she could take them with her, but any more would stick out, and besides, she needed to raid some needles. So instead, she shifted the remaining canisters to the shelf's front, providing a passing concealment of her theft.

Beep.

She jerked to attention. Behind her, the slate blinked. Now or never. She started to rise but stopped, her fingers cold on the cabinet's door as its refrigeration continued to pour out. On the upper shelf, she spotted a common sedative and pocketed it. If she were cornered, it could be an easy exit. It secured; she shut the cabinet, and its locking mechanism clicked into place.

Katya lurched to her feet and darted to the computer, its secrets laid bare. Activating a fast transfer storage application, she sought Sotiris's data and transferred it to the slate. She then moved to the cabinets and thrust needles into her other pocket, separate from the medicine. From time to time, she glanced at the data flow. Sotiris's folder seemed to be larger than she'd expected. She returned to the computer and started browsing some files, later ones.

A flicker caught her attention behind her, and she turned. Nothing. Inhaling, she refocused on the screen in front of her: its formulas, observation notes …

Her limbs trembled, and she had to rest the bulk of her weight on the control panel's flat surface to stop from sinking to the floor. The open file brought an acidic, coppery taste to her mouth. They'd used her and Mina as test subjects for the Tizzet people. Blinking, she swallowed while her mind reeled. The drug gap. It'd never been a break for Sotiris or a chance to retool the formula. They'd pumped another drug into their quarters using the water system while leaving their distant neighbors unprotected to Sotiris's mental nocturnal wanderings.

Her estimates on that second drug had been correct: It safeguarded against the Oneiroi mutation ... somehow. Katya couldn't make sense of the notes, detailing the how. But Garbi and Isla had labeled it as a success.

Katya squinted at the notes. *"Untreated individual reported insomnia and poor sleep to station doctors. One stated they'd suffered from nightmares, though they could not recall them. Said individual also noted migraines the next morning. Rated nine on the scale. The headaches were again noted on following days but lower on the scale. One subject felt like they'd run a marathon. Displayed paranoia. Believed something was hunting them."*

Katya flexed her fingers against the smooth surface. She knew those headaches all too well. Exhaling sharply through her nose, Katya scrolled further.

Her blood chilled reading what appeared to be Isla's clinical and detailed notes, which were surrounded by all kinds of postulations about the Oneiroi species. A queasy sensation rumbled in her stomach. She'd given a terrorist organization the blueprints to harm an entire species—because that was precisely what they would do if the Oneiroi didn't comply. Isla's notes prepared for every inevitability.

She should have known. She gritted her teeth. In the back of her mind, there'd been an inkling, but she'd ignored it. Far too focused on the moment, the immediate need of care for Sotiris. Strom was Strom. She wouldn't care what method removed the Oneiroi from battle; it only mattered that they were. And now, even if her virus wrecked this computer, there was likely a digital backup elsewhere.

Her eyes returned to the medicine cabinet, tempted to steal or destroy the second one. She and Mina had perfected it after all … but that would run afoul of her new allies. How much had they known about its creation? She ground her fist into the control panel. She had a pistol and a Magistrate registration chip. They had more than paid to keep the drug. And tampering with it could not remove it from Plasovern's arsenal.

She glanced at the slate. Its clock informed her she'd been in the clinic for at least ten minutes. Any minute, someone would come. Her slate flashed upon the transfer's completion, and she switched over to the virus. Her trembling hand tightened around the connector cord, ready to rip it from the computer. The upload line crept further and then froze. With her free hand, she wiped sweat from her brow. Hurry. The green line leaped forward again. Stopped. Chewing her bottom lips, she closed her eyes momentarily. Almost there. Glancing at the clock. Add another minute.

She ripped the cord from the console when the line reached one hundred percent. After pocketing the slate, she powered down the console's screen. By now, the virus had spread across the network, sinking its teeth in.

In haste, she scrambled from the console and focused on the stuffed toy, maneuvering around the space until she reached its hiding spot under one counter. She bent to retrieve it and almost hit her head against said counter when the door shot open.

Garbi, gaze wide and out of breath, jumped once she caught sight of the crouched Katya.

"What-what are you doing in here?" Her hair stood in complete disorder, and one sharp finger aggressively pointed at Katya. So far removed from the calm, bubbly woman she presented herself to be.

Katya held her hands aloft in a sign of nonresistance. "Sotiris dropped his toy during our last appointment." She nudged her head toward where it lay on the floor after she'd fished it out. "I didn't want him to wake up tomorrow and find it gone."

Garbi stared at her, then the stuffed forest cat before her hands lowered to her sides. Her gaped expression made her look winded.

Katya took it as an opportunity to pick up the toy. "I hoped it wouldn't cause a big fuss. Me popping in here."

"The code was for regular visits to help reception. You shouldn't have come after hours." Garbi took a huffy tone. "This is a closed lab. Such intrusions can compromise or contaminate our work."

Thinking of the virus doing just that, a sense of pride blossomed. Externally, Katya feigned remorse, even managing a blush. "I'm sorry. He's already hard to manage in the mornings." She rubbed her eyes like a haggard mother. "I just couldn't deal with this"—she waved the toy about—"on top of the hide and seek."

Garbi's mouth formed a thin line, her eyes shifting to the side. Quite a cross expression. "I need to decontaminate. Please leave."

"Yes. Right away."

Flustered, stuffed animal pressed to her chest, Katya bounded from the space. Given Garbi's attire, a crumpled set of medical scrubs, she'd been in a rush to reach the clinic. If a live feed of the clinic existed, she hadn't viewed it before coming, or else Katya's gambit would have ended.

Katya rushed back to her quarters, almost surprised when she successfully reached it. She imagined Garbi's intensive search of the clinic had uncovered tampering by now.

Inside, Sotiris slept soundly where she'd left him, not appearing to have moved a single muscle to reposition himself.

No Mina. She tried to com her again, using their quarters' com system. No answer.

Wiping sweat from her brow, Katya hoisted the packs—after loading a couple of Sotiris's favorite toys into her own bag—on to both of her shoulders. She then lifted Sotiris in a bridal carry, more comfortable for both of them. The boy had added weight, a good thing, though it turned her current endeavor into a more strenuous exercise.

"You're in for a surprise when you wake up," she muttered into Sotiris's ear. One way or another.

Like a thief, Katya progressed through Jomsborg, taking routes known for their low traffic during her runs. If she heard people, she shifted her path. Her current loaded-down state would raise alarm.

She entered one of the main common spaces and maintained cover using its foliage. A group of Plasovern agents didn't detect her as she crept by.

Proceeding into another corridor, she arrived at the correct hangar bay. The machinery and ships protected her movements. While mostly deserted, a group of mechanics had stayed behind to disassemble a pleasure craft, part by part. Heavy chunks had been blasted from its exterior, the results of a firefight with something much stronger.

Sotiris shifted his head, bothered by the heat and fumes of the bay. He wouldn't wake. He couldn't. The drugs in his system were too potent.

Passing between two freighters, Katya arrived at her mark. As with all off-duty vessels, its back hatch was down, allowing anyone entrance. Through its blackened interior, she inched, clearing every room. When satisfied, she took Sotiris to the cockpit and laid him on to the cool metal floor, using Mina's less bulky bag as a pillow. Her scan for any enemy devices uncovered one listening device, which she destroyed. She then ducked under the navigation console and helm, tweaking wiring to avoid any sudden power cut-off or remote tampering. Anything else she'd have to mess with after a jump. Probably several just to be safe.

She removed all of Sotiris's medicine from her jacket and the cumbersome slate, keeping only the firearm. As she unloaded the needles, she filled a couple with the sedative and placed them, recapped in her exterior pocket. What remained in the bottle stayed in the cockpit.

She glanced at the time on her slate. Almost midnight. She rubbed her furrowed brow. No alarm rang yet. Her mind flickered to Garbi. Had the virus taken down the clinic's systems? It might have even jammed the doors, trapping and isolating her. A blessing, if true.

She took out the Tizzet com device and reset its frequency to Mina's. No response, no pickup.

Mina, where are you?

Bowing over Sotiris, she brushed his hair away from his face. "I'll be back."

She exited the ship as stealthily as she'd come. She had left the toddler in the open. If her escape plan became a shot in the brown, she wanted him found. Her heart fluttered, recalling Isla's and Garbi's detailed notes about how their research might be applied to Oneiroi unhindered by the defect. Still, she banked on a future where Sotiris would be reunited with his people, the research wouldn't be wielded as a weapon, and she wouldn't be damned for her role in allowing it.

Mina. Focus on her. She tried the com again, but the hundredth time wasn't a charm. She shoved it into her pocket, not once breaking from her frantic run. The time window was closing. She forced herself to slow. She needed to use her brain. Blind stabs in the dark weren't getting her anywhere. Her mind poured over spaces she knew Mina and her friends liked to frequent ... factor in the hour. Checking the café and the two central commissaries turned up nothing. All were vacant except for third-shift workers, who couldn't understand a word she said.

Her heart banged in its cage, and a cold sweat lined her brow and back. What if Mina was no longer on the station? She wiped her mouth. Strom wouldn't have, at least not so soon. What if Strom hadn't been as unaware as Kahina said and made a move? Could she be hunting for Mina, who wasn't even on the station?

Rubbing her sternum through her shirt, Katya swallowed. When did she have to give up? She froze when a wave of sickness struck her. She would have to. The plan was now too far along to stop. Not with the virus. Not with the stolen drugs. Dragging her fingers through her hair, Katya tore a path to the observation space, with its benches and extensive span of space-grade synth glass. Popular with the station's youth.

She wasn't leaving Mina. She couldn't. A younger Mina, beaming up at her, refused to budge from her mind. Katya's action would hurt her, but she would live on and not be devoured by a crusade.

As she encroached on the observation deck, she paused in the hallway. She skimmed the benches for one figure.

The benches near her proved deserted, but farther down, a few people lounged on the backless benches, some on their backs to stargaze. Giggles punctuated the near-silence. It echoed from the far corner and drew Katya from the hall. As she approached the group, she noticed a collection of bottles. Someone had smuggled the forbidden on board, it would seem. One group member, a boy caught in that awkward in-between stage on the cusp of adulthood, blew smoke out, little bits also escaping through his nostrils. His fair features, despite his purple hair, suggested he was Varraganarian.

Katya inched closer, scanning the other teens and twenty-some-year-olds. Bright turquoise hair, with an underlayer of bubble gum, caused her heart to jump. Mina.

The teen had stretched out on a bench, with her legs dangling over both sides. Dag stroked her left wrist and arm from the floor before touching his lips to her pulse point. It drew a smile Katya had never seen on her face before.

Mina would hate her. Yet Katya didn't slow in her approach. Her footsteps caused several members of the group to lift their heads. Mina slipped her arm away from Dag, her face pink.

"K-Katya?" she sputtered, potentially affected by the smoke lingering in the space too vast for the recirculation system to erode completely. Or maybe she'd imbibed some of the alcohol.

"I've been trying to com you for the bulk of the day."

Mina bit her lower lip briefly and dropped her gaze to the ground. "I lost my com. I'm sorry." She lifted her face. "Is everything all right?"

"Oh, yes." Katya forced a smile. "I just need some help real quick. You'll be back with your friends in no time."

Dag snaked his fingers through Mina's and squeezed her hand before setting his blue gaze on her. The bulky muscles in his neck stiffened when he shifted his weight to stand. "I hope you've decided to not make a fit about Mina joining us."

Mina's eyes widened, and she tugged at his hand, scowling up at him. Having several inches on Mina, he didn't even notice, too busy bearing down on Katya like a guard dog.

On the second tug, he shook his head and rolled his eyes. "No. You have a right to do what you want to do. She may have extracted a promise from Mistress Strom, but she can't control you. You're more than capable of deciding for yourself."

The others shifted toward Katya like a pack of wolves, gauging her reaction and forming a supportive wall. They would back up Dag no matter what, and it seemed—her gaze never left Mina, who wiggled under it—they'd been fed interesting information about her. But that is what teens did. Rebelled against parental figures and sought any ear willing to hear it.

And she wouldn't debate Mina's maturity or her role in the teen's life. "I'm sure she'll learn a lot in Medzeci."

Mina gaped at that, her eyes like platters. Dag's posture loosened while his lips parted.

Katya slipped her hands into her pockets and shrugged, mostly to cover the emerging shake. "Strom made an impressive case." She then gestured the way she'd come with a nudge of her head. "It'll only take a bit. You can come right back."

Without even asking what her task was, Mina came to her side and followed her. Katya kept a fast clip, eager to put distance between them and the teen's friends. She couldn't take them all in a fight, even with the sedative. She'd seen their toned arms. They were trained.

"So, what *do* you need?" Mina walked backward in front of her as she asked, eyes narrowed. "It's awfully late to be needing favors, isn't it? And aren't you normally asleep?"

"I'm not geriatric," Katya muttered.

Mina snorted. "Maybe not, but you have a set sleep pattern." The skepticism morphed to humor as Mina beamed, eyes lit with energy despite the late hour. "Something with Sotiris, huh? Though he should be out by now." The smile faded. "The medicine is working, right?"

"Yes, don't worry about that. The real reason is I'm heading out on a mission." The lie exited her mouth without a hitch, though really was it a lie? She never said it was a Plasovern mission.

"You said I could go back to my friends." Mina pouted. "I can't do that if I'm on Sotiris duty."

"I don't leave until later tomorrow, but I wanted to get some adjustments done to the freighter."

Mina frowned. "You're letting me leave? Knowing that Sotiris will be on his own?"

The teen had always been clever. One day, Mina would give her a run for her money. "I'll be back before you leave. I'm not going far."

"You'd better." Mina swung back around, both hands slipping into her hoodie jacket's pockets.

"Strom wouldn't have it any other way," Katya assured.

An irregular cadence beat in Katya's chest as the hangar grew closer. Mina's side glances grew more frequent when Katya declined to take any lifts, forcing them to take the long way. That constant observation paired with others prowling the halls summoned her hand's shake; she dropped the offending hand from sight. As she steered the teen from others, Mina's eyebrow rose. She'd noticed. Their time on the run wasn't so far removed, she wouldn't miss the signs of evasion. During that time, it had been vital for her to read Katya's intention.

Katya's fingers, still hidden within her pocket, tapped an erratic pattern against her body. The virus had to be seeping into the station's systems. She wanted to have Mina on the freighter before then. She knew her too well that a sudden change in the station would set off warning bells in the teen's mind.

She stilled her nervous twitch as they reached the hangar bay. At the door, she nudged her head toward the right wall. "It's over this way."

The path provided coverage, even though the space had gone quiet. Those who'd been working on the other ship had set the task aside for another day.

"Are you doing a courier mission?" Mina asked. She cocked her head toward the rows of freighters.

Katya shrugged. "It's what I do."

"You could do more than that. You just need to build trust."

Katya shrugged and diverted the conversation. "Here we are." Katya traversed the ramp, breaths coming easier when Mina's footsteps followed her.

As they crossed the dark cargo hold, Mina cleared her throat, her feet going silent, all forward momentum lost. "What exactly do you need my help with?"

Finally facing her, Katya's chest tightened. Mina had grown a couple of inches somewhere between Reznic and here. Her face had lost some of its youthful curves, particularly now as she watched Katya like a hawk, arms crossed, lips forming a thin line. Almost an adult, just not quite all the way there.

The teen rolled her eyes and tapped her foot. "Well?"

The lights flickered behind her, just a slight thing, barely noticeable.

"Over this way." Katya stepped toward the ladder.

"No, tell me here." When met with silence, she said shriller, "Now!"

"We're leaving."

Mina's eyes widened while her mouth opened and then closed. She recovered, shaking her head repeatedly. Then, with clenched fists, she ground out, "You don't get to tell me what I get to do. I'm staying." The last part, almost a shout, reverberated off the metal walls.

"Keep your voice down." Katya leveled her tone. She kept her posture loose and facial expression neutral. "I can't stop this. The parts are already in motion. If you alert them, they will kill me."

"What have you done?" Mina brought her voice to a whisper, but her face was beet red.

"Uploaded a virus."

The teen gawked at her. "What?" She jerked her head toward the hangar bay as if expecting explosions.

"I went with disruptive, not destructive." She stepped forward, causing Mina to do likewise in reverse. Katya held up her hands, rooting herself in place so as not to spook the teen into running. "It'll just disrupt the lights and some security components, allowing for a seamless exit."

"They saved us!"

"And they've experimented on us. So I think we're even." Katya bit the side of her mouth, cursing the heat in her tone.

Mina's fists shook, the inner workings of her prosthetic hand creaking. "I'm not leaving."

Katya ran her hand against her wet forehead. Sweat. She even caught its salty flavor on her lips. Across from her, Mina stood strong, ready to combat whatever left Katya's mouth. What could she say? Nothing would get through. But how had she differed from Mina? She blinked. She hadn't. She'd discovered a cause all her own. That was the power of belonging. Something familiar to Katya, now gone.

Mina sighed and shoved her hands into her hoodie, turning from her. "I'll keep quiet until you and Sotiris leave, but I'm not going."

But this wasn't like her petition to join the academy. That hadn't entailed the same things joining Plasovern did. She'd gone into it, eyes fully open to what she was signing up for, only slightly blinded by the luster of Magistrate blue. Mina ... hadn't reached that stage. She was still so clouded with pain. In her pocket, Katya uncapped a syringe.

She then stepped forward, concealing the syringe in her jacket's sleeve. The motion drew Mina's attention back to her.

There was no going back.

Katya extended both hands out, gesturing for a hug. The skin around the girl's eyes bunched, as if resisting the urge to cry. After a moment of hesitation, she rushed forward, burrowing her face into Katya's shoulder. She clasped the trembling girl. This would be the last time she would—

Tears clouded Katya's vision when she sank the needle into Mina's upper right arm and delivered its payload.

"What—"

Katya supported the teen's weight as her legs buckled and sank with her to the floor. Sniffling, she laid Mina out before pulling her farther from the opening. Her breaths came in huffs, and she leaned over her, wiping a strand of hair from the girl's face. When the lights outside in the hangar bay cut out, an almost electric reaction shot through her body.

She needed to move. By now, the virus should have crippled the station's communications systems. The getting wouldn't get any better.

Katya climbed the stairs, skinning her knee on one rung. A hiss escaped her lips, but she didn't stop. In the cockpit, she descended on the console, working the controls in rapid succession: closing and securing the ramp and firing up the freighter. She plugged in the firewall that the Tizzets had loaded on the slate while continuing to monitor the data on the viewscreen, hunting for any line hinting to some undiscovered device hampering operations. Normal so far.

All the systems kicked on, the engines ready. Katya lifted the freighter and activated the gravitational shielding, prepared to use a previous trick that'd worked well. Building speed, she veered toward the shield, intent on breaking through it. The massive freighter collided with it, catching, grinding the pace to a crawl before breaking into space. Control, already fleeting after the shield, evaporated when a blast ricocheted off the freighter's hull, spinning the craft. The interior gravity kept them from bouncing off the ceiling. Small comfort when they faced destruction or being retaken.

The virus still hadn't removed the threat of Jomsborg's armaments. Clenching her teeth, Katya rocketed between two blasts, using the freighter's nimbleness to her advantage. The navigation system flashed red, noting debris. Krezk. Screaming, she pulled the freighter from the spin.

"I suppose we now have our answer," Strom's sultry voice said from behind her. "The blue runs too deeply."

Katya stiffened at the helm, spinning her head, expecting Strom to be standing there, gun cocked, ready to blow her head off her shoulders. But the space was empty. Shifting her gaze, she spotted a speaker. Had the virus failed to down the communications or was Strom using something unconnected to the station's systems?

Despite herself, her left hand removed the firearm and trained it at the door behind her.

"Not blue," she said, testing to see if Strom would hear. Surely, some device would record her words. "Morality."

Strom sniffed at that.

The navigation console lit up with short-range fighters exiting Jomsborg. She had to bluff her ass off.

"I wouldn't do that."

"Oh? Why not?" Strom purred.

Katya sent the freighter careening back at the station. "I've rigged it to blow. If they don't back off, I'm taking you with me."

Strom burst into laughter; it surrounded her in the cramped cockpit. "You have the boy and the girl with you. You'd never—"

"I'd rather take them with me than leave them in your care. I've seen what you've been up to, and it's ending"—she swallowed hard—"either with us parting ways peacefully or by me ramming this freighter into your station and letting it detonate. The shielding won't take all the damage."

Silence. Strom likely calculated whether her fighters and station cannons could remove the threat before the freighter got close enough to dent the station. Katya broke out her skills deftly maneuvering between two fighters, which overcompensated, one so much so that it drifted into another's path. Newbie pilots. Plasovern likely had little need for short-range fighters at the moment, and their training was lacking. Katya increased the freighter's speed, eyes on the navigation screen, waiting for the fighters to close in or give.

She gained distance from them. Come on. Call it, Strom. The station loomed closer. Katya opened the jump program, picking the nearest coordinates that dipped them into the Fringe.

The fighters dispersed.

Air hissed through her teeth as she exhaled, recognizing that her bluff had won the day. She redirected her acceleration from the station to open space. No blasts followed her, perhaps silenced by the virus.

"Watch your back, Cassius." Strom's tone curdled her blood. "I will not forget this."

Katya snorted. "Clean out your eyes, Strom. You're no better than the Magistrate. Wrecking worlds, turning people into weapons … You've completely lost yourself. And the Medzeci will devour you."

Any retort cut out the moment the jump figures clicked and Katya punched it.

CHAPTER ELEVEN

Panel covers laid spread out around Katya as she tore into the circuits and wiring they'd been protecting. By this point, bags had formed under her eyes, yet she didn't break. The search for trackers and other nasty surprises was too important. Over the hours, she'd dismantled several devices and buried codes. Sinking to a seated position on the floor, Katya exhaled and brushed her damp bangs to the side. Her shirt clung to her frame. She wanted to collapse, cave to sleep. Using Jomsborg's time zone, it would be close to three o'clock in the morning now. She aired her shirt, pumping its fabric back and forth. Strom's threat, however, provided all the incentive she needed to keep working.

She glanced at the viewscreen, which was relaying navigations. Empty space. Not another ship in sight. She'd set the navigation console to alert if that changed, but paranoia kept drawing her eyes to the screen.

Standing, she stretched and surveyed the mess of metal around her. They'd been stationary for too long. She stepped over her handiwork to the helm, where she cycled through a series of coordinates, plotting several jumps to get distance and confuse any Plasovern agents giving chase. She would have to find someone to continue Plasovern's work with Sotiris, but before that, she needed funds. Her father flickered to mind. She needed to contact him, and he might have some guidance. As for funds—she set the last jump near the Reello System—she hoped Barsaa would prove fruitful. With luck, the couple had wisely invested the proceeds from their wrecked ship.

She returned the panels and tidied the destroyed components into a compartment for now. Dusting her hands against her pant legs, she muttered to Sotiris's sleeping form, "I'll be back."

Upon exiting the cockpit, déjà vu enveloped her. The tasks ahead were nearly identical to what she'd performed with *The Maelstrom*. Only it'd been easier with two sets of hands—three if counting Mina in the cockpit. Her stomach clenched. She couldn't think of Rein. The guilt clung like putrid tar, and no matter how often she told herself he'd gotten what he deserved, it wouldn't dislodge from her.

That was then. This was now. Interior and exterior, it all fell on her. She couldn't rely on Mina as she had in the past. Even when she woke up, the girl would never forgive her.

She descended the ladder and checked on Mina, who remained under the sedative's sway. Like with Sotiris, the ship's adaptive artificial gravity had saved the teen from severe damage. However, she'd slid from her original spot.

"I'll change out the card, jump again, and get you somewhere more comfortable." She straightened out the teen. "It'll just be a bit longer."

The sedative would delay the dreaded conversation long enough for them to be deep in the Fringe of Magistrate space ... reducing Mina's ability to connect with her Plasovern friends.

Face downcast, Katya proceeded to the engine room.

Confined in the space, she cracked open the registration chip and tethered it to her slate, something she wished she'd had the luxury to do earlier. But time and circumstances hadn't allowed it. Briefly, she wondered if Izem's people had succeeded in their own mission. The blank screen that popped up drew a smile. She had a completely open, unhindered chip—no hacking required. She could build their identity and history. Unlike her circumstances with *The Maelstrom*, she didn't need to cultivate a complex one to hide her tampering. Their new ship, *Pollux*, had been purchased from a dealer a month ago; it was a complete retrofit.

Finished, she resealed the chip and slid it easily into place. The green light signaled success. Swiveling around, she inspected the engine room. Given Plasovern's nature, few identifiers hinted at the freighter's origin or past uses—thus requiring few cosmetic changes. She checked the engines. Not top of the line—as she'd known—but they would pull through in a pinch.

At least, when they'd fled Jomsborg, it had been with a full tank of fuel. But if Barsaa wasn't a lucrative stop, there would be trouble.

She ditched the engine room and returned to Mina. Hoisting the teen over her shoulder, Katya trudged up the ladder. Her chest heaved as she pushed Mina on to the catwalk, then worked her own way up. Returning Mina to her arms, she picked one of the three crew quarters and settled the teen in one of its four beds. She placed a blanket over her before squeezing her upper arm and returning to the cockpit.

Sliding into the pilot's chair, Katya tightened security — limiting access to the helm and com system to herself — while waiting for the next jump to occur.

"Now, we need some allies in our corner." Her gaze shifted to Sotiris. "And to get you to bed." She hadn't adjusted the freighter's set temperature, so his brow creased with stress.

Through the metal, she felt the hum as the jump drive kicked on. The freighter's newer system almost wholly eliminated the pull as they sped through space before dropping to impulse after reaching their destination: nowhere.

Slipping from her seat, she activated the communications station. She should call her father, but she was unsure if he was still on Pestor or had returned to Meracus Domus or Vergo. A horrible excuse since she had his static com number. His likely monitored com number. They would expect her to reach out to him.

Her mind ran over the list of people she trusted. Most were Magistrate military contacts and out of the question. That left her adoptive siblings. Would the Magistrate monitor them as closely? Main lines likely. But if she took another approach ... after finding a relay signal, Katya typed in a number.

"Faverra's. Fashion ascended," a perky voice greeted her. "How may I direct your call?"

"Anaïs Cassius, please."

"Madame does not accept unsolicited calls. I can direct you to her secretary, Miss—"

"Tell her Squeak is calling. Trust me. She'll want to speak with me."

The line went silent, and Katya could practically hear the operator mentally grumble. Finally, "Please hold."

Don't blow it off. Katya willed the operator to share the message. Would Anaïs even want to speak with her? She supposed it would depend on what she'd been told. Though they had always been close, closer than she and Zhihao, her oldest sister, had ever been. Their personalities had clashed, and the age difference hadn't helped.

Minutes ticked by. If Anaïs was heavily involved in a design, that concentration would not be broken, even by her assistant. The line beeped, causing Katya to sit straighter. If she hung up on her …

"So, little Squeak … long time no talk." Her sister's voice ringed across the line. "I'm in a subordinate's office, so the line should be fine. Papa came for a visit once his dig on Pestor wrapped up. He's literally beside himself with worry."

"Literally?"

Anaïs snorted. "So he says. And I believe it. He's dropped some weight because he can't stop worrying. And he has a right to be. You've made no contact for months. You could've been dead for all we knew!"

Katya pressed her lips together; they'd come close a time or two. But her sister didn't need to know that. With a constricted throat, she said, "I've made a bad step." Her hand ran through her greasy, sweaty hair. "I was cornered. Now I need a place to"—she stumbled for the right word—"to regroup."

"Obviously you can—"

"No. You need to understand before you agree." Katya swallowed. "I've been with Plasovern."

A hiss of air was audible over the connection. Her sister then said something rapidly in her native tongue. She'd always been so talented with it, whereas Katya had stumbled with hers—and really any language.

"What were you—" Anaïs cut herself. "No, no, you can tell me *that* in person."

Tears welled in her eyes. "No, it needs to be now. I think I've made a clean break from them—at least, I can't find anything more on the ship. But I can't be sure. There are so many of them, and they are everywhere. You need to be aware of that. I've pissed off Hedda Strom. There will be repercussions for that. And"—she shifted toward Sotiris, the limited supply of drugs close to mind—"I have a metaphorical ticking time bomb on board."

"Your latest ward?"

"Papa was talkative, I see."

"He was." Anaïs then asked, "Your other charge—the girl I'd sent clothes to a while back—is she with you as well?"

"Yes ... but that is a delicate matter." Katya grimaced. "She ... she wasn't as inclined to leave. I kind of forced her hand."

Anaïs clucked at that. "You have become Papa."

And yet, she didn't want her relationship with Mina to resemble Papa and Seneca's.

"Still," Anaïs cut through the thought. "You're going to come here to—what was it?—regroup? I'll patch in Papa. He won't come in person; he rightly fears he's being watched."

"I'm making a quick stop beforehand," Katya said. "I suspect it'll be four weeks before I can make it to Trides."

"Where are you going?"

"I can't say, not over a line. But it's securing some funds."

"I can help—"

"No. There can be no large money transfers. Besides, what you're taking on is more than enough ... It's too much." Rolling her tense shoulder, Katya added, "Besides, this route will work, and it's no risk. I promise you that."

Anaïs sighed, and in the background, she heard a door open. "Occupied!" her sister called to someone. "Just a few more minutes." Then, after the door closed again, she said, "Four weeks? It's poor timing, Squeak. Trides's chief port will be hopping." She groaned. "It's Joining Day. They practically shut down the capital for a week of festivities, which could be a boon or bane for your arrival. There'll be more security, especially this year. Some Magistrate bigwig's coming for a big legislative motion. Bernat can talk of nothing else, but you know me, politics hold no interest."

"Will there be Elites?"

"Just the Mercena escorting the official. Trides isn't unruly, so I doubt they see the need to bring anything more than the regular guard."

The Mercena were a common sight in Meracus Domus's capital city. For centuries, they served as guards, their fealty spanning the empire and current republic eras. A Core species, they'd been long prized for their martial skills. They stood out with their historical uniforms with puffy shoulders and three shades of Magistrate blue. They would be a challenge in direct combat, but they weren't a threat on the level of Jar'rasks or Oneiroi. Their sensory abilities merely captured vibrations, allowing them to avoid attacks with their speed. Their focus would not stray from protecting their charge.

But to enter Trides on Joining Day, when citizens celebrated its inclusion within the Magistrate, could be challenging, though the hullabaloo might let them slip on to the Mezzo world more easily. Izem's people had left a facial kit in the hold, which they could use to blend. Besides, there was nowhere else to turn.

"I'll ring you before we head to Trides for any security changes. We have methods available to conceal our identities."

"Stay safe until then. Oh, and use N.999.312.456. It's a private com that no one knows about. It's not registered under my name either. I figure it'll be safer."

"Thank you. I look forward to seeing you." She swallowed. "It's … been far too long."

"It truly has." Her tone pointed the finger at Katya before the line went dead.

Katya blew her bangs from her eyes and slouched against the console. She angled her head toward the viewscreen and its small window to the stars. Light-years separated them from Strom now, but she couldn't wait for the next scheduled jump to put every inch of space between them.

After the next, she would work on exterior cosmetic work. Until then, she carried Sotiris from the cockpit and put him to bed in the room they would share, giving Mina much-needed space. She lowered the temperature before scrounging up an armful of blankets from a built-in cabinet. After setting her slate's alarm for six hours, she cocooned herself on another bed as cold air poured in from the vents.

Adjusting the blankets, she couldn't believe she actually missed her shoebox on Jomsborg with its comfortably regulated temperatures.

Katya didn't dawdle after her respite. Her adrenaline burst had abated, replaced by soreness and fatigue. Six—no, maybe four—hours hadn't been enough. As she trudged into the locker room from the airlock, she rolled her head back and forth. She set the helmet on a bench and stripped the suit. They never were comfortable, but this model rode up so much. She kicked it where it lay on the floor.

"Stupid thing," she muttered, leaving the locker room for the cockpit.

There, she returned the freighter to impulse and reactivated the countdown for the next jump. Two until the Reello System and Barsaa, their first test. But she felt confident she had missed nothing.

The door opened behind her. She startled and angled toward it as Mina stumbled against its frame, still affected by the drug. Her hair was in disarray, and her eyes had a glazed quality, somewhat sleep encrusted.

"W-where are we?" Mina slurred the words. "What did you do to me?"

"We're in the Fringe," Katya answered the girl's first

question, earning a blink, the words being slowly processed. "As for your lethargy, I gave you a mild sedative before extracting us from Strom's organization."

Mina leaned into the doorway, her frame trembling. "You had no right!" Tears streamed from her eyes. "You drugged me—took everything from me! You can't just override my life to be what you want it—" She sank against the frame until she reached the floor. There she sat, daze, shoulders trembling, legs drawn up to her chest.

Katya bit her lip to stop its own tremble. She couldn't have left her. How could she have? She jerked from the sight to the data on the screen.

"I want you to have a life," Katya said. "I don't want you to throw it away on a cause you think you know, only to realize too late that it's not what you thought it was."

The teen snorted. "That's not for you to decide! If I want to fight against oppression, I can. No debate!" Mina slammed her fists against the floor. "You're not my mother!"

Her teeth ground together. How many times had she heard that shouted, brandied as a weapon by Seneca toward their father? Now she understood its sting.

"I'm not." She breathed in a deliberate pattern. Control. Keep it. "But … I brought you with me from Reznic. I took responsibility for your well-being. I brought you to Plasovern. That is why I couldn't leave you."

The prosthetic moaned. Mina's flared nostrils screamed she'd ruined her life.

"You have a good heart, Mina," Katya said, practically a whisper. "I know you want to make a difference, to right wrongs. But what Strom offers won't help you on that mission. She only spreads more pain, more sorrow." She fully faced Mina, hating the heat in her eyes. "The galaxy doesn't need another Hedda Strom, Mina. It needs more good hearts, and I don't want you to lose yours."

Mina stared stonily at her.

"The moment you turn eighteen ..." Katya's throat constricted. "If you want to go back, I won't stop you. But until then, I want you to think about it, without the peer pressure, without the surrounding fervor, just really think—"

Lurching to her feet, Mina punched the doorframe before swiveling on her heels and storming off. Her feet banged against the metal floor as she went who knew where.

Pressing her hands against her eyes, Katya wiped tears away. She feared experience would become Mina's teacher as soon as she turned eighteen or found a chance to run. Should that happen, she couldn't guarantee she would catch her this time.

CHAPTER TWELVE

Katya's lungs bled as she tore through the ship, syringe in hand. Not perturbed by new surroundings, Sotiris had transferred their hide-and-seek games from Jomsborg to the freighter, only now he had more than tripled his possible hiding spots. Despite Mina's rage, Katya had enlisted her in the search. The girl's fear of the defect proved far greater than her icy anger. She was lucky the girl had been sleeping in her bed and not doing her own hiding game.

Hissing through her teeth, Katya dipped into the engine room. Its machinery glared at her, bringing imaginings of how Sotiris could injure or kill himself. The boy had grown too secure with his new surroundings and harbored too little appreciation for their dangers.

The space was too warm for the Oneiroi; he wouldn't have stayed long … unless he'd fallen asleep. Maybe on Barsaa, she would find locks to keep Sotiris somewhat contained, or at least from the ship's more dangerous aspects. Plasovern had stripped such mechanisms from the freighter, even the cockpit. Such safety measures were apparently worthless in their operations.

Ducking down, she scanned each crevice and space between the consoles and equipment. She moved onto the engines and FTL drive, slinking back toward the coolant syst—curly black hair.

"Out with you!" She snatched Sotiris's arm before he could burrow into the system's inner workings.

He hissed and grabbed one of the plastic lines connected to the *ressennian* reserve.

"No, no, no," she sputtered through clenched teeth while prying his fingers from it. A substance used to cool engines, ressennian was the last thing Katya wanted to clean up or have touch Sotiris. "Enough of that."

She hefted him in her arms, popped the cap on the syringe, and shot the drug into his arm. It earned a wail that didn't let up as she transported him from the engine room. On the catwalk, Mina rolled her eyes before shutting herself off behind a closed door.

Of course.

With Sotiris screaming in her ear, Katya climbed the ladder. She paused in front of Mina's room, sighed, and walked away. For now, they would remain at an impasse. Let the emotion chill further. But what if it turned cold, well, colder?

In the cockpit, she seated Sotiris in the communications console's chair, holding him in place when he tried to squirm off.

"Time out. You can't just run around a spacecraft."

Meaningless words. And the lingering presence of her hands rooting him in place only encouraged more escape attempts. When he didn't stop, she brought him over to the pilot's chair and contained him in her arms.

He pouted, huffing, chin pressed against his chest. Mentally, she counted the drug, now severely depleted. She should cut the dosages, spread them out better. She frowned. Dangerous … they would balance on a line. One dip too far, and Sotiris's defect could break through. She blew air into his hair, earning side-eye from him. From Barsaa, it would be another three weeks to Trides. Then, she would hit a brick wall. Sighing, she gazed into Sotiris's icy blue eyes, with their barely visible pupils. She did not want to be on a ship with him if the drugs were removed from the equation.

She would have to tread the line.

"You're still too young to understand," she muttered.

Katya flipped on the radio, and the familiar tongue soothed her. Home. She chuckled. She was too ingrained.

One Magistrate broadcast noted a shortage of the ever-in-demand *proxizeeum*, a key component for manufacturing FTL drives. "The shortage is linked to a production disruption on Aedelsten," the reporter said. "Production is expected to resume in the next two weeks."

Katya whistled. That was not something one wanted to hear regarding a highly combustible substance. And on one of Strom's sister planets.

Sotiris ground his tailbone into her leg, drawing a groan. "Little imp." She slid him to the floor. "Stay in here."

The moment the words left her mouth, he'd already bolted through the door. They needed locks. After setting the navigation console to autopilot and locking it, she pursued.

Months ago, Barsaa had lacked a solid Magistrate presence; it'd enabled them to land the crippled *Minerva* without a fuss. Now, they wouldn't be so lucky. Several warships had created a temporary relay for the planet. Their clean, unassuming freighter—family-run, of course—didn't draw a second glance in space or on the ground. More Magistrate blue guarded the port, specifically its fuel supply.

As Katya guided a reticent Mina and a wonder-struck Sotiris on to a tram, her eyes nearly popped from her head upon catching the fueling prices. Since she'd been away from Magistrate space, the price of *caeliset* fuel had tripled.

Had there been a production or supply line issue?

Mina's boasts of the Fringe cracking echoed in her mind. If caeliset was this expensive everywhere, it added another complication for her to surmount.

She glanced at Mina, who'd angled herself away and numbly stared at Barsaa's scenery as the tram went, her lips pressed into a slim line. Settled between them, Sotiris had climbed on to his knees and leaned against the tram's ledge, his sunglass-clad face bobbing this way and that, not wanting to miss anything.

The city had changed little, though Katya caught more signs in the windows. They were in the native language, with the Magistrate translation too small underneath to be read from the moving tram. She recognized the corner street that connected to the scrap yard and signaled the tram driver to stop. Gathering her kids, she retraced their steps from months ago to the neat—and expanded—shop. She almost commented on it, but the words died when met with Mina's down-turned lips. The camaraderie wasn't there … at least not at the moment.

Inside, they'd added more shelving and display units, though the wares were spotty. Katya discovered most common repair items, going from the labels, had been cleaned out. The vacant store suggested everyone knew its supplies were low.

Chest tightening, Katya approached the main counter and rang the bell.

The woman from before—Lilian, she recalled—left a backroom and greeted her with a smile. "Welcome to Harbonet's Ship Supplies." Her hand rested on a small infant nestled against her chest in a carrier. "I apologize for our lack of supplies. Lines are still struggling to keep up, but my husband is very talented, and we've been able to come up with workarounds for most ship problems."

"This time, we're blessed to not have ship problems," Katya said.

The woman blinked, and recognition flashed in her eyes. "You! I see you've found a new ship." Lilian bobbed as her baby fussed. "Your kids have both grown so much."

Mina stepped away. Katya followed her footsteps with her ears as she walked a short distance away.

"I'm surprised by how much," Katya replied. "Business seems to have picked up."

"It really did," Lilian smiled. "We were able to expand with your investment. Though, things are a bit crazy at the moment."

"Is a supply line down?"

Lilian's eyebrow rose. "You must have been out of the Fringe for a while, though maybe it's not like this everywhere. There's been strikes, factory issues, shipments being targeted. The Magistrate is working to clamp down and remove Plasovern agitators, but I suppose it's easier said than done."

"We've been out of the Fringe, but a run brought us back. We're actually heading back to the Mezzo." Katya tightened her grip on Sotiris when he tried to stray. "I was hoping to reclaim some of that investment before we do and hopefully get a few ship locks."

"Hard currency again?"

"If possible." She tried to appear contrite. "We're still trying to sort out accounts after that attack. The investigation just never ends. And after it happened, hard currency just feels safer."

"I suspected as much." Lilian snorted and reached for a slate, working its screen. "We've been keeping some around in case you came back. We can't do a complete payout, but"—she extended the device to Katya—"we can return a decent percentage with some of the interest. It's been lucrative lately, even without price gouging customers, unlike other merchants who will go unmentioned."

Katya could've whistled. The store had done well for itself to afford to give her more than one hundred thousand aurums. Still, factoring in the cost of fuel, they would burn through it without an income to supplement it. She pressed her thumb against the screen, and it read the print.

"It's more than fair," Katya said. "The remaining interest can continue to support your business."

"It's appreciated." The shopkeeper beamed and spread her arms out, startling her infant. "To have a Core-worlder investing in our little Barsaa shop, it's incredible. Give me a sec, and I'll get the funds. As for locks, you can look, but I think we only have a few, if any."

Katya browsed the aisles, the displays' emptiness promising disappointment. She stumbled across a space for magnetic locks, which contained one. Mina stepped next to her, lips still stuck in a petulant frown.

"What's that for?" she asked, an edge to her voice.

"To keep Sotiris out of the engine room," she returned. Though, if she used it to keep Sotiris in their room, there would be no engine room excursions. But—she glanced at Mina out of the corner of her eye—she didn't relish leaving the engine room open to tampering. Not just from Mina ...

"You could just keep him in his room."

Katya shrugged and picked up the lock. "I'm too used to protocol. You don't leave the engine room unlocked."

"You don't trust me."

Her throat tightened, and she faced Mina. "If given a chance, wouldn't you go back?"

Folding her arms, Mina jerked her head away. She remained silent for so long Katya gave up on a response.

"Yes." The teen squared her frame and glared at her. "But I wouldn't put you and Sotiris in harm's way to do it. But you obviously don't believe that." Moisture grew in Mina's eyes, but she turned to hide it. "Whatever ... I don't care."

As Katya's mouth opened to refute, Lilian returned with a nondescript case. "I'm hoping this won't draw too many eyes. There are desperate people in the city. I highly recommend not advertising you have a case full of money." She set the case on the counter and popped the lid.

Katya leaned forward and inspected the funds, adding a small sum to her jacket's chest pocket.

"The lock's on us," Lilian said.

Snapping the lid shut, Katya smiled. "Thank you. I hope business continues to go well."

After trading niceties and leaving, the three purchased food supplies from another store before catching the tram to the spaceport. Katya secured fuel, but not a full tank's worth since the Magistrate was rationing.

Fueling completed, Katya stowed the supplies in the kitchen before returning to the cockpit. Mina had holed up in her room, leaving her with only Sotiris for company. Cuddling with him in the pilot's seat, she used the private com signal to reach her sister.

The call didn't go through, and there was no inbox. It wasn't her regular com ... she might not reach it right away.

In the interim, Katya warmed the engines and submitted their flight plan for Trides. An approval greeted her soon after. Come on, Anaïs. She called again.

"Squeak?" Anaïs asked on the other end.

"Any changes on your end?"

"They're breaking out all the stops already. I don't think I've seen this much blue since the last time I was home on holiday. But the procedures are the same basic ones rolled out for such state visits. Bernat's going to drive me mad." Anaïs chuckled. "But if you play it smart, you'll be fine."

"Don't walk through security with contraband, huh?"

"Something like that." Her sister stifled her giggles. "I'll pick you up in the city. Bernat will be rubbing shoulders with the others, so no worries there. He'll be staying at the Plaza. He's unaware … I love him, but I don't know if he'd turn a blind eye. I've given our staff the week off."

"Our faces will be changed." Katya winked at Sotiris. "Look for the brown-haired woman carrying a kid with a slick pair of shades and a long-sleeved shirt no matter how hot it is outside. With a broody teenager in tow."

"You won't be hard to spot at all."

"See you in a couple weeks."

"Until then."

Katya severed the connection, her heart beating heavily. Shifting to the helm, she left Barsaa, never expecting to reclaim the rest of the interest. To enter the heart of Magistrate space and actually visit her sister. She'd thought both had been lost to her. Still, to enter the Mezzo … Her fingers clenched the edge of the console.

So much could go wrong.

Gaining clearance to Trides's capital, Tres, with their vessel's clean registration proved easy, especially with no cargo to claim. Katya slipped their freighter through the planet's rippling ecosphere shielding, which protected against radiation while healing its ozone layer. Past it lay a green gem of a planet, a complete one-eighty from the highly industrialized world it'd been, now confined to photos. This marked her second time visiting Trides. How long ago had that been? Anaïs's wedding. Ten years ago? Too long. But leave had its limits, and in most cases, she'd remained in the same system.

"Follow the pylons and guides to Section 30, Lot 120," a woman's voice advised her. "Limited searches will be performed on all vessels."

"Understood." All Medzeci items—anything with Plasovern inklings—had been long cleared.

Katya brushed her bangs from her forehead. They were now red, a brilliant red she would have never chosen, but it was what they had on hand. Mina had claimed the deep plum box for herself. From the smirk on the teen's face when she'd grabbed the box, she'd purposely chosen the least showy option to poke at Katya.

The game of avoidance had continued, and she was lucky to even get a word, let alone two, from Mina.

Grimacing, Katya resisted the urge to touch her nose. They'd used the facial kit from the Tizzet people, and her reshaped nose drove her crazy. The facial clay dried to look and feel like flesh but added weight. Caving, she prodded at the foreign object. Her entire face felt weighted. Her hand skimmed the clumps on her cheeks, making them plumper while not crossing the line of absurd. It'd been a fine line. Little tweaks. Here, there. Expanding, changing existing features. Then, eventually, you would find a stranger in the mirror.

She bent and picked up her bag, which contained enough for a day visit for herself and Sotiris. Within, she'd slipped a partial vial of Sotiris's medicine, labeling it as seizure medicine, in a refrigeration bag. She wanted to pack the gun but knew it would never pass through port security. She left it in plain sight in her bedroom. It was a Fringe manufacturer, and hiding it would draw more attention.

"Come on." Katya extended her hand to Sotiris, taking him to meet Mina in the hold.

The teen had gone overboard on her nose, making it slightly too large for her face. But it didn't scream facial clay. "I still don't know what you expect a fashion designer to do." It dripped with layered sarcasm. A slight smirk graced her lips afterward—not unlike a fresh recruit.

Katya's fiery instinct begged to wipe the smugness from Mina's face like she would any tyro. However, she killed that instinct.

"I expect nothing," she replied instead. "It's more about Anaïs's connections. And she won't turn us in."

Mina lifted an altered eyebrow. "Are you sure?"

One never truly knows another being. The saying flickered to mind, unwelcomed. The muscles in her back tightened. "I know it."

The teen scoffed.

Sotiris tugged her hand. His face remained unmodified beyond a concealer to warm his skin tone. She'd been afraid to even apply that to his fragile Oneiroi skin that had only healed.

Katya activated her com. "It's Squeak." She shifted from Mina when the teen chuckled. "Where are we rendezvousing?"

It took a minute or two before Anaïs replied, likely through bared teeth. "Traffic's horrible!" Background noise filtered through the connection, mainly traded insults. "Get to the Trit Sector; it's still largely open. There's a small café, Mennis." A rustling noise followed as clothing moved. "Yeah, asshole, I hear you! We're all stuck here!"

Katya's eyebrows shot up. "I didn't know you had that in you."

"What was that, dear Squeak?" Anaïs said more clearly in the com. "I didn't catch it over this oaf."

"I don't think I've ever heard you cuss before."

"Traffic brings out the worst in us all." A clap sounded. "Excellent, traffic's moving again. Just meet me at the café. We can pick up lunch and leave this blasted city."

"Copy." She could feel her sister's eyes roll with that, even as she cut the line. Habits were hard to break.

"This is a mistake."

Katya shrugged, facing the teen. "We're here." She opened the hatch before Mina could offer a pithy response and lowered the ramp.

Two port officials waited. They wore Trides's colors and uniforms with the green piping against Magistrate blue.

The one in front, a native Tridetarian, beamed as he reached the top of the ramp. "We'll be quick!" Like his greeting, his amber-hued eyes harbored warmth. He swiveled to survey their empty hold, then made notes on his slate with his fingers, longer than most humanoid species. "Just need a quick look at the rest. Engine room?"

"Just this way." Katya led him to it.

Mina stayed with Sotiris. Stiff. Expectant. She might as well broadcast she expected to be arrested.

Katya traded light conversation with the officials as they did the broadest search of the engine room. They talked about the weather, their added workloads, and, of course, the festivities in the city beyond. The younger of the men chuckled, sharing he planned to take his girlfriend to the rides.

"Going to pop the question?" the older one asked, elbowing his partner while following Katya out of the engine room and up to the freighter's upper levels.

"I have the *temesse* band ready to go," he said from the ladder before pulling himself on to the main level's catwalk. "Just don't know if"—he peered first into Mina's room— "now's the time. Ya know?"

The older peeked into Katya's room. "Can't get better than this. All the decorations. Fireworks throughout the week. She won't be able to say no."

"A girl does like a good fireworks display," Katya added, earning a thumbs-up from the senior officer.

"See," he said. "Start carrying it around. Wait for that right moment."

They moved to the cockpit, where they conducted another search, but nothing too thorough.

"All clear," the senior officer said into his com. He then faced Katya. "Welcome to Trides, Ms. Tulius."

She saw the pair off before guiding Mina and Sotiris through the packed port. To keep Sotiris from being trampled in the crowd, she hefted him into her arms before deciding to place him on her shoulders. He was getting too big for her to carry long. He huffed into her hair.

"Yeah, yeah," she muttered. "We've got a trek before us." She hefted the bag she set down. "It's going to be a hot one."

Trides's capital city, Tres, was approaching eighty degrees Fahrenheit with its famed high humidity. It caught the oily, fatty aroma of festival food that cooked in stalls throughout the port. Music lit the air, and blue cloth, adorned with either the Magistrate eagle or its laurel, had draped the port's walls.

Ship crews had established several picnics between the parked freighters, their crews trading stories and playing cards. The aromas stirred Katya's stomach, but it needed to wait.

Sotiris ground his chin into her head, enjoying neither the heat nor the noise. Katya rolled her eyes and picked up her pace while making sure Mina didn't wander. The teen could easily disappear into the crowd. Even if she did, she would find it difficult to return to Plasovern from the Mezzo, especially without funds, which Katya had hidden to avoid pilfering.

"He won't last long out here," Mina said. Her eyes shifted everywhere, though she lingered on the Trides and Magistrate officials patrolling the crowds.

"Don't stare." Katya nudged Mina on, weaving them through the masses. "And we'll get him out of the heat as soon as possible." They joined one line for the port's custom counters. She leaned closer to Mina. "Act normal. Don't give the custom agents a reason to be suspicious."

The line shifted forward. Next to her, Mina toed the concrete, the perfect moody teen, annoyed at the world. Little fingers pinched Katya's shoulder. She groaned and jabbed them with one of her own, getting Sotiris to let up.

Good. No one was happy.

When a Magistrate official pulled a person about a foot in front of them out of the line, Katya stiffened.

"Step this way." The official's navy blue uniform with gold insignia set him apart from his Trides counterparts.

"I did nothing!" The male Csek stepped back even as he raised his hands. "You—"

"This way." The official snatched his arm and pulled him to the side as other soldiers surrounded him. "We have a warrant to discuss with you, Mr. Bastni."

Mina's jittery frame rattled against Katya, who wrapped her arm around her, partly to provide comfort but mainly to prevent bolting.

"Stay with me," she whispered as the soldiers carted the Csek away, ignoring his declarations of innocence. The line moved again. Katya pulled Mina forward with her. "Keep calm."

The girl pressed her lips together, some retort likely burning at her tongue, but she held it.

They were so close to the customs table. Katya watched as an agent dumped a purse and inspected its contents before shoving it all back in.

The elderly couple in front of them took their place at the table, where officials poked through their bags. Once their items were returned, the pair departed, and Katya and Mina placed their own bags on the cleared table. The soldiers divided their bags between them, opening every pocket and leaving no privacy as they littered items across the metal surface. The one scrutinized Sotiris's medicine but returned it to the refrigeration pack on the table. Next to her, Mina blushed and jerked her head away when her port official uncovered feminine products.

"Cleared."

The two women scurried to return their items to their bags, not nearly as neatly as they'd been packed. As soon as the zippers were closed, another port official ushered them into the next line of security, where they passed through the scanners without fuss. Beyond the machines, they entered the spaceport proper, with its information centers, screens galore, supply purveyors, and anything else to aid the weary traveler. Katya inhaled the air-conditioned air.

Walking over to the port map, she found their route and led the way. Sotiris's head rubbed against her scalp each time he redirected his attention. The boy drank in the sights and the various species traveling the corridors. Probably the most he'd ever seen, now that Katya thought about it. With his parents, his own kind had surrounded him. With Katya, he'd either been asleep, left on the ship, or covered.

His hand collided with her face when he spun around to follow a group of Baspettes. The black insectoids—with shiny blue, red, and gold shells resembling gems—each wore masks that supplied them with plenty of iron-enriched oxygen. One shell split partially when glimmering wings fluttered underneath, just like gossamer. The light from the synth glass above cast beautiful patterns on their shells.

The massive building married modernity with traditional Trides architecture. Pops of green mingled through it all, the people no longer divorced from it. Beyond the skylights, there were walls of synth glass, and past them, barricades and so many people. She wondered if anyone was working or if they'd all called it a week.

Katya walked around a gentle water feature comprising several sizeable hammered copper bowls with patches of patina. Trides's native fauna, including its vibrant pink, orange, and turquoise blooms, filled the in-betweens. A stunning welcome to the planet.

Sotiris rested his head on hers, eyes fixed on the moving water. He grunted when Katya took them through a set of double doors back into Trides's heat.

"Stick close," Katya reminded Mina. "We don't want to get separated in the crowd."

The teen rolled her eyes in response.

Katya kept them on route, only diverting when crowds and activities dictated it. The city had set up beer gardens throughout the second and third block, barricading off sections of the road. Stringed lights dangled from the wooden frames that set off the gardens. Music, sometimes clashing, serenaded them everywhere. A couple, both native Tridetarians, had taken to dancing. They cackled like maniacs and stumbled into a table. It actually drew a chuckle from Mina, the first Katya had from her since Jomsborg.

She almost said something, but drifted instead to a screen. It relayed sector trade talks, which had been the primary draw for the Magistrate official. Anaïs had likely zoned out on the details. She'd never been one for politics, even though she had mastered negotiations. Her sister had proven adept at business, which wasn't too removed from politics.

In front of them, at least twenty children chased each other, trying to capture a miniature Magistrate flag. They squealed, darting to and fro. One, a young boy, scrapped his knee upon tripping over another youth's leg. The latter careened into a wood barricade, earning a scolding from the adults on the other side.

It drew a smile to her lips and lulled her into memories of Meracus Domus and games played with her siblings.

Mina glowered at her surroundings as if by will she could turn it all to dust.

Inhaling, Katya embraced the festive air of food, flame, even sweat. She glanced at Mina again and sighed. "What do you see?"

The teen started, eyes flickering around as if she expected drones or officers moving to intercept them. When met only by the raucous celebrations, she sought some other thing of note, the corners of her mouth sinking. "What am I supposed to see?"

"You look like you're sucking a lemon."

Mina balled her fists and glowered at the sky before redirecting it at Katya. "Can you blame me?" She pressed her lips together, lifting her nose to the festivities. "They're bathing themselves in blue while other worlds are swallowed by it."

Strom would be so proud. Katya monitored those around them, being careful of eavesdroppers. "And what would you like to do?"

"Show them."

"What?"

Her mechanical arm creaked. She could read the teen's mind: show them exactly how she'd been hurt.

"Breathe. Look again."

She didn't, choosing to scowl at the sidewalk instead. But Katya wouldn't fail to impart this lesson.

"Fine. Let me tell you what I see." She cleared her throat. "Children playing. Old men complaining about their joint pains. A mother desperately trying to feed her baby — sound familiar?"

Lines deepened on Mina's brow, but beyond that, she gave her nothing.

"I see people living their lives," Katya continued. "You're hurt, but I don't want you to lose sight of this. The moment you do, you repeat a cycle of injustice. You become capable of creating greater atrocities than the ones you're supposedly avenging." She discreetly gestured to the boy with the flag; he was hoisting it high to keep it out of a much smaller child's reach. "He's a Magistrate citizen, holding the flag. Should we cut his hand off?"

"No." Mina gritted her teeth. "But that's not—"

"It's exactly that. Strom has long lost sight of actual people. On Ereago, they shot people trying to get their children off-world. Military targets are one thing, but when shooting citizens becomes acceptable, you've lost yourself."

Katya closed her eyes, remembering Reznic, its decay, crime, death … She'd reached a moment where she'd wanted it to burn. Guilty and innocent alike. "The closest I've ever come to that point was on Reznic."

Mina straightened at her homeworld's name.

"I was burned out … just sick of sending my teams into a meat grinder and seeing no change. At my nadir, something reminded me that there were people just trying to live their lives the best they could. People who deserved better. Do you know who reminded me of that?"

Mina rolled her shoulders.

"A certain girl who snuck on to a military base."

The teen's chin practically touched her chest to avoid all eye contact.

"Just something to think about," Katya said, resuming their walk.

By the time they arrived at the small sandwich shop, the sun had tilted marginally farther to the west. They found the shop nestled in an old-fashion shopping corridor with wood-framed structures dwarfed by dangling trees, which lined the street. Their modern metal and synth glass brethren towered over them. Twisted metal street lamps dotted the street's length, adding a taste of whimsy. The shop's facade used old-fashioned glass pane windows framed in knotty pine.

Katya recognized her sister in a heartbeat, sitting idly at one of the shop's outdoor tables. Dressed in a tailored navy blue dress and suit jacket, she traced the table's wood grain as she waited. She'd added a Magistrate eagle pin to her lapel. She definitely looked the part of a dutiful planetary senator's wife. Her amber-hued eyes jerked up and met Katya's; even with the cosmetics, a spark of recognition flickered. Perhaps the unaltered gray eyes had clued her in.

Anaïs rose and crossed the space between them, enveloping Katya in a hug that knocked the air from her lungs and drew a squawk from Sotiris, who yanked her hair.

"My dear, you've arrived," Anaïs said, her smile so broad on her face. "You'll love the samples I've found. Including some rather exclusive options." She pushed a strand of golden hair not confined to her messy bun behind an ear. "Have you heard of Morhoven muslin?" At her vacant stare, she careened forward. "Very few have. It's a technique we've reclaimed. But where are my manners" — she waved them to the counter — "let's pick up lunch, and then I can show you the designs."

Katya only blinked. Anaïs could talk a mile a minute if given a chance. She stumbled forward after catching her sister's subterfuge: "I'm looking forward to seeing them."

They claimed their sandwiches, and from there, Anaïs escorted them to her open-top hydrogen microcruiser deluxe, two blocks from the café. It'd been painted a vibrant yellow and stood out among the parked vehicles.

"Everyone shuffle in," Anaïs said. "It's time to leave this disaster. Every year. Close hundreds of streets, and the traffic system can't accommodate the strain and BAM! I'm cussing in traffic."

Katya snorted as she plopped Sotiris in the vehicle's backseat and buckled him in place. "I suppose we all have our limits."

"I normally prefer to avoid it all," Anaïs continued. "You should appreciate my effort, Squeak."

"And I do." She slid into the passenger seat.

Behind them, Mina sat next to Sotiris and kept him out of the bulging sandwich bag Anaïs had settled on the floor between them. No one spoke as Anaïs manned the helm, taking them from the side street on to the more congested highway. It took them from the city proper and into one of its ritzier enclaves, where traffic thinned out.

"We've got to make good time," Anaïs muttered. "We're cutting our time window short."

In the corner of her eye, Katya saw Mina stiffen. Clearing her throat, she asked her sister, "Time window for what?"

"Papa is on Vergo, and he's *eager* to speak with you." Anaïs flicked a glance at the rearview mirror. "Settle down back there. I'm not turning you in. And don't fret about Bernat. He'll be staying in the city with his fellow senate members."

"Who exactly are they hosting?" Katya muttered.

"High Regulator Junius. Just one head short of an actual magistrate being on-world."

"No Uncle?"

"Nope," Anaïs said. "Or else I might have already been playing hostess. Bernat would have insisted." She snorted. "He corresponds with Bernat, you know? Politics." She shook her head and rolled her eyes. "And where Uncle goes these days, Zhihao often follows. I think she's being groomed to inherit."

"Inherit?" Mina echoed from the backseat.

"Whatever Uncle Pontius does for a living," Anaïs answered as she redirected them into a walled-off community nestled among trees and vibrant blooms.

Distant water rumbled over the mild hum of the vehicle's inner workings, particularly as their driver slowed and turned on to a private drive. The Baieretel Mountains crafted a beautiful backdrop.

At the end of the driveway, a white mansion stood, constructed mostly of synth glass, delicate arches, and intrinsic columns. The same weeping trees with blooms of blue filled in holes around the building. Anaïs took an offshoot that looped back to a smaller building, mimicking the main house in architecture. A decent-sized pool, lined in mosaics, filled in the space between. A waterfall circulated its water.

Anaïs parked by the secondary building. "You'll be staying in my studio. I don't allow anyone else in there, except for clients and colleagues. Though Bernat will ignore my rules when he's lonesome."

Katya helped Sotiris from the back. The boy cried as he panted in her arms. Poor kid. Through his sunglasses, she could see his eyes were mere slivers.

"I hope you have a good AC unit," Katya muttered. "We're going to need to crank it up."

"We can make him comfortable." Anaïs grabbed Katya's bag before she could. "Just worry about him."

She then ushered them inside, where the organized chaos of a creative mind greeted them. A massive glass-topped drafting table stood at the ready, designs and notes lining its surface. Fabrics, storage units, scrolls, and massive sketchbooks topped other tables. Dispersed through the space was a series of mannequins donning clothing items in varying stages of completeness. Ample seating had been provided, all plush and crafted from crushed velvet.

Anaïs flung her purse and Katya's bag into a chair and pushed one table's contents aside before gesturing for Mina to place the sandwiches there.

She waved to one door. "There's a guest room there. Two beds. Go ahead and leave your items there." She messed with the thermostat, and cold air poured into the space. She also darkened the glass, cloaking the studio's interior. "My office's through there." She pointed to its neighboring room. "Head in there once you're done. Papa's been waiting long enough for answers, I think."

Katya nudged Mina into the guest room, where they unloaded their bags. Katya laid Sotiris in one bed, resting his head on the pillow.

"Stay here and cool down," she said.

His eyelids crept downward, and her chest constricted. Heat exhaustion? Or had she lessened the dose too much? She brushed his bangs from her forehead. "I'll fetch you when it's time to eat."

When she did, would he rally or still cling to his dreams?

Mina started into the attached bathroom.

"Leave the clay on," Katya instructed her. "I know it's a pain, but our faces can't change even by a bit when we go back through customs."

The teen groaned but nodded. She still proceeded into the room.

Sighing, Katya slunk from the room and met her sister in the next. There, Anaïs fiddled with a highly illegal, black market com unit. Superior encryption. She'd seen ones like it on Reznic and knew their value and the cost of owning one, if discovered.

"Where did you get that?"

"Channels," Anaïs muttered before hissing something at the device. "Papa has one too. He actually bought this one. He figured if Kat'ee would contact anyone besides him, it'd be me. He knows you well." She snorted.

"I'm nothing less than predictable." Katya slumped in a red armchair positioned in front of the com unit. "So Papa is back on Vergo?"

"Yep, his dig wrapped up. He had a brief campus tour but retired from it early." Anaïs paused her efforts and swiveled on the balls of her feet to face Katya. Her hands rested on her upper thighs, elbows making sharp points. "Having three wayward kids is wearing on him. Seneca's been institutionalized. His last spiral ended with him assaulting a peacekeeper, so he's not getting out. Then he's losing one daughter to his brother, and another has apparently been hobnobbing with Plasovern."

Anaïs rolled her eyes, huffing. "Of all things! I cannot believe by-the-rules Kat'ee has Seneca beat. He would've had to *burn* the peacekeeper station to the ground to get anywhere close."

"I was bleeding out." Katya ran her shaking hand through her hair. "Mina had been gravely wounded. Sotiris—well, he ... I didn't have very many choices."

"Bleeding out?" Anaïs's eyes narrowed further. "What had gone so wrong after your visit with Papa?"

"Our ship got trashed, my lieutenant stabbed us in the back, and Jar'rasks picked us up." Katya ran her hands down her face, forgetting the clay. "Mina's right hand is a prosthetic. She's still struggling, understandably so. No matter how—" her voice gave. She concealed her mouth until the tremor of her lips settled. "She drank in what Plasovern promised. I had to knock her out with a sedative to get her away. It'll be a long time before she trusts me again. If she ever does."

She sank into the overly stuffed armchair. Her limbs felt so heavy. "Plasovern had managed a temporary fix for Sotiris, but I'm already down to six vials. That's with me already cutting the regular doses."

"What happens when you run out?" Anaïs scooted across the floor on her knees, drawing nearer to Katya. Her amber eyes traveled over Katya, wary, undoubtedly spying cracks that only a sibling could.

"I don't know."

The tremor passed through Katya's hand like it hadn't in days. She slid it under her leg. Sotiris would eventually seek connections, the need baked into his DNA. Her mind drifted to Jordah and the wide reach that Oneiroi teenager had shown. She pressed her weight down on her hand. Only Magistrate scientists knew the full scope of power held by a child with the defect. Her mind drifted to Jomsborg, how the defect had paralyzed the station, killing innocent—

Anaïs cupped her cheek. "We'll hope Papa has answers."

What answers could he possibly have? She didn't vocalize the thought as her sister returned to the device, adjusting its settings. Static echoed.

"Whew!" Her sister slumped on to her butt. "The signal's live. Now we just have to wait."

"Does it have visuals?"

"You better believe Papa wants to look you in the eyes when he scolds you."

"Wonderful."

The door behind them cracked open.

"Mina," Katya said, turning in her seat. "Go ahead and eat."

The girl said nothing, simply retreating, though she left the door cracked. Katya started to rise to close it, but the static disappeared.

"Anaïs?" their father's voice boomed from the com. "Is she there?"

Anaïs flashed her teeth at Katya before bringing the visual component to life. "She is."

Her father's stern face settled immediately on her; the camera even caught his crossed arms. "What did I tell you on Pestor?"

"There were" — his eyes narrowed, but she pressed on — "extenuating circumstances. I couldn't contact you where I was."

"Plasovern."

"Yes." She tried not to blanch as her father shook his head. "I'd run out of options. I didn't have the time to think things out. They'd offered a viable solution for Sotiris, and it paid off for a time. But ..." Her mind reeled, searching for the right words.

"You reached an impasse," her father supplied.

She nodded.

"How far have you gone?" Her father pressed.

"A few courier runs. The most egregious was delivering supplies to Ereago." Phantom ice rushed along her back. No, the worst had been giving Plasovern access to the Oneiroi genetic makeup. There'd also been the gift of a Magistrate black ops vessel. Low on blood and options, she hadn't entirely grappled with the ramification of her choice. "I tried to avoid providing too much support, but Strom became adamant. My refusal would've ended with my corpse being jettisoned."

Her father lowered his head, which shook ever so slightly. The com unit barely picked up his sigh. His facial features were downcast when he lifted it again, lines showing around his mouth and on his forehead. "No, no, we don't have time to address what a misstep you've made.

There's no coming back once that's revealed." A muscle along his jaw twitched. "Why didn't you approach a neutral system? That would've been so much better."

"They would've turned me over to the Magistrate," Katya cut in. "You know just as well as me they won't cross the giant next door. And you know how horrible I am at picking up other languages. I'd stick out like a sore thumb for their immigration services."

"What's done is done," her father waved away the subject. "You're removed from that organization; that's all I care about. And we have limited time. I've no doubts that I'm being monitored. It's only a matter of time before they detect the signal and try to break in." He swallowed. "I did what I said I would. Made discreet inquiries. And I've found a new potential solution for your boy."

Katya leaned forward, her elbows pressing into her thighs.

"Aleksandr Lomonosov. He's a prodigy who has dabbled in genetic disorders among a cornucopia of other disciplines. He resides near Velikaya Stolitsa on Mramor."

Heat flooded Katya's face as if it were being held to a flame. "Now's not the time for me to explore my past."

Her father huffed at her, dramatically rolling his eyes and head. "Explore or don't. But Lomonosov is your best bet," he retorted. "The only others who are capable of what you need are within the Core. They're heavily tied to the Magistrate and are more likely to turn you in." Rubbing his brow, his eyes harbored tiredness. "I can't guarantee he won't as well, but you have a better chance of breaking away from Mramor than from a Core world."

Despite the pounding steadily building behind her skull, she asked. "What do you know of him?"

"He's a recluse, I'm told. He was supposed to be at a conference I was attending but never showed, and I never heard why. It seems he seldom leaves Mramor, if at all. His contact with the Magistrate's Upper Brass is limited, another plus. I only know of three projects with his involvement; the tech is beyond me."

The roaring in her head hit a fever pitch, yet she kept her hand burrowed under her leg. Snow, blood, gunpowder—

"It's a month's journey from here. I"—her jaw ached—"don't have enough of the drug to last that long. There has to be something else, someone closer."

The look her father gave her, brimming with sympathy, only increased the heat on her face. "Kat'ee, there's no one else of Lomonosov's caliber. I know you're afraid. But you can't allow it to cloud your judgment. Just like you can't let any misplaced sense of loyalty prevent you from exploring your history." His eyes welled, though he dabbed at them before tears could form. "You will always be my child. No matter what."

Biting her lip, she glanced to the side, pointedly not seeing Anaïs, who still sat by the com unit on the floor. Her shaking left hand clawed into the velvet cushion. She didn't want to go back. Couldn't ... but given only one option. Still, a month. Her mouth dried at the prospect. She'd already stretched each vial to six doses versus the original four. Could she get more out of a vial? There was no choice but to. Otherwise, only thirty-four doses would remain. Not enough. If she ran out ... if this Lomonosov couldn't replicate the formula ...

"I don't have enough of the drug." Katya met her father's gaze. "Mina and I will be at the mercy of Sotiris's whims."

"Have you tried working with him?"

She gaped. Yes, the Magistrate had managed it, fashioning children into unseen weapons. She recalled devices that'd clung to the Oneiroi teenager's body, passing through flesh in places. She winced with the recollection. All of that, for control.

"I'm not equipped to 'work' with him," Katya said. "The Magistrate uses these devices"—she tapped her temples—"for control."

At the lift of her father's eyebrows, she elaborated, "They've turned them into targeted weapons. The Jar'rasks were handling a teenager; he pinpointed Mina and me on Jordah and incapacitated us. If I had to wager, I'd say the devices act a lot like the drug Plasovern formulated: creating chemical responses that invoke wakefulness and sleep as needed. I don't know how widespread the Magistrate's use of the children is—or how much the Oneiroi know—but I know they're using at least one on Tizzet."

Her father's jaw tightened, and he dropped his gaze. "I see."

Katya pressed her lips together and shifted in her seat, liberating her left hand that'd gone numb, little pins prickling under the skin. Undoubtedly, he was wondering about the Oneiroi child that'd once been in his care.

"I'll speak with Pontius."

Blood drained from her face. "Is that wise?"

He shrugged. "Like you'll always be my child, he'll always be my brother. He won't kill me. The worst he can do is lock me up here on Vergo or haul me to Meracus Domus. But at least this dancing around each other would end. It's been getting ridiculous. He's monitoring me, has been for most of my life, but it's gotten worse since your defection. He says nothing about it. Lies by omission to my face."

"You're certain he knows."

"I have no doubts."

She leaned toward the projected image of her father. "What does he do?"

He shook his head. "That's between him and the magistrates themselves."

Her eyes flew open.

"You shouldn't attempt to contact me again," her father said. "After this and my impending conversation with my brother, they will intercept any calls. We cannot allow them to uncover your location." He smiled at her. "One day. One day we'll meet again, b-but—" his voice cracked—"it won't be for a while." He pointed at her with authority."Until then, keep yourself well."

"I will," she nearly choked on the words.

"I need to end the transmission," her father said. "I'm sure they are aware of it by now."

Katya bit her lip before blurting out, "I love you."

"As do I you." His eyes were definitely brimming with tears, and hers followed suit. "I always will. No matter what."

The line then went dead, her father cutting the feed. Katya buried her face in her hands, wiping away the moisture in her eyes. She choked when her sister's hand squeezed her leg. She couldn't bring herself to look at her.

The touch vanished, her sister wandering off. When she returned, she dabbed a handkerchief at Katya's eyes. "Don't look at me like that; it's perfectly fine to cry. Just like it's perfectly fine to accept help from your sister." She grinned, though a bit muted. "I do it at least once a month. Usually over fabric, but that matters not."

Katya still pulled away, and like a child, her jaw jutted out.

Anaïs sniffed and rose, shoving the handkerchief into Katya's hand. "Oh, keep your aura of unflappability. After you're done, you can join us for lunch as if it never happened."

Dusting herself off, Anaïs left her.

Katya flinched when the door shut. Pulling at the soft cotton handkerchief in her hand, she caved and rubbed it against her face. Her hands shook with the effort. Mramor. He'd purposefully narrowed his search to ensure her return to that planet. Her chest tightened while her heart became off-kilter. Damn it. She settled her breaths, forcing the vise to loosen.

She hated this. This plan, this weakness of hers.

Rocking to her feet, she crossed over to the doorway and cracked it open. Her sister chattered with Mina, who was halfway through her sandwich. Sotiris—awake, albeit with heavy eyelids—lounged on the sofa, taken by a screen, which had cartoon figures dancing about. His sandwich rested on his chest, untouched.

Mramor. Their best option. His best option.

She ran her fingers through her disgusting hair before glancing back at the com unit. No one else. And he was a relatively unknown quantity at that. Three projects with the Magistrate. She would need a plan in place if he proved to be a dead end. A month's journey. There would be time to plan alternative courses of action while calculating a safe, lesser dosage for Sotiris. In between that, she would dig into this man and glean more information, get a better read on him and his allegiances.

She inhaled and stepped from the small room.

"You still use the Cassius name, though?" Mina asked, sandwich suspended in front of her mouth.

"It has its perks business-wise. And dearest Bernat is quite fond of it too." Anaïs shrugged. "Cassius carries sizeable political clout."

"But it's a Meracus Domus name," Mina pressed. "Surely, he should take pride in his Trides name. And you, couldn't you do just as well with your own?"

"I don't have my own." Anaïs kept her smile even as Mina plodded without thought on to dangerous terrain. "Much like Katya here, I was an orphan without one. Cassius is very much who I am. And Trides has bound itself to Meracus Domus for centuries; our cultures have morphed and blended with each other. Our names have morphed over those times."

"Doesn't that make you sad?"

Anaïs took a bite from her sandwich, chewing to buy time. Gradually, she lowered it. "But isn't that nature? We can't simply wrap ourselves in bubbles. And it is within humanoid behavior to share and adapt. It was Trides's merchants who instigated the trade centuries ago. I know others have not so freely started that trade, but Trides was never conquered. We have autonomy over our planetary affairs. We are leaders in our quadrant, and our voices are heard on Meracus Domus. We aren't alone. The Magistrate has always tried to maintain voices."

Anaïs gestured to Katya, who stiffened by the sandwich bag, dread filling her. But she never prompted her to join the conversation. Instead …

"Take Mramor, for example."

Katya's stomach clenched. If she didn't need the energy, she would have ditched the sandwich entirely.

"It is a part of the Fuusi Arm planets. Some call them the New Acquisitions."

"Acquisitions? Sounds like they were bought," Mina said, brow narrowing as she lowered her sandwich to her plate.

"They are solely called the New Acquisitions because they're beginning their transition into the Magistrate's form of governance: establishing their own planetary senates, launching their own regional legislative assemblies, and eventually acquiring seats in the *Legiferi*," Anaïs said, referring to the building on Meracus Domus that housed the republic's overall government.

"And how long do they have to wait to have a voice in matters affecting them?"

Anaïs tapped her chin. "It varies. Some already head their own senates. However, for others in the Fuusi Arm, the Magistrate was invited to solve various planetary catastrophes. In Mramor's case, a massive world war had decimated the planet. Because of the gravity of such catastrophes, it may take longer for enough stability to be restored. Many of them weren't as technologically advanced as the rest of the Magistrate."

Mina's gaze darted to Katya. The girl knew she was adopted, but Katya had never told her about Mramor, its conflict, and how she'd come into Faustus Cassius's care. The only person she'd come close to doing that with since leaving her family for military service was Sotiris, and her brain had unwittingly done that. Even Valens, who'd been allowed access to so many of her inner thoughts and history, hadn't been given that part of her past.

"Katya was one of many children the Magistrate saved from the turmoil on-world," Anaïs commented, reading Mina's thoughts.

"It was a long time ago," Katya supplied, taking her sandwich to sit by Sotiris. The boy barely registered her presence, only grunting when the cushion sank. His attention remained on the cartoon. "I don't have any memories of Mramor, so there's really nothing to say." She shrugged at Mina's scrunched face.

"Katya was very young," Anaïs said. "But she'll be making new memories of Mramor soon enough."

Katya really wished at that moment that looks could kill. If they could, her sister would be dead.

"We're going to Mramor?" Mina asked.

"So it would seem," Katya muttered.

CHAPTER THIRTEEN

Katya put off Mina's questions about Mramor, opting instead for a troubled nap in the guest room that'd amounted to little actual sleep. It hadn't stopped Sotiris from snoozing beside her. Her mind grasped for any excuse—blaming the heat—but she knew the truth in her bones: The dose had been too little. A month. There was no way. Though, as she watched the slow, steady rise and fall of Sotiris's chest, she noted the quiet in her own mind, the lack of touch. His eyelids displayed no signs of the dangerous REM sleep.

Maybe, even without a full dose, enough remained in the bloodstream to prevent him from fully exercising his abilities. She curled her toes when she stretched, hissing when her calf clenched. Groaning, she shifted in the bed and waited for the muscle to loosen. Through scrunched eyes, she saw Sotiris didn't even flinch. She pulled the leg up to massage it, the tightness and pain ebbing while the tingling remained.

If that hypothesis proved true, they might have a fighting chance. It remained a gamble.

The door cracked open, and Anaïs slid in. "You're both going to struggle to sleep tonight if you keep napping."

"I haven't napped at all." Katya groaned into the pillow before swinging up, straightening out her hair as she came to a seated position. "Did you keep Mina entertained?"

"I've been showing her my private collection. She tried to pull the moody teen shtick, but I got a smile! Just kept digging. Despite trying to be *so* dour, she has a good fashion sense."

"She likes your designs, I take it?"

"What's not to like!" Her sister bumped her shoulder with her own. "I'll send plenty with you. I understand you made it out with little more than the clothes on your backs."

"It's appreciated, but please don't overload us." Katya hoisted Sotiris into her arms, though he locked his arms, pushing away and back toward the bed.

"I insist," Anaïs said.

Carrying Sotiris into the shared space, Katya spotted Mina, face in a binder stuffed with designs.

"Just keep it tame. Contrary to what Mina might think"—the teen froze mid-page turn—"we need to travel somewhat light."

"There's no need to look like vagabonds, though," Mina muttered. "Not that you—"

"Here!" Anaïs handed Katya another binder. "Make yourself look interested. An assistant is bringing over supper."

"I should have left Sotiris in the bedroom."

"She's a Trides native," Anaïs said, a flutter of movement as she cleared the coffee table of its sketchpads, magazines, and an assortment of papers and slates. "Never left, has never seen an Oneiroi. Just keep the binder up, and she won't see his eyes."

Katya did as instructed before a Tridentarian woman, with the same light blue skin as her sister, wheeled in their meal a few minutes later. Her sister chatted up the assistant, directing her attention from the "clients." Which proved wise since Mina tightened up and stared, resembling a guilty woman. The interaction between the Tridentarians was amiable as they traded jokes back and forth.

"All right, dig in!" Anaïs clapped. "And be sure to tell me about which designs you favor." She added the last as the maid exited.

"Definitely have quite a few," Katya said.

Anaïs rolled her eyes and filled the plates with food for each of them. "If only you would try some of them. Even now, you cling to the same-old, same-old." She waved her hand at Katya's practical pants, basic shirt, and still militaristic jacket. "No color, no personality. And never any dresses."

"And as Papa said, there's nothing wrong with not liking dresses."

Her sister erupted in laughter. "I've missed you, Squeak."

They ate, Anaïs dominating the conversations. She sat close to Mina, regaling her with tales from the fashion world, never allowing the teen to sink back into herself. Anaïs was hard not to like, not to orbit around, and Mina resembled herself more than she had in weeks, so animated, the smile coming more frequently. To top it off, she was actually engaging. Katya had been skittish when she'd come to the Cassius household, but Anaïs had worked the same magic.

"One minute," Anaïs said, her hand activating her ear com device. "Hello, love, how has your day been with your movers and shakers?" She winked at Katya and Mina. "Very good." She frowned and moved to the screen, where cartoon critters engaged in a game, and switched it to a news station.

On the screen, politicians swarmed a woman wrapped in a tailored suit dress of silk. Its scarlet hues suited her warm beige complexion. Her violet hair had been twisted into a classic bun.

"Regional Governor Dennette is on-world," Anaïs said. She whistled at something Bernat said. "It must be a big deal indeed."

Anaïs continued to converse while Katya set aside her plate and moved closer to the screen, eyes scanning those surrounding the regional governor. Within her shadow was a man draped in equally expensive garments with a floral design. Her lips pressed together. Snapping her fingers, she pointed to the figure so her sister would see.

"Who's that with the governor?" Anaïs asked. "The man?" Silence. "Ah, a speaker."

A speaker. There. She spotted the medallion under a partial fold in his robe; while its engraving was indistinguishable, Katya knew the roaring eagle. Speakers were the visual representative of a magistrate, who, meanwhile, draped themselves in secrecy—unknown, incorruptible, and forever bound to service. This was not a minor trade deal. To garner a speaker, it had to be something that expanded past the system.

In the background, a platoon of Mercena, their antiquate uniforms of blue separating them from the shadows, flanked the speaker. The camera caught the gleam of their traditional "one hundred and eighty-nine" pins attached to their uniforms' collars. A testament to a storied history of service, even against overwhelming odds.

The feed bled to the revelry outside of Trides's capitol building. A group of men draped their arms across each other's shoulders and belted out a song, their words slurred and interrupted by fits of laughter. Then the camera shifted to dancers entertaining a packed crowd in one of the city's squares.

Rising, Katya cleared the plates. Mina poked around a woven basket filled with an assortment of colorful yarn. Long needles of varying sizes and materials shot up along its edges.

"Stop snooping," Katya whispered. She'd only met Bernat two times—when he'd been introduced to the family and then again at the wedding. But he'd also been in the background during some of her calls to Anaïs, and she wasn't chancing her voice being recognized. "Some"—she nudged her head at the yarn—"are super expensive."

"She won't hurt anything." Anaïs settled on the loveseat by the bin after ending her call. She sorted through its contents before removing a small ball and a pair of pink-marbled needles. She tossed the ball to Mina. "Here. Let's teach you a new skill!" She clacked the two needles together before handing them over to Mina.

The girl, bug-eyed, stared at the needles, her mouth agape. "I-I—"

"Will be a pro at it." Anaïs patted the vacant cushion next to her. "Hopefully, the lesson will stick better with you than it did with a certain someone."

Katya rested her hands on her hips. "You'd be surprised. I can still do repairs as needed."

"Repair is one thing. Creativity is another." Anaïs beamed as Mina joined her and launched into her instructions, showing the teen how to make a slipknot. "We're going to show Miss Mina how to create."

Mina's hands shook while Anaïs demonstrated casting on using another set of needles. Her right hand struggled to replicate the motions, the fine motor movements elusive to the gears and pistons inhabiting the prosthetic. As they progressed, Mina's brow knotted and beads of sweat formed. With every slip, she bit her lip. A slight flinch followed every moment her mechanical right hand released too early or tightened too much.

"You're doing fine," Anaïs intoned every so often.

A great exercise for Mina. They'd neglected those fine motor skills, settling for the ability to use utensils. At that point, Mina had sworn off physical therapy, rebuffing any further attempts. It'd grown too challenging, and Katya had let it slip. She shouldn't have. This exercise, however, slipped under the teen's guard, because even the most dreaded activity became positive in Anaïs's presence.

They moved on to the actual knitting part, and Katya hoisted Sotiris from the couch to retire him to the bedroom. After she tucked him in, she administered a portion of the drug, leaving enough for the following day. Then, slate in hand, she returned to her sister and Mina, situating herself in a chair away from them.

She typed Lomonosov's name, misspelling it at first, before being directed to several news articles about his no-shows at several conferences. Why they continued inviting him, Katya didn't know. Photos of him were nonexistent. Similarly, she found no direct contact for him, except for a message service that he never responded to, according to some obscure forum. She stumbled across articles about one of his Magistrate projects centered on agriculture and the last ... a military contract. What it had been wasn't noted.

A string of curses erupted from Mina, and Katya dropped her slate. The teen shook her head, clenching her project—now about three inches—in her lap. Her shoulders shook.

Anaïs reached across and encompassed Mina's hands in her own. "It's fine. I promise."

She then got Mina to release the project, allowing her to examine it. While Anaïs did this, Mina kept her face averted, hands clenched in her lap. From a distance, Katya couldn't tell at first what had occurred until Anaïs took two frayed ends in hand. The yarn had snapped mid-stitch.

"It's just yarn." Anaïs squeezed the teen's arm. "Mistakes and misfortunes are remedied. Some are easier than others, but it's never the end of the world. Drop a stitch, pick up another. Snap your circular needles? Cry, yes, then painstakingly move all your stitches on to a new pair. Break a strand of yarn" — she took the strand still connected to the ball — "you join it with the new." She demonstrated this before carrying on to the row's end. "There! Just like new."

Mina dabbed at her eyes, her lips trembling. "It's not. You have two ends sticking out in the middle of the project."

Her sister returned the project to Mina's hands. "If you leave it like that, yes. If you continue on, you'll eventually work them in, and it'll be as if they were never there. Sure, you'll always know, but you'll also know the effort poured into the piece, the lessons learned, the accomplishment of finishing something, no matter the adversities. Trust me, there will be. Stitches will fall off your needles. You'll drop a stitch and not realize it for several rows. But in the end, it doesn't matter. Very few people will notice."

Mina gritted her teeth and glared at the small knitted rectangle. "You're not talking about knitting."

"Aren't I?" Anaïs raised an eyebrow. "What else would I be talking about?"

"My hand."

Anaïs deadpanned. "I'm afraid I'm only qualified to speak on needlework." She shrugged and rose to her feet, heading to the kitchenette. "But if it has other applications, I'm fine with that."

Mina's glare redirected to Katya, but she simply shrugged under it. "We have to leave early in the morning. Why don't you head to bed? I'll follow shortly."

The teen shoved the knitting project into the bin and sulked from the room, cradling her prosthetic hand as she went.

Katya reclined further in the chair, at a loss. How could she help heal that invisible wound, at least as best as it could be? Her chest ached as solutions failed to materialize.

Clenching the slate, she realized there were no solutions. Her gaze drifted to the yarn bin. But perhaps little steps … if Mina would touch the hobby again.

Glasses clinking broke her reverie. In the kitchenette, Anaïs popped a cork and poured a deep purple wine into two glasses. Taking them in hand, she nudged her head to a side glass door, which led to a veranda. Thick vines climbed its wood structure, providing privacy.

"Let's talk." She opened the door wide and extended a glass to her.

Katya's innards shriveled. She curled into the chair, trying to decline the invite, but ultimately, she followed.

The air outside had a welcomed warmth compared to the studio, which had chilled dramatically for Sotiris. The moon, a crescent that cut through the pitch-black of night, illuminated the area, catching on the pool's water. Anaïs flipped a light switch, and lights flickered on among the vines, whimsical in a manner befitting her sister. It wasn't overwhelming light, not detracting from the celestial display above them.

Anaïs settled the wine glasses on a metal table in the center of the veranda before climbing on to one of the tall, matching metal barstools.

Katya did likewise, stiffening when her sister slid her fingers through her hair.

"I like," Anaïs said. "It really suits you." She retracted her fingers and picked up her wine glass. "I'm glad you're finally going your own way."

Katya glared darkly over the rim of her own glass as she sipped from it. It was almost too sweet. She scowled and set it aside. "All that from a haircut? I cut it to pass under the radar, not as some form of parental rebellion."

"Still, you're not beholden to Papa's choices."

With hooded eyes, she lifted her face. She didn't say that her hands had shaken as she'd cut it. That she'd been queasy, peeling away an element of herself that'd become a part of her identity. She downed some more of the wine. It didn't bother her anymore. Now she hacked away at her hair whenever it got too long, or her bangs obscured her vision. Perhaps the betrayal had already happened, making it easier to move forward. And really, that was all there was to do: move forward.

Anaïs sighed. "Papa means well. But he misses the intricacies, details only people within a certain culture will know. It's the little things that don't always make it into papers or anthropology textbooks." Her sister took a deep gulp of wine. "My debut on Trides wasn't without its ... missteps"—she waved her glass a bit, her cheeks darkening with memory—"little faux pas. Papa tried his best to prepare me, but yeah ..."

"I don't plan to reintegrate myself into Mramorian society." Katya took a massive swallow of wine. It went down like syrup. "I'm going to get Sotiris the help he needs."

"And you don't have to." Her sister leaned nearer. "But—now hear me out—I hope your trip to your homeworld will be as"—she pressed her lips together as if struggling for the right word—"as enlightening as it was for me. Hard, but rewarding."

"Rewarding?" Diverting the conversation, Katya asked, "Are you and Bernat trying?" It'd been one call homeward for her sister. As she'd worded it herself: If there was any hope for anything sexually satisfying, it would only be with another Tridetarian. Having a child also depended on it.

"We still have time. He's pursuing his career like I am mine. But we've been talking." Anaïs played with glass. "I think I'll be comfortable in a year or two. I have a good team behind me; I think they're almost ready to pick up the slack."

"You'll be great at it whenever it happens." Katya smirked. "You've always mothered me."

"Oh, Squeak, someone had to." Anaïs chuckled. "Such a tiny thing. You were so quiet and removed when you came. I doubt you said even a word in those first weeks. You also didn't like being touched. The boys learned that the hard way." Some memory stoked a deeper laugh. "Do you remember punching poor Harsha in the face? He was too rambunctious for his own good. Then Cyprianus ... he was too old to want to interact with a four-year-old. Someone had to be that bridge. Let you know you weren't alone. I'm afraid I made a project out of you."

"I don't want to go back." Katya clenched her hands under the table, hiding the shake that stirred. She used to be unflappable, but now, the slightest stressor threatened to undo her. If she was still on duty, they would've said her nerves had cracked. Commanding officers would've ordered psych sessions, possibly even a discharge. "Mramor is a tougher situation than Trides."

"Do you remember anything about it?"

The lie poked at her tongue, likely dyed purple now, but the warmth in her sister's eyes halted it.

"Sotiris has dug"—she tapped her forehead with her right, tremor-free hand—"literally dug up memories ... fragments. So distorted." Tears prickled at her eyes, but she vanquished them with her sleeve, shaking her head as she did so. "I-I don't want to know."

Anaïs seized her shaking hand under the table and held it for several minutes until Katya composed herself. Concern radiated in her amber eyes, threatening to brim with tears of their own. That she, the ordinarily solid one of their father's children, would sink so far. Katya clenched her teeth. Her mind flickered to the charts taken from Plasovern, the scans of her own brain.

"You've been through so much in so short a time." Anaïs tightened her grip. "Give yourself some slack. Breathe." Her sister looked her dead in the eye. "Promise me you won't just focus on the kids. You need to prioritize your own well-being too." Her long fingers traced a circular pattern against Katya's skin. "Maybe take up knitting again. It's quite therapeutic."

Laughter erupted from deep within her, and Katya withdrew her hand. "It's not my ideal method of relaxation. But thank you for sharing it with Mina. I think it could be a good thing for her."

Anaïs's shoulders slumped while her eyes took a veiled appearance. "I'll send it along with you all. Sneak it into a bag. I'll give you some money—"

"That's unnecessary. I picked up some funds through a previous transaction." She didn't mention how quickly fuel's rising prices would deplete it, but she believed they would reach Mramor with some to spare. After that … They would make do.

"What type of transaction?"

Katya groaned and finished her wine glass. "A legit sale of a vessel, which I had legally purchased."

"Entirely legal then?"

"Mostly."

Anaïs emptied her own glass and stood; however, rather than clear the table, she embraced Katya, holding her tight. "Just remember to take care of yourself too." She squeezed tighter, almost reminding Katya of a *polypus* and its many tentacles. "Also, remember no matter where you may go, what you may discover, you and I will always be sisters. We may not share blood, but no one will understand us like we do each other. Our time with Papa—roving the galaxy, being shoved in front of so many musty books, putting up with his eccentricities—only we will ever have that shared past."

She released and took both glasses between her fingers. "Best to get to bed. You'll want to leave early to avoid the crowds." She sauntered into the studio, calling back, "Don't stay up too late."

Katya grunted in response. She lingered on the veranda for a few more minutes after she heard Anaïs return to the main house. She blindly stared at the stars, both eager and dreading her return to them.

A commotion in the main room startled Katya from her sleep. Thrusting her unkempt, greasy hair from her forehead, she rocked to her feet, leaving Sotiris to slumber on while she crept to the door. She cracked it open to watch her sister direct her maid to set up two breakfast trays in the kitchenette. A man donning a tailored suit laid three lumpy bags against a wall.

"Oh good, you're up." Anaïs beamed at her.

Beyond her sister, Katya could see—even through the tint—that the sun had yet to rise.

Katya rubbed a kink in her neck. "When you said early, I didn't imagine it would be quite this early."

"I apologize," Anaïs said. "I received a call late last night from another business associate whose husband is an elector visiting Trides. I hate to rush you, but she's arriving later this morning, and I knew you wanted to be on your way early, so I didn't think you'd mind." She gestured to the man. "Agustí will drive you as close to the spaceport as possible. I apologize for rushing you out."

"No, no, you're right. We need to be on our way. We'll review everything and be in touch."

Anaïs winked at her and then crossed to the sofa, removing three neatly wrapped clothing boxes with deep blue ribbons tied around them. "A parting gift for all three of you." She nodded to the bags. "And there's some more in there. I spoil all my business associates."

Katya accepted the boxes, grateful Anaïs had stopped at the backpacks and the wrapped clothes. Taking them to the bedroom, she dropped the box with a stylized "M" on Mina's bed. The girl sputtered awake, fighting with the covers.

"W-what?!"

"A gift from Anaïs," Katya said, biting down on a smile. "Fresh clothes for the journey. We're heading out early since she has an incoming guest."

Katya opened her own package to discover a navy blue fitted blouse with quarter sleeves and a series of off-center buttons to the right side so its collar formed a V. She would blend in with all the Magistrate blue in the city. Beneath was a pair of lighter-washed jeans.

She glanced over when Mina opened her own to find a navy blue shirt. Hers featured long, sheer sleeves and a gathered collar with cutouts on each shoulder. Her smile split her face as she hugged the silky fabric, silently squealing.

Together, they dressed in their new clothes before Katya set about dosing and clothing a drowsy Sotiris, who struggled to open his eyes. Anaïs had continued the blue shirt and white pants motif with Sotiris. Apparently, Anaïs deemed the children as cleaner than Katya. She probably wasn't wrong.

After brushing their teeth, they joined Anaïs in the main room.

She pressed her fingers to her lips and made a smacking sound as she pulled them away. "Beautiful! You all look great. I bet you can't wait until you're wearing your own faces again."

"I want to shower so badly," Mina mumbled, withdrawing her hands from her hair. "Disgusting."

"As soon as we break atmosphere," Katya intoned. She craved it too. Her scalp itched, and her pores felt plugged.

Anaïs turned on a news feed while Katya and Mina helped themselves to Tridetarian pastries filled with a native fruit that started tart before transitioning to sweet, almost flabbergasting the brain.

"A signing is expected today for the new trade deal, which will see the removal of levies on select products within the Mamercus Sector. After the signing, the deal will be sent to the Mamercus Legislative Assembly for approval," a newscaster said. "It is expected to pass without protest."

"I think you'll have a much easier time getting to the port," Anaïs said. "Traffic will be light this morning, though the port itself — well, it is a spaceport. You'll see I kept it light." She waved at the packs. "A week's worth of outfits, heavy-duty and warm, for where you're heading."

"I appreciate that." Katya finished her plate and now tried to entice more bites from Sotiris, who displayed little interest. Clearing her throat, Katya asked, "This guest of yours?"

"Pushy and untrustworthy. I wouldn't put it past her to steal designs, but the polite things I must do for dear Bernat." Anaïs lowered the volume when a loud commercial overtook the screen. "While I'm not letting her in my studio, I don't want to chance her spotting you and asking questions. She's always looking for opportunities." She chuckled. "But don't worry about me. I guard my business well."

Mina finished her meal, and Katya gave up on forcing food on Sotiris, who'd flopped into the pillow emitting a high-pitch whine. Fine. She let him wallow, twisting, groaning. Withdrawal, maybe? She ran her hand through her grimy hair. They had a month. Closing her eyes, she rubbed his back. Off to the side, she heard her sister summon their driver.

"Mina," Katya said, "make sure you have everything."

"He'll be around soon," Anaïs said as Mina left them. "You'll remember our conversation, right? Take care of yourself too." She hugged Katya when the latter stood, holding her for a good minute before releasing her. "Don't forget any of your things. I won't be able to return them."

"That's probably true." She smiled, but it was hollow, echoing the chasm in her chest. "I likely won't be in contact soon. It's always been risky, but I think it's more so now."

"Likely so, now that they've probably detected Papa's illegal signal." Anaïs stroked her chin. "I doubt they have me under the same level of scrutiny. If they did, the signal would have drawn them by now."

"Such a pleasant thought." Katya rolled her eyes and headed to the bedroom to ensure all of her and Sotiris's items were safely stowed. If any agents had intercepted the signal, they could be waiting for them to leave the compound. A quick grab, no drama, no shame heaped on to a senator and his family. The right team could pull it off seamlessly.

She tried to banish the thought as she gathered hers and Sotiris's packs before taking the toddler's hand in hers. He remained unenthused about reentering Trides's tropical heat. He still allowed her to guide the way to the waiting vehicle. There, the driver stepped up to load their bags after opening the doors for them, an action that dropped Mina's mouth open. There had been little of that on Reznic.

As she fastened her seatbelt, Anaïs chattered about business dealings, designs, and the like. She added canned responses that wouldn't betray a lack of knowledge, though they probably did all the same.

As the driver slammed the trunk, Anaïs teared up. Through the window opening, her hand found Katya's wrist and squeezed it. Katya's chest swelled. The pressure around her wrist lessened, then withdrew. Anaïs stepped back when the driver slumped into his seat.

The two waved to Anaïs until the vehicle swept them out of sight and on to the highway. Katya sank into her seat, arms encircling herself. She'd never visited Anaïs ... she could have seized leave to do so. Yet, she never had. Her fingers curled against her ribs. And now, she would never visit again. Finality settled heavily along her shoulders. *"No one will understand us like we do each other."* She rubbed at her breastbone. The bond would remain, but they could never return to that nursery, that time. Only forward.

"Are you all right?"

Katya lowered her hand and nodded, not trusting her voice. The breeze lapping at her face settled her stomach fractionally. She ignored Mina's lingering gaze and allowed the rush of air to calm her.

The driver whisked them into the city proper, getting them as close to the spaceport as possible. There, Katya and Mina weighed themselves down with their bags while Sotiris panted. Katya thanked the driver, took directions to the port, and started around a barrier separating the downtown area with its political delegations and partiers.

The streetlights provided most of their light, casting the barest orange glow against deeper shades of blue.

Sotiris plodded along, falling behind hers and Mina's longer steps. The early hour made the temperature comfortable—at least for the older two. Katya estimated it wouldn't be long before she had to carry him again. The street remained largely vacated, though they crossed a few passed-out forms who'd partied too hard the night before. A few maintenance men cleared copious mounds of trash from the sidewalks and overflowing trash cans. A slight hum followed as a street sweeper passed them.

Katya shifted away from a drunk who'd passed out on a bench. The aroma of vomit clung to the air, and Katya scowled when it reached her tongue.

Mina, who had the good fortune of having a free arm, used her long-sleeved shirt to block the smell. There were also a sizeable number of abandoned bicycles and hoverboards.

"It's going to take them weeks to clean up," Mina said.

Katya grunted, her right arm cramping with the added weight. "I'm sure once the hangovers lift, they'll get everything back in order."

She reclaimed Sotiris's hand after it slipped. The boy was practically melting.

"We can't stop," she said, earning a muffled moan.

They took another street heading east, where a line had already formed outside of a bakery. Fresh bread permeated the air, coating any undesirable odor from the previous day's revelry. Despite having had a full meal, Katya's mouth watered. Bread always held a special place in her heart, especially when it was fresh and warm.

"When we get to the ship," Katya said, "I'll send our itinerary to the port. As soon as I have us en route, you can have dibs on the shower unit." They each had their own, but a cognizant Sotiris required monitoring.

"I guess if we don't want a repeat."

"We don't."

The teen glanced at the panting boy. "We should carry him. He won't last long."

"You up to it?"

Mina shifted her bags with some effort and situated Sotiris on her shoulders, all with zero cooperation from the toddler, who provided nothing more than deadweight. Around labored breaths, Mina slung a potshot. "If we hadn't left, he'd have been better off. He'd have—"

"Not now."

Mina rose with Sotiris on her shoulders, his head buried in her hair. "But you know it's true."

Katya stepped in front of her. She still had height on the teen, but Mina was growing so fast, narrowing the difference between them. "We're not having this conversation on a public street."

The teen's flared nostrils suggested she would dig in, but she followed Katya like a turbulent wake.

By the time they reached the port, the sky had a vibrant pinkish tinge. More early risers dotted the streets, conducting business or patronizing eateries before the area once again swelled with celebrations. The port itself, like any other massive port, never slept. Sentients of all species milled, awaiting the subsequent transport, browsing stores, scoring breakfast, or coming and going from their ships.

Security surveyed all activities like the Magistrate eagles perched on their patches.

Mina paused at the entrance fountain, using its ledge to make a quick bag adjustment. Katya joined her, as hers also cut into her skin and angered her muscles. She rolled her head to relieve the ache. At the same time, a young Tridetarian child drew her attention when she flung herself into the arms of a disembarking traveler. The man's hair, a lustrous silver, suggested a grandfather.

Her blood froze in her veins when a familiar face poked through a crowd farther down.

"I will personally extract the price should you betray us."

The woman's face disappeared amongst the surging crowd. The fleeting glimpse heightened the tension between Katya's shoulders. Without a doubt, Bodil had arrived on Trides.

Katya nudged Mina with her elbow. "Let's head out."

The girl grumbled but lifted her bags and moved around the fountain, which Katya hoped would act as a buffer. As they moved, Katya tracked the incoming crowd and caught another glimpse of Bodil. She wore the same severe bob, her eyes straight ahead, unmoved by her surroundings. She wasn't alone. While dressed unassuming, four men and one woman—blonde with fair complexions— stood too close to Bodil to be a separate party. They shared the same grim-faced expression, the targeted vision. They'd come on a mission. Her? Or something bigger?

Katya twisted her bag's strap. If her, how had they tracked them to Trides? She'd been so careful, dismantled everything to remove any trackers or monitoring devices. Plasovern had eyes everywhere. Her face chilled.

Mina's gaze darted around. The teen knew her far too well, had read that something was off. Releasing the strap, she caught Mina's arm instead, keeping her near. Katya's heart clambered as she dragged Mina to a point where the fountain was at its tallest.

What would the teen do if she spotted Bodil and the other Plasovern agents? Would she expose them? Would she rush after them? Sweat pooled at her pits, drenching the light fabric. She couldn't allow Mina to spot them.

"What's—"

"Keeping going." She prodded Mina's back, forcing the girl forward even though her foot almost tripped on one step's lip. It was enough to distract the girl from looking, an action Katya did.

Bodil and her group mirrored them, only they were descending the staircase.

Pick it up, pick it up.

Mina grunted and glowered at her over Sotiris's leg, which rested on her shoulder. The boy remained inert, unaware of any turmoil. When they reached the second-floor landing, Katya continued to egg the teen forward. Meanwhile, Bodil and her group below never broke from their path to the city proper.

Krezk. Katya's lungs burned, and she couldn't tear her eyes from the doors the Plasovern agents had exited through. Had they come for some other purpose?

The festivities, the signing, the dignitaries—they all made too tempting a target for Plasovern. She had to warn someone. But how did she explain recognizing a Plasovern agent who had just calmly walked through spaceport security without a disguise?

She swallowed. Her head thrummed, vision narrowing … She wasn't having a panic attack, not here, not now.

"Are you all right?" Mina pressed.

"Yes." It came out snappish and only increased the teen's frown.

Mina didn't comment, especially as they entered port security and went through its rigmarole, including answering export questions and ensuring no exotic or endangered fruits or animals were being concealed in their bags.

Cleared, they returned to their freighter. Katya remained alert as they approached it. If Bodil and her agents had been in this section of the port, there was no way they would have missed their stolen freighter.

Pursing her lips, Katya lowered the hatch, her heartbeat an odd staccato as she pulled Mina back. The ramp connected with the ground, and the half-expected explosion never came. Katya extended her arm in front of Mina after she stepped forward.

"What is—"

Katya silenced Mina with a sharp jerk of two fingers in front of her own mouth. "Stay here with him," she whispered. "If you hear anything, run and get help."

Explosives were Plasovern's stock-in-trade, and she'd half-expected the ramp to trigger one. It would've been ideal. Knock them out and make a massive dent in the port. She prowled through the freighter's darkened, quiet interior, seeking anyone or anything that didn't belong. Her gut tightened as she entered the cockpit. No one. Nothing a miss. She removed her pistol from her quarters before clearing the other crew quarters, the mess, and even the locked engine room. At that last destination, she examined the ship's mechanical components with a fine-tooth comb. No nasty surprises.

Returning the pistol's safety, she slid it into her belt and returned to the cargo hold.

At the ramp's end, Mina waited, hands on her hips. "What's going on?" Her tone sliced.

Katya waited until Mina was onboard to say, "I saw a familiar face," as she started closing the ramp.

Emotions rampaged on Mina's face, confusion, anger, uncertainty. She faced the closing hatch, possibly considering running out while she still could. "Strom?"

"No." Katya picked up her bags. "Watch Sotiris while I get us underway."

Mina, however, remained rooted before the now-closed hatch. Hope flickered in her eyes. Almost breathless, she asked, "Was it Dag?"

"Bodil." Then upon seeing Mina scrunch her eyes, Katya explained, "Strom's second in command."

The teen leaned toward the mechanism.

"If you follow her"—Katya fought the waver in her voice—"you will regret it the rest of your life."

"And how do you know that?" Mina spat.

"Because I know Bodil well enough." Katya stepped toward the ladder. "Nothing good will ever come from getting close to her." She climbed up, leaving Mina to war with her desires. She'd already made one decision for her. She massaged her chest, trying to calm her breaths, the ache. This one would be Mina's.

When she reached the cockpit, Katya brought the *Pollux* to life. The display showed the main hatch remained latched, and she locked its operations from the cockpit. Mina had had her chance. Warming up the engines, Katya relayed a flight plan to Gort for refueling. She left the final destination vague—Fuusi Arm—and their goal: seeking work. Nice and bland. Satisfied, she sent it to the central tower.

While waiting for approval, she inspected the cockpit again for anything she might have missed. Bodil's group had to have come from another section of the port. There was no way Bodil would've passed the freighter without some manner of sabotage. Katya opened and closed another panel before launching a system scan. After several minutes passed, a beep drew her attention. Official approval from the port.

Katya climbed into the pilot's chair and froze. Plasovern was on-world. Her sister's and brother-in-law's world. Report it. She ran her hand through her hair, her toes tapping unsteadily against the metal floor. A heads-up about suspicious behavior? No, that wasn't grave enough. It wouldn't heighten their security enough for the danger represented by Bodil and her team. Katya twisted her shirt's fabric. There are Plasovern agents on Trides ... It would be followed with, how do you know? She ground her teeth together.

Through the active viewscreen, an uptick in life streamed through the port once more with the sun's return.

"Port to *Pollux*."

Katya's heart skipped. Clearing her throat, she opened her line. "*Pollux* to Port. Responding to port's request."

"You're cleared for departure. Please vacate your space in the next twenty minutes," a brusque voice ordered.

Katya bit her lip, her molars grinding together. They needed to leave. Time was slipping away with Sotiris's medicine dwindling. But still ... "Port, there was a party entering the city." She swallowed as her throat tightened. "Two women, four men. I hate to profile, but they appeared to be Varraganarian ... and I think I saw a Plasovern pin on one of them."

Silence. "Did they appear to be carrying anything?"

"Luggage."

"How long ago did you see them?"

Katya moistened her lips. "About twenty to thirty-five minutes ago. They'd passed by the fountain in front of the main exit."

"Why didn't you report this to customs?"

"I don't like to profile, but the more I thought about it, the more it didn't sit right."

The port official didn't respond immediately. She imagined a conversation was occurring on the other side. "We'll check in on it."

Katya tapped against the console. They needed to act now. Bodil wasn't a lightweight. "I appreciate it. *Pollux* to Port. Directions received. We are taking off now." Then on the ship's intercom, she called, "Mina, we've been cleared. Lifting off in three ... two ... one."

Working the helm, she lifted the freighter from its spot with the atmospheric systems. Below, life continued, more people pouring into the spaceport structure, ships landing in its many hubs while others like theirs departed. Through the viewscreen, that action grew smaller. She lessened the exterior display in favor of an enlarged navigation chart. Standing, she tracked the port's route for them and kept a respectable distance from other crafts. In the background, she turned to regular com traffic. Captains trading gossip, traffic alerts, and fuel prices calmed her mind, settled the unease goading her mind.

Katya yelped, her knees buckling when some substantial force tossed her—no, their ship—like driftwood in a roiled sea. Alarm after alarm bayed, red light engulfing her. Sputtering, she staggered up, the choppy waves knocking her from the helm. Had something hit them? Shielding beyond those regulated to atmospheric travel sprung to life on their own accord, some safety mechanism being tripped.

Groaning, Katya latched on to the helm, holding it for dear life, the vibrations rattling through it, jarring her bones. She wrestled command from the autopilot and tried to keep them upright. They had to break atmosphere. Her teeth clattered against each other, one possibly chipping.

The readings on the screen—the thermal heat. Krezk. The external view, what little she'd left on the screen, had become blanketed in grime. Only flares of orange bled through; an ill omen of what occurred outside the ship.

Mina staggered into the cockpit on her hands and knees. "What's happening—"

Words morphed into a scream when something hit the freighter; the piercing sound rising even above shuddering metal lifted Katya's hair and chilled her to her core.

The camera relaying the exterior never cleared beyond the fiery flashes. The navigations console blared, and she caught a larger freighter careening toward them, caught in the same force.

"No, no, no—" She forced as much power into the thrusters as possible, and her breath caught in her throat as the seconds stretched seemingly into minutes, promising catastrophe. Only the other ship didn't rip through their hull. She pressed the thrusters, burning through fuel—then the *Pollux* leveled, greeted by calm as jarring as the concussive waves they'd transcended.

The alarms continued to blare, and somewhere in the background, Mina cried, a heap on the floor. Katya coughed, a horrible coppery concoction building in her mouth. Prodding her mouth with her tongue, she discovered punctures on both sides.

Now, in the safety of space, she increased the exterior view. Scratched and muddled, the scene the viewscreen presented, like a gut punch, rendered her breathless. Smoke—debris—billowed, enshrouding the once-vibrant green and blue world of Trides. Katya's knees, already tense, shook. The only color seeping through the black and brown was the flicker of molten orange—blooms of destruction.

What-what had they used? Krezk. How far had it gone? A sickening sensation enveloped her. There was no doubt Bernat had been in the blast zone, but … had Anaïs? Tears poured down her face. The exact damage was impossible to tell.

She opened the communications system; however, Trides lay silent. It'd lost not only its relay but other essential communications infrastructure. The only traffic came from the ships that had been coming to and from the planet. It amounted to captains and their crew members trying to make sense of what had happened.

"What's the radius?" one voice asked.

"Hard to judge. Too much smoke," a man said over the com ways.

Another man, voice wavering, choked on tears. "We were coming in … when it happened. It started near the capitol building … it just, it just kept going, like air fueled it."

Someone else opined, "Had to have been a good chunk of the city."

Katya dry heaved. Stepping away from the helm, she tried to settle her body, but retched further when a foul taste entered her mouth. Stop it. She sucked in air, only it wasn't reaching her lungs.

Then, a crackling cut over the communications system, supplanting the shocked masses with the singular voice of a ghost.

"For longer than I've drawn breath, the Magistrate has coated our worlds in blood. Taken what is not theirs, subjugated peoples, not their own." Bodil echoed through the cockpit. "This is just a foretaste of what's coming: the blood that will drench your own soil. You will reap what you've sown."

CHAPTER FOURTEEN

Land, Katya's mind screamed. Yet she remained frozen, arms clutching her abdomen. Through the viewscreen, massive swirling clouds—smoke and debris—blotted the planet. It wouldn't allow any landing. And with her current status as a wanted woman who had stupidly connected herself to the bastards who'd done this, she couldn't. Her stomached churned. It'd started near the capitol building ... there was no way her brother-in-law had survived. And Anaïs—her jaw popped—her fate would rest with on-world emergency professionals.

Com traffic, no longer co-opted by Bodil's programmed last words, stirred and at some points made no sense as words bled together. Questions, inquiries, emotions being processed. Katya collapsed in her seat, resting her head between her legs, breaths steadying. Bodil's words … there was no way she'd escaped the explosion, nor had Trides's relay.

How had she sent that last message?

A chill crept across Katya's spine, and she straightened. Blue dots, signifying Magistrate-registered crafts, surrounded them on the navigation chart. Somewhere amongst them had to be a Plasovern agent, if not a crew of them. Her mind spiraled from there. Trides's downed relay left the quadrant blind … ripe for another attack. Wiping her mouth, Katya couldn't pull her eyes from the static blue dots, questioning which one had relayed the message. Her skin itched while her mind played the damage one ship could do with so many others clustered together just sitting. They needed to leave.

"Anaïs?" Mina croaked from the floor, where she hugged herself. Tremors passed through her body.

"We—" Katya's voice cracked, forcing her to try again. "We can't help her."

The com was once again commandeered, this time by one of Trides's patrolling A-Class warships. "All ships are to remain in place. Trides is off-limits to landings," a robotic voice, unaffected by emotion, stated. "Any vessel that disobeys this order will be disabled, its crew contained."

The message repeated.

"But, but we could help. We-we really could." Mina hiccupped, her head shaking as if she could banish the sight on the viewscreen. "But …" Tears and snot streamed down her face, her expression so lost.

Katya slumped next to the girl, encircling her and hugging her close. They shook together, tears streaming.

Around hiccups, Katya spoke. "T-They can't chance a second team entering atmosphere. And spacecrafts aren't designed"—she nudged her head to the viewscreen—"for that."

Mina burrowed into her bum shoulder, causing Katya to wince.

Katya swallowed. "They need to manage the situation. Contain it, not add to it." She didn't mention her suspicions of a second Plasovern team, not out of distrust but to spare her.

Mina swallowed hard, trapping her trembling lips between her teeth.

Katya rubbed the girl's back. "Just breathe."

"Ship *Pollux*?" a female voice inquired from the communications station. "This is Lieutenant Bover."

Squeezing Mina's upper shoulder, Katya approached the station, found the caller to be from the warship *Caeso*, and activated the mic. "This is her captain. Aelia."

"You're from the Core?"

Her accent gave it away, but in the current circumstances, she hoped it would smooth nerves. "Yes. My family had been visiting a business associate. We left just before"—Katya tried to draw moisture to her mouth—"the explosion."

"Please open remote access to your helm data. We are redirecting traffic to alternative ports for service and interviews. Our sensors show your vessel is leaking radiation."

Katya hesitated, not liking the sound of interviews or their helm being inspected. She'd cleared their time in the Medzeci Empire from it, but if they compared it to the registry, it would be like they'd appeared from nowhere. She glanced at Mina, who watched with wide eyes. She doubted the teen's ability to get through an interview without triggering suspicions. However, with all the warnings still flashing and the sizeable amount of burned fuel, there was no outrunning the warship and its brethren, which now walled off Trides.

She crossed over to the helm, fumbling with its controls and clearing several warnings to comply with the warship's request.

"We're going to ask you to divert from your flight plan," the lieutenant said. "With the damage to your vessel and your fuel supply, it's unlikely you'll reach Gort. I'll have you go to Station T-45. Magistrate officials will get any details you can recall during your departure. It's a matter of Magistrate security."

And Katya suspected, for that reason, their ship was now marked. "Understood."

"Your navigation system says Gort was for refueling. Where is your final destination?"

"The Fuusi Arm."

"Which planet? And purpose?"

Katya's jaw popped. Her brain weighed options before selecting truth, given the circumstances. "Mramor. To meet a potential business associate about picking up a load of alcohol." It was the chief export she could think of to lend any plausibility for a freighter to want to visit Mramor for work.

There was a pause before the lieutenant returned to the com. "Continue to T-45."

Katya cut the com and shut down safety measures she'd never had to deal with in the past. The radiation levels being displayed didn't sit well with her. It'd been a near miss leaving Trides. At least the leak was on the exterior, not the interior—though something chemical clung to the recycled air. Of all the things, she couldn't afford a massive repair bill or wasted time.

"We're not going, right?" Mina pressed.

"There's no choice. We need fuel and repairs, and every ship in Trides's air space is going to be tracked as they investigate." She pulled away from the planet, gathering speed toward the station. She kept them at impulse. She didn't want to chance falling apart along the way. "I don't expect we'll get too much of their attention: a single woman with two children."

"I'm not a child."

Katya broke from her duties to face the teen. "You're a minor, and you'll embrace it with every legal protection it provides."

That sunk into the teen's mind, and she sat straighter.

"You'll let me handle this." Then Katya froze. "Sotiris?"

"I left him in your room."

The bumpy ride wouldn't have been less harsh in there. Concern burned in her chest, but she didn't want to leave the damaged freighter unmanned. "Stay with him. T-45 is about two and a half hours at our current speed. Leave the facial clay on and add more blush to his face. With luck, they won't pay him any mind as he sleeps."

The teen, still hugging herself, staggered to her feet. The girl from Reznic filtered through, lost and alone.

"It'll be all right, Mina. Just let me take the lead."

She nodded and trudged from the cockpit. Now alone, Katya crumpled into the pilot's chair and sobbed.

Armed guards didn't greet them at R-45, but Magistrate inspectors did, combing over every inch of the *Pollux*'s hull. Not just its exterior. They swarmed other ships that had been leaving Trides and taken the explosion's worst. While workers conducted triage, Magistrate officers escorted victims, looking like the walking dead with vacant, red-rimmed eyes, to the Magistrate on-station offices.

As Katya had hoped, the station's Magistrate investigators paid Mina and Sotiris no mind, leaving them in the hallway's uncomfortable, straight-back chairs alongside other survivors. Two officers, however, cornered Katya in an office and grilled her for recollections. Not that she had much to give them. She'd been too focused on the helm, not the exterior view, and by the time she had looked, it'd been obstructed. She omitted having reported suspected Plasovern agents. All records of that were lost with the city, and it was best they remain buried there.

Within a couple hours, her interviewers, two Tridetarian Magistrate officers, released her to the hallway and its muffled sobs. She extracted Mina and a grumpy Sotiris and flitted back to the ship. There, she eyed the workers with trepidation. They didn't have time to wait, but that choice was out of her hands.

"Take him on board," Katya instructed Mina. "I'll be along."

Moving around equipment, at one point lifting her hands to her ears to protect her hearing, she cornered one worker.

"Hi," she shouted to be heard. "What's the verdict?" She waved at the patches being welded in place.

"Cosmetic damage," the man responded. "Also needs a system flush. The debris was something else."

"The cost?" She already ran her own calculations.

"None. It's all being handled by Relief."

In a little over a few hours, the Magistrate Relief Fund was already dishing out its reserves. A wave of sickness swept through her. That she would benefit from it when just months ago … she buried the thought before it triggered a bodily response. Her stomach had never really settled. She shoved her shaking hands into her pockets.

"How long until we can leave?"

The man sighed. "A couple hours. We've got an incoming second wave. Ships like yours need to be cleared to make way. We'll fill you up a bit, but you'll want to factor in a stop along the way. We have to ration it."

"Thank you."

"We've all gotta help each other out."

Katya nodded. Any response with words would have caused the bulge in her throat to erupt. She trudged back toward the *Pollux*'s ramp, only to freeze. In a cascade of hooves hammering against metal, horses burst from the hold of a badly crippled ship next door. Despite herself, Katya backpedaled and gaped, the dissonance of the scene throwing her. The horses threw their heads in complete upset and tugged at their handlers. Of the five, one had a noticeable limp and a deep red gash along its side.

Unused to the creatures, Katya edged up her ship's ramp, eyes never entirely leaving the mass of billowing muscles and nervous energy. Her father had often commented on humanity's primal tethering to the species, even after their use was rendered obsolete. One didn't just ditch an old friend. All the same, she found their presence on a space station jarring.

"So?" Mina asked, still waiting in the *Pollux*'s hold with Sotiris on her back.

"A couple hours, and we'll need to clear out." She squeezed the girl's shoulder before taking Sotiris and placing him on her own shoulders. "Keep the facial clay on. As soon as we're underway, I promise you can take it off. We'll be in the cockpit." Swallowing, she said, "Try to eat something in between."

"And what about you?"

"I'll get something once we're underway." Her stomach rebelled at even the thought.

Mina twisted her hands in her pockets, wrinkling the fabric. "And Anaïs?"

Swallowing, she struggled to respond. Trides's wrecked relay would hamper reports and recovery efforts. In the place of hard reports, misinformation and speculation would rush forward to make sense of what had happened. People would bandy names about. Her chest clenched, knowing Anaïs's would be among them.

"It'll be days before there's anything concrete," she said. "And with the relay gone, there'll be no long-range communications in this sector. But as soon as we're in range of another relay … I'll try to reach Anaïs."

The teen nodded, and with Sotiris firmly on her shoulders, Katya climbed to the second level, a weight settling within her.

A week later, they'd docked at another Magistrate station as the *Pollux*'s fuel reserves metaphorically flirted with fumes. Katya had stretched it far longer than she'd intended, but Trides's misfortune shot outward, hindering supply and stirring hoarders. Their initial destination had been drained of fuel reserves. Without the relay, she hadn't realized until arrival, wasting time they didn't have.

Katya massaged her jaw. But their alternative refueling station—SMR-13—came with a bonus: It was within range of a relay. And thus, the floodgates opened.

Barricaded in the cockpit, Katya tracked the refueling that'd begun outside the hull while a news station blared in the background. Using her slate, she uncovered an official Magistrate page set up for those impacted by the tragedy— "the greatest loss of civilian life experienced by the Magistrate in centuries." Her fingers curled around the slate as the live coverage detailed aggressive terror attacks in the Fringe and a botched assassination on Skogarld. Intermingled within the deluge of information were snippets about Magistrate counters, which were akin to a giant flailing while a nest of hornets stung it.

"I don't think we'll ever know the true cost of this attack," one woman reporter, clad in a dress suit, said. The hologram recorder captured her lean toward a male co-host. "So many people come and go from Tres each day, more so because of the holiday and the trade legislature's passage. With the port and its records' destruction, there's no fathomable way to accurately calculate the loss of life. Families with relatives they don't regularly communicate with—they'll always wonder if their freighter pilot uncle was on Trides. Was he lost in the explosion? Is that why they can't reach him?"

Her co-host bobbed his head. He was a Borelle, his antennae raising and lowering like a gentle wave. "That will be a real challenge. With eighty-five percent of Tres destroyed, some are simply gone—"

Katya cut the stream. Heart pounding, she started the call using the frequency on the next of kin page. None of her attempts to reach Anaïs directly had panned out, but there was still no relay in the Trides sector. Yes, the Magistrate had placed bandages, but those were restricted to recovery efforts, not for the masses.

The line connected. Her chest constricted. Breathe. Breathe.

"Trides Victim Assistance," a woman's voice emitted in Katya's earpiece. "If you are calling to verify the status of a known Trides resident, please say one. If you suspect—"

"One." It came out barely a whisper, but the system still registered her response. A prerecorded service announcement relayed challenges faced by the assistance line and rescue workers on Trides, begging those calling to try again if disconnected. The automated message cycled through other resources.

Click. The connection ended. She tried again, the cycling repeating ten times. On the eleventh attempt, she expected the telltale click.

"Hello. You're calling regarding a Trides resident?" A new voice, indistinct in gender, asked. Their tone harbored an air of tranquility, with a strain of fatigue clear in the pauses and vocal cracks.

Katya's breath caught. The words circling her head vanished.

"Hello?" the operator prompted.

"Y-yes." Katya sat straighter. "Yes, I'm calling to get the status of"—she fought with a leaden tongue—"Anaïs Cassius. She lives in the Trachep suburbs of Tres. I know … I know her husband didn't make it." New agencies had blared the loss of all Trides's senators, alongside visiting governmental officials and dignitaries.

"And your relationship with Anaïs Cassius?"

"I'm—" Katya bit down on her lower lip when a sob threatened to hunch her entire body. The words "I'm her sister" barreled forward, but they couldn't leave her mouth. She swallowed them, tears leaking down her face. "I-I'm a close friend, a business associate." Her throat threatened to close off with each word.

"I'm sorry," the voice sounded properly apologetic. "At this time, we're only releasing statuses to verified family members."

Katya didn't answer, her fist pressed into her mouth. I'm her sister. Tears obscured her vision.

"Ma'am? Ma'am, I think they plan to have an official database available in three to five months. Ma'am?"

"Of-of course." I'm her sister. Her face contorted painfully, and she sobbed into her hand. "Thank. You."

She disconnected the call and curled in on herself. With trembling hands, she massaged her face. What other option did she have? She couldn't call Pa—her eyes flew open. He would have no way to know she'd left Trides safely. She clenched her hair between her fingers. She couldn't contact him, even if she suspected his minders would be preoccupied. She couldn't reach out to her older brothers, couldn't draw them in. She'd—she bit her lower lip, this time drawing blood—she'd already dragged Anaïs into it, and it had possibly gotten her killed.

No. Her arms tightened around her frame. That was ego. It'd been the festivities, the visiting dignitaries, and the relay that had drawn Plasovern. She repeated this to herself in unison with the corner of her mind that spewed Strom's and Bodil's threats. Strom definitely had a file on her, possibly even knew her sister lived on Trides, but this wasn't a message to her—that it had impacted her came as a bonus. Their intent, as always, was to stab the eagle's heart.

Katya wiped her face with her sleeve. How had they gotten through? The interceptor flashed to the forefront of her mind. She sucked in air, wincing at the twinge in her lungs. The tremors set in. She had …

"Station to *Pollux*," a voice like ice water cut through her darkening thoughts. "Fueling's complete. Clear out."

Sure enough, a green light flickered on the viewscreen. SMR-13 specialized strictly in fuel with no habitation and had heightened its security … her simply sitting after fueling had probably stirred concerns.

She activated the com. "Copy station. Detaching in five."

She couldn't blame their diligence. Being attached to the station unsettled her and dredged up reports of past station attacks by Plasovern. It was too tempting of a target. Pulling from the station, she warmed the FTL engine and set course. To Mramor. A heaviness cloaked her frame with the thought.

Once underway, Katya slipped from the cockpit and headed to Mina's room. The girl had become absorbed in the news reports.

Outside the room, she knocked, but when no answer came, she entered. Mina laid curled in a cocoon of blankets on the floor. A pile of the ship's thin white pillows poked out from beneath her. The teen's focus never broke from the display before her. Another newscast.

"Ereago has returned to Magistrate hands after a multipronged attack broke Plasovern strongholds."

Sotiris, who rested his head on Mina's hip, shifted, giving Katya his full attention and a toothy smile. She shot him a small one in return, though she didn't feel it. She continued across the space to the display.

"Other operations are underway in the Fringe. A public campaign is being run on Skogarld, Varis, and Aedelsten to root out any funding sources for Plasovern. There has been an uptick of violence on Tizzet, but the Brek's support is expected to stem future acts of sectarian violence."

Katya rubbed her hand across her face, thinking of Izem and Kahina. What had become of them? Had they put their plans into motion, or would they shelve them now that Strom had created an inferno?

The voice droned on until Katya clicked off the stream. "There. It's not healthy to just sit and listen." Sure, the signal would die as they pulled away from civilization, but it was time to break the fixation, the ongoing horror show.

"Anaïs?" Mina asked, not moving from the floor.

"It'll be months before we know."

Mina brought her knees up, showing no signs of wanting to leave the floor.

Pinching her nose's bridge, Katya fought for words; however, she found none. She turned from the blank screen and froze. Pink loomed against the white sheets on Mina's stripped-down bed. The pink knitting needles and equally pink yarn. The knitting project that'd been abandoned on Trides had grown an inch or two. The stitches were uneven. Mina's prosthetic hand had struggled to maintain consistency; nevertheless, it was progress. Anaïs would have been so pleased. The ache in her chest returned. Would have. A bitter taste swept into her mouth. *Could* still be. Hope remained for now. And to keep its kindling intact, she blocked the twisted remains of Trides's capital from her mind. She wouldn't give up on her sister.

"Get up," she said, steel returning to her voice.

Mina didn't even blink. "Why?"

Katya swallowed the acidic taste in her mouth. "We're not wallowing. Get up."

The teen bristled at her tone and tightened her hold on the surrounding blankets.

"Up!" Katya poked Mina with her boot-clad foot, not letting up even as her target tried to evade—not even after earning Sotiris's glower for disturbing his pillow. The boy stalked away and flopped into an unused lower bunk.

"We're alive." Katya bit out. "We're still on the outs with the Magistrate, and I've pissed off Plasovern. We're not crumbling now. So get up."

"I don't want to!"

"No one ever wants to," Katya pressed, tugging one blanket away. "But we do it, anyway. No matter how many times we get knocked down, you and I are going to get back up." She ripped another one away. "And now? We can't sit still. I'm going to teach you some self-defense. Something I should've done a long time ago."

On Reznic. On the run with Rein besides giving Mina the stun gun. She'd believed too much in her own ability to protect Mina—and where had that gotten the girl? No, she wasn't a girl anymore. She was an equal partner in this dire game, and Katya should have realized it months ago. The minute they'd deserted. Her age had only ever been an excuse. Strom hadn't been wrong about that. Age didn't matter, not to Plasovern and not even to the Magistrate when it came to traitors.

"Meet me in the cargo hold. We'll start in ten minutes."

Mina lurched upward. "What good does self-defense do when they have bombs?!"

"Plasovern is many." Katya hefted Sotiris from his perch after deciding he could watch. "And not all of them have bombs. For those, you'll need to know how to hold your own with or without a firearm."

She left the girl with that and moved to the cargo hold. There, she placed Sotiris to the side before working through stretches. Moving felt good, offered an opportunity to forget the cloud of uncertainty plaguing her. A smile flirted with her face when she caught Sotiris trying to replicate her stretches, sometimes losing his balance before hopping about to regain it. She'd become so engrossed with his antics she missed Mina joining them. The teen wore loose sweats, the same she slept in.

It was time to break the funk … for both of them.

"Stretch, and then we'll get started."

Seeing Mina's half-assed efforts, Katya stepped forward and guided her to deepen her stretches.

Adjusting the teen's side lunge, Katya began. "If you're confronted by Plasovern agents, never let them take you to a secondary location. It's better to stand and fight where you are rather than where they're comfortable. Trust me, in a lose-lose situation, it's better to be taken by rank-and-file Magistrate soldiers than either Plasovern or Elites."

Mina grunted as she reached for her ankles, stretching her back. "Better?" She snorted. "I don't think so."

"Ideally, avoid all of them. But I'm talking about worst-case scenarios. The grunts are bound to be humanoid with humanoid scruples. Elites are often removed from them and usually more predatory." She winked at Sotiris. "Most of them."

Mina rose from her stretch and waited.

"No kiddie gloves," Katya continued. "You get your wish. I'm treating you like an adult, and I won't hold back."

She entered a loose posture, rolling her shoulders as she did so. "In an ideal world, you'd be able to evade and blend into your surroundings, never having to engage. Always pay attention to your surroundings, dredge up all the instincts you had before ship life. Everything Reznic imparted."

Memories of Reznic flared in Katya's mind: she and Valens wearing civvies at bars among the world's residents. Despite being off the clock, they had constantly scanned their surroundings, knowing they were targets even outside of Magistrate blue.

"No matter where you are, always have an escape route. Mentally mark items that can aid your retreat," Katya continued while widening her stance. "But today, we're talking worst-case scenarios, meaning engagement. Now, I want you to attack me."

Mina stiffened, her eyebrows lifting. "What?" She breathed the word. While days ago she might have been more than willing, she'd calmed enough to know what she would be attacking: a soldier with years of martial arts training.

"You heard me." With four fingers, she waved the teen toward her. "No kiddie gloves. Now come!"

Hesitation was her only answer, and Katya almost used that to drive home another lesson. But then Mina rocked forward, rushing her. Clumsy. With only a swipe of her foot, Katya sent the girl toppling hard to the metal floor. She yelped when she hit.

"The most important lesson I can impart on you is this: Always take control." Katya offered Mina her hand and pulled her up. "Don't cede control to your opponent. The moment you do, you die. How did I take control?"

"You cheated!"

"No." Katya crossed her arms in front of her chest. "There's no cheating in life or death; you use whatever means are available. Here, I used your momentum against you. Something to keep in mind when your opponent is larger than you. Go for the knees; they're the best point to throw off balance. If your opponent is coming at you recklessly, like you did me, you'll be able to topple them with the slightest of kick."

Mina ducked her reddening face.

"If your opponent isn't rushing you or has already invaded your space, go for the weak parts of the body."

"Nose?"

"It'll work. Eyes are also good." Katya pushed Mina's chin with two fingers, forcing it to the side. "Any part that brings control back to you. You have an advantage with a prosthetic. If your opponent isn't aware of it, they won't be expecting power behind it."

She highlighted other target points. Then she worked Mina through different frontal attacks and ways to turn them to her favor, either by attacking weak points built into a humanoid body or turning momentum and an opponent's own weight against them. They'd carried on for a good hour until Mina heaved for air and staggered to her feet after Katya had twisted her arm until she'd buckled. The teen's hair was even more of a tangled mess than it had been because of the constant grappling.

"I think that's good enough for today." Katya's own heart rate raced by this point, and she wanted a shower. "We'll work on attacks coming from behind. Once we have the basics down, I can train you in the tenets of Copre an. I noticed Plasovern uses it, so you'll have a better idea of what to expect."

Mina's eyes glowed at that, even rubbing her hands together.

"It's for worst-case scenarios only," Katya intoned. "We don't have allies or safe holds. You're not engaging to win. You'll be using it to get away."

"Run away, you mean," Mina muttered.

"Yes." Katya gestured to their surroundings. "Which brings us back to the first lesson. Always know your surroundings. Always have an exit. As soon as you have an opening, remove yourself from the situation."

She crossed the space to a wide-eyed Sotiris, who'd sat through the lesson aptly watching them, gasping each time Mina hit the floor before leaning forward each time she rose.

"Come on you." He blinked at her words and tensed. "No," she muttered, "I'm not teaching you." Yet.

His arms wrapped around her neck as she rested him on her hip. She faced Mina, who winced as she stretched her left arm, which Katya had wrenched badly. Mina, despite being right-handed, had so divorced herself from the prosthetic that she relied on her weaker left throughout the exercise. Or perhaps she'd been worried she would hurt Katya if she didn't.

"Stretch out thoroughly." Katya clapped the girl's shoulder. "Eat. Enjoy the signals while they last, maybe watch a movie instead of the news."

"And you?"

"I'll shower and monitor the cockpit for a while." She started to the ladder but stopped short of it. "I'll be training you in the engine room. It's a struggle for me to take on both, and"—her neck corded—"if something happened to me, you need to know."

Mina's fists clenched, and she likely mentally counted the remaining doses. They both knew they were cutting it close.

"I'm lessening them," Katya said. "I don't know if it'll be enough, or if … or if he'll be able to reach out." Her gaze drifted up to the catwalk. "If we divert our course, we can reach the Cresnee Wormhole. It'd be both out of the way while also being a shortcut. Shave off maybe a week."

"What if the doctor can't help or turns us in?"

"We'll deal with it then." Possibly flee into a neutral system and hope to pass under the radar or receive asylum. She kissed Sotiris's cheek before moving him to her back to climb the ladder. From the top, she called, "But we'll get through."

She then slipped into her quarters, playing with Sotiris and toys until he became enthralled enough for her to shower. She'd been reusing the same clothes repeatedly, unable to bring herself to open the bag Anaïs had prepared for her, but …

She unzipped the duffle bag and dumped its contents of thick sweaters and durable pants, all dark in color. She bit her lip upon finding a wad of Magistrate hard currency. Always a giver who never acknowledged "no."

Lessons in self-defense and the engine room operations continued right up to their arrival at Cresnee Wormhole, where freighters lined up for their turn to cross over to the Fuusi Arm. A C-Class warship oversaw the traffic and served as a deterrent to pirates. Wormholes had proven too tempting for them in the past, as freighters were often easy pickings without heavy armaments.

The *Pollux* had too little in the way of defense, though it at least had some maneuverability. More punch would be ideal, especially as they entered the Fuusi Arm, a wilder slice of space infested by pirates.

The cockpit door opened behind her.

"The engine room?" Katya asked as Mina hobbled into the cockpit.

Mina groaned and sank into the communications station's seat, rubbing her calves. While she'd built up muscles over their sessions, Katya kept finding new ones the teen hadn't realized she'd had. She hadn't moved Mina into the realm of Copre an. The teen had to accept the prosthetic before Katya would. Her mindset would also have to shift from offensive to defensive. Mina was too aggressive, trying to one-up Katya only to give the older woman copious flaws for exploitation.

"I saw nothing amiss." Mina exhaled. "And I'm not going back down the ladder again. My legs are killing me, and I have a massive bruise on my bone." She pointed to her left shin.

"Bones don't bruise."

Mina puffed out her cheeks before reiterating: "On my bone!"

Katya sighed, though her chest filled with warmth. The familiarity, the ease. It sparked hope their relationship had begun to heal. After Jomsborg's rocky departure, she hadn't envisioned their current level of partnership.

"If you insist."

"I do," the teen muttered.

The line shifted forward. Their turn through the wormhole would come soon.

"About Mramor ..." Mina rocked toward her. "What's the plan?"

Katya closed her eyes, a wave of fatigue hitting her. She needed to reestablish a sleep pattern even while not tethered to the ebb and flow of a station or planet. Substituting actual sleep for catnaps was a rookie mistake, and she wasn't getting any younger. *"You need to take care of yourself."* Where was the time for that? She had no place in the galaxy where she could unwind, address everything.

"Katya?"

She shook herself from her thoughts. "We'll land at the spaceport in Velikaya Stolitsa. The scientist—Aleksandr—lives somewhere in the city's orbit, but it seems he's scrubbed his address. So, we'll have to ask around." She tapped her slate, resting on the helm. "I've found some universities that have published articles by him. We'll start there." She shrugged. "He's an unknown factor. If it wasn't for those articles, it'd be like he didn't exist. If he rejects us, we'll leave Mramor immediately. If that route is blocked, we'll have to find another way off-world."

"Hmm ..." the teen hummed.

"A lot of moving pieces," Katya said before taking more control of the helm. Their turn had arrived.

Following the scripted transmission, Katya maneuvered the *Pollux* through the jump gate while cutting the still badly scratched exterior viewscreen—she'd never cared for wormhole innards. Three. Two. One. Momentum picked up, with the data relaying their progress until they broke out in the Fuusi Arm. One week to go.

Setting the autopilot with a heading to Mramor, Katya stood, taking her slate in hand. "Let's get some sleep. We both need to start an eight-hour sleep rotation to sync with Velikaya Stolitsa's time zone."

"Aye, aye!"

Katya rolled her eyes, but a smile tugged at her lips. "I'm going to check on Sotiris. Don't stay up too much longer."

Mina's head bobbed, but she said nothing. The moment the door closed, Katya heard the communications system fire up. Her smile broadened when it tuned to music. Steps in the right direction. She continued to her room, where

Sotiris waited. He would need another dose, even as the amount grew minuscule. A week and she was down to three vials. Lomonosov had better not be a dead end.

In her shoes, Katya curled her toes. So cold, so detached. She pressed her back into a wall for grounding while her eyes traced familiar ivy wallpaper before landing on the closed door. Light poked from its bottom, the sole source of illumination in the hallway. She squinted. Something—she couldn't place it—roiled her stomach. A wrongness. A wispy sheen of purple overlay clouded her vision. In moments, her surroundings winked out, then solidified. She knew this hallway despite the removal of its clutter, which had screamed hoarder of antiquities and curiosities.

Katya dug her nails into the coarse wallpaper, inhaling. It wasn't enough. She spared another glance at the door … her father's study.

She'd wanted to tell him something.

A derisive snort drove her attention to the far end of the hallway. Her oldest sister, Zhihao, stood wearing an academy uniform, arms crossed. Katya dropped her gaze, unable to meet the other's. They were wearing the same uniform. Tingles webbed their way across Katya's scalp. Something … something had gone horribly wrong. Yet she couldn't place what.

Katya swiped at her eyes with her cardigan's sleeve.

"You're wasting your time."

She bristled at her oldest sister's comment. Sweat trickling down her brow, Katya forced herself from the wall's support. "It doesn't concern you." The words tasted weird, familiar—wrong.

Zhihao chuckled, covering her mouth as was her habit. "He's never going to approve. All that effort put into cultivating that brain of yours, and you're going to throw it away to be a meathead. He'll never approve."

Katya ground her teeth and faced her sister, her tightly spun bun, the air of ease.

"The galaxy is literally open to us, Cassiuses, and you choose to be a cog. What do you hope to achieve? Propaganda's just that: empty. You'll squander your life 'making your difference.'"

"It doesn't concern you," Katya reiterated through clenched teeth.

"But I'm your older sister, aren't I? It's my job to watch over you." Her smile morphed into a thin line. "Isn't that what sisters are supposed to do?"

Katya stepped back into the wall as if slapped. A combination of nausea and dizziness threatened to pull her to the floor. Why? Her left hand shook, even as she clenched it into a fist.

"What do you think she felt?"

"Who?" Katya whispered.

The elder tilted her head. "Don't ask dense questions, little *Squeak*." She emphasized the nickname's first part while transforming its latter into almost a click. "And all because you didn't think. Not now, not when you got in over your head."

Zhihao shrugged and turned away. "The saddest thing is she died for no reason." She glanced back at Katya. "You'll never find who you're looking for. You know that. Deep in your bones. And you'll regret this decision for as long as you live."

Katya's shaking legs threatened to buckle. Would she regret it? Images, amorphous, churned and were snuffed out before they could ever be realized. Her hand shot to her temple, applying pressure. She hissed as the film rippled, rocketing pain through her skull akin to a six-inch nail being driven in. The hall broke apart.

"Absolutely not!"

She flinched, trying to gather her bearings. She stood before her father's desk, the antiquated clock ticking in time with her heart's rapid beats, which echoed in her head. She felt hot, cold, every bit aching like a fever. She gripped the chair's arms. When had she sat?

Her father skidded his chair back when he shot to his feet, fists colliding with his desk. Katya flinched. The light cast a ghastly pallor on his lined face and quivering lips. She couldn't recognize him for the man he was.

"You have such a brilliant mind, yet you want to waste it doing this?"

Sweat crept from her brow. "I …" she tried to verbalize why only it wouldn't form. Why did she want to enlist? The reasons had been so clear; now, they were like smoke wafting through her fingers.

"I could get you into any university. You'd make so much more of yourself there, not be taken from post to post. Please, at least visit some campuses, explore some of the programs," he implored, sounding more himself. He reached for something. "Do it for your sister." He extended a framed photo of Anaïs, and Katya muffled a scream when confronted by her sister's bloodied corpse. "Doesn't she deserve to live?"

Katya recoiled, moaning into her hand. "I-I didn't—"

"Didn't you?" Her father soothed. "Didn't you give them a tool? Didn't you assist them? Piece by piece, and here we are … and she is not. You know that. Deep in your core."

Nausea swelled, and she wretched.

"If you'd only listened, she'd still be alive."

Katya looked past the chair's back to the closed study door. The light shifted darker, murkier.

"Would you deny her life? No? All for a dead end that'll ultimately bring you nothing but pain? What good did you ever really achieve?"

A rattling breath escaped her lips, and she turned back to her now-balding father. The pain rippled through her head. "So-tir-is …"

Her father blinked at her.

Katya rocked to her feet. The office was a blank canvas, not her father's study, which was always filled to the brim with books and trinkets. This conversation wasn't theirs. Yes, he'd been hurt, disappointed, but he'd never raised his voice. And Anaïs ... her heartbeat escalated.

"Sotiris!" she screamed. "Let me go!"

She tore through the space and fought with the door, mentally keeping up the racket. Anything that might get her released from his control. There was still enough of the drug. Mina should notice before long and dose him. A kernel of doubt settled in the pit of her stomach. If the teen was still able to do that.

"Let me go!" she shouted into the hallway, which had grown cavernous. She ran, hitting at the walls. "Let go!" Tears kept coming with the waves of blinding pain.

Katya plunged on, not knowing to what end. She banged until the walls dispersed, and snow enveloped her legs, slowing her momentum and threatening to topple her. Coldness sank into her skin, but she wouldn't buckle.

"You've had your fun. Let me go!" Flecks of red dotted the snow. "I'm not afraid of that anymore."

A lie. She was lying. She didn't want to see further. She didn't want to go to her supposed home. It petrified her. "Sotiris!"

Hard, cold metal rubbed against her cheek, a rivet cutting into it. She wiped her nose with a shaking hand. A torn chuckle followed. She'd never been so relieved to see snot in her life. She lifted herself. A view screen, consoles ... she was in the cockpit. They were dead in space. Had she ...

Sotiris. She ran, bumping into the wall and almost falling as she raced for the drug. She measured a greater dose than she'd been giving him and then rushed to her quarters. With each step, the tendrils pulled at her mind, messing with her vision. He wasn't in their room. Spinning, she stumbled to Mina's room, where she found the teen splayed on the floor.

Damn it.

Gritting her teeth, Katya backpedaled, tripping on the door frame and skinning her knees after she struck the floor. She pulled forward using her hands and lurched to her feet, her vision wavering.

"Not now," she hissed. Where was he?

She leaned into the wall for balance while she sought Sotiris's hiding spot in every room on the main level. She winced, her vision growing muddled. She held on to a spare bathroom doorframe as she peered in. It was the same old game, and Sotiris never picked the same place twice.

She blundered through the other two vacant crew rooms. The pressure ballooned in her brain, sight and thought wavering. In her ears, screams erupted, muddled and distorted. She hissed after clipping her knee against a chair.

The lower level then. At least with the locking mechanism in place, he wouldn't get into the engine room, not again.

One rung at a time, Katya descended, only to land on her butt after misjudging a step. The room swayed as her vertigo roared, drawing forth an overpowering desire to retch. All that followed was dry heaving and mucus collecting in her throat.

Damn it.

Crawling forward, she collapsed, consciousness being snuffed by the screaming in her ears. Katya dug into her lower lip and propelled herself forward. She tore through the hold's nooks and crannies, even impossible spaces where she doubted he would fit. As she proceeded, phantoms bumped and touched her, eliciting goose bumps.

Another trenchant assault drove her to the floor. It amounted to a tantrum, with Sotiris railing against the threat to his playtime she represented. Unlike other four-year-olds—she bit hard into the side of her mouth—he could kill. She wormed her way to the storage hatches along the far wall. One was ajar.

She threw herself at it, ignoring her battered legs. Inside, a piece of pale skin glared against the dark polished metal; she jabbed the needle in, pushing the plunger before collapsing.

Wails, red, hot ones, startled her from her stupor. Sotiris thrashed. The howls echoed in the cramped hatch. Gasping, Katya buried her face into her hands. Each scream caused her to wince. Terming it as play was shortchanging what they were doing to him. They were robbing him of something so woven into his species; it was akin to taking a white-hot poker to another species' eyes.

A frantic, bloodcurdling shriek covered Sotiris's own.

"Mina."

Katya scuttled to the ladder, her balance still shot. Above, the teen roared hysterically. When Katya reached her room, she found the teen contorting on the ground, digging the heels of her palms into her eyes.

"Mina!" Katya grabbed her and forced her hands from her face. "Look at me. Breathe. It's OK."

Now, yes. Later … she had her doubts. They couldn't dilute the dosage any further, and she didn't know how long they'd been dead in space.

She hoisted Mina into a sitting position and stroked her back in a circular pattern while the teen gulped and sobbed. When it decreased to a whimper, Katya fetched water for the teen from the small bathroom. Chilly water poured from the faucet. The system had gone into energy savings. Not good.

Upon returning, Katya discovered Mina had taken to rocking. The teen locked her arms around her legs, which pressed into her chest.

"Drink," Katya said, holding the glass to Mina's lips.

For a moment, she did nothing. But when Katya tilted the glass, she sipped. The action of drinking slowed her breaths, her frame calming as well.

"Do you remember anything?" Katya asked.

Mina faced away, lines forming on her face. Her eyes were puffy. "Cold. There was something—someone—I don't know." She ran her hands through her hair and kept them there, puffs of plum hair with faint hints of her natural brown sticking out between her fingers. "I can't—I just remember cold, the fear." Her breaths rattled in her chest. Then Mina wiped her nose. "I can't remember. Just *so* much fear."

Katya resumed rubbing the teen's back while stretching for a blanket on the bed. She draped it over the girl's shoulders.

It mirrored Katya's own first experience. A flash in the pan. The clarity and imagery had faded, leaving only slight impressions ... at least most had. The snow, meanwhile, clung to her psyche, just like the figure and fear did for Mina. But it had always been an element of memory sitting too close to the surface. The rest, whatever had been, evaporated. This time, however, the conglomeration of memory and falsities remained vivid. She could clearly recall her eldest sister, the academy uniform she wouldn't have been wearing since she'd moved on to university. Katya refused to think of her father.

The difference between the first and second occurrences ... The brain scans in the Plasovern files loomed. She couldn't truly understand them without the guidance of a medical professional. But she knew Sotiris had irrevocably altered her.

Had it enabled her resistance? Possibly. But the realness kept her ensnared. *"Doesn't she deserve to live?"* Katya choked against her gag reflex and the tears that threatened to burst. Dabbing at her face, she forced herself to her feet.

"I'll prepare some tea. It'll help calm you further."

"So—" Mina licked her lips. "Sotiris. Where is he?"

"Having a temper tantrum." She rushed to add, "I've dosed him enough that he won't do it again."

"Until we're out."

"Until we're out," Katya agreed.

Silence hung between them, neither moving.

Mina lowered her gaze, and her left hand tightened on the blanket. "We know nothing about the Oneiroi." She toyed with the blanket's edge. "Because he's humanoid, perhaps we're ascribing characteristics that simply aren't in his genes. We like to think he's harmlessly playing, trying to speak with us in his way. But what if it's more like how an apex predator plays?"

A chill traversed Katya's spine. In her mind, Strom smiled, describing Sotiris's mother as a cat amused by a mouse that had dared to address her. Yet, Strom had hoped to negotiate with the Oneiroi. If that weren't a possibility, she wouldn't have bothered with Sotiris. But more so, Katya knew it in her own bones. Each smile, the way he replicated their movements, the cuddles ... He was simply a child speaking a different language.

"He's not malicious." Katya's tone drew Mina's focus from the floor. "At four, even a human child doesn't fully understand right from wrong. It's why the Oneiroi had to seek the Magistrate's help. Even they couldn't avoid" — she gestured aimlessly through the air — "this."

No, it had dragged them not only to an endless sleep but also into the Magistrate's endless conflicts. If that hadn't been an act of love, she didn't know what else it could've been.

"It may not be right to impose certain emotions on him," she continued, "even if he's humanoid, but ... he wouldn't have killed the Jar'rasks if some part of him wasn't fond of us."

"And he could still kill us with that fondness."

"He could." Katya stepped toward the door. "And undoubtedly children with the defect have accidentally killed their own parents." She swallowed. "In one way, we're carrying the fate of an entire species. If we can find a viable alternative, it'll change circumstances for the Oneiroi."

A sharp intake of breath issued behind her, the idea new to the teen. Just as it had been to Katya before she'd seen Plasovern's files. She'd suffered from tunnel vision centered on Sotiris. But hadn't that always been one of her greatest flaws? She tore after one goal; consequences be damned.

"I'll make the tea," Mina said. "We shouldn't let him wander. He might find a better hiding spot."

Katya snorted. "He's good at doing that."

She opened the door, but Mina called her before she could leave.

"How far behind schedule are we?"

"I don't know. But since we aren't starving, I'd wager it's just hours."

Katya fetched Sotiris from the hold and dragged him, hiccupping, to the cockpit, where she reactivated all the systems that'd gone dormant. Her hunch had been accurate. They'd only lost four hours to Sotiris's high jinks. She had probably cut the engines to prevent them from drifting into something the moment she'd detected Sotiris's powers in use.

She resumed their progress while calculating dosages—avoiding the dream apparently mined from her subconscious. She angled toward Sotiris, who lay on the floor, his near-pupilless eyes glaring at the ceiling. The surrounding skin was puffy, a mottled purple.

"It's your nature," she muttered, drawing those eyes. "But we can't keep this going." She didn't even want to think how they would carry on if Mramor proved to be a shot in the brown. Could they carry on? No.

Swallowing hard against the knot in her throat, Katya resumed her work at the helm.

Minutes later, Mina entered with a teapot and cups on a tray. She'd gathered ration bars and artfully spread them into fans around the teacups, creating, depending on perspective, rising or setting suns.

She said something in a language not embedded in Katya's head, drawing a raised brow from her.

"It's 'let's eat' in Moscanov," Mina said, settling the tray on the communications console while giving Sotiris a wide berth. "I downloaded a learning program and am trying to learn as many basic phrases as possible, but it's difficult. It's nothing like the Magistrate tongue, and I'm not sure my pronunciation's any good."

"Don't look at me." Katya snorted. "I don't speak a word of it."

"Does our contact speak Magistrate?" Mina asked, her forehead bunching together.

Katya shrugged. "I'm assuming, yes. He's submitted scholarly articles, and there weren't any notes about translation." But there had been notes of edits for clarity. Still, she doubted there would be massive understanding gaps.

Mina poured cups for both of them. They each ate a ration bar while enjoying the tea in silence. Sotiris toddled to the tray and set about rearranging the remaining ration bars. He stuck one in his mouth only to return it to the tray, face caught in a scowl. He sauntered over to Mina—the master food giver.

Katya noted how the teen's breath caught and how she marginally flinched as Sotiris leaned toward her. Sotiris mouthed at Mina, unperturbed, unable to comprehend her stalling.

"Will there be enough?" Mina asked, not moving to fix Sotiris a more palatable meal.

"Just." Katya clicked her tongue against her teeth, drawing the toddler's attention from the teen. After setting aside the teacup, she outstretched her hands and curled her fingers, beckoning him to her. "I'll make a couple jumps to shave some time. I just don't want to eat too far into our reserves in case we really need to use them." As Sotiris's fingers wrapped around hers, Katya pulled him into her lap.

Mina clasped her hands, knuckles paling on her left one. "And do you have a plan if … if we don't find help?"

The vice tightened on Katya's chest. "Yes." She stood preparing to take Sotiris to the galley. She stopped before the door and said, "Watch things up here. I think you could use a break from our little Elite."

"You didn't say what the plan was." A knot along the teen's jawline popped up beneath her round cheeks.

"It's not out of lack of trust, Mina," Katya said. "I just can't bring myself to say it. For now, just keep watch."

Mina's mouth formed a grim line, but she made no further comment, allowing Katya to leave the cockpit. As she walked to the galley, she rested her cheek against Sotiris's soft black curls. It had an overly floral aroma from the powdered shampoo they'd found onboard after suffering dirty hair for days because of the facial clay. Her hold tightened on the boy, and she swallowed so hard against the tears that welled up.

She imagined Rein would feel vindicated beyond the grave.

CHAPTER FIFTEEN

Mramor truly resembled a marble, with its swirls of white, swatches of greens and browns, and varying shades of blues, showcasing rivers, lakes, and the deepest oceans. Its varied climates of haves and have-nots had resulted in bloody colonial spats over resources and strategic points. The country of her birth had harbored an ever-present appetite for warm-weather ports, pushing it to a disastrous war, which preceded the war that broke it. Casting aside muddy history, Katya had to admit the planet was a beautiful marble, indeed. A true match for its name.

Still, its picturesque tranquility did little to relieve the storm brewing in her. Katya tapped against the helm, a staccato rhythm with no semblance to any song she knew, and stared. Even if she couldn't remember the planet, it triggered a strong flight instinct. Her chest ached. Focus. With a deep inhale, she throttled the tapping.

Her homeworld. It'd been a simple factoid all her life; however, Meracus Domus had long supplanted it. Yet, as she took in every detail, including the light traffic moving in and out of its atmosphere, questions she'd thought dead rose. She rubbed at irritated eyes. She wondered if someone on the world below had once loved her ... if anyone were still alive to remember her.

"Are you all right?" Mina asked from the communications station.

"Have we received notice?"

The teen frowned, cheeks puffing out. "Yes, sending the clearance now."

Katya pointedly ignored the attention, each movement under a microscope searching for fractures. And there they were, splayed like broken glass. Instead, she immersed herself in the instructions being distributed to the helm.

Some cities were visible from space, but the planet lacked the buildup of more industrial worlds. Katya eased the freighter into the planet's controlled traffic patterns, which were sparse. A New Acquisition, Mramor lagged behind others in technology. The Magistrate had imposed regulations to guide its development, a slow, deliberate plod into modernity. It had then built spaceports and relays, forever tying it to the republic. Other advancements in infrastructure followed. The Magistrate had poured funds into projects aimed at improving productivity and bolstering Mramor's individual economies, many of which the war had devastated.

However, some had sidestepped those measures, despising being hobbled. And that was how you got Mramorian pirates, Katya supposed. Ex-soldiers, disenfranchised, snatched older defunct models of salvaged corsairs and somehow made a lucrative run, shaking down easily cowed merchants. Said funds then purchased better vessels, and the scale of their conquests exploded. No matter how the Magistrate stomped, it hadn't crushed them all.

Katya kept their course in line with Velikaya Stolitsa, the former capital of the Moscanov Imperiya. Where she'd been found. Her jaw ached. That discovery's circumstances, however, remained nebulous. At least, the on-world officials hadn't bothered to record any details before flinging her across the galaxy.

The city featured circular planning, a lingering design from an era when walls served as a defense. Within, a forked river passed through and created a waved appearance in the city's stacked buildings. The port was moderate in size, yet the largest on the planet. During the war, Katya understood the Magistrate had sent observers. Among the opulent, gemmed existence of the Moscanov emperor and his domain, they'd found their foothold. That fondness had translated to establishing operations from the old empire that'd crumbled rather than the less tumultuous nations that had also existed on-world. Or perhaps they had felt they had no choice if they wanted to save Moscanov from itself.

As they reached cloud level, snow swirled, washing out the viewscreen. It held no impact, the ship's navigation and computers guiding them unhindered to their designated spot.

Once parked, Katya started the cool-down sequence between answering the port official's digital inquiries to their stay. She opted to sound like a tourist interested in picking over the remains of a sub-modern culture that, just decades ago, had fought with gunpowder. It drew no red flags.

At least the port was open, unlike Gilga's Kazeeme port. If faced with stringent entry criteria, she doubted they would pass. But the Ka'ze people had been isolationists before joining the Magistrate; in fact, they'd approached the table first to maintain it through the induction process. Like the Sarchin, they'd seen the writing on the wall and had chosen to join rather than be absorbed—if not by the Magistrate then by the Medzeci Empire.

"Lock down," Katya instructed Mina. "Then put on your warmest clothes. If we don't make lead way before dark, we'll come back to the ship and spend the night." There was no sense burning through money when they lacked a steady income.

"Where do we start?"

"There's a scientific academy." Katya lifted Sotiris into her arms, groaning lowly. He was getting too big. "I'm hoping it'll have means for contacting him."

"If not?"

"There are a couple other universities."

She banked on him maintaining some relationship with at least one, given his scholarly articles published through them. Surely, one had a better contact method than the man's unchecked message system.

Sotiris wiggled in her grasp, regaining the ground. She sighed; she knew a lost cause when she saw one, and at least, he didn't take off. As they walked to their quarters, he stayed a step in front of her.

Inside, she layered herself in clothing: a thick coat, two layers of sweaters, a faux fur-lined hat, scarf, gloves, and boots. She kept Sotiris as light as possible without screaming neglect to natives who didn't need to know about his Oneiroi biology. He issued a chorus of noes as she did, puffing out his cheeks and trying to undo everything each step of the way. She had to grab his hand several times while packing her slate, some funds, and Sotiris's spare shades, the simple plastic ones with tinted lenses.

His resistance continued until they, along with Mina, exited the *Pollux*. And then he stopped. Every movement ceased as he took in the snow, mouth parted, enraptured. He held out a mitten-clad hand to catch it. Katya wondered if it snowed on Demos Oneiroi. It was a frigid world, so likely yes, but one couldn't assume with alien planets.

"Come along!" She clapped her gloved hand against her leg.

The boy, however, remained riveted, bending to scoop up the snow, packing it together between his hands. Katya stopped him before he could eat it and all the chemicals compiled within.

"He really likes snow," Mina muttered, dusting some from her shoulders. "I could do without." She huffed, following Katya toward the port's terminal. "It never snowed on Reznic. One thing we had going for us."

Katya merely rolled her eyes. "You'll live."

She grabbed Sotiris, who tried to stumble back, not wanting to enter the heated building. Despite her reassurances that they would be outside again, he either didn't understand or didn't believe her. Mina swooped in the help, pushing Sotiris from behind. Inside, he complained, but didn't pry free of Katya's hand.

Being in the early afternoon, the terminal bustled. Both products and people were being moved, some going somewhere on-world while others went abroad. A mix of Mramorian port officials and Magistrate officers mingled throughout the unadorned, sterile interior, overseeing everything and inspecting all items. Like on Trides, a strident customs gauntlet greeted them: bags emptied, contents inspected with a fine-tooth comb, and a full-body scan. Only this agent, who spoke in a heavily accented voice, interrogated their purposes and planned movements more thoroughly. Katya's vague sight-seeing itinerary drew suspicion to the man's wizened face. While he scowled, he let them pass after a few pointed questions. They then had to walk through a scanner before reaching the building's center. Like any other spaceport, it offered benches. These seat offerings mingled between multistory statues of bold, stylized people. The equally stylized murals contrasted with the vast white walls from the ceiling.

Katya strained her neck, peering at the faces above. The mural's subjects struck heroic poses, then as they stepped into a section with a circular, concave ceiling, a midnight blue sky with patterned suns, stars, and crescent moons took over. The gold paint glittered as they walked through.

A hand seized Katya's coat and tugged backward, drawing a loud grunt from her and throwing her off-balance. A frail woman, who carried deep stress lines and the lingering aroma of medicine and decay, accosted her. Her thin, knobby fingers clawed at Katya's coat while she blubbered in Moscanov. Katya stumbled and lost her grip on Sotiris's hand. The old woman with her frayed braids didn't let up, her grip twisting the coat's fabric.

Mina gawked.

"Ma'am," Katya bit out. She attempted to seize her attacker's boney wrists. "Please let—"

The woman's grip never broke, and she cried into the fabric before spouting Moscanov.

"Mina!" Katya yelped.

The teen blinked from her stupor, though she remained transfixed by the Mramorian.

"Mina!"

The teen tugged at the woman's sleeve, then attempted something in Moscanov.

The woman frowned, the wrinkles around her mouth deepening, before spewing a heap of words. Mina's eyebrows shot up while her wide eyes lifted to Katya.

"I only know a few basic phrases," Mina squeaked. "I can't translate that. And I think my 'Where's the bathroom' failed."

Katya liberated her arm and toppled backward, almost on to Sotiris, who had tears streaking his cheeks. The woman followed the movement, trying to reclaim her sleeve. The action halted when another woman, wearing an official spaceport uniform, intervened.

She shouted at the woman in Moscanov, waving her away with her hands. They traded words in a lightning fashion. In the end, the old woman, scowling, slunk away, casting glares back.

"Forgive her," the port officer said, her voice not as accented as Katya had expected. She looked to be in her early twenties, meaning she'd been born after induction. "She waits here every day and harasses people. We put her out, but she just keeps coming back."

"What did she want?" Katya asked, still catching her breath.

"Her daughter. She targets anyone with the right hair color and same rough facial structure."

"Doesn't she know what her daughter looks like?" Mina muttered.

The woman shrugged. "I don't think she's seen her since she was a toddler."

Katya stiffened, a chill coursing through her frame. She shook it off, clasping Sotiris's hand again. "Thank you for your help."

There was no point in interacting more with the official. It would only create opportunities for missteps and draw further attention—and they'd already received too much. She began to shuffle Sotiris and Mina away from the scene.

"Are you from Mramor?" the port officer called as they set off.

Drawing short, Katya mulled responses before settling on one. "At one time, I suppose I was."

The port official smiled. "Welcome home then."

Swallowing, Katya guided her charges farther into the port. The ceiling continued its elaborate star motif. She wondered how long it'd taken to complete. As they moved into a massive hallway, it faded from midnight blue to black with silver stars. Beside her, Mina took a sharp intake and stopped.

Katya froze as her gaze leveled. An array of photos lined both sides, floor to ceiling, in places overlapping. In stark black and white, children gazed from tattered, fading prints.

Was she among them?

Katya swiveled from face to face while a chill emanated from her very core. She walked, absorbing each one while tugging Sotiris along.

Had they all been orphans?

Her stomach sank, a burr of a thought sticking. The woman who'd accosted her had been waiting for her daughter for thirty years. Gripping the strap of her satchel, she stared. Dead parents didn't hang photos of their children in hopes of someone recognizing them. Some small voice asked: Was someone waiting for her? Had her father known this? That not all the orphans were that? Her chest constricted. She pulled forward, eyes darting over the images for any female child with similar features. A sign. An implausible task amongst the sea of faces.

A hand — Mina's — grabbed her shoulder. "Katya?"

Katya jerked at the gentle gesture, but it freed her from her spiraling train of thought.

"Y-yes?" She choked on the word and dabbed her gloved hand against wet eyes.

"Are you all right?"

Sotiris yanked hard, and Katya realized she'd been holding his hand in a vice-like grip.

"Sorry," she muttered, loosening her hold. "I'm fine. I—" She swallowed hard around a knot that'd formed. "We have places to be." And thirty years removed ... There was no point digging now. Not when Sotiris needed more medicine.

Mina fell into step behind Katya as they resumed their path, passing a group of elderly Mramorians in the hallways, fixing photos that'd peeled from the wall. The group of four women, all clad in bulky clothes, inspected them out of the corner of their eyes but didn't descend on them like the previous woman had. They did, however, converse in Moscanov. A low steady stream lined—going from their narrowed gazes—with suspicion. Katya hefted Sotiris on to her hip before picking up her pace, rushing through the long hallway until she barreled into a spacious room with a series of multistory windows. Katya still felt like she was being smothered.

She didn't slow until they were once again out in the snow, where she stopped and fought to catch her breath. It came in ragged huffs, creating puffs of clouds in front of her face. She grimaced when the moisture froze to her skin.

"You're really not," Mina said beside her. She crossed her arms as she scrutinized Katya with narrowing eyes. "What was that back there?"

Pressing her lips together, Katya faced the lines of hovercars, which swerved up to the curb while others left. In the background, Velikaya Stolitsa loomed with its unique architecture and colorful facades. The hovercars themselves were a hodgepodge of new and antiquated models probably imported shortly after induction, going off their rust patches.

"A shrine to children long gone," Katya said under her breath.

"Gone as in gone? Or, gone as in dead?"

She shrugged in response and waved to a taxi. But as she talked about the destination—one institute that'd published a paper for Lomonosov—it became apparent the driver didn't speak an ounce of Magistrate. She shuffled down the line, reaching the fourth cabbie who understood her destination, or at least he nodded and repeated what she said in his heavily accented voice. He also leaped from the cab, his six-foot frame towering over her as she took her and Mina's satchels and shoved them into the trunk.

"We go now," he said, taking none of Katya's further questions to ensure there were no misunderstandings. "Yes, go now."

Peeved, Katya slipped into the backseat, settling Sotiris between her and Mina. Without even signaling, the driver sped up, causing all three of them to lurch to the right. He revved the car through the spaceport's drive and on to the street without stopping.

Mina yelped as she gripped the door's armrest with white knuckles. Meanwhile, Katya slid into the door after their drive initiated another hasty turn. In her arms, Sotiris stiffened, his fingers pressing into her arm. Outside, horns blared. However, once on a highway, the driver steadied their pace and fell in line with traffic.

Katya exhaled, though the crowded traffic surrounding them kept her muscles clenched. Much of Velikaya Stolitsa's traffic remained ground based. Pressing her sweaty face to the ice-cold window, she found the clear blue sky almost whimsical. When had she ever seen a sky so clear of air traffic? Never.

The city blared the Magistrate's slow development plan with its mix of hundreds-of-years-old buildings and pockets of high-tech infrastructure. As they sped past, Katya even caught a few buildings clearly built within the past thirty years in a Magistrate manner. Official Magistrate offices, she guessed. They passed one with its white columns and front of synth glass that caught the sun. It was a sore thumb along the side of the road, pale compared to its colorful neighbors, packed so close together they resembled walls with windows and doors.

Katya leaned back as the cabbie traveled on a narrow street for a mile or so, then gunned on to a six-lane road.

Mina cursed in Reznic, her prosthetic grip denting the armrest's cheap metal. Katya would pay extra for that, she briefly thought, even as she fought queasiness.

Sotiris tugged at her shirt and pointed against the glass to the massive river just beyond the road's stone and metal safety rail. The Black River, Katya recalled. Its fork wound its way through the western portion of the city, and as it did, its turbulent course created white rapids. There were also several canals in the capital.

"River," she told him.

In front, the driver clicked his tongue against his teeth when a Magistrate armored vehicle drove by in one of the distant opposing lanes, dwarfing the surrounding cars. Another followed. Then a third.

"Has there been an uptick of military traffic?" Katya asked, meeting the man's eyes in the rearview mirror.

He returned the gaze in the mirror. Through his rough beard, she caught a muscle clench along his jaw. He shrugged. "Since madness, yes." He swallowed. "But I know not these things." His focus reverted to the road.

Mina relaxed as traffic slowed, and she folded her hands in her lap. Still, her foot tapped against the floorboard. The teen seemed transfixed by the city's statues as snow swirled around them. Katya had to admit it was like being trapped in a snow globe. Surreal, beautiful. Though, a few bullet-riddled statues and pedestals featuring only legs marred the illusion.

The sidewalks were as busy as the roadway. People, utterly unfazed by the snow, carried on, ducking into different businesses. She briefly caught sight of two men with long gray beards drinking from mugs on a bench. Snow formed mounds on their fur caps, but they didn't budge.

"Hey, sir," Mina said, leaning into the gap between the driver and passenger side seats.

The cabbie grunted while turning on to a quieter street.

But Mina didn't give up. "At the spaceport, there was a hallway with photos of children. What was that about?"

Katya's spine straightened. The cabbie once again looked at them in the mirror, lingering on Katya, before he shrugged.

Mina's lower lip protruded, and she whipped back to the window, one finger drumming against her prosthetic hand.

The buildings grew more residential. In fact, the apartment buildings towered over them. Katya wondered if the population had rebounded enough in the years after the war and purges or if large swathes of the units remained vacant.

Children—four boys and a girl—rushed from the street ahead of them. One boy hefted the ball they'd been playing with over his head, sending the others a stony glare. The girl, who had to be no more than five, wore her hair in an all-too-familiar fashion—the bangs cut long on the edges, two braids dangling before wrapping around a bun. And thinking about it now, Katya realized all the women she'd seen had their hair braided into a tight knot bun, no loops. That, or they wore their hair in a crown braid.

Warmth flooded her face. Her father had saddled her with a young girl's haircut. What would the surrounding people have thought if she'd returned sporting the hairstyle? How massive of a blunder would that have been?

A woman shouted at the children from a front step, gesturing for them to come to her. One set of words struck Katya, chilling her bones. Their sound triggered something within.

"Institute is just ahead," the driver said.

Wrapping her arms around Sotiris, Katya abandoned the sensation percolating in the back of her skull.

The cab turned on to a drive, and a sprawling snow-covered lawn soon surrounded them. Pockets of trees dotted its expanse. Severe dark-colored statues stood vigil, one holding a book. Brick hardscapes created flowerbeds, which were currently bare. A couple of young women in long-flowing skirts sat on one, talking. Beyond a few others strolling, the area was relatively quiet, leaving Katya to wonder if there was a holiday.

And at the drive's end, a massive sandstone structure with far-reaching towers waited. When the taxi pulled in front of it, the driver rolled down his window as they got out, and Katya settled the fee after she and Mina fetched their satchels.

Leaning down, she asked the man, "Can you wait?"

He stroked his silvered beard while the corners of his lips twitched. Then he shrugged. "If you pay."

She gave him a little extra and gathered Mina and Sotiris, leading them toward the massive concrete staircase to the main entrance.

"Why don't I stay outside with Sotiris," Mina said before they even reached the first step. "He'll fuss if we force him inside." She nudged her head toward Sotiris, who'd bent to play in the snow.

His expression seized Katya's heart. The wide, toothy smile. The bubbly nonsense coming out of his mouth. He was in his natural element.

"Stay mindful of your surroundings," Katya said before climbing the stairs. She paused at the top, watching as Mina directed Sotiris further off to the side to untouched snow. A smile spread across her face, ignoring concerns.

Opening the large oak door, she sucked in her breath when heat struck her. Around her, exquisite marble spanned the large grand entrance on both its floor and walls. Above, elaborate designs in gold decorated its vaulted ceiling, and amidst it, a crystal and gold-encrusted chandelier hung. Her lips parted while she stood enamored by it and the way it sparkled.

"It originally was in palace," a young woman in a brown suit said to Katya's right. Her accent was less than the cabbie's had been.

Katya placed the woman as being in her twenties. She zoned in on her metal nameplate — Belova.

The university official clenched a slate in her hands. "Can I help you?"

"I'm hoping" — suspicion reared its head the moment the other woman heard Katya's own accent — "this institute might have a way to get in touch with Aleksandr Lomonosov."

The woman snorted before descending into a full-out bout of laughter. She moved her rose-gold braid to her other shoulder. "Lomonosov is not associated with this institute," she said between chuckles that refused to die. "He does not associate with anyone. He is ghost."

"But he's published articles here."

"He sends them whenever he pleases." The woman shrugged and pressed the slate to her bosom. "He reaches out to us, not vice versa."

"Surely, the institute has some means to at least watch him, given his skills."

"One does not monitor ghost."

"Is there anyone here that might have the means to contact him?"

Belova lifted an eyebrow. "Not likely."

Katya pressed her lips together, tempted to seek someone else with the institute. She didn't know what role this woman played here. She could just be pushing Katya off, but given what she knew of Lomonosov, she assumed the woman was being honest. With slumping shoulders, she turned to leave.

"Why seek Lomonosov?" the woman asked.

Katya swallowed and glanced back at her. After hesitation, she said, "His research into genetic ailments. There's a disease that's passed through my family, and I was hoping he might help my son."

The woman pursed her lips, giving all appearance of being done with Katya. She flipped up her slate and scrolled, tapping to select something. Then she spun the slate around and extended it so Katya could see a list of maybe five names.

"If you need geneticists who aren't ghosts, I recommend these," she said, her eyes still partially cloaked. "If you want excellent ones, go to Core. Mramor does not compare."

Blood rushing to her face, Katya recorded the names in her own slate before thanking the woman and retreating from the institute. She paused at the top of the stairs and inhaled Mramor's frigidness. This did not bode well. A shout—too familiar—reached her from a distance, and Katya barreled down the stairs. Mina.

She cleared a small decorative wall to find the teen in a screaming match with a group of three boys. They pushed the teen, throwing off her balance and landing her in the snow. Katya's cheeks flamed. The girl hadn't listened at all. In a panic, she scanned for Sotiris and found him standing near a tree, mittens over his mouth.

"Hey!" Katya screamed. "What's happening here?"

Mina whipped her reddened face toward Katya. The young men, probably students of the institute, stiffened at her tone—no, the Magistrate-ness of it. She channeled her past as a soldier into her walk.

"I said, what's going on?" she barked again.

Mina rocketed to her feet and clenched her fists. "They're hurting it!"

Past her, she saw it. A small cat-like creature battered and hunched in the snow, a crude rope tied to its neck like a leash. It cowered as if that alone would save it from more cruelty.

"We don't want problems," one stammered.

And neither did she, but she glanced at Mina's hardened brown eyes and Sotiris's tear-streaked face, and she ground out with drill sergeant flare, "Then drop the leash and run."

The fact they did stirred so many questions in Katya's mind. "Grab the cat; we need to move."

Mina did as told, scooping up the quivering creature. Katya did the same to Sotiris and rushed them back to the cab. The cabbie dropped his newspaper against the steering console, glancing over their frazzled appearance before landing on the cat. His eyes then locked on Katya, his bushy brows knitting together.

"I apologize," she said. "Please let—"

The man rolled his eyes before snapping his fingers and extending his flattened palm. Grinding her teeth, Katya added currency to it. The man nodded and faced forward while they slipped in to the backseat, now more cramped with their bags and the cat, which was the size of a small dog. It purred a broken melody and shuddered for the effort.

The cab pulled forward, and they continued to the following colleges, where they met the same results. Lomonosov was a ghost, one who worked under copious layers that obfuscated anything but cursory personal facts. Vacating the last such stops, Katya wanted to yank her hair out by the roots. She had, however, received an address to an attorney he kept on retainer. However, she wouldn't be surprised if they communicated by some form of carrier bird—that was how isolationist Lomonosov had proven to be so far. And she had only obtained this little kernel of knowledge as the sun lowered. She estimated maybe four or five hours of light were left. At least the snow had stopped.

Sliding the attorney's address into her pocket, she slipped back into the cab where Mina, Sotiris, and their new companion waited. The pair had been well-occupied by the creature. She noted as she closed the door that the cat flinched and bunched in Mina's lap. As Katya buckled in, Sotiris curled against her. She sighed, frustration swelling before it ebbed. Exhaling through her nose, she laced her fingers through Sotiris's curls. They would find Lomonosov.

"Where to now?" the cabbie asked. He'd never complained as they dragged him around the city and to its suburbs. Not as long as she doled out hard Magistrate cash.

Exhaling, she ran her hand through her hair and leaned into the seat. Sotiris draped himself over her lap so he could rest his head against her left leg. His eyelid appeared to be growing quite heavy. With one and a quarter vials left, they were out of time.

Her hand stilled in Sotiris's hair. She couldn't keep running around the city, especially as most offices would be closed. She considered eating in the city, but funds were finite. The interest from the scrap on Barsaa would hold them for a time, as would the money Anaïs had slipped into her bag, but she couldn't afford to throw money around. If they had to leave Mramor in a hurry, fuel would consume it in a matter of two months without income.

Mina leaned toward her, giving her best puppy-dog face.

Katya clicked her tongue against her front teeth and caved. "Where can we get a bite to eat?"

"With fiend?" He seemed to ponder this for a while before deciding: "Moshchonaya Ulitsa. It is not too far from spaceport. Plenty of restaurants. And you can walk back to the port. Surely, one will let you in with fiend."

Fiend? Her gaze dropped to the cat. That didn't bode well, though Mina had determined some monster had stripped the poor thing of its claws and teeth. It was hardly a threat. Rather than press, she gave her consent, and the man drove them to said location, a street converted to pedestrian use. For that reason, they had to walk to their destination from a parallel street.

Katya held Sotiris's hand while paying the man well. Mina cradled the fiend in her arms and waited. She smiled at the girl, then maneuvered along the sidewalk toward a lit narrow alleyway. Young lovers made use of the benches lining it, leaning into each other, whispering sweet nothings, and stealing kisses. One pair shared a cigarette. The walls had been painted in a bright array of colors and conflicting images that bled into each other: faces, animals, flowers, wording—a general mismatch. One couldn't look away, every inch packed with a confectionery of art. It reminded her of the street art on Reznic in a way; only Mramor's artists favored bolder lines. However, both on Mramor and Reznic, the artists shared the same love of color and movement.

She stopped in front of a black-and-white print that'd been tacked into the sandstone. It featured a man decked out in a dress uniform complete with a billed service cap that Katya recognized from the old photos she'd seen in history books about Mramor's war. Across his eyes, the artist had diagonally slashed vibrant red paint, sending splatters across the blank white surrounding the man. Under a well-manicured mustache with a slight curl, he smiled lopsidedly. The soldier held one hand in a Mramorian saint pose: two fingers extended to the sky, while the thumb burrowed itself between the hand's last two fingers. Examining it, it was very much like the icons she'd seen from Mramor that'd come as part of a traveling exhibit to Meracus Domus. Her father had dragged her and her siblings to it. At the print's bottom, a bold text declared something in red paint.

A hand slammed against the poster and then ripped it from the wall. A red-faced man in an official-looking uniform, not Magistrate in design, glowered at her and shouted in Moscanov. He bore down on her, and Katya pushed Sotiris behind her.

"I can't understand—"

It was like the flip of a switch. The man retreated and instead beset the youth in the alley, who bolted. He gave chase.

"What was that about?" Mina whispered.

"I don't know." Katya's gut tightened. "But I suspect there are undercurrents the Magistrate"—or some internal force, given the man's non-Magistrate uniform—"is trying to clamp down on."

Katya kept them moving until they reached the mouth of the alleyway, which opened to an old-fashioned cobblestone road. Sotiris squeezed her hand, and she returned it. With the darkening sky, his sunglasses looked misplaced, but there was nothing for that. She sighed when fat flakes fell again.

Great.

Still, Katya lifted her face. It had a magical effect amidst the strands of lights dangled in a zigzag pattern over the pedestrian walkway. She maneuvered Mina to the side to avoid a large group of people going in the opposite direction. They belted out songs at the top of their lungs and reeked of alcohol. It was far too early to be that drunk.

"Let me know when you see a place you want to try," Katya told Mina. "Tame your taste buds, nothing too fancy."

"Have you had Mramorian food?"

"Presumably, when I was a kid." Katya deadpanned. She didn't know if she could count her father's later efforts as authentic, but he had tried.

Music exited one establishment, an upbeat, raucous tune composed of stringed instruments. The area, despite the cold, hummed with chatter—a mix of languages—and music, but not so much to be overwhelming.

"Torvarish!" a man's voice called from a connecting pathway's umbra.

When Katya shifted toward it, she froze, the blood in her veins chilling. Captain Zakhar, their unlikely savior, who'd given them a tow. An associate of Hedda Strom's to some degree. Once again, she put Sotiris behind her and reached for her pack, forgetting the weapon's absence.

The motion, however, caused the man to thrust his hands in the air, palms facing her. Very little had changed about his appearance in the months since they'd parted. Still overweight, his hair might be a tad bit grayer, and his beard fuller.

"Now, now," he said in that baritone voice. It lacked the overly thick accent he'd used months ago. "There is no need for that."

Katya didn't relax, keeping her hand next to the satchel. He didn't know she was unarmed. From behind, Mina pressed into her, the cat still in her arms.

"Don't move." She packed venom into the words.

But Zakhar only snorted. "You've been asking after Aleksandr Lomonosov, no?"

"What's it to you?"

"I am Zakhar Kozlov. His attorney." He rolled two fingers in the air. "I handle all of Aleksandr's affairs."

She could only blink at him, recalling the name that'd been scratched on to paper. Lomonosov's attorney. The freighter captain who'd been working with Plasovern. Only he'd never really been a captain, had he?

He didn't wait for her to respond. "The only way to Aleksandr is through me. No doubt through your inquiries, you have discovered he is private" — he waved one hand as if cooling a pastry while still keeping both in the air — "person. You will never find him."

The snow swirled around them. A few people walking by shot them dirty looks but made no moves to intercede.

"Are you still in touch with Strom?" Katya asked, lowering her voice.

"Answer to long story: no." He lowered his hands but kept them seen and inactive. "Her way is not our way forward. But she is also not woman I want gunning for me, so I drop line that boy she didn't want me to know about is still very much alive and where I saw him. We parted on good terms, but communications are not had."

Katya mulled this over. Mina had clenched her coat, no doubt wanting them to run for it. But they were out of time. Yes, Zakhar had ties to Plasovern, but that meant he was not friendly to the Magistrate. So by extension, Lomonosov likely wasn't either. This was their one shot.

Zakhar came forward, going around them. Katya swiveled to keep her back from being exposed to him.

"Come." He waved them to follow him. "I'll feed you and tell you of Aleksandr. You can even bring your little taiga fiend with you." He chuckled. "To have such companions will make for an interesting night."

Katya didn't move; instead, she stared a hole into the man's back. Her mind raced through his potential motives and traps. There was only one carrot: more medicine for Sotiris. It was enough.

Sighing, Zakhar faced her, now a good foot ahead of them. "Besides, you still owe me that drink."

CHAPTER SIXTEEN

Just down the street, Zakhar ushered them into a narrow establishment with a pair of dingy windows bookending an oak door. The heat from a roaring fire in a hearth halfway into the building greeted them, along with plucks on a three-string instrument. Melancholic, yet quick, the musician coated the space in music; every so many notes, a discordant stroke stirred the hair on the back of Katya's neck. It bounced off the establishment's coffered ceiling.

Pulling Sotiris close, as three patrons passed them to depart, Katya knew the boy wouldn't last long with the heat. The thought vanished when she realized the rough-looking patrons had abandoned their endeavors to follow their every move with a wary and hard light.

Zakhar belted something in Moscanov, and the attention dispersed; however, Katya still caught surreptitious glances cast in their direction. Their newish associate paid no mind and approached a large woman clad in a long-sweeping black dress and white apron embroidered with colorful flowers. Her expression soured at Zakhar, and she dusted her hands across the front of the apron as he spoke. Her only answer was a grunt before walking around the counter and opening the door to the backroom. Zakhar followed her, and Katya and her charges did likewise.

Like the dining room, the backroom was dimly lit, except where a cook worked, chopping vegetables. The knife stilled as she stopped to glower at them. Her eyes landed on Zakhar, and she chuckled and resumed her work.

Their hostess took them past a massive rack of casks and paused in front of one with wine. This she unlatched from the wall, swinging it forward to expose a concealed room.

"What are our odds of being murdered in there?" Mina whispered into Katya's ear.

She shushed the girl before following Zakhar in. Like the outer room, its walls were brick, but more cobwebs clung to its corners. The rough slated wood that composed its ceiling would probably give splinters if touched. It was a tight space, the bulk of it filled by a sturdy oak table with intricate carvings vining the legs and baseboards. In the far corner, a miniature, old-fashioned cast-iron stove provided the only heat source; red coals brightened and faded behind its grill. It made the space comfortable.

"Paka has long history of hosting *lively* discourse." Zakhar pulled back three chairs for Katya, Mina, and Sotiris before sitting on his own. "It seems like centuries ago when a few other enlightened intellectuals and myself would discuss current events and like."

"Hiding in a backroom," Katya said while scooting her chair forward.

"When criticizing the emperor who is autocrat"—he shrugged—"it is best not to be overheard."

Ah. Her fingers curled into her palm as she wondered what degree of revolutionary he'd been. The type that had engulfed not only the autocracy in flame but swelled to consume ordinary people? Something in between? Or something other? There had been so many factions within the Moscanov Imperiya.

A forlorn smile shaped Zakhar's lips, almost as if reading her thoughts. "We were many things, Ms. Cassius. But in our hearts, a desire for free thought and speech bound us." Lines deepened across his brow. "But with all passions and ideas, there were … divergences."

Images of the burning world and the remains of people dragged from their homes and sent shivers. "And your own?" She needed to know who she was dealing with.

Beside her, Mina leaned forward, likely to better see Zakhar—for what good it would do her. The man before them closed himself off as if he were playing a card game, sealing away any emotion.

"I have been many things," he spoke the words slowly. He wove his fingers together, his brow knitting together. "When I was quite young, I shared many things with Hedda Strom. I believed true revolution could only be achieved with the removal of the emperor and other government officials who supported the autocracy. By any means, but mostly bombs. Crude things that required tossing into carriages and cars. Some would explode early. But all we achieved was severe curbing of any existing freedoms. A complete crackdown. It found my younger brother hanged for it. And I, I lost my taste for that particular violence."

"But not revolution."

"No." His jaw set. "You have never lived in an autocracy. The emperor, the entire system, it needed to fade to history. People were starving, being murdered by the state for thoughts. There was never such a thing as a good emperor: inept, cruel, regressive—the list of failing stretches for miles. But with age, I understood change needed made not through bombs in radicals' hands but through the people's will." Chuckling, he leaned into the chair's back. "Which could not be stirred by little expeditionary excursions to the *people* that some of our out-of-touch members undertook. Conditions had to stir the change."

The light in the man's eyes lacked the maddening fervor Strom's often possessed, but it burned no less brightly. Reformed terrorist, then—she shifted in her seat— and her sole gateway to Lomonosov. She gripped her pant leg with her shaking left hand. She'd already taken a catastrophic misstep with Plasovern in desperation. And now ... And now, a sinking sensation enveloped her frame.

Swallowing, she turned to darker waters. "And your role during the purges?"

"I was member of the provisional government. When I backed it and what it was trying to achieve, I lost face with segments of my former compatriots." His eyes lowered to the table. "Circumstances became as they were. It all went 'puff' like smoke. I was fortunate to keep my life."

"And Lomonosov's role?"

The corners of the man's lips dipped. "He was child."

The word hung in the air with unexpected weight. The moment didn't last as their hostess flounced through the open door, a tray resting on her hip. She slid it, laden with food, on to the table, followed by the second tray of beer she'd been holding in the air. There was no other drink offering.

"Do you have anything nonalcoholic for her?" Katya asked, pointing to Mina.

The woman scrunched her face and inspected Mina. "Is something wrong with girl?" She hacked deep in her throat, scowl deepening. "Is she princess? It is good enough for princess."

Further insistences met eye-rolling and clucking before the proprietress barreled from the room, shutting the hidden—heavily insulated—door behind her. Katya imagined a knocking inspector would never suspect a room hid behind it.

Clattering returned her attention to Zakhar, who filled the bowls with a yellow soup featuring vegetable strands. He also gave each person a thick bread slice before he served the main course, a meat dish. Once finished, Zakhar moved to the stove and lifted a kettle from a cabinet. He shook it, head bobbing at the slush of water. Setting it on the stovetop, he returned to the table.

"Do not fret. Your girl can drink tea. Ulyana is proud woman. Particularly proud of her stout. She will hear no insult toward it. The deposed emperor *himself* needn't have imported stout had he sampled hers." He settled into his chair with a chuckle. "She also makes the best cabbage soup. It really warms one on snowy night."

Katya sipped the soup from her spoon and found a delightful blend of beef broth mingled with hearty vegetables. She drank from the goblet, and her lips puckered. A strong stout, indeed.

Spoons clattered against ceramic with the occasional slurp. Around it, Zakhar peppered them with questions, which Katya helmed. Mina, for once, caught the tension and didn't enter the conversation, which amounted to a fishing expedition. He was digging, trying to gather a fuller picture of their time since they had initially met and then parted ways on Barsaa. When Katya kept giving vague answers, he engaged Mina directly.

"And what did you think of the Medzeci Empire, Ms. Mina?"

Katya's jaw tightened. Despite steering the conversation from Plasovern, he knew. Mina looked at her, her wind-knocked expression all Zakhar needed to learn he'd hit the mark. Swallowing, Katya addressed the man.

"I thought you didn't speak with Strom anymore."

"I don't." He pushed his empty bowl to the side, moving to the main dish. "I only have to see boy awake for so long to know. What other options were there but Strom?"

"Apparently, Lomonosov." Anger blossomed in her chest. At that moment on Barsaa, he could have saved them from the months with Plasovern.

His grip loosened around his fork, facial features softening. "I told you, you should come home." He raised his free hand as her mouth opened. "I could not bring the boy here, not without risking losing everything. The time was not right."

"The time for *what*?" Katya ground out as dread blanketed her shoulders like a heavy cloak. The effect her accent had on Mramorians, the significant military presence, particularly the home guard, the poster—she almost didn't want his answer.

The moment shattered when Mina sputtered and hacked.

Katya spun to face her, concern shifting to annoyance as the teen hastily replaced the beer goblet to the table. Mina's already-strawberry-red complexion deepened under Katya's glare, and she ducked her head, tears forming as the coughing fit didn't ease. From between Katya and Mina, Sotiris stared at the teen with saucer-sized eyes.

"Strong, huh?" Katya deadpanned.

Zakhar smirked. "It is *acquired* taste."

The girl eyed the goblet.

"Wait for the tea," Katya pressed.

Mina snapped. "I-I'm … fine."

With a soft chuckle, Zakhar rose again and removed the boiling kettle from the stove. He drew a tray, four cups, a teapot, and a canister from a cabinet to the side. He then prepared tea as if it were a meditation, each move slow, deliberate.

"I'm finishing it," Mina muttered while toying with the goblet.

Katya shook her head, but let the teen make her mistake because she would regret it in the morning.

Meanwhile, Zakhar returned and situated the teapot, a shiny red, on the table between them. "I have been poor host," he said. "We have not even finished our meals. Eat now, talk business after. I will explain all. It is important since Aleksandr's involved."

And there, the rock settled in her gut. Still, she continued eating while helping Sotiris, who otherwise had picked at his food. His eyelids were growing heavy, and with the hour, he would succumb to sleep soon. Further down, Mina nursed her stout, occasionally sipping from the teacup as a palette cleanser. Their four-legged friend had curled up under the table, munching on a finely shredded piece of meat Mina had given it. Pity welled within Katya as the creature gummed at the meat, unable to do anything else.

In the silence, Katya savored the meat dish and its rich sauce until her stomach felt it might burst. It'd been a long time since she'd been so full. She stretched her legs under the table and sipped her tea. Mina, unused to alcohol, let alone one touting an alcoholic content that the stout did, had slumped against the table, snoring. Sotiris had slipped from his chair and curled next to the cat, fingers looped through its long fur.

"Ah, now the adults can talk," Zakhar said, his own teacup nestled in his hands. "Tea in hand just like the old days."

"The old days really aren't that removed, are they?"

He smiled ruefully around his cup's lip, dragging out his sip. "No, I suppose not. Once a revolutionary, always one. Only this time, I seek to expel a foreign entity and banish former brethren from their seats of power."

"And Strom's ways couldn't accomplish that?"

Sighing, he closed his eyes. "Her ways had already failed Old Imperiya. All they brought were bloody change and the almost realization of different type of authoritarianism." He rested the teacup on the table but didn't relinquish it. "Though perhaps, no almost. The terror never stopped. It merely changed tactics."

"How so?"

"In the chaos of war and revolution, an outsider like the Magistrate couldn't make heads or tails. Their clumsy stabilization efforts gave Alyypriliv too much power. After all, it had seen it was losing its standing to its fellow *true* revolutionaries in Sila. So it requested intervention." He took the teapot and poured more of the black tea first into her cup before his. "This gesture garnered Magistrate support. They leaned on Alyypriliv, and while the Magistrate brought other countries into the planetary governance, Alyypriliv moved in shadows to ensure it maintained a majority, often by wiping out opposition."

"And the Magistrate did nothing?"

"Even a giant only has so many eyes." Zakhar rotated his cup. "Assassinations, disappearances, arsons … Alyypriliv has convenient scapegoat: Sila." He chuckled. "It forced internal rebranding on Sila's part to Tsitadel, the true revolution's citadel, under assault. But to Magistrate, Sila is still Sila."

Drinking deeply from her cup, Katya mulled over the information being dumped on her. One only had to look at Ereago to know how badly the Magistrate could misstep in its intervention. "The spaceport pictures didn't raise any eyebrows?"

A mirthless laugh left Zakhar. "Shooting women en masse is bad look for colonial overlords to see." He shrugged. "And Magistrate was keen to look other way. Best not be reminded of complicity in mass kidnapping, especially when there are no plans to strip Magistrate households of their gains."

She refused to entertain the thought forming in her mind—just as she dismissed the twisting in her gut. She still saw her father torn with worry. She hoped the name *Pollux* in the Magistrate's meticulous records would give some comfort. Despite the warm ceramic between them, her fingers felt icy.

"If you'd only listened, she would still be alive." Sotiris's phantasm stirred. Would he think she'd led them there?

Some of her turmoil must have filtered to her face because Zakhar asked, "How old were you?"

She shook her head. "That's—I love my family. I'm not—it's not this. All I can think about is my sister. She was on Trides. In the Trachep community around the capital."

"We have heard much about Trides's situation, but I cannot say I have heard of that place." He bowed his head. "I am sorry."

She bobbed her head, no words springing to mind. Her nails dug into the ceramic.

"It's spreading like wildfire," Zakhar continued. "The Magistrate is rampaging like it has a demon on its back, and Plasovern and other enterprising sorts are making their moves."

"Like you," she stated.

"Yes. It is now or never. Being in Fringe and in Fuusi Arm will be hard task for Magistrate."

A hard task for the Magistrate seemed practically impossible for Mramor. Thirty years. That was all that removed the planet from its world war, where countries tore into each other's throats. That didn't heal in decades. She wasn't even factoring in the divisions that had sunk several of those former countries.

"And when the others don't join you? What will you do then?"

A knowing smile answered her. "I have not been slacking these past years, my dear. It is amazing what common enemies can do. Those who do not go along, what can they hope to do if they lose the sky?"

"And how do you even hope to take the sky from the Magistrate?"

He shrugged. "That is too early to discuss."

"You've already shared a lot."

Zakhar chuckled. "Who will you tell? You are a woman with too few options, and that boy"—he pointed to where Sotiris slept under the table—"has you over a barrel. Aleksandr is heavily involved in this endeavor as our resident inventor. If you tattle, you lose your shot at helping the boy. Because I do not doubt Aleksandr could help him."

She was over a barrel. One and a quarter vials, and Sotiris needed another dose yet tonight. But no matter how calmly Zakhar spoke over his vague plans, she only saw catastrophe and another hole for her to bury herself in.

"What is your goal?"

"Mramor ruled by Mramor."

Katya hummed, her index finger tapped against her cup's lip. "Which Mramor?"

His eyelids lifted, and he sat straighter in his chair. His lips twitched as if trying to formulate a response. She didn't allow it.

"Mramor didn't exist until the Magistrate's intervention. When you remove that moderating force, will this coalition you've established hold together? Or will old grudges destroy it? I'm an outsider, but I can't help but think when pressure is applied—as the Magistrate will— your coalition will crumble."

"But that is when we are at our best." He stood and stretched his back. "We are stubborn creatures no matter country."

"And when the common enemy is removed?"

He sobered. "Perhaps in the shared shedding of blood, we will avoid the power struggle, especially if our groundwork holds." He set their empty cups and the teapot on to the tray. "Our meetings have been productive, and I enjoy seeing the passion not only in us old birds but in our youth. Ms. Cassius, this is not something pursued blindly."

He clucked as he returned from depositing the tray back to the cabinet beside the stove. "But now, it is late. I'll return you to spaceport and can pick you up in morning ... if you still wish to meet with Aleksandr."

She pushed back her chair. "I will meet with him." What choice was there really at this point?

Zakhar clapped his hands, startling Mina from her stupor. "Excellent. Tomorrow morning indeed." He doubled back and helped Mina with her coat and to her feet. "It is a distance from city, so I would pack bags, especially if Aleksandr plans to keep you. He's plenty of room. You will be quite comfortable, I assure you."

He supported Mina as they crossed to the hidden door. Katya, meanwhile, gathered a sleeping Sotiris and the taiga fiend's lead. The creature set its baleful embers on her but surrendered to the leash's pressure and scrambled after her. In the hall, Zakhar spoke animatedly with their hostess.

"As always, thank you for your hospitality." He shook her hand before slipping into Moscanov, a parting phrase Katya actually recognized: "Til we meet again."

Zakhar guided them from the establishment, keeping the swaying, staggering Mina in tow. The pedestrian-only Moshvhonaya Ulitsa area remained crowded despite the time. Street performers delighted Magistrate tourists, who surrounded them, clapping along as instructed.

"Do a lot of tourists come?"

"We are popular with Magistrate tourists." Zakhar changed directions into an alleyway lit only by strands of light. "I suspect we are novelty to them."

Snow swirled again in thick flakes. No one had cleared the alley, so the snow crunched beneath their feet. Katya shivered, a prickling sensation covering her scalp. A familiar poster drew her to a stop. The same soldier print, only this time with a topaz swath.

Footsteps punctuated by the snow drew her attention back to Zakhar.

"One of yours?" she asked.

"Another's." He tugged at his beard. "It's grown popular with our youth."

The way his face darkened, lines etching into his forehead and around his eyes ... Was he troubled by this?

"What does it say?"

"I know the Magistrate has no such beliefs, but it is best translated as, 'Give them hell.'" He straightened a dipping Mina. "They mean it to represent everything we've cost ourselves. It is why paint goes through the face. So many were lost. We burned them all." He exhaled sharply. "But I feel it is best not to summon so many ghosts. One person's martyr is another's devil."

His eyes gazed down the alley, not focusing on a single point. "We need to build a Mramor that is divorced from our baser instincts. I will die happy if this can be achieved." He resumed his walk. "Come, we must get you to your ship."

"Why not use the Magistrate Exit Policy?" Katya asked, following his lead.

That drew a chuckle. "How many planets have?"

None.

"We could never get fair votes to push it through. And even if we did, it would not be true independence. It only creates puppet state, one financially and militarily bound on Magistrate. The fine print is burdensome."

He directed them into a nice hovercar on a side street and drove the rest of the way to the spaceport, maybe fifteen minutes away. It would have been less if not for traffic. Pulling along the curb, he stopped and allowed them to exit. Katya shepherded Mina from the car. The teen had regained some of her faculties, at least enough to stand on her own and hold the cat creature's leash. Then Katya returned to lift the sleeping Sotiris when Zakhar cleared his throat.

He glanced to the other side of his car before looking her directly in the eye. "I didn't want to say anything over supper, not with the girl, but Trachep was in blast radius. I have heard no survivors."

She froze; her hand of its own accord sought the car for support. Air grew sparse, and she could only nod her head.

"Take your time to grieve," Zakhar said. "I will not come until around two o'clock. I think it is best we get that boy on whatever medicine he needs. Not only for you but those around him." Through the window, he handed her a small scrap of paper. "My com number. Call me for anything.

Katya nodded again and took the paper. She then stumbled away from the car, Sotiris draped in her arms.

Anaïs … gone.

She swallowed her tears, biting her trembling lip. Mina, still not registering the world around her, took no notice. Katya walked beside her, having the teen drape and arm around her for stability.

A litany of "she's gone" circled through her head. Hollowness accompanied it. She was gone. A foreign concept. She couldn't feel much, just a gaping shock. As she carried Mina's weight, she decided to wait until morning to tell Mina; the girl was in no state for that information. She rested her cheek against the crown of Mina's head, smelling her floral shampoo. For now, one of them could hold on to the delusion.

Thick gray clouds promised snow but had so far held off as Zakhar drove them far out of the city's limits where houses grew far and few in between, replaced by soaring trees that stretched for miles.

Zakhar cleared his throat in what had been a relatively quiet drive, excluding the quiet rambling of a talk radio show in Moscanov. "I warn you. Aleksandr … he is …" He mulled over his words "… eccentric. But he has a good heart."

Katya shifted from the window. "Oh?"

"He can startle people with his enthusiasm."

It reminded her of her father in a way. Touch the right subject, and unaccustomed people might label him eccentric too. She didn't comment further, gaze lowering to Sotiris, who pressed into her side as he played with his Skogarld wildcat. Forehead against the opposite window, Mina absently stroked a very real wildcat. With puffy red eyes, the teen observed the forest and seemed lost in her thoughts. The taiga fiend, which had taken to Mina, sat like a good lapdog, purring with each stroke of the teen's fingers.

"Look!" Sotiris chirped.

Katya's eyes widened as she diverted her attention to Sotiris, who beamed at her, extending his toy. It had a ribbon sewn around its neck that could be tied and untied, and Sotiris had made a simple, lopsided bow.

"Very good." She pecked the crown of his head.

Queasiness rose in her. She needed to put more time into his education—her gaze landed on Mina—both their educations. The craziness around her provided an easy excuse, but she needed to do better. Her chest tightened as she took in Mina's morose brown eyes that lacked the light ordinarily present. She was running out of time there. The girl would be an adult in a flash, then all she could do was offer guidance when sought, but perhaps that was all she could do now. She wouldn't return to Plasovern now, but she also couldn't linger in Katya's shadow. She needed a purpose and goal of her own.

She wrapped her arm around Sotiris and laid her head against the headrest. And he needed to learn basic things: reading, counting, shapes, colors, etc. Basic subjects she hadn't taken the time to teach him.

Circling in the back of her brain was, like Strom had insinuated, her own void of purpose. Beyond the kids, there was no driving force. As a person who had always been driven by ambition—from primary school through her career—it terrified her.

Zakhar fiddled with a com and clicked his tongue off his teeth, muttering something in Moscanov.

Still unarmed—too unwilling to bring the Renmark through security—Katya considered how easy it would be for Zakhar to kill them and deposit their bodies in the forest.

She pressed her lips together before asking, "Is something wrong?"

"Just trying to reach Aleksandr, but I am not getting anywhere."

"Could he be away?"

Zakhar laughed at that, a full-bodied one. "Highly unlikely." He turned on to a rural one-lane road that wound through the forest's umbra, stoking Katya's nerves. "More likely, he's buried in project."

He smiled about that last bit, though Katya noted it vanished as the minutes ticked by and his repeated contact attempts failed. They were twenty minutes along the roadway when they reached a clearing with a driveway and expansive snow-covered lawn. There, Zakhar's attempts grew incessant.

"Are you really his attorney?" Katya asked, leaning her head in the gap between the driver's and passenger's seats.

"Yes!" Zakhar balked. "And I know my client well—"

He yanked at the steering column, tossing Katya into his headrest. Her vision temporarily blackened at the impact. Her mind jumped to various conclusions, namely Zakhar had tried to knock her out. Blindly, she caught the fabric of the man's coat, twisting it. Her brain could barely manage more than that. In the background, Mina screamed while Zakhar was muttering a string of what—not knowing Moscanov—she assumed were curses.

An explosion ripped soil into the air—it pelted the car. Katya dropped her grip on Zakhar and gaped at the turrets that had popped from the ground.

"What—"

Zakhar cut her off. "Keep calling that signal. Do not stop!"

He sped up, abandoning the road. Despite being a hovercar, the ride proved bumpy, throwing Katya's fingers from the com. She pulled her body through the gap to better reach it and kept hitting the call-back button. At the wheel, Zakhar seemed to anticipate the booby traps, staying ahead of them. Still, as he drove, sweat seeped from his brow, his face ashen.

Still patching through the com signal, Katya hissed. "How many times has he almost killed you?"

"I've lost count." His jaw tightened, creaking even, as he swung around another explosive bolt. "Paranoid bast—" The com line went live, and Zakhar unleashed a torrent of Moscanov.

Katya exhaled when the turrets retracted into their hidden housings. "What a greeting."

"He is a paranoid b—" He cut himself off, glancing at Sotiris in the rearview mirror. "He is … paranoid."

Sighing and muttering under his breath, Zakhar returned his vehicle to the drive. He drove the rest of the way, carrying on a conversation in Moscanov over the com until it petered out, and he turned the system off.

At the end of the mile-and-half driveway, a grand palace greeted them.

Katya's jaw loosened as it emerged from the trees. Three stories with railing at its top and a spire—it was massive. Its white columns and arches had been weathered, and their paint was cracking, just like its cheery yellow facade. The homeowner had boarded some windows, and through the crevices, Katya caught broken or missing panes. A shame, as the craftsman had spared no detail in shaping them. The unaffected windows had been closed off with thick curtains, probably velvet. Around the grounds, unkempt evergreens stood clustered together in barren landscaping beds.

The home of a recluse.

"Should we be concerned about him shooting us when we enter?" Katya asked sardonically. Even with the vehicle stopped next to a side entry, likely used by servants, she stayed rooted.

"No, not now. He knows it is me, and I bring a curiosity. He loves curiosities." Zakhar lurched from his seat, his bones creaking. Then he opened her door before ambling over to do likewise for Mina. "You'll have to forgive Aleksandr. He means no harm."

"Hard to tell that to someone who comes foul of those turrets."

"Good thing no one knows where he lives to visit." Zakhar gave a flat smile. "He survived the purges and carries that with him always."

He opened the palace's side door, entering a code into an improvised panel that had been inserted into the mortar, leaving it chipped.

"You don't get to go in through the front door?" Katya asked, ushering Mina, taiga fiend in her arms, and Sotiris toward her. She wanted to keep them close should their host prove to be more unstable than she'd already assumed him to be.

"Oh, it is not some classist slight. Much of the palace is closed off in disrepair. Aleksandr only uses fraction of its space. He has money to renovate but chooses not to." He waved Katya and her charges into a hallway, and as she entered, he added, his tone gravelly, "There is danger in living with too many ghosts."

She raised her brow at this.

The hall led to a kitchen where pots and pans hung from the ceiling alongside herbs. An old, wizened man sat at the table reading an old-fashioned newspaper. Covered bowls surrounded him, as did a patch of flour on the tabletop. The substance had even collected on his jacket's elbows. He grunted at Zakhar's greeting and flipped the page.

They proceeded up a wood staircase, which bore scuff marks from service. At its top, Zakhar popped open a door that blended with the wall on the other side. The residents needn't know the servants existed. The hallway to which it opened was devoid of furniture and adornments. It only harbored an expanse of marble that echoed their steps as they continued. Mina whistled when they entered a high-ceiling room with a large, dangling crystal chandelier. If not for the curtains, it would glisten, casting shimmering light on to the marble.

Katya imagined the room in its heyday: an immaculate table dressed in the finest fabrics, silver, and porcelain; richly upholstered chairs; artwork; and statues. Then, among it all, gemmed nobility moving about in their own finery. The space almost breathed with those haunted memories, its former residents clinging to the room through their absence.

A danger of living with too many ghosts. A passing sensation of stepping on a grave lifted her hair as she treaded behind Zakhar.

She halted and did a quick circle, drinking in the embellished trim and minute details etched into the room. Adopted into the Cassius family, Katya knew grandeur, but this was a distinct style of opulence. Haunting, dead.

"Aleksandr will be on second floor. He has his workspace there," Zakhar said, putting her back on task. "Perhaps once settled, I can give quick tour of rooms not boarded up."

Ahead of them now, Mina proclaimed, "Shit!" The word echoed in the cavernous setting, devoid of furniture and décor.

The girl stood slack-jawed as she faced the grand staircase, which stretched upward. Its white railing popped against the greenish-blue walls. But, Katya supposed, the teen was more taken by the extensively paned, vaulted skylight. Along its bottom, gold leaf designs gleamed under the natural light and glory of a massive crystal chandelier.

Zakhar smiled. "This way."

It was a straight climb to the second floor, which, like the main floor, was a husk of what it'd been. One could spot where portraits and other artwork had hung by the slightly off-color wallpaper and the mini holes in the plaster. A few pieces of furniture remained. Their elegantly carved and curled legs poked out from beneath the heavy white cloth draped over them.

Ahead, light, an electric sort, spilled across the floor from a room with a cracked door.

"Oi! Aleksandr!" Zakhar bellowed before lashing out at the other man in Moscanov.

A man in the other room launched a rant of his own. It continued as he—Aleksandr—tramped into the hallway, barefooted, pants hiked up to his knees, exposing hairy legs. Katya blinked. He appeared to be approximately five or six years older than her. He waved his hands in the air while he traded words with Zakhar, who wagged a finger at him. Then, the older man clapped him into a hug while laughing. The action was reciprocated.

"Ah!" Zakhar turned and gestured to them with one hand while keeping the other dangling over the younger man's shoulders. "This is Katya Cassius, one of our Lost Children. Mina. And this is your new patient, Sotiris. He is Oneiroi, one with an ailment that brings sleep to those he sets his magic on."

Aleksandr's steely blue eye snapped to Sotiris. "Fascinating." Like Zakhar, he spoke with an accent when he switched to Magistrate. He entered the three's space and hovered in front of Sotiris's face. "I have never seen one before but have heard much discussion on boards."

Sotiris jerked into Katya. She couldn't blame the boy. The man before them resembled a madman with his wild, wavy brown hair sticking at all angles. His entire frame bubbled with manic energy. And he remained completely unaware of the fear he was stoking. Unperturbed by

Sotiris's eyes, he even reached for his face, though Sotiris batted his hand away. This only earned a chuckle from the man.

She fished into her satchel and removed the last full bottle. As she'd hoped, it bought Sotiris space. "Plasovern created this formula, specifically a woman named Usha."

"Ah, I am familiar with her work." He snapped the bottle from her hand before she could say anything and scurried into the room he'd exited.

Katya followed close on his heel, unwilling to let the precious liquid out of her sight. In the room, Aleksandr hopped from table to table, messing with the equipment.

The room, like the rest of the palace, was massive and equally closed off by curtains. Unlike the rest, it gave the appearance of being lived in, though tech and machinery consumed its bulk.

"Hey!" Her attention jerked back to Aleksander as he added a decent sample of the drug to a machine. "We only have that vial!"

"Yeah, yeah," he muttered, too engrossed in his work to even look at her. "Crack eggs, make omelet."

She bit her lip, wanting nothing more than to throttle the man.

Sotiris bumped into her, and she carded his hair with her fingers, meeting a few tangles. He wrapped his arms around her leg, owlishly drinking in his surroundings—and what surroundings they were. Discarded clothes dotted the room in piles. There were also dishes in various stages of finish. Katya scrunched her nose as she passed one with what appeared to be a half-eaten sandwich, complete with fuzzy, green mold. Somewhere, a radio played music at a low volume. She discovered a buried cot in the corner; it resembled military surplus. She spotted a slight impression of a human body at its center in the muddled chaos of blankets and clothes.

Did he ever leave this room?

Along its walls, an odd mix of religious icons and scientific posters gave personality. Though—Mina leaned toward one poster of a person having their head measured—Katya felt discomfort.

Aleksandr settled on to a tall stool in front of a microscope and scratched at his stubble. His hand dropped to the tabletop, one finger tapping incessantly against it.

Upon joining Katya, Mina tugged at her sleeve and shot her the best shell-shocked expression she could manage.

"You thought *I* was messy," she whispered between gritted teeth.

From the intent in which Aleksandr was inspecting the slide he'd prepared, Katya doubted he would have overheard, even if the teen had spoken normally.

Zakhar moved about the room, clearing its debris. He grumbled under his breath but sorted through the items. An attorney well beyond the purview of his profession. Katya approached him.

"He seems ... off." Not polite, but still politer than the word her mind wanted to say. She'd seen soldiers who had cracked, no longer able to manage the horrors they'd witnessed. Aleksandr could have been one of them. The way he moved, the minute tics.

"He functions." Zakhar placed the pile of plates he'd collected into a plastic bin. "And as long as he has something to focus on, he doesn't dwell on the darker elements in his mind."

"He's not a serial killer, is he?" Mina asked.

Zakhar laughed and shook his head. "No." He wiped his mouth. "Aleksandr is mostly harmless unless you are visiting unannounced. The darkness only engulfs him, not others."

"How did you meet him?" Katya asked, unable to imagine the man ever leaving his home.

"Chance and good fortune. For both of us." He glanced at Aleksandr hunched over a pad of paper, scribbling away, before poring over data printed by the machine. He never stopped his low muttering. "He needed a branch to society and, conversely, a person who could keep society away; I stepped into that role. And I needed such a brilliant mind to realize my own goals. Mramor has been behind curve technology-wise, and without such minds, we would have no hope in our endeavor for liberation."

Katya shifted her weight, which caused Sotiris to sink his little fingers into her leg. Meanwhile, Zakhar resumed tidying. There was genuine care there, far more than a professional relationship.

"Good news!" Aleksandr exclaimed, slamming his hands together, startling the three elopers, while Zakhar didn't break from his task. "I can replicate and make better."

"Excellent!" Zakhar beamed, placing a folded shirt on to one table. "I think that calls for celebratory drinks all around."

Katya stared at the wild-haired man in front of her. "Just like that."

He tilted his head, one eyebrow lifting, as if to question her intelligence. "Da."

"It took months for them to—"

"And I only need replicate work they did and then perfect it." He snapped his fingers at Sotiris. "Boy, this way. We will attach you to machine."

Sotiris's grip tightened on her leg. His face scrunched in confusion, likely from the thick accent that probably sounded like a completely different language from the one she and Mina spoke. She placed herself between Aleksandr and Sotiris.

"He's not a dog."

"Yes, yes. But this way!" He patted his hand against his pant leg, completely ignoring her statement. Then he completely shifted gears, approaching Mina. "I can make better."

Mina's face went slack, and she ineffectually uttered, "Umm ..."

When Aleksandr took a step toward her, she darted behind Katya.

"The arm," Aleksandr said and tapped his own, mirroring Mina's prosthetic. "I can make better."

Katya witnessed Mina's face redden from the corner of her eye, but Zakhar saved her from interceding.

"First, make the boy better, and leave poor girl in peace."

"But I can add mobility and weaponry."

"Weaponry?" Mina peeped.

"No," Katya said, her tone flat.

He held his hand to his face like an old-fashioned telephone. "We talk later."

"No," Katya reiterated after the rustle of clothing suggested Mina had reciprocated the gesture out of her line of vision. Of course, when she turned, Mina sheepishly lifted her face to the ceiling. Aleksandr simply smirked, though it morphed into a scowl.

"Who let wildlife into my house!" He pointed at the taiga fiend.

"Focus on boy. It's domesticated. Maybe even more than you," Zakhar chided. "Come now."

Aleksandr's bushy eyebrows almost formed a unibrow as he glared at the creature. Grumbling, he fired up a machine, and Katya helped settle Sotiris on to its bed.

She tried her best to soothe him, but having been weeks removed from the routines instilled in him at Jomsborg, he revolted against their potential return. And whereas his previous doctors had practiced good bedside manners, Aleksandr was brusque and easily frustrated. His Moscanov ramblings resumed when Sotiris moved to escape for the fourth or fifth time.

Pushing aside his wheeled desk, Aleksandr stood and began pacing while running his hands through his hair.

With his absence, Katya eased Sotiris back on to the bed and calmed him by humming a light ditty.

By the time they'd gathered the scans Aleksandr had demanded, their stomachs growled. The old man from the kitchen wheeled in a covered tray, saying not a word before leaving. By the time of its arrival, Zakhar had cleared enough space for them to eat the sandwiches, which they had to do standing. There simply were no chairs in the room besides the solitary stool.

"I will want blood as well," Aleksandr declared around his sandwich. His smacking caused Katya to cringe.

"It can wait," Zakhar said. "We will eat, and I will then show you your rooms. Research can resume after full night's rest."

Katya stepped toward Aleksandr. "If I find you trying to harvest blood in the middle of the night, I won't be responsible for what happens to you."

He held up his hands. "No midnight blood drawings. I got it!"

She sorely regretted not having the Renmark.

Zakhar chuckled and took his sandwich and bowl of soup to a far table. He ate there peacefully while Katya and Mina ate, standing around the cleared table, not exposing their backs to either man. Sotiris recoiled from the soup and picked out the meat from one sandwich to devour. When that was gone, he dismantled the bread and scattered it across the floor.

"That is not how we behave." Katya grabbed his arm before he could do the same to the second piece. At his complaints, she put him on the floor, where he could no longer reach the plate.

Across the way, Aleksandr moved on to a slate, scrolling through its contents and using a stylus to make digital notes. He approached Zakhar and struck up a conversation in Moscanov, blocking her and Mina from the discourse. The older man inspected the slate's screen, nodded before passing it back to Aleksandr, adding some additional comments.

They wrapped up the conversation by the time Katya and Mina had finished their light meal, and Sotiris had further mutilated the bread already on the floor.

Aleksandr inspected it dourly before stating, "Joke on you, little brat. The rats will clean it for me."

"Hire a maid," Zakhar said.

"They never last."

"Then improve yourself. *Then* they will stay."

Zakhar beckoned them to follow him out of the room. "I have two rooms for each of you."

"Just the one," Katya replied, earning a groan from Mina. "I'm not leaving you alone in a strange environment with a strange man."

"Rein was strange."

Katya stumbled on her tongue as if struck. She had left Mina alone with him, but she'd trusted him. He'd been trustworthy enough before ... before it'd all fallen apart. She warred with the burning in her throat, the guilt.

Zakhar narrowed his eyes as he observed the exchange, but he made no comment. He had to remember that they'd been traveling with a man who was now conspicuously missing. One that neither of them had mentioned.

"I shouldn't have. And I won't repeat the mistake."

"But it's a palace! When am I ever going to have my own room in a palace again?"

"The two rooms are connected with door." Zakhar smiled. "It is only door besides the two front entry points. They lock from inside, and you can put chairs in front of them if you like. Both have bathrooms with functional plumbing—if only all of building could say the same."

The moment they stepped into the first room with its rich trim and light blue walls, massive bed with canopy, gorgeously carved wardrobe, fireplace, and chandelier, Katya knew it was a lost cause. Mina already rushed to the connecting door to scope out her digs, and Katya found it was no longer a hill she wanted to die on. Sotiris, meanwhile, pried himself from her grip and darted to the bed, the medicine in his veins waning in potency.

"Lock the door and put a chair in front of it," she called after Mina.

Zakhar burst out into laughter. "Ah, you'll get along just fine. Here" — he directed her to a digital display — "you can make comfortable for boy. But problem with palaces is they are drafty. You shouldn't have to adjust much."

"Why is the room already ready?" She squared herself beside him.

"Aleksandr has hosted members of my faction before. They usually stay in these rooms. There are others available on the main level and the servant quarters if Aleksandr doesn't like them. Though those normally go to members of other factions."

"They don't take affront to that?" It didn't feel like the best approach to cementing a solid alliance. It would make more sense for Zakhar to cow Aleksandr into being accommodating.

"They know what they did." He approached the door. "Rest for the evening, make use of the facilities. You have my com. Do not hesitate to call."

When he slipped from the room, Katya locked the door and moved a chair from a desk with an assortment of birds carved into it so it rested under the knob. She would take no chances.

She crossed over to where Sotiris burrowed into the down comforter and pillows, curling up in the sea of a bed's center. Fishing the almost empty serum vial from her satchel, she pried his arm from the cocoon he'd created and dosed him. The last dosage now remained in Aleksandr's workshop. If he couldn't start production quick enough …

"So awesome!" Mina swept into her room, jumping up and down. "My bathtub! It's like a small swimming pool!"

"Did you move a chair?"

"Yep."

Katya gave her a small smile. She hadn't seen her this animated in a long time, and it was a far cry from this morning. But grief was like that. It came in waves, all-encompassing one moment, less heavy in others. Glancing at the coffered ceiling, the ache in her chest prickled again, but it was easy to lose oneself in a place like this.

"Enjoy your bathtub. I'm going to settle in for the evening. Don't stay up too late."

When Mina left, Katya approached the heavy dark blue curtains and pulled them back. Removed from the city, the stars—the ones she'd been born under—glistened with an intensity that overwhelmed her. It brought back the memory of her and Anaïs, their last conversation on the patio.

"You and I will always be sisters ... No one will ever understand us as we do each other."

Katya wept into the glass, fogging it.

CHAPTER SEVENTEEN

The following day, Katya enjoyed her own mini-pool bathtub before dressing in a long-sleeved, fitted black shirt. Her sister had designed it with flared sleeves—likely to break her propensity for military-style civvies. What could she say? They just felt natural. She fingered the fine lace that made up the sleeves' ends and wondered if Anaïs had crocheted it herself. The vice in her heart tightened. She would never be able to ask. Her eyes burned, and she dabbed them with the towel before tossing it aside.

In the main room, she passed a drowsy Sotiris spread in the bed, his glossy eyes staring at its canopy. He might stay in place, or he might hide in a hundred-some-square-foot palace, something she wasn't chancing. She called Mina in before leaving to get his morning dose from Aleksandr's room.

She hugged herself as she walked down the almost cavernous hall. Her shirt was almost too thin. At least, she wouldn't have to worry so much about Sotiris. Stroking her cold arms, she tried to not feel like an interloper in the emptiness surrounding her. Like a child, she touched the velvet curtains concealing the windows as she went, stirring up dust and a series of coughs from her. She wished she could yank them away and bathe in the sun, but she resisted, following the lattice-patterned floor to Aleksandr's cracked door.

She didn't barge in, choosing to knock loudly against the trim beside the opening. She recalled Zakhar's statement that he'd survived the purges. Who knew what he'd outfitted the interior with? After all, the turrets remained fresh in her mind.

"Are you decent?" she called, still not touching the door.

She caught an exclamation and a clattering of items; something ceramic shattered against the floor. Then, a dower Aleksandr pressed his face against the door crack, causing Katya to stumble back.

"It is ungodly hour."

"It's nine in the morning."

"Ungodly."

She smiled, which seemed to deteriorate his expression further, his lips really dipping.

"I need some of the drug for his morning dose," she pressed.

"It is needed here."

She gritted her teeth, trying to maintain a pleasant expression. "If he doesn't have it, he may drag us under with his genetic disorder."

His eyebrows raised, the manic energy flashed across his face like lightning. "You think he might?"

Her jaw slackened. This was not the route she'd expected their conversation to go, but she could see the gleam, the same one the doctor who'd patched Sotiris back together had had. The desire to explore every aspect that made an Oneiroi tick. She'd already betrayed their secrets to Plasovern. Who was she to say Aleksandr's intentions would be better?

"He could kill us all."

He tapped a finger on his temple. "But think of the experience."

"I am. It's not pleasant." She shoved past him and liberated the bottle, her frame shaking to find it a quarter full. She swung around. "What did you do?"

"As instructed, I duplicate formula. This is how you duplicate formula."

"So you've made a batch?"

"It takes time."

Katya growled and ran her free hand through her still-damp hair. He had sunk them all. Her nostrils flared, the urge to hit him brewing.

"We," she said through her teeth, "need another dose in ten hours."

"He will be right on it," Zakhar said from the doorway. "Is that not right?" He narrowed his gaze on Aleksandr, who slumped under it. "Come, I have breakfast ready in more hospitable area. And I opened the drapes. Not all of us are averse to sun."

"I'll put Sotiris's shades on." She, for one, wanted the sun. For all its space, the palace felt claustrophobic with its mausoleum-like atmosphere.

Aleksandr didn't join them for breakfast, which buffeted a solid wood table in an airy blue room on the main level. Eating a mixture of pastries, fresh fruit, and porridge, they basked in the light streaming through the wall of windows; the layers of snow made it all the brighter. Beyond the glass, the back garden offered interest with its overgrown hedges and broken statutes.

It was a warmer space, more intimate with its gold trim and ceiling motif—the crackling fireplace also helped. Likely it'd been a private, relaxed room for the family who'd called the palace home. Had Aleksandr had some tie to them? From what she knew of the revolution and its resulting civil war, most nobility had abandoned or been forced to leave such structures.

"Was this one of the emperor's palaces?" Katya asked.

"No." Zakhar passed a basket with a dark-colored bread to Mina. "It belonged to a noble family. I believe, *many* decades ago, a princess had married in, but other than that, they didn't have royal blood. But they had plenty of money."

Katya fiddled with her spoon, a sinking sensation rooting itself in her stomach. "Aleksandr's family?"

Zakhar nodded, elaborating no further as he cracked open a soft-boiled egg.

The conversation dropped off, but Sotiris's fruit excavation enterprise filled the void, his spoon clattering against the bowl. The boy hated fruit, and conversely, it seemed to hate him, upsetting his stomach. *Clang*! Katya grabbed the spoon from his hand and pulled the bowl away. With Sotiris's toy removed, the munching of the taiga fiend under the table echoed in the room.

"Can we get something more bland or savory for him?"

Zakhar handed her a small gold container. "Try this."

Inside, little black orbs filled it to the brim.

"Caviar?"

"Aleksandr is fond of it." He waved his spoon at Sotiris. "The boy strikes me as having similarly high tastes."

Almost as if by the flick of a switch, Sotiris perked, eyes widening even behind his sunglasses. He dove into the little container with his fingers before she could set it next to him and popped the little eggs into his mouth, not stopping.

He'd had caviar before. Actually recognized it as edible or even something to be preferred. And now that she thought about it, he'd tolerated most seafood-related meals. But most records had always described Demos Oneiroi as a frigid wasteland; she couldn't see it having much in the way of seafood. Perhaps it'd become a gained taste after they'd joined the Magistrate.

Zakhar watched Sotiris with interest. "One shared commonality. Food the great reconciler." He folded his hands across his abdomen and leaned back in his chair. "He looks better than that first meeting, so you have found some balance with his diet."

"Some." Katya warred with whether she should pace Sotiris, who'd decided on the shovel method, or allow him to devour something that may be the most natural meal he'd eaten in over a year. "I know nothing about their official diet … but he is better. I'll content myself with that."

It marked one successful battle.

"Aleksandr will probably be able to provide more insight." Zakhar stretched for his teacup and drank from it. "I will leave it to him."

She stiffened.

Zakhar lifted a hand and had the good grace to look apologetic. "I must return to society. I will procure any supplies Aleksandr requires for the new batch of medicine. I must also take care of other affairs. Be warned. I will not be returning alone."

Mina squinted at this and then redirected her focus to Katya. The girl had been so sloshed when Zakhar had spoken of his plans for Mramor, and Katya hadn't enlightened her, not after telling her Anaïs's fate. That had been hard enough.

"When done, this space" — he gestured to the room with his free hand — "will be filled with delegates for important business. Some are quite crude and opposed to interlopers. I would suggest giving wide berth when I return." He took another swig of tea and discarded the cup. "I will get papers around to transfer your vessel to here." He pointed out the window. "We will park it somewhere out there. I will see about getting workers to clear space. It will take days and maybe after we move."

"Move?" Mina echoed. "What does that mean?"

"It is of no concern," Zakhar replied. "I only ask that you four do not kill each other in my absence. I will talk to Aleksandr and impress upon him the importance of doing better. But have patience with him. Sometimes, I think I have gained the patience of saint." He shook his head as he pinched the bridge of his nose. "I will check in to make sure boy also doesn't pull you under his spell if Aleksandr can't get dosage around. But I have faith."

Standing, he stretched, his round stomach bouncing with the motion. "Explore, connect with the Net, make use of one of Aleksandr's screens." He pointed at Mina. "And be wary of exploring too densely in the woods. If you get lost, you may not be found, and since the property is not as active as it once was, some carnivores come closer than they once did. They'd easily take boy with them."

Mina's eyes shot up, her mouth a gaping hole. "What carnivores?"

"Worry about wolves," he said. "Not all taiga fiends are fangless. Though, despite their fearsome name, they avoid people." His gaze shifted to the table's far end, under which the wild cat continued to eat moist food. "Wisely so. Still … don't cross one unless they are like your little friend." He frowned at the vast window. "There are also bears and wolverines. We haven't seen many of them, but that doesn't mean they aren't nearby."

Aleksandr popped his head into the room, causing Zakhar to beam.

"Ah, good! You saved me a trip upstairs." He grabbed the scientist by the shoulder, waved at them, and then pulled him from the room. "You can walk me to car. There are things to discuss."

"What's happening?" Mina blurted out, leaning into the table. "Something is definitely happening. You said it yourself: undercurrents. But it's more than that. He's found another path beyond Plasovern. That's what's in motion."

Mina, as always, remained clever. Katya sighed. "They're planning to overthrow Magistrate control on-world. How? I'm not privy to those details."

"Our game plan?"

She snorted. "We don't interfere. We just watch and hope the effort doesn't deteriorate in the manner I'm afraid it will."

"And why do you think that?"

Katya ran her tongue against the backs of her teeth. She then took the small gold container from Sotiris, who'd taken to licking its empty interior. Mina narrowed her gaze even further when Katya stood and picked up Sotiris.

"Because," she said slowly, turning to leave, "Mramor has never stood as one before."

Life in Zakhar's absence mirrored Jomsborg with routine examinations for Sotiris. On the third day, Aleksandr hooked the boy to another machine after Katya shared details about the teenager on the Jar'rask ship. While he'd replicated the Plasovern formula, though the supply remained sparse, he was dead set on pursuing all angles — to make perfection. His latest quest was theorizing the devices' roles while bemoaning her inept descriptions. Her defense that she'd been experiencing massive, blinding pain earned no sympathy or understanding.

Standing beside Sotiris, she managed his movements to keep him in place. Aleksandr seemed incapable of handling him, either from inexperience with children or indifference. In the background, Mina would roll her eyes at their antics.

Unlike Jomsborg, Mina had nowhere else to be, no other person to interact with beyond her new pet, but the creature proved prone to long naps. And so, the teen grew mad with boredom. On day two, she'd crafted a game of opening all the drapes, which had not ingratiated her with their host. Aleksandr had cussed in Magistrate to convey his upset with them. And now ... Katya winced when the girl threw a ball she'd found among Aleksandr's collection of garbage, bouncing it off the wall. Her eye twitched with each thud. *Thud. Thud-thud-thud.*

Unable to take it anymore, Katya snatched the ball on its subsequent rebound. "Watch TV."

"It's not in Magistrate." Mina exhaled with enough force to lift her overgrown bangs by a fraction.

"Channels two hundred and forty through two hundred and forty-eight," Aleksandr shouted, not deviating from the settings he was programming into the machine.

Sotiris sat serenely, munching on caviar given as bribery for good behavior. Grudgingly given. Under his breath, Aleksandr had muttered caviar thief.

Mina changed the screen repeatedly through the channels. She groaned. "It's all news. Is there anything better?"

"Go on to the Net and find other content," Katya advised.

The screen's rolling bar dispensed information about attacks in the Fringe, including one that had crippled a fuel refinery. It would send prices skyrocketing and impede the Magistrate's operations in the Fringe. There was no mention of damaged relays or communications blackouts. The hysteria following the Trides Bombing probably heightened the Magistrate's inclination to hold information close to its chest. She was shocked so much was being dispensed as it was. She imagined some planets within the Magistrate might keep tighter lids on what was being disseminated. The closer to the Core, the more trusted you were to receive more detailed and accurate information—full-right citizens demanded it.

"They never give all the details," Mina commented as she lowered herself to the floor to sit cross-legged while propping herself up with her hands. "From what Dag had said, I bet the Fringe is on fire."

"Bah!" Aleksandr stepped away from his project to join them. "News is actually much improved. In days of emperor, we would have heard nothing of this. Only glories of empire and ignore those corpses over there—unless they were revolutionaries. Then it was look, and do not repeat. Any paper that said differently? Well, its publishers didn't last long." He shrugged. "Compared to that, this is wealth of information."

Mina sighed and claimed another ball from Aleksandr's mess. Katya grimaced after it struck the wall and bounced back.

Tilting her head, Mina pointed to the poster near where her ball hit, an old science print showing different skulls with measurements. The language was in Moscanov. "What's that about?" the teen asked.

"Rubbish." He shrugged. "I keep to remind myself to science wisely." He resumed checking his data. "My father entertained all sorts of crackpots in the day. It was fashionable."

"But what is it?" Mina pressed.

He glanced at the teen, eyes lingering on her face. "That some of us are better than others."

Her eyebrows pinched together. "How?"

"It is delusion, but these scientists believed breeding determined it."

"That's stupid."

"Incredibly."

Passing the ball between her hands, Mina rolled it toward the taiga fiend that'd nested in Aleksandr's discarded clothes. It cracked its eyes, stared at the ball, and then, with a sigh, curled tighter to resume its nap.

"Well, I'm done." Mina rocked to her knees and then stood. "I'm going insane. I want to explore."

"Knock self out." Aleksandr adjusted a setting. "Don't go into west wing. Everywhere else, fine."

"What's in the west wing?" Katya extended her hand to stop Mina from leaving.

He squinted his eyes at her and threw up his hands. "Why does it matter what is in west wing? It is my house. It does not matter why I don't want people there—only that I don't."

"Are there bodies?" Mina asked.

"What is it with you thinking I am some crazed murderer?"

"You were the person who said you could add weaponry to my hand." She bandied her prosthetic limb in the air.

"For self-protection!" He cleared his throat, almost as if gagging. "If any of us have murder on brain, it is you."

Katya lowered her hand in front of Mina. "Stay out of the west wing. Remember our host installed turrets in his front yard." And before Mina reached the door, she added, "And, Mina, break nothing. Keep your com with you."

While Mina left, Katya remained next to Sotiris, especially now that he'd finished his snack.

"Go?"

"Not yet."

He puffed his cheeks. Ah, he'd adopted one of Mina's traits. Katya smiled and brushed his hair with her fingers. She would cut off the experiments soon. Take him outside to play in the snow, maybe set up lessons to push his vocabulary forward.

"There's shared DNA."

"Pardon?" Katya faced Aleksandr.

He flipped through some documents on his slate. "Oneiroi. There are common threads between them and humans."

Which explained how Kahina had been conceived—not that she planned to share her existence with Aleksandr. That would only spur his mind into new directions for discovery when she needed him to focus on one task.

"I am familiar with your adoptive father, Faustus Cassius," Aleksandr said.

She must have looked shocked because he further explained.

"I have read some of his papers and theories about humanity dispersing from a central hub of planets or colonies. Similarities in different cultures' artwork carried through, even if history or technology was lost, leading us to this point—mass dispersal with fewer commonalities and hybridization. One colony happened upon Demos Oneiroi, and mankind has never met an alien that it didn't"—he stumbled under Sotiris's big-eyed gaze—"it-it didn't want to passionately ... hug."

"Nice save."

He chuckled. "I will not be one to corrupt. But there was definitely a hybridization event in their evolution somewhere. If I had more specimens, that would be fabulous." He set the slate aside. "In another time, I could see doing further research into that theory, tracing genetic lines to prove or expand upon theory, but there is no time. Not on timetable Zakhar has dictated."

"Is that why you're involved in this liberation effort? Zakhar? Or do you have another goal with it?" She grabbed Sotiris's hand before he yanked off the sensor attached to his forehead. "He shared you come from a noble family."

One of his fingers tapped rapidly against his pant leg. Then he stilled, his rampant energy vanquished.

"Do I want to see restoration of some power?" His voice was a mere whisper. "No. I enjoy the beautiful picture painted by Zakhar of a functioning republic. Though I know it won't be easy. It may even fail. But, we have seen it partially realized in the last thirty years if not for Sila and Alyypriliv guerrilla tactics."

She swallowed. "You were young when it all happened."

Aleksandr moved along his assortment of lab tables, weird devices, vials of liquids—a bizarre assortment fitting of a horror flick featuring a mad scientist. That moniker wasn't too farfetched for Aleksandr.

His head bobbed.

"I"—she swallowed—"I was probably about four when my father adopted me. I don't really remember anything before."

"Count your blessings."

"You carry it." She couldn't stop herself. The reddened snow sprung to her mind. She carried it. Couldn't remember it but carried it all the same. *You know in your bones.* Her toes bunched in her boots.

His head bobbed while he fiddled with a few vials, but did nothing with them. Lowering his head, he balled his fists against the table and leaned into it.

"Do you want to know what is in west wing?" His voice was gravel. "Ghosts. Ghosts and blood." He chuckled, not leaving the table, his eyes trained on it. "They all linger. There. In here." He rapped an index finger against his head. And then he laughed, pinched, distorted. "Long ago, there was market for blood. Blood of martyrs, saints. People would pay to say they had blood of such saints on cloth, in reliquary." A flat smile spread across his face. "I have a house. Does it bring good fortune? Who knows? But here I am. When I shouldn't be."

Silence. Katya regretted broaching the subject, sympathy welling. He'd survived the mass murders, a civil war, and an illness that had swept the world, all as a child.

"Shut the mouth!"

Warmth crept across Katya's face, and she stepped back at the shout. She should have done just that: kept her mouth shut. She'd opened the door to this man's trauma, and why? To find someone else with similar memories? To spark something in her mind while not wanting to touch those macabre memories?

His hand slammed into the table. "Bang!"

Both she and Sotiris jumped. Her heart stuttered.

"Bang!" Another clap reverberated. Then in quick succession: "Bang! Bang!"

Swiveling, Aleksandr faced her and pressed a finger to his mouth. "Not a peep. Not even when the blood, the brain matter, seeped down. I kept mouth shut and lived."

He lifted one of his bare feet, and for the first time, Katya saw beyond the lack of shoes to the scarring that remained from frostbite.

"I ran into snow. I couldn't stay. They might return. And they were all gone." He lowered his foot and slid on to the table, sitting upright on it. "I hide in plain sight, a nobody. When children were being rounded up, I dodged it.

"From there, I used my brains and continued to live. Inventions, here and there, enough to build up my fortunes. I gave plenty of patents to a greedy company, but I kept the superb ones for myself. Took back my home and filled its forest with turrets." He shined his teeth at her. "They'll never get me. No, no … I'll blow them to smithereens before that ever happens."

"I'm sorry." It sounded lame, even to her.

Aleksandr shrugged and stood again, once again becoming a flurry of motion flitting from table to table. "No bother. Everyone in Old Imperiya has ghosts."

Including her hung in the air.

He lifted his slate, a slight smile returning. "Interesting." He only hummed when she inquired what was. "Let us …"

Sotiris yelped and stilled in shock before he tore at the devices on his forehead.

Stunned, Katya shifted to Aleksandr, whose eyes were wide. They stared at each other before he leaped over the table, scattering its contents in haste to put it between them.

He had actually shocked Sotiris. She balled her fists, tempted to follow him over the table, but Sotiris collided with her legs and sobbed into her.

"You—"

"I was testing—"

"You don't shock a child!"

"But what if Magistrate is? Huh?" He held up both his hands, backing away while eyeing the door. "Electricity to override biologic mutation. Eventually, one small device, no need for drugs."

She recalled the teen, the many devices. The Magistrate hadn't narrowed them to one microdevice over the decades, but maybe they hadn't really tried for such an outcome, as it was not conducive to their goals. But why not? It would make the children easier to move, particularly as they got older. Or perhaps they'd become too hard to manage. Or maybe they'd sought to magnify their abilities.

She hoisted Sotiris into her arms. "Just make the medicine digestible." She flavored the words so they screamed the underlining threat.

She held her withering glare longer, then left with Sotiris nestled in her arms.

A week passed, and Aleksandr trod as if on glass around Katya, not pressing to conduct any experiments. With forced cheerfulness, he kept the supply of medicine growing while reexamining the formula. This included developing a digestible option, per Katya's wish. Ever the survivalist, he would drop off daily vials outside her door before retreating to his room.

Freed of obligations, Katya and Sotiris spent leisurely hours exploring the defunct garden's endless snow and patches of dead brown plants that poked through it. The snow delighted Sotiris as nothing else had. On other occasions, they'd explored the palace with Mina, avoiding the west wing as requested. Following her conversation with Aleksandr, Katya favored letting any ghosts rest.

As the week concluded, she lifted an eyebrow when Aleksandr knocked on her door mid-morning rather than just leave a vial. She'd been curled on the crushed velvet sofa with Sotiris, reading him a story on her slate, taking great care to emphasize words with their accompanying illustrations. She handed Sotiris the slate and went to open the door.

"I want to test for reactions to new drug. I call it 'ne spat.'" This left his mouth before the door had opened even a fraction of an inch.

"What does 'ne spat' stand for?"

"No sleeping."

"Is it digestible?"

"Likely. We must first see if there are adverse reactions of any kind before we give in mass dosage to treat disorder."

Across the way, Sotiris played with the slate, running his fingers against its screen as he'd seen her do. She thought of the skin rashes he'd endured in the pursuit of any type of drug. She didn't want to relive that.

"What side effects are you worried about?"

"Upset stomach, hives, headaches, heart palpitations, so on, so on, and death." Aleksandr shrugged at her physical recoil. "Unlikely. One must always add death to potential side effects. Always possibility. But fret not, I put after so on and so on."

Her throat burned. She was going to murder him. One day, he would find the right combination of buttons to press, and she would snap.

"Are you unwell?" He cocked his head.

Exhaling through her nose, she shook her head and collected Sotiris. She allowed him to carry the slate, which he continued to read as they walked. She froze at the threshold of Aleksandr's room. Mina sat on the floor in front of his screen. She had a bag of some type of snack food in her lap, munching on its contents while watching what appeared to be a musical in Moscanov on the holoscreen.

Katya came to stand behind the teen. "Do you understand any of it?"

Mina popped another doughy-looking piece into her mouth. She chewed, tilted her head at the screen and the brightly costumed singers, and said, "Not a word. But I think there's a love triangle between those three. And that old man is creeping on her. Truthfully, I'm just admiring the costumes and makeup, then creating my own story."

"Not too far off," Aleksandr said and patted the small stool he'd scrounged up from somewhere for Sotiris. "It ends with duel, and both lovers are killed. Making sensible decision, she marries old duke and embarks on lonely, loveless life—but with great wealth!"

"Spoilers," Mina muttered and bit down on another snack.

Katya hoisted Sotiris on to the stool and stood next to him. "Why don't you have chairs?"

"Revolutionaries carted them off." He poured a brown liquid into a spoon. "I show them. Chairs are worthless to me."

"You have chairs elsewhere."

"It is not my fault that Zakhar is weak." He brought the spoon over to Sotiris. "Now, open up."

The boy, of course, did not.

Rather than descend into a huffy fit, Aleksandr grabbed a familiar container, and Sotiris instantly perked. "I had thought as much." The man snorted. "I will give you this if you take your medicine."

Sotiris tried to bypass the spoon, but Aleksandr yanked the caviar container well out of reach. "Medicine first."

The toddler blinked and assessed the situation, sucking in his lips and shooting Aleksandr a withering glare. Then he capitulated.

Once the medicine was swallowed, Aleksandr relinquished the container to Sotiris. The boy popped open the lid, stared down, and then threw the container across the room with a scream.

"No contaminated results." Aleksandr wagged a finger in the boy's tear-stained face.

"That was mean."

"And fighting him wouldn't have been?"

He had her there. The fight would've ended with Sotiris in tears, likely with bruises as they forced the medicine into his mouth. The sample likely would've been thrown up. It was better to use a little lie than to engage in the struggle.

"Now what?" Katya asked, after deciding to drop the point.

"We wait and monitor." As had been his habit, Aleksandr disconnected from them through busy work around his lab.

Despite her aching bones, Katya joined Mina on the floor to watch the rest of the opera. Beside her, Sotiris kept opening and closing his mouth while pulling his face into an odd expression. He shot plaintive glares at her. She imagined the medicine tasted horrible for him since Aleksandr likely cared very little for what his young patient thought of that aspect. He would only care about its effectiveness.

Time passed with no changes in Sotiris's behavior or his breathing. He only sat with a dour expression that reminded her of a drenched kitten. His disposition improved after lunch when Aleksandr deemed he'd satisfactorily earned the right to caviar.

From there, their host dismissed them from his room. Katya took Sotiris outside to play with Mina and the taiga fiend before returning to their rooms to begin further lessons. Mina griped when she realized she was being included.

"I'm too old for this."

Katya guided the girl to an upholstered chair. "You're going to study Mramorian history. I'm starting you with Old Imperiya before Magistrate intervention. I need you to be more aware of what's happening around you."

"Are you?"

Katya rolled her eyes. "I doubt it."

She reflected on her own readings she'd begun in the evenings when Sotiris slept beside her. While perhaps lacking, her materials had freshened her memory of Mramor's recent history. As a side reading project, she'd tried to find Aleksandr's family. After uncovering nothing, she decided he'd shed his original surname. But having people break into your house and murder your family would make one want to hide. "*They'll never get me.*" In his mind, they were always coming. Maybe not that day, but eventually.

Reaching for her hairbrush, which she'd left on the stand next to the bed, she took to brushing out her longer hair. She would need to cut it or begin braiding it again, or else she'd go crazy. She swallowed. "The history's only going to get us so far. We'll miss intricate details. No matter what, tread carefully."

"When do you think Zakhar will be back?"

Katya wondered about that. She had his com, and the temptation to call had arisen frequently. Was he held up on business or getting the paperwork squared away to move the *Pollux*?

"Hard to say."

"Do you want me to trim your hair?"

Katya narrowed her eyes, and the teen buried her nose in the slate. Discarding the brush, Katya helped Sotiris with a Magistrate alphabet and word game. He thrived under the attention and parroted the words with bubbly enthusiasm.

They'd been at it for an hour when Aleksandr interrupted.

"Time to test."

A caviar container had been positioned next to the stool in Aleksandr's room. Sotiris rushed it, scrunching his face upon discovering it was half empty.

Aleksandr sighed. "You aren't getting all my fish eggs."

He plastered sensors to Sotiris's body and completed a series of readings, bobbing his head as he did.

"Is it on track?" Katya asked.

"It shows promise, but I have concerns that dosage or formula will need adjustment." He moved aside a bunch of his instruments to the edge of one table. "We'll let scanners monitor his brain activity for a while."

Mina peeked into the room, her slate absent, as she slinked into the room and its screen. And plop.

The teen met Katya's glower with a shrug. "It's research." She circled through the stations. "Social studies."

In the background, Aleksandr hummed a deep, canorous tune. Airy, yet forlorn. The hum morphed to a susurrus of words. Katya closed her eyes to hear their impressions, as she couldn't understand the language. He continued for maybe a minute or two, then fell silent; whatever had compelled him released its hold.

"It's beautiful," she said.

He hummed in response. "It's about two sisters. Despite having each other, they still froze to death."

Katya blinked. "Of course."

Mina stood and ran to the windows and opened the curtains despite Aleksandr's complaints. "There's cars!"

Katya rushed to her side, and sure enough, there were at least ten, including Zakhar's. "Stay with Sotiris."

Running into the hallway, Katya barely heard Aleksandr sputter. As she neared the stairs, she shifted her pace to a creep and rolled her feet to muffle her steps on the marble after recalling Zakhar's words about keeping a low profile. When the wall met the stairs' railing, she stopped and peeked around the corner to the grand foyer below.

Zakhar ushered a delegation of men and women into it. Some stood in awe of the remains, even devoid of their prime grandeur. Though Katya would be the first to admit, the bones were awe-inspiring. Others, however, remained unmoved, a few even scoffing at their surroundings, noses turned up, or mouths in narrow lines.

One such man, who had a murine appearance, complete with beady eyes and a pointed nose, scrunched his gaunt face as his eyes roved over his surroundings. His hair, a dark gray, signaled that he was probably a contemporary of Zakhar's. Katya shrank back when his head lifted to scan the upper railing. Seconds later, when Zakhar spoke, she poked around the corner again.

He faced the delegation as he talked in Moscanov, gesturing to a rack the silent cook had drug out. Hangers dangled from its center rod.

All of them spoke in Moscanov, placing Katya once again at a disadvantage. One by one, they stripped off their thick winter coats and hung them while Zakhar continued to speak in a tone Katya could only describe as amicable.

He made his rounds, and in following his movements, Katya latched on to a gruff man, built with muscle, whose tangled hair formed a bird's nest when he removed his fur hat. A deep, white scar cut across the left side of his face, reaching his ear where a snippet of the lobe was missing. Whatever misfortune had befallen him had likely exposed his teeth, possibly even shattering or cracking them, depending on the type of weapon used.

"Matfey Sobol."

Katya jerked, stifling the sharp intake of breath she wanted to take when she spun toward the voice behind her. She swore her heart had stopped.

She cursed under her breath and rounded on Aleksandr. "What are you doing?" The words passed through her teeth in a whisper.

"Answering your question." He pointed to the gruff man. "Matfey Sobol. He is veteran of war, now pirate, and, I suppose, would-be revolutionary."

"Did he receive that wound in the war?"

"It came after during madness: Bitvaza Trypu—Corpse Battle."

"He carries clout?"

Aleksandr shrugged. "He is, if you like, folk hero. Served directly under General Volkov in war. Now he is pirate. What's not to love? People like someone who hassles rich and Magistrate alike."

"And him?" She discreetly pointed to the rodent-like man.

"Yakov Kuznetsov." Aleksandr curled his toes into the marble. "He and Zakhar have … turbulent relationship. Once friends, then enemies. He views Zakhar as an enemy of true revolution. Kuznetsov has been long-time Sila member. A real piece of work." His face pinched into a menacing expression. "Devil you know. Devil you know."

Below, the delegation shifted toward the dining room, though a handful broke off from the rest and headed further down the main floor hallway.

Aleksandr groaned. "They brought helpers. Hate guests. Meddling in my rooms." He shifted from foot to foot and then nudged his head toward a closed door. He opened it and waved her in. It was empty, save for a simple cot and a side table.

"Someone might stay here tonight, but for now …" He hit a decorative piece of trim, exposing a servant corridor. "This way." He pressed a finger to his lips before guiding her down the darkened hall with its peeling beige wallpaper. He stopped halfway and crouched in front of a vent.

Katya followed the action, eyes widening a fraction when voices rose from within. Aleksandr shrugged when she looked at him, all but confirming he'd eavesdropped on Zakhar's meetings before.

Though it did her no good. Whatever meeting occurred below, it was in Moscanov.

"They are just exchanging pleasantries," Aleksandr said in a hushed tone. "Prepping for other former countries' representatives to arrive—ah, tomorrow." He rolled his eyes. "Hence I play host or more like delegate to Zakhar. When they arrive, the proceedings will switch to Magistrate. It is common tongue now between continents. Irony, right?"

A man shouted, which was answered by another.

"Oh! The snipes have begun." Aleksandr stuck out his tongue. "They trade them right after pleasantries. Get it out of way. Sets good tone for meeting."

"Does it? I think it doesn't instill much hope for any partnership." If the Old Imperiya delegates couldn't manage civil discourse, throwing in their continental enemies would provide all the ingredients for a clusterfuck.

A third voice—Zakhar's—reined them in, projecting a gravitas that commanded respect and silence.

"And ringmaster takes over," Aleksandr said. "Mutual, blah-blah. They are discussing ..." He trailed off and tilted his head from side to side, weighing something while sucking on one side of his mouth as he did. "Why not? You will find out eventually. They are discussing a league of planets. An official accord has been solidified between all parties, and our delegation—all former countries in new proposed government—need only sign. Tonight it seems the goal is for Old Imperiya to hammer out its differences and then pressure the others into accepting terms and our lead."

"Huh." Katya processed this. History rhymed, the dominant country bullying the others. It did not inspire thoughts of sustainability. "How likely is that?"

"Hmm ..." He lifted both palms as he shrugged. "We outnumber them. But common enemies can be positive driving force. But there will be a reckoning when that enemy is removed. Then the desire for power will consume. For now, the pressure is to solidify a functional provisional government that can withstand war and hopefully beyond."

"Some would say it's impossible."

He bobbed his head. "I would be one, but I have high faith in Zakhar's skill to butter people and get them in line with his goals. He has that persuasion on others." He leaned closer to the vent's grate. "He's doing so now. Painting picture of republic that creates stability and a voice for all."

A clamoring ricocheted up the vent's metal.

"Our faction's support," Aleksandr clarified.

What followed was a high-pitch cacophony where compatriot voices blurred together to bend the others to their wills by drowning them out. Who leads what, who does what—the verbal skirmish raged for over an hour. Aleksandr narrated the drama for her. It amounted to petty squabbles about who would attend the planetary league meeting, what concessions were allowed before cementing the league deal, what their partnership should be with their foreign allies, but equally so with their Mramorian ones. Through it, Katya discerned vitriol from a decades-old war still smoldered.

"That is minority member. Not strictly imperialists but also not fan of 'emperor must die' approach—albeit it is late for that. But they were very keen to continue the war," Aleksandr explained as one man raged below, bellowing up a storm. "He just wants to seize all control and force other countries along. Says they should pay war reparations."

Aleksandr hesitated in places, dropping a series of umms and then not finishing the sentences before jumping to new topics of discussion downstairs. Censoring. She smiled at that. She was a foreigner here, with deep ties to their ultimate enemy, no matter where she'd been born. It showed he cared for the grand enterprise being embarked on.

"Ah, they are descending into the military conundrum again." Aleksandr massaged his forehead. "None of the countries have had military in over thirty years, and no one wants to give others edge. Nothing like mutually assured destruction." He snorted at that. "Joke's on them."

"What joke?"

He smiled, baring his teeth. "No good joke is ever explained."

"I imagine it's something akin to what the Magistrate has been doing to their firearms."

"Could be, could not be." The lilt in voice suggested it was.

Below, discourse swelled into a verbal brawl. Aleksandr closed his eyes, his nose's bridge scrunching as he strained. He didn't translate, simply listened. Then his eyes flew open. His eyebrows all but disappeared into his unkempt hair.

"What happened?"

"We are done here." He stood and marched to the door, leaving her alone by the vent.

"What happened?"

He retreated to the servant's door as if the hall had caught fire. Throwing open the door, he waved her through and, as she passed, stated, "I am not touching."

Before she could get another word out, Aleksandr darted to his room. She stood in the main hall, bewildered. What had happened?

The old man delivered their dinner to Aleksandr's room, and he spoke for the first time. Of course, it was in Moscanov, which robbed the momentous moment of its full potential. Aleksandr informed them it was a message from Zakhar, warning them to stay upstairs. After dinner and Aleksandr's last inspection of Sotiris, the man himself appeared.

"Ah, you all live!" He extended his arms as far as they would go, his smile stretching as if to match them. "Is medicine squared away?"

"We are trying improved formula," Aleksandr said. He didn't break from his examination of the data on his slate.

"But there will be no slip, right?" Seriousness encompassed Zakhar's face. "I cannot have slipup. Not now."

"It will hold." Aleksandr set aside his slate and switched to Moscanov.

Katya pressed her lips together as they shunted her from the conversation. Zakhar stumbled a bit, his lips turning downward during Aleksandr's rapid stream of words.

"Will the medicine work or not?" Katya cut in, forcibly loosening her balled hands.

Aleksandr hoisted one finger in the air. "My formula is without reproach!"

"Then why shift the conversation to a language I can't understand?"

"So I can broach topic I gathered eavesdropping!"

Zakhar yanked two fingers across his throat, silencing Aleksandr. "Enough. Ms. Cassius, a word."

Aleksandr rolled his eyes and waved his slate toward Sotiris. "I suppose I will babysit."

"Mina," Katya said, drawing the teen from whatever new program she'd found. "Watch them."

"Ay-ay!" The teen placed her hands on her hips and narrowed her eyes at Aleksandr, who returned the pose. The pair had established an odd friendship of sorts, but really, the scientist was practically an eternal teenager, so it made some sense.

Katya walked alongside Zakhar as he took her, not to her room, but to a more isolated section of the floor, close to the west wing's entrance. He opened an ornately carved door, which creaked. She doubted it saw many visitations.

Resting her hands behind her back, she followed Zakhar inside. Unlike every other room, this one had no curtains, though a few windows had exterior boards. The light passed unrestricted through the massive remaining windows' dust-encrusted panes. The walls, a faded yellow, contrasted with the floral carpet's patchy remains. The sun had bleached it. The room was narrow but had an arched ceiling that created a sense of spaciousness. It housed a chandelier at its center, though it wasn't as grand as the main level ones. Its gold had tarnished and lost its luster. Only the two gray marble pillars appeared unblemished, though cobwebs hung off them. No furniture. Instead, crates had been stacked around the room; they were all locked with digital mechanisms. A couple of slashed icons, gold still lucent despite the damage, hung.

"Aleksandr's mother's drawing room." Zakhar dusted off one crate and then sat on it before gesturing her to do likewise on the one across from him. "When it gets bad in here" —he pointed to his head—"he will come here. Just sit. Bask in better memories, perhaps. He never lingers, though."

Katya nudged her shoe against a hole in the carpet. "Why not restore it?"

Zakhar's shoulders rose as he inhaled. He held his breath for a moment and then released it in one long exhale. "I imagine because he can never restore the most important part."

And so, he lived with the metaphorical corpse, allowing it to display the decay of time.

The man rubbed the side of his face and shifted on his crate. "But Aleksandr is not what I want to talk to you about."

Katya crossed her legs, the crate's edge already cutting into her tolerance.

"Imperiya's three majority factions will each have battle fleets." He folded his hands in his lap. "Sobol has garnered support as admiral from his faction and others. He is seasoned, and it makes sense. Kuznetsov is other. Seasoned on ground, not in space." He snorted, his eyes growing stormy. "More seasoned in butchery of unarmed people, but the more radical components favor him, and I need them in line — give them this one thing, and then not the whole pie. I feel these two men will balance each other out."

"And your faction?" Katya ground her hands into the crate. Something sour reached her tongue.

"There is … dearth of the right military experience, not unlike with Kuznetsov. We have people who served on ground during war or partook in what followed. No notable candidates." He folded his hands in his lap. "But against Sobol and Kuznetsov, we need more. Someone who might not be as popular as them but has the right amount of gumption and knowledge. Who should they swing toward authoritarianism can act accordingly." Zakhar pressed his lips together and allowed silence to drag. "Then I remembered I had professionally trained Magistrate captain waiting here."

A pinched laugh passed her lips unfettered. Was he insane? "You don't even know me, and you want to give me a command post? That can't bode well for your faction."

"Many said as much tonight." Zakhar entwined his fingers. "But I can only see wisdom in using our enemy's knowledge against them. My faction agreed after much persuasion."

"I can't even speak the language, let alone manage all the" — she struggled for the term and settled — "bad blood. I have no buy-in to this cause. In fact, I think it's a fool's errand."

He chuckled in response. "It is madness, but … but if it succeeds, I think it will heal our people more, better us even. We will no longer be hobbled. We will no longer be at mercy of a foreign power or a much-hated internal faction. People will not disappear anymore. We will not be as were … we will forge a new identity. A Mramorian identity, removed from nationalist tendencies."

"Rosy, but divorced from reality."

"I think not." He twisted his hands in his lap. "Not if we reach the youth. Bond them, no matter where they hailed from." He scooted forward on the crate. "This, you could help us achieve by establishing a training regimen, using the guideposts given to you by the Magistrate." Her hand ran through her hair, a slight tremor traveling through her fingers. She thought of her father, Anaïs, Valens, and countless friends still wearing the blue. What would they think, her returning to Magistrate space helming an enemy vessel? She clenched her eyes shut, blocking the floor. She couldn't even picture herself in another uniform. She blinked at the patchy carpet and its rotten roses. Her throat burned, and she settled her glare on Zakhar.

"You realize what you're asking me to do? Not just to fight a war against former friends and my family" — her throat cracked — "but against other factions in Imperiya who will only see a usurper. They'll constantly try to stab me in the back." She swallowed against the sour taste. "Who would serve under me? Really? Who would serve under someone who had been a dedicated Magistrate officer and may still have sympathies for it? No one in their right mind."

She rocked to her feet and paced, keeping her hands wrapped around her torso, hiding them underneath her upper arms.

Zakhar sat serenely on his crate despite the building tension, though the bags under his eyes appeared darker. Or perhaps it was more to the angle or the deepening blues and purples outside the window. It was getting late.

The man shrugged. "You offer insider knowledge. A perspective of Magistrate operations we lack. We have some younger members engaged in the home force that the Magistrate formed to prepare in a century or so to provide our own security. These children, they would serve under you. They would likely appreciate consistency you could provide with your background and experience. Most of our young people speak Magistrate tongue now so that is no problem. As long as you prove useful and willing to support cause, the rest will comply. I am also convinced you could be bridge with other former countries. Yes, you were born in Old Imperiya, but you've been stripped of all its trappings. It will make them more willing to listen."

Here he stood, his joints creaking. "And what I propose is a partnership between you and me. I am politician. I have no military experience, but I can navigate the many landmines on Mramor. I will keep other factions at bay, allowing you to work unanchored to them. You have the military knowledge to go toe-to-toe with Sobol and Kuznetsov. Together, we can create a unified front and see this to success. Because of current proposed structuring that includes representatives of other former countries, you would be vice admiral positioned behind Sobol. He is lesser evil."

"They will never accept me."

Zakhar's features softened. "Not all. But ..." His eyes grew glassy. "You are one of our Lost Children. That will speak to many people. Remind them of what was lost. Bring hope."

Katya clenched the fabric of her shirt. "Of what?"

His face, so vulnerable, startled her.

"That they will come home."

The simple words staggered her, and she couldn't respond.

Sighing, Zakhar rubbed his chest. "Yes, not all will be swayed by sentimentality. But some will hope that their missing child will see you and know that they too have a place—that they are welcome to return." He turned away. "That is why they must make room for you and capitulate on this demand."

Shrugging, he added, "As I have said, my faction will back you."

Pressing her lips together, Katya crossed over to a window and fixated on the murky landscaping beyond. Snow clouds moved in, blotting out the stars.

"Say your ragtag internal alliances hold" — the muscles in her neck ached — "how can you hope to take on the Magistrate?"

"For one, we don't try to win."

Zakhar lumbered forward until he stood next to her, breaking her concentration from the billowing clouds and flecks of snow.

"We make ourselves unpalatable. Drag out the war. Make it so costly the Magistrate people, and thus their leaders reject it." His icy blue eyes didn't break from the window. "It will not be an offensive war — we cannot afford to go toe-to-toe with the Magistrate. Our aims are solely to push them off our world, out of our space and keep them so off-balance they cannot return." He faced her. "I cannot give you all details, not without firm commitment, but know we are not alone in this endeavor. We have forged strong connections with other Fuusi Arm planets. Between us, we will make a good go at it."

The league Aleksandr had told her about. Balling her hands in her armpits, she swallowed against the lingering sourness. She couldn't do this. Couldn't fathom how to even manage the request. She bit the interior of her mouth. If she did this, what would it mean for Mina and Sotiris? Her face chilled.

"If I decline, will Aleksandr's work end?"

"I am not a cruel man. Aleksandr will be busier, but he could continue or maybe outsource its production." He cleared his throat. "I will not use him against you. You have sacrificed enough for that boy. This command is not Magistrate, but I thought perhaps I could give you something back. A career, focus, safety, home, and maybe even answers.

"Perhaps, by the end, some sort of agreement can allow friendlier relations, and you can speak to your family again without fear of reprisals. But for now, you and your children would no longer be on run." He squeezed her shoulder before turning back to the room. The pressure remained even after his hand dropped. "And no, I am not threatening to throw you out. But you would own part of the change, the betterment of Mramor—it would truly be your home. Take time but not too long."

Rage boiled in her chest. Once again, someone had maneuvered her to the precipice of horrible decision-making. At least, Hedda Strom had seen fit to give her plenty of time to run out of rope by her own actions.

A dull laugh left her. "You purposefully waited to ask me until the last minute, hoping I'd make a rash decision."

"It was rash decision of my own," Zakhar said. "When options did not materialize, I made one. But I have good gut feeling about it."

Katya didn't feel the same, continuing to glare at Zakhar's retreating back. Lowering her arms around her abdomen, she faced the growing snowstorm. She'd been sentenced to a sleepless night.

CHAPTER EIGHTEEN

Unlike Usha's formula, this new one didn't result in a complete evening crash, which proved unfortunate for poor Sotiris, who Katya jostled awake with each turn. Her brain formed a kinetic mess of scenarios and jumbled emotions. No matter how she situated herself, the chorus never stopped. Eventually, she freed herself from the pile of warm blankets she'd amassed. She tucked Sotiris in—his heavy eyelids closing as she did—with the single blanket covering him. Without her blankets, she shivered.

Despite slipping on a sweater and socks, she still trembled. The night chill had truly sunk its claws in. She shuffled to the window and edged her way to the other side of the velvet curtain. Pressing her forehead against the frosted glass, she gazed into the dark garden, no longer concealed by the snowstorm. There were a few traces of light emitting from the lower level. Apparently, she wasn't alone in her insomnia.

She wondered if Zakhar was one of them, potentially planning a replacement military consultant—he would be a fool if he wasn't. She had no call to this fight; instead, she felt numbness. She had never had a command of the scale Zakhar proposed. Yes, the training was there, but it amounted to nothing when compared to experience. The man was insane. He had to be to give so much control to a person he didn't really know. Why was he betting so heavily on her?

She knocked her head against the glass. But where did she have to go? Nowhere. Neither location-wise nor personally. She had no prospects, only an offer from a crazy man, a long-time devotee to hopeless causes. She shifted until her cheek and temple rested on the window. And if she picked up his latest hopeless cause, what happened when it went sideways? Why even ask that question? She'd dabbled in Plasovern; that already damned her with Magistrate officials. There was no return there. There'd never been once she'd run.

Removed from the heat of the situation, she picked apart that decision. Perhaps she, Rein, and Mina would've made it through fine. Still, Sotiris would have vanished, absorbed into machinery. Alongside him, the *Aletheia*'s true fate would've been lost much like its fragments to space.

She snorted. The most she'd done to expose its fate was to tell the Oneiroi special ops team, and they possibly never made it off the Jar'rask ship. And so, the Magistrate would continue to use children as weapons.

Exhaling on the window, she created a patch of frost. Like a child, she etched into it with a fingernail. The motion was familiar, yet divorced from memory. She could have answers, even though she didn't want them. This wasn't her home—hadn't been for decades. A phantom touch spread across her hand. Flinching, she dragged her nails through the cartoon tree she'd sketched.

"You're up."

Katya pushed the curtain away, catching Mina as she glided into the room and sat on the sofa.

"What did Zakhar want?"

"That's not important."

Even in the darkened room, she caught the teen's exaggerated eye roll that involved rolling her head as well. Dramatics settled, Mina patted the cushion next to her, and Katya joined her, slumping into the sofa's corner. She drew her legs up away from the cold floor.

"It couldn't have been that bad."

It could be. Clearing her throat, Katya muttered, "He wants a military consultant. A vice admiral."

Mina whistled. "That's more than the Magistrate ever offered you, and he doesn't even know you."

"It's insane."

"Are you going to do it?"

A mix of a snort and shrill laugh poured from Katya's mouth before she could stop it. But given her recent past actions, crazy matched her modus operandi. The scary part was the notion had set its hooks into her: a chance to restore her own normalcy, a return to the rigid structure of military life. She burrowed her fingers into her hair.

"It's your home."

"Is it?"

Mina rolled her eyes. "Of course it is. You're just disconnected from it because they ripped you from it."

Katya smirked at that, hearing Strom's talking points. "That simple, huh?" She left the sofa and folded her arms behind her. She fought the urge to pace like a caged animal. "I love my family" — the girl winced, perhaps thinking of Anaïs — "and they supported me when I had nothing. I was happy." Cotton coated her mouth, and she turned to conceal her face. "Emotions — senses of loyalties — they don't just vanish. They can't be brushed away or forgotten."

Part of her wanted to see if Aleksandr had encrypted communication methods she could use to reach her father. She knew neither the scientist nor Zakhar would approve. Exposure would sink their fragile cause, and despite everything, her father was Magistrate, born and raised. He would not support her if she pursued this cause — and after Anaïs, he might report it.

She curled her toes against the cold wood.

The three of them sat in a precarious position. Zakhar and Aleksandr may be compassionate toward their plight, but they were alone. One shift in circumstances — such as the removal of Zakhar by an opposing faction — could find her and the kids fleeing or in even worse straights.

Why not solidify their position and kill the delusion there was a going back? But faced with a Magistrate vessel, would she be able to give the order to fire?

She tilted her head from side to side to relieve the pressure building there. Even if she could follow through with such an order, there was no guarantee she would achieve the stability and good graces needed to safeguard Mina and Sotiris. Not if others undercut her at every turn.

"We have nowhere else to go," Mina said, echoing her thoughts. "We should make our stand here."

Katya snorted and gave into her inclination for movement, tracing a circle in front of the sofa. "*We* will not. At least not until you hit eighteen. I don't care if it's an arbitrary number. Take that time. Really consider what you're potentially sacrificing your life for."

Mina straightened as she spoke.

Katya continued, "Never give your allegiances on a whim or out of petty revenge. Remember the lesson from Trides."

The teen dropped her gaze to the floor.

"You have roughly five months. That'll help you decide with a rational head." She placed her hands on the teen's shoulders. If only she had those months. Her grip tightened. "Until then, I'll take the first step in."

Mina's face rocketed up. "But you don't believe—"

"I believe in my promise to you all those years ago. Not about making you a pilot. The unspoken part, that I would take care of and protect you." To build something for her and Sotiris, she'd sacrifice logic, her own doubts, herself even. Kneeling, Katya rested her hands on the girl's knees. "There's only going forward. I've been trapped in a past that no longer exists for too long." Her mouth tasted of ash. "And if Zakhar's dream comes to fruition, all the better."

She squeezed the teen's knees before returning to her feet. "Get to bed. I want to have a brief conversation with our host. Everything else can wait until morning."

They parted in opposite directions: Katya entering the hallway and Mina reentering her room. In the blackened hallway, Katya navigated using her memory until she spotted the sliver of light that declared Aleksandr was still awake. As per usual, she knocked.

"Are you up?"

"Yeah, yeah."

He didn't break from the work he was doing on his desktop console. Suspended over it was a warship blueprint. Katya drank in the design, its smaller size and sleek lines built with speed and maneuverability in mind. Aleksandr had tailored it to compete with current Magistrate models, which were marginally larger. Zakhar's words about a war of attrition seemed confirmed by their design. This vessel could outmaneuver the Magistrate's three main classes and avoid engagement. But if it came to that—she traced the cannons—it would put up a fight.

"Just a blueprint, or do they exist?"

"Are you taking Zakhar's offer?"

Katya sat on the corner of his desk, twisting her fingers together. She struggled to tear her eyes from the blueprint. It would be a lie to say the design didn't excite her. One positive in a no-win situation.

"I'm leaning toward it, but"—she met Aleksandr's gaze—"I want to know more about my partner, and I think you're the one to tell me. Why is he betting so much on me?"

"Shame," Aleksandr muttered. "I was getting used to houseguests."

"You could make more friends."

"Too much effort. Though"—he glared at the blueprint—"he is going to be dragging me from my hole." A long-suffering sigh left him. "But you need not worry about Zakhar backstabbing you. He's taken shining to you."

"Why?"

Aleksandr cut the holoprojection. "He is man who has lost much. His son in the war ... his wife to pandemic ... daughter to the mass theft."

The way he'd talked about Mramor's Lost Children struck her. Of course one was his.

"He's never been able to find her?"

"No." Aleksandr rubbed at his eyes. Bags had formed under them. They were all getting very little sleep. "Very few have ever come back or been traced. He never stopped looking as best as could be ... though it has fallen to the side. She would be in her thirties, likely have a life of her own. Who is he to derail that? But you? Your life is already derailed. By helping you, it will bring some joy to him. And it burns the light of hope further. For him, for others."

"And what do you think?"

He shifted his weight. "I trust his judgment of character." Then he chuckled. "Members of intellect surround him, but he needs might. I think given your violent tendencies, you can give that to him." He maneuvered around a table and plunked two small glasses from a cabinet. In each, he poured a clear liquid. "Sleep aid and"—he extended one to her with a smile—"toast to new partnerships."

She accepted and practically inhaled the liquid. It hit strong, scorching her insides on its way down, and she swayed. "Krezk!"

Aleksandr burst into a fit of laughter. "You will sleep well tonight."

"Wh-what is this?"

"About one-ninety-proof grain concoction. I call it, Sweet Dreams." He set his empty glass aside and massaged his face. "And boy? Does he sleep well?"

"It—" She gagged. Krezk, her tongue felt swollen—swollen and numb. "It doesn't knock him out as quickly."

"Yes, it's more gentle nudge. Less extreme." He slumped on to his cot and flopped over. "Plasovern sought quick sledgehammer to problem. They knew they were dealing with ticking bomb on their station and could not afford it going off. Me? I have time to create something more natural." He threw his blankets over his head, leaving only the top of his wild hair exposed. "Sweet dreams. Shut light off on way out."

Katya stumbled to the switch and then, by some miracle, to her room, where she collapsed on the sofa and watched the stars through the curtain gap she'd created until they bled.

The next morning Katya groaned, her vision blurred by a brewing headache. Objects had a distinct double edge to them. That alcohol. Krezk. She hated the sun. It assaulted her through the askew curtains, needling her head. How late in the morn—the thought died as Sotiris leaned against the sofa, his warm breath spreading across her face. If he was up ...

She needed to see Zakhar.

"You were out like a rock." Mina walked into the room while toweling off her hair. She'd apparently used the morning to cut two to three inches off her head. The deep plum dye was fading to her natural brown. "I don't think I've ever seen you out like that … not since, well, Sotiris."

"Can you watch him?" Katya asked while stumbling to her feet. She gathered a fresh, albeit wrinkled, shirt and pants and traded out the old with them. "I want to catch Zakhar before the proceedings start." The other former countries' representatives would arrive at any moment.

To reach the lower floor, she took a secondary servant's staircase she and Mina had discovered during one of their expeditions. They had uncovered a lift too; however, it had been locked by their host's silent employee. Neither Mina nor Katya had gathered the nerve to ask him to leave it open. Besides, the secondary staircase opened close to the room Zakhar had claimed for bedroom and office.

She exited it through the hidden door, which blended with the paneled wall, and when she did, she stiffened. A group of five hardened men, ranging in age from around twenty to at least sixty, broke off their conversation and faced her, exposing empty holsters at their hips—or with the youngest, chest—likely in compliance with some agreement for no weapons at this assembly. Among their number, Katya recognized the scarred face of Matfey Sobol. The man who would become her CO. The lesser evil. His lips pinched in obvious distaste at the sight of her.

She nodded to them in universal greeting and beelined to Zakhar's room. Behind her, one man said something in Moscanov.

When she didn't stop, a loud voice shouted, "Hey!"

She froze, her jaw aching. With no other choice, she faced that voice while gripping her hands behind her back.

"Is that any way to treat comrades?" Sobol asked with his gruff, heavily accented voice. The accent held a distinct flavor, separate from Zakhar and Aleksandr's. He'd come from a very different region of Old Imperiya, Katya wagered.

Around him, his men chuckled, adding commentary in Moscanov—their eyes alight knowing she found the words meaningless. They slid in beside Sobol, forming a wall with their muscular frames; however, they never overstepped him, highlighting their respect for the man. Katya twisted her hands. Fighting just one would be a problem, but there would be no taking on all of them if it came to it.

Having garnered her full attention, Sobol grinned, revealing stained teeth. "So, you are Kozlov's would-be champion?"

"What's it to you?" She loosened her stance, hoping she appeared unperturbed.

He smirked, the scar along the side of his face pulling and whitening. "Merely curious to what he dug up." His teeth poked out from the mockery of a smile. "And I see his purported military genius is a used-up Magistrate soldier who's given into shakes."

Her right gripped her shaking left hand tighter. Around the pounding in her ears, she snapped, "What do you know?"

A snort. "I know it all too much. I have seen too many soldiers crack under pressure. They carry selves similarly. I recognize it in you." He shrugged. "I am sympathetic to such soldiers, but would I give them commands? No. Yet Kozlov rushes to put you in situation you have no business being part of nor have fortitude to see through. You may think me cruel, but he is far crueler."

Forcing aside her first few responses, Katya lifted her head, her chin jutting out. "You know nothing about me." She hoisted up her shaking hand. "I may shake, but I'll never break. Not in command and not to the likes of you."

Sobol's smirk returned. "We shall see. I just hope it doesn't cost too many lives."

The man ambled away with his entourage while Katya clutched her hand, which tremors refused to release. He'd hit the mark dead-on. She never would have passed a

Magistrate psych exam. Yet some part hoped a uniform and a military regime would overpower this mental tic. She was a fool. Still—she glared at Sobol's back—she wouldn't give him the satisfaction of bending her.

"What is going on?" Zakhar asked from his doorway, causing her to jerk.

Doubts flared, coursing through her like electricity. Decline, some part screamed. No, there was no going back.

"I just had a wonderful conversation with one of your associates."

Zakhar stepped farther out, his gaze trained on Sobol's retreating form. "Wonderful? But was it pleasant?"

"Can we talk?"

He nodded and directed her into his room. Like hers and Mina's, he had fully furnished it, complete with a desk coated in paperwork and a few slates. The wheeled office chair, which featured maroon crushed velvet, reminded Katya of something her father would purchase.

"You've decided?" Zakhar shut the door behind them.

"I have. With a caveat."

An eyebrow rose, but he waved for her to continue.

She inhaled. No going back. "I'll join you in this partnership, but I need you to promise if I start to slip, replace me."

"Slip?"

She nodded. She felt no pull to this cause, but she wouldn't be a reason for its collapse.

"I—" She struggled on words to describe the past year—Krezk, it'd been a year. "Before Strom and Plasovern, we were guests of Jar'rasks." No change passed over Zakhar's face, and she wondered if he'd heard of the species. "We ... we made it out by the breadth of a knife, and since then, I've struggled." She didn't think of the sore, often stiff shoulder where the bolt went through. She wouldn't think of Rein, the sound of his body hitting the floor. "It lingers."

She swallowed. "If I stumble because of it, I need you to replace me."

Zakhar stroked his beard, and Katya half-expected him to reject her after all.

"I will do this, though I do not think it will come to it." Zakhar went to his desk and collected some papers and a slate, creating a neat pile in his hands. "You are made from strong material. You were calculated extracting self from Plasovern. I can only imagine the pressure to escape Jomsborg. But you didn't break. Not then, not in navigating through Fringe to Mramor. Your will wins." While holding the stack close to his chest with one hand, he extended the other.

Katya stared at it for a few seconds before taking it with her own. They shook, Zakhar applying tremendous pressure and zeal to it.

A knock separated them.

"Enter," Zakhar called.

The woman from the university, Belova, peeked in, her braid swinging in front of her as she leaned in. So, that was how Zakhar had found them.

The woman inspected them before saying, "The other delegates have arrived. Are things settled?"

Zakhar glanced at Katya before nodding his head. "We are in good order. Shall we, Miss Cassius?" He gestured to the door with a sweep of his arm. Then, as they started off, he nodded to the other woman. "This is my protégé, Miss Militsa Belova. I am old friend of her father."

"One of your revolutionary friends?"

"Discussion buddies." Zakhar took the lead as they traversed the hall, heading to the dining room. "Blazh was always more freethinker than actual revolutionary. Yes, he wanted change, but he was never one for sparking revolution."

Militsa added nothing as they went, though her grip on her slate tightened.

Something had happened to her father, Katya realized after pairing her reaction with Zakhar's choice of "was."

"Alyypriliv murdered him. Magistrate turned blind eye."

"Not for long," Militsa said under her breath.

"During course of meeting, stay with me," Zakhar said over his shoulder to Katya.

Her eyes lowered to her mussed clothing before considering her unbrushed hair and teeth. A room full of dignitaries ... "You can't expect me to attend."

An eyebrow rose. "You will be fine. Follow my lead. Try not to paint a target on yourself. No matter what, do not speak."

She glanced at Militsa, hoping she would see the issue, but the woman remained impassive.

Her breath seemed to sour with defeat and the stirring ghost of last night's alcoholic drink. "What can I expect?"

"We will iron out details and sign League of Fuusi agreement."

He stopped shy of a room with an open set of double doors. At its mouth, others had gathered. They talked in clusters in front of the dining hall, some hushed while others gabbed and belted out good-natured laughter. Their clothes varied from group to group.

Zakhar faced her. "After today, as long as signing goes as planned, we will take the accord to Tausafira to a great convention for ratification."

"Under the Magistrate's nose?"

Zakhar tapped at his own nose. "That is plan."

Katya frowned at him. "How have you avoided Alyypriliv's and the Magistrate's radars?" He would have been a prime candidate to vanish.

He shrugged. "I am cagey old bird."

He then guided them into the larger formal dining room, dismissing further questioning. Someone had cleared the windows' fine layer of dirt, brightening the space. Katya barely recognized the room from their explorations of the palace. For one, it now housed furniture. A large wood table, lined with chairs along its sides, dominated the space. More chair rows orbited it. She noted no chairs at the table's ends, perhaps to prevent one faction from feeling superiority over the rest. Given the massive room, plenty of standing room was available.

To one side, a group wearing traditional Old Imperiya dress, smocks with gold patterns, chatted. In contrast, a group with darker skin tones still clung to their coats, appearing just as displeased with the palace's drafts as Katya.

Zakhar prodded her forward toward an old woman, who wore an old-style smock dress with a red and gold floral pattern; gray fur lined its long sleeves and collar. Over it, she wore a long black velvet vest. She'd braided her hair in a crown, adding to her noble visage. She very much belonged in her surroundings, as if she'd waltzed from some Imperiya storybook.

Her wrinkled face tightened when Zakhar greeted her in Moscanov, adding age lines. She had to be in her seventies, if not early eighties. She responded in the same tongue, to which Zakhar responded; amidst their dialogue, Katya caught her name intermingled. The woman's icy blue eyes inspected every inch of her, lips downcast. She said nothing to Katya. Instead, she uttered one more thing to Zakhar and faced the opposing delegation.

Zakhar tugged at his collar like a scolded schoolboy. He then ushered her and Militsa to the room's periphery.

"You will remain here for meeting's duration. Keep mouth shut and observe. You will learn much." He shifted away as more people shuffled into the room. "Militsa, see that no one harasses." He then departed them, taking his place at the table beside the elderly woman.

"Who is she?"

"A woman of old realm, but too radical for her family. Jekaterina Mikhailovna Menshikova. She is actually a relative of some degree to the former emperor. Yet, she tried to push reforms and was actually a proponent of a constitutional monarchy." Militsa tossed her braid to her other shoulder. "She survived the purge, ironically, because her family had sent her to another country to shut her up partway through war. I think she is the sole survivor of her immediate family. She speaks several local languages but never picked up Magistrate tongue."

"What did she say to Zakhar?"

"Largely that she hopes he didn't misjudge."

Katya's throat tightened. This would be her life until she proved to be a sound investment. She wondered how arduous that task would be. Rubbing clammy hands against her already wrinkled shirt, she once again regretted her apparel.

In front, Zakhar unfurled a piece of parchment while another man helped him lay out pens. Around the table, more factions settled; their spacing split them into eight distinct groups. Some had donned traditional garb, while others had selected clothing that would be as equally at home in the Core. Seeing them all gathered, Katya could not fathom the groundwork Zakhar had done to get them civilly sitting around a table. Many were stone-faced, but there was no goading, no insults, no violence. Zakhar might not have done it alone, but she imagined he played a pivotal role in accomplishing this in thirty years. However, it was a far cry from the planet's thirty former countries.

"How were these representatives selected?" Katya whispered.

"Varies. Most are well known in their homelands and were elected in whisper votes or selected by existing separatist movements."

"And this"—Katya gestured to the filling room—"won't catch notice?"

"We use pirate methods to bring everyone here." Militsa smiled. "Much happens in Taiga that no one knows about."

"And the former countries not here?"

Militsa flipped her braided ponytail back. "It is imperfect."

Sobol strutted into the room. His gaze caught her, but the only acknowledgment had been his downward lips, which rivaled Menshikova's. He loathed her existence here, even if he didn't voice it upfront. Compared to the others' entourages, his men gave the appearance of bouncers, and people shifted from their path as Sobol took his place at the table as if he owned the place. His seat was only a couple removed from Zakhar. His entourage sat just behind him.

As the chairs filled, the standing room became tighter. Katya had a rather large man beside her. A tangy, sweaty aroma wafted from him, and even as Katya stepped away from him, it followed her.

A knocking distracted from the horrible musk. A scraggly man with a beard that stretched past his belly stood at the head of the table, a small wooden mallet in hand. Sickly thin, he gave the impression that a strong breeze would carry him away. He cleared his throat and leaned against the table, using both hands for support.

"Ratification of Mramor's entrance into the League of Fuusi," he said with an incongruously booming voice, which had an odd lilt on the Magistrate words. "All parties have individually read the terms. Altennette. Baast. Kairnet. Mahaan. Old Imperiya. Oriaat. Terrn. Zetne." As he referred to each country, he would extend one hand toward its delegation.

Katya tilted her head to press Militsa on the excluded countries but fell silent when Aleksandr poked his head in, disappeared for a few seconds before stepping in. For once, his pants covered the entirety of his legs, and he wore shoes, which created an awkward gait. His wavy hair had even been slicked back. He carried a small holoprojector in his hand, scuffing the floor as he went.

The speaker sighed, looked to the ceiling, to which he muttered something, before he continued. "If all parties agree to terms, they shall be signed and in a week be transported to Tausafira by representatives Menshikova and Kozlov."

Across the table, a member of the Mahaan, wearing a bright red caplet and white linen shirt, stood. "Should our representatives not show the breadth of Mramor's cause? Old Imperiya is quick to throw its weight around. It always has been. It dragged us into a war, which served us on a platter to foreign interlopers."

A ruckus boomed from his side of the table, a mix of shouts and claps that drowned out other rumblings. Katya shifted between her feet, dread building. Sobol's laugh, however, ascended the rabble. When he too slogged to his feet, a hush fell.

He flicked a finger at the other delegate. "You all rushed in to that quagmire with no help from us!"

"We are not here to rehash war," Zakhar broke in. "We must bury it as it is only means for us to continue."

"So says you," the man spat, his tawny brown skin reddening. "Yet here, instead of equality, it is Imperiya charging to represent us all." He waved his hands as if to elicit support from those on his side of the table. "Who are we to say that it won't lead us into the same trap that Alyypriliv did? I, for one, refuse to be subservient to another Imperiya radical group!"

The table rumbled when those surrounding it rapped their knuckles against it.

"Had Grega not been arrest, you would have had representative!" Zakhar shouted. "As is, goal is travel with small group without rousing suspicions. A crew of multiple Mramorian countries will raise suspicions. You know this." He beckoned the man and Sobol to sit. "I am familiar with details and have good rapport with planetary delegates."

Zakhar inclined his head to the elder stateswoman beside him. "Madam Menshikova"—said woman had a much younger woman with red hair relaying the discourse to her—"will not arouse suspicion traveling with servants. And Madam Menshikova's lineage will be pleasant with our hosts. As monarchists, they do not want to see their establishments burned to ground. Having one of their own kind will ease them. She is also shrewd businesswoman with close ties to Altennette." Zakhar extended his hand to a delegation further down the table dressed in modern attire. The first republic in Mramor before the war and the Magistrate derailed it. "Since she still lives majority of time there, it is her best interest to support its well-being."

The old woman rolled her eyes while her lips puckered in distaste. Not moving a muscle, she spoke in a language decidedly not Moscanov—and the room listened, all eyes trained on her. Her voice carried authority with only the slight crackle of age.

Katya leaned toward her minder. "What did she say?"

"No idea. Likely, it is just the act of fluidly speaking it than anything else. It is also respect."

Katya could see that; however, it had to be more. There had to be a substance behind the act, but in the grand scheme, it didn't matter. All that did was it had calmed the nerves around the table.

"Aleksandr," Zakhar said, shifting attention to another topic.

The scientist activated his projector, and the ship blueprint sprung to life. "Production has concluded on first round, and they are ready to be staffed from shipyard. We are speeding up timetable to coincide with league meeting so we can move in concert with our allies."

He flipped to another display, the planet itself. A second later, the floating, transparent image glimmered as something resembling a grid enveloped its surface like swash rushing the shore. Katya's breath caught. The similarities between what was being showcased and the shielding around W'yrea were remarkable. Her gaze shifted to Zakhar, who still stood, a smile lining his face.

"Our planet will be secured," Aleksandr said. "This technology will ensure no one enters or leaves when we make our move. It will kill communications from Magistrate officials; I have created workarounds for our ships."

"What does the first wave entail?" A man from Baast with sard-toned skin asked, his accent melodic. He had been one delegate to keep his coat, a brilliant teal, which had pops of white fur as trimming. "How will the new warships be dispersed?"

"Evenly among all delegations here," Zakhar said.

"Mutual destruction assured." Aleksandr plastered a smile on his face. "Each will receive two A-Class warships of new design. Rest will be filled out with hodgepodge of crafts pressed into duty or shared with us from Fabrocore. Compared to strength of Magistrate fleet in the Fuusi Arm, we will be more than able to put up fight and back up allies."

"Does that include all Old Imperiya factions?" The man in teal pressed.

"No," Zakhar answered quickly against the brewing storm the question created. "It will truly be equal between all former countries here. Just as it will be in our new parliament structure. Our two warships will go to Sobol and Kuznetsov. In sign of cooperation, my faction will settle with the Fabrocore models until our shipyards can complete more of our own warships. Production is being ramped up."

"To get a Magistrate officer among our ranks," Kuznetsov, who'd settled farther down from Zakhar, said, projecting his voice. A sneer dominated his rat-like face, and once his words sunk in, the delegates searched for the Magistrate officer with darting eyes. Some shouted their questions and demands. In the confusion, Kuznetsov slinked back in his chair, folding his hands across his chest.

Bastard.

Militsa dug her nails into Katya's arm. "Say nothing. Do not react," she said into her ear, barely audible against the pandemonium Kuznetsov had unleashed.

"Quiet!" Zakhar rapped against the table.

"What is the meaning of this? Why were we not informed?" An Oriaat woman, about Katya's age, zoned her pointed finger on Zakhar. Bathed in shimmering red silk, Katya thought she resembled a judge. "This is not in the spirit of open partnership."

Zakhar pursed his lips and seemed to inspect the table's wooden grain before clearing his throat. "After league conclave, I would have brought this forward as I had just this morning received a firm commitment. The person in question is not a Magistrate officer, not any longer. She is one of our Lost Children, returned to us, trained by our very enemy. We use that knowledge against them."

"You can say that, Zakhar, but we need more information," the woman said.

"I second Isi," the man in teal said.

Zakhar chuckled. "She has completely burned bridges with the Magistrate, injured its soldiers, spent six or so months on the run from them, including evading Elites and crippling an A-Class Jar'rask vessel from the inside. There is no going back. She has also brought us a future olive branch with the Oneiroi."

Katya saw red.

Militsa pinched her harder. "Hold tongue."

Her face, however, burned as the sensation of betrayal took root, even though she understood Zakhar's underlying strategy to build her up and reduce opposition. Despite that, she wouldn't let Sotiris be a pawn to be moved when lucrative.

Isi leaned forward. "Olive branch?"

"She rescued a member of their species from nefarious Magistrate intentions." Zakhar shrugged. "It was spark for desertion. Just as it will spark the Oneiroi's desertion."

"Is she present?" Isi asked.

"Ms. Cassius, please come here," Zakhar called.

Before Katya could follow his instruction, Militsa squeezed her arm tight enough to bruise and hissed, "Say as little as possible." She released her hold and allowed Katya to amble forward, her back a ramrod and her arm throbbing.

Zakhar welcomed her to his side, clapping her shoulder with his hand. "Katya Cassius," he said as an introduction. "She was a captain and trained at one of Meracus Domus's top military academies. She will serve as a vice admiral under Sobol. I feel that will put everyone at ease."

Sobol grunted. "I will impose rigorous standards and will not let any treachery pass without response."

"And what of you, Ms. Cassius?" Isi prompted. "Have you nothing to say?"

Katya struggled with how to answer. Her true motivations wouldn't inspire confidence or trust. She settled on: "I'm ready to serve. Zakhar is a brilliant talker."

Isi snorted, her eyes closing with the action. "That he is."

The man in teal ground his fists into the table. "We will have a full examination of her past and skills before giving her a command. You cannot sweet talk your way out of this, Kozlov."

Zakhar merely beamed. "But of course. When we get back from the league conclave. For now, all military plans will continue as have already been discussed and ratified." He then waved Katya away.

She rejoined Militsa, who nodded her approval, before absconding with her from the room. "We will make you scarce now. The fewer people can talk with you, the better. It'll be easier when you go with Zakhar."

"What?" Katya froze in the hall.

"You will go with Zakhar to Tausafira. He can't leave you here, or else someone might act against you."

"I can't leave the kids here."

"They will be fine. Aleksandr will ensure it."

"If he can ensure their security, why not mine?"

Militsa rolled her blue eyes. "For one, they do not know that children exist. And for second, Zakhar wants you with him where he can continue to observe you. Yes, he trusts you, but he is also cautious, as he should be. This will ensure no bungling that will reflect poorly on him and our entire faction. We rest on your back. Never forget that." Militsa brought her to the stairs. "We are in this together. We will fall together ... if it comes to it."

"I understand."

Her minder chuckled. "We all think we do. But we will never fully grasp it until such a moment comes. If it does at all." She then headed back to the meeting, pausing only to add, "Start packing for at least a two-week trip."

Katya ascended the stairs, her stomach twisting like it had when she first boarded Strom's ship. Only now, she couldn't blame blood loss.

CHAPTER NINETEEN

As the sun crept upward, Katya swung her satchel across her shoulder, prepared to meet Zakhar and Menshikova. She'd packed light, opting to bring fewer pants, which she could wear again throughout the journey. If they became stained, the ship had washing facilities she could use. That same reasoning applied to her eight shirts, which were lighter since the section of Tausafira they would visit was classified as tropical. She braided her hair once again, mimicking a style favored by women in Old Imperiya: two side braids spun around a bun.

From the bed, Sotiris glowered at her and the bag. He'd understood the gist of what he'd been told last night, or so it seemed.

"Have you been to Tausafira before?" Mina asked.

"Nope. I've never visited New Acquisitions planets before."

"And you're sure I can't come?"

"Yes." Katya bent over and picked up Sotiris. He could at least see her off. "You'll stay with Aleksandr and make sure he doesn't traumatize Sotiris."

Mina rushed to open the door for her, and she proceeded toward the stairs. All the delegates had already departed—a staggered affair to avoid attention. It'd been midnight by the time the last group left, and Zakhar informed her she would pilot the next day. Instead of the *Pollux*, their ride would be a beaten-up Messertev "Hog" that would have given *The Maelstrom* a run for its money in terms of age and wear and tear.

"*It won't draw attention.*" Zakhar had explained.

"Keep Aleksandr from scaring him too badly or going overboard with his testing. He may be a genius, but he doesn't understand kids."

"I'll try my best." Mina ran her fingers through her long hair and sighed. "Things exit his mouth so quickly."

"Don't I know ..." Katya trailed off at the foot of the stairs, the eyes of Madam Menshikova on her. Her posture, head high, nose slightly up, and eyes narrowed, struck her, summoning memories of her illustrious Uncle Pontius. Oh, the judgment. Beside her, her attendant mirrored the expression to near perfection.

"Ah, good!" Zakhar clapped his hands upon entering the foyer with Aleksandr in tow. "We're set to go."

"I just need a moment alone with our host." Katya beckoned Aleksandr to join her off to the side, which he did like a skittish critter.

"Is this where I am threatened with violence should anything happen to children?" He drawled before shoving his hands into his pockets and leaning back. His freed toes curled against the marble floor.

She snorted. Within the week they'd been trapped in the palace, she'd grown fond of him. "Exactly that. But it's also more than that: Be patient with them. No songs of children freezing to death. Nothing like that."

"So no tales of semi-cannibalism?"

Her brows lifted. "Semi-cannibalism? No. And there is no such thing as semi-cannibalism."

"Well, witch turned mother into sheep before she was devoured, so *technically* not cannibalism. But yet, she was also human at one time."

Her right eye twitched. "Definitely no stories like that."

He actually pouted, leading Katya to wonder if those were the only type of stories he'd been told as a child, but then he grinned broadly, his frame once again bursting with energy. He removed one hand from a pocket, bringing with it a little baggy.

"I perfected a chewable!" He fished out one little square and offered it to Sotiris. "Candy."

Sotiris perked from where he'd buried himself in Katya's shoulder, the dour expression lifting from his face. Like any other child, he accepted the offering with greedy abandon. But the moment he plopped it into his mouth, his lips contorted. Before Katya could get a free hand up, he spat the medicine on to the floor. Several raspberries followed, which Katya believed Sotiris purposefully blew in Aleksandr's direction, as he struggled to banish the taste from his mouth.

Aleksandr scowled at Sotiris, lines forming deep ridges on his forehead. "Ungrateful, caviar thief."

"What did you make it taste like?"

"What do *I* care of taste?" Aleksandr raised his voice. "All I care is that it works."

"He's a child. He's going to be repulsed and not take it if it tastes like crap."

Aleksandr's brows scrunched together. "Brats should be grateful and take their medicine."

Katya ground out, "Children don't work like that."

Under his breath, Aleksandr muttered something sounding vaguely like "they should." He then shifted to a full fake smile. "I will work on flavoring for caviar thief." He swung around and marched up the stairs, not looking back.

Her heart heavy, Katya handed the still sour-faced Sotiris to Mina. She then hugged them both. "If it goes sideways and the Magistrate gains control, stay hidden. However, if you can't, steal a ship. Get away. Break off to a neutral system. Lie about your age. Two children refugees will probably get through. Do you understand?"

Mina stiffened in her arms. Tremors then spread through her frame as Katya held her.

She tightened her grip. "No matter what, stay alive."

Mina nodded her head against her cheek, hair scratching Katya's skin. "I-I understand."

"Good." Katya released them and stepped back, drinking the pair in. "I'll see you when I get back. Don't go overboard with improving your arm and keep Aleksandr in line."

Mina smiled, though she'd gone gaunt. "Yeah, yeah."

Then with Zakhar, the madam, and the latter's attendant, she departed. It snowed heavily as they crossed the lawn to where Zakhar had parked the freighter.

"How seriously do they monitor traffic?" Katya asked when she came beside Zakhar. She knew none of the delegates had flown into the property, yet they would be leaving in a freighter from it now.

"Thoroughly. But being a lawyer, I am very knowledgeable of paperwork and the shipments Aleksandr routinely receives. Since he still gives useful patents and research, they will not cut flow of materials reaching him." He adjusted the thick scarf around his neck. "We will be fine to leave from here. As for Tausafira, there's a staggered approach for delegates to avoid attention. It was more technologically advanced planet when inducted, so it receives more traffic than Mramor."

Inside the freighter, the madam and her lady-in-waiting — Katya didn't know what else to call her — retired to their quarters while Zakhar and Katya headed to the cockpit. There, he flopped into one of the side seats near the communications console.

Katya fired up the freighter, checking over all of its systems and the data she was receiving. "We should have a mechanic with us."

"I figured you'd be able to manage that. I can pilot, though I figure, leave it to the young." He fiddled with his console, probably sending their departure information. "But I wouldn't worry. These Messertevs are quite sturdy."

No active warnings. It showed some promise. But the vessel's age summoned concerns. The ship was not much younger than *The Maelstrom* had been. Boita had a track record of stability and longevity ... Messertev was not a manufacturer she would place her wagers on.

"We're approved for departure."

"On it." She activated the atmospheric thrusters and lifted them. A pang rang in her chest as the palace grew smaller and disappeared in the forest of soaring pines. It conjured emotions from Jomsborg and the runs Strom had dumped on her.

"They will be fine," Zakhar soothed. "Aleksandr will see to it. Or his turrets."

"It's still ... hard. Things have been so hard lately."

"I understand that."

In open space now, Katya glanced at the man. He gave all appearances of being lost in the stars visible through the viewscreen. Of course, he would understand. She guaranteed he was thinking of his own daughter.

"Aleksandr told me about your daughter."

Zakhar sputtered to alertness from his stupor. "Ah ..." he uttered airily. "He would do that, I suppose." He scratched at his beard and shifted in his seat. "She was … not as lucky as Aleksandr. It happened so fast … I couldn't hide her." His hand stilled, and then he slowly lowered it to his lap, where he clasped it in his other one. "I did search, but you can only get so far in a gigantic universe with no help. Some guidepost to narrow your search. The fragility of the mind also obstructs you.

"It's been so long. Little details evaporate, leaving only impressions in shifting sand. But I remember her smile, her dimples. I have no photos anymore. There'd been a fire in Velikaya Stolitsa, and my house was among the casualties. All that remains is in here." He pointed to his head. "There are times I wonder if perhaps I might have passed her and never known it was her. Perhaps she's changed so much since she was a child, making my memories useless."

A silence fell between them.

Katya set their course and let the autopilot bring them up to FTL speed. She would monitor the cockpit for a while before retiring into whatever space Zakhar had set aside for her. However, she forgot the display when Zakhar stood.

With a thick voice, he said, "I couldn't continue, not as I was. It was only rending my heart to pulp. Unless the Magistrate opens its records, if they even exist, as I know Alyypriliv gave them little, I can only wait and hope she returns home."

He clapped her shoulder and headed to the door. Before slipping out, he added, "There is database started for Mramorian parents. You should really consider testing." His voice filled with gravel. "It's not just answers for yourself."

"Her granddaughter?" Katya disregarded the helm to face her copilot, who did none of the required work.

Arms folded across his stomach, Zakhar shrugged. "It was different times."

With this latest tidbit, Katya reexamined their other travel companions, who'd cloistered themselves in their quarters, with only the attendant, Kadri Tamm, leaving to fetch food. She made the perfect shadow as she moved with practiced grace to not draw notice. To think Kadri was actually her employer's secret granddaughter. Meanwhile, Menshikova, who preferred to be addressed as madam, had once held the title princess, the actual daughter of a Moscanov emperor and a great aunt to the last one.

"Does Miss Tamm know?" Katya prodded.

"Yes, but some matters are just not discussed outside closed doors." Zakhar removed his slate from the navigation console. "Even when systems were dismantled decades ago."

Katya couldn't understand why not. The concept proved so foreign. While illegitimacy had been a part of Magistrate culture, it'd lacked such stigma. A child conceived outside a union would not sully a family's name. And if a patriarch decreed a person, with or without shared blood, would be stitched on to the family, it was done.

He passed his slate to her. "It's good to prepare. This will give better understanding of League."

She cringed to see walls of text. Written in Magistrate, she could read the document cementing the confederation — all two hundred pages. After the preamble, which stretched two pages, she took to skimming, finding most sections pedantic.

Zakhar had shared summarized parts through the trip as he injected himself into her routine of ration bars, exercise, and monitoring the helm. While he shared some relevant information about their present mission and their longer aims, he'd sprinkled in Mramorian tales and Imperiya gossip. He'd avoided mentions of Mramor's Lost Children, for which he had Katya's gratitude.

Rubbing an eyebrow, Katya preferred Zakhar's colorful summaries.

The drafters had been keen to maintain planetary independence while crafting functional tendons between league member planets. While each member safeguarded their own system, the confederation document laid the groundwork for joint operations, mutual aid, and the sharing of materiel in war. It painstakingly separated governance. Though the league had co-opted the Magistrate's regional system, only it would be more limited in its power. Trade, new planet admission, and resource management would be its duties.

She cast aside the slate as the lines blurred. "They seem to have thought of everything."

"I should hope!" Zakhar grinned. "Do you have any idea how many lawyers it involved to craft this?"

She snorted. She could imagine the staggering number, with each planet demanding their own partake in the drafting. Flipping her bangs to the side, she tapped a finger along her pant leg. Yet Mramor had sliced a sizeable number of former countries from the table.

"Why only eight?"

Zakhar tilted his head, then his bushy eyebrows lifted. "Oh." He shifted in his seat. "Yes, that. Like all things Mramor, it is complex."

"We have time."

He chuckled, but then seemed to mull over his words. As he did, his fingers rolled against each other. "Some old countries destabilized even worse than Old Imperiya; it would be too risky to invite them in. Others—particularly the smaller ones—have opted to watch. We keep their representatives informed, but they maintain plausible deniability. I imagine if our initial expulsion works, they will become more engaged." His hands clenched, knuckles whiting. "And then, there are the Fourth Coalition countries."

Leaning into his seat, he sighed. "The wounds haven't healed there. Those at table had become allies during the war. Most still clamor for reparations. They will not have them at table."

"And you?"

He bowed his head. "Perhaps me too." The words hung until Zakhar clapped. "Let us not be troubled with this. We have enough to consume our time with. When we reach Tausafira, you will be bodyguard. Keep eyes open and mouth shut. You speak not a word of Magistrate. And tread carefully. This planet is landmine of taboos. Do not walk under woven archways; only priestesses and the queen can. Never make direct eye contact with anyone. Bow or nod, depending on their rank.

"Their queen is mythological figure in their culture. A uniting figure who brought planet together," Zakhar continued. "The Magistrate, as you know, is not one for what they deem superstitious, but she is so revered, they keep her in place. But at sixteen, she is largely an imprisoned figurehead. She is paraded to be seen and largely locked away. Her liberation will be key to continuation of Tausafira's position within the league."

"If she can't be secured?"

"The people will not follow the leading proponents for independence. Her safety is utmost. I cannot stress enough that these people believe she is divine."

He reclaimed his slate and closed the league documents, switching to an old-fashioned ink sketched seal on worn leather. While faded, the nude figure of a woman could still be made out with her full curves. Her hair waved outward, a jeweled crown at its center. Meanwhile, a type of ivy wrapped around her body and bore fruit. Fragments of the fruits had been cut open, revealing many tiny black seeds.

"Their tales speak of an original queen, the unifier," Zakhar explained. "She took the throne, brought all countries under her. How? That is up to debate. But the continued legend, which stretches to now, is that original queen has continually been reincarnated. Her soul passing into each queen's womb and then being reborn. The kicker? They are all virgins."

Katya raised a brow, expecting that he was pulling her leg, but he only returned her gaze earnestly, face deadpanned.

"You're serious?"

"Very. There is ritual, from what I gather. Secret ritual. My understanding is Magistrate has been against its practice. It makes sense they'd like the line to end. While the Magistrate has made concessions for most planets' traditions, one can imagine they wouldn't want a 'divine being' to conflict with their authority. I understand the current queen owes her existence to some sleight of hand from the faithful." Zakhar shrugged. "But I do not judge. Sizeable portion of Mramor still believes in unseen supreme being, and most of our countries had rulers with divine rights. Sure, most were deposed and murdered, but to each their own."

"Keep our opinions to ourselves."

"Exactly." He twiddled his thumbs. "I am just glad we have no stake in absconding with the queen. That falls on others."

The surrounding gravity shifted, bringing them another step toward matching their destination's own. The freighter lacked a sophisticated system, and each notch was noticeable, building pressure in Katya's head and drawing out aches in her joints, especially her shoulder.

"And what do you believe?" Katya asked.

Zakhar chuckled and wagged a finger at her. "Never talk politics or religion. I talk too much politics; I shouldn't add religion." His joints creaked when he rose. "I will inform our companions we're few hours out."

Katya filled the silence following his departure with available stations. What chaos was occurring in the Fringe went unmentioned on the news channels she'd found.

Trides was also absent. It seemed the Magistrate had Tausafira on an information diet. What coverage she found related to the planet's weather, trade news, and ongoing infrastructure projects, with human interest features sprinkled in between. The next channel featured the type of celebrity gossip Mina would have enjoyed.

She shifted to music, choosing a channel with slow melodic vocal tracks, which were only accompanied by an odd stringed instrument or sometimes an assortment of them. She could only describe their strokes as happy or plucky.

Another tweak in the gravity drew a grimace. That had been more than a single-level shift. She rolled her right shoulder while massaging it and uttering curses.

A notice flashed across the viewscreen, the navigation console chattering. Increasing traffic ahead. Air control broadcasted several routes to the helm, and Katya selected the one to the spaceport Zakhar had secured for them. It would be nearest to their lodgings, and he'd memorized several escape routes if needed.

Katya adjusted the freighter's speed. As they met other vessels, she integrated the freighter into the stream of traffic heading toward Tausafira. It was another couple of hours before they waded into the planet's atmosphere, past a few widely dispersed warships patrolling the planet's space. Their presence wasn't disturbing. Like Mramor and other New Acquisitions, entrance to Tausafira was more guarded. She cataloged five C-Classes and one B-Class, going from the information on the navigation console. No A-Classes. No Elites.

The pathway on the console blinked, diverting them to Zakhar's chosen port, a smaller one that was a remnant of Old Tausafira's merchant guild. They'd had several across the planet and had controlled commerce with an iron fist. Following the guild's dismantling, it'd become another public port.

Through the viewscreen, Tausafira resembled Trides—tropical and brimming with an array of colorful and exotic flora. Though larger chunks had been cleared for massive cities. Still, much like Trides, nature had been intertwined into civilization. Lush green ivy and flowering vines climbed older sandstone structures' sides and dangled from balconies. Where modern metal buildings had been constructed, plants were also cultivated, trelliswork giving footholds. Vines looped around architectural arches. Amidst the green, bits of gold peeked through, catching the sun.

The similarities set her teeth on edge, but she banished thoughts of Tres and Anaïs. Instead, she bent her focus to the now: the seditious meeting she would be attending. She brushed her tongue between her lips and followed instructions to slow her speed further. The path looped around one city corridor before approaching the port. Air traffic control skirted around the area, but their vessels were incapable of transcending the stratosphere, imperfect for chasing spaceships. Though, the Magistrate could rally more capable ships. If they had to run, it would be luck interceding on their behalf.

Finishing the loop, Katya slid into the designated port opening and parked, starting a cooling sequence that hissed and moaned. She hated this freighter.

"All clear?" Zakhar said when he poked his head into the cockpit.

"For now." She tapped the console. "We should have taken the *Pollux*."

"It has too much history. And not right type." He clapped his hand against the freighter's metal. "This one has made many missions to planets within this sector and abroad in ports where it was thoroughly inspected and observed to have diligently been used for freight. It is not Trides vessel. And it is not Plasovern vessel. There is too much risk of agent visually confirming it." He chuckled. "Besides, the princess rests more comfortably in something Mramorian made."

She rolled her shoulder and stood. "I'm not sure how. That gravity shift is a beast."

"And yet the old do not complain." He sloughed off his coat, casting it on to the communications console chair. "There's no need for winter wear. It's boiling out there." Then after clapping her shoulder—ignoring her wince—Zakhar added, "Come now, we must settle ourselves and prepare for tomorrow."

Katya blinked at his retreating form, then at the current ninety degrees readings on the screen. Boiling indeed. After finishing the lockdown routine, she left her coat in the cockpit and caught up with Zakhar, who waited in the main hold with their bags. He handed Katya her bag, which she strung across her good shoulder.

He then dipped his hand into his unzipped bag, removing a holstered pistol, which he offered to her. An Avitus AVI-14. Newer than her old trusty sidearm, but not too new. "Ready to upgrade to bodyguard?"

"Definitely" She fastened the holster to her hip, the added weight a comfort that'd been missing for far too long.

He shot her a smile. "I legitimately registered it. It will pass through any checkpoint. No problem."

The princess, clutching a cane with a carved sodalite ornament at its top, and her attendant—her granddaughter—descended from the freighter's lift to join them in the hold. Miss Tamm rolled a suitcase with a large handbag on its top, fastened to the retractable metal handle. She nodded to Katya and Zakhar while the princess maintained an air of imperial indifference. The princess's hair, pinned in a regal coiffure, held a golden band with emeralds that resembled a tiara; it completed her ensemble. She said nothing to Katya and Zakhar as she passed them. As she went, Katya noted the cane's carving was a bird's skull.

Zakhar spoke in the Old Imperiya tongue as he lowered the ramp. The princess returned his comment before sweeping down it, the red-headed woman rushing after her. Zakhar struck his tongue against the roof of his mouth and gestured Katya forward.

Fitting her new role, Katya scanned their surroundings and stuck close to the other women. They had their own separate port pod, which wasn't surprising given its age and design. Vines scaled the walls, stretching toward the curved semiopaque ceiling that took a golden hue as it allowed some light to pass through. A man approached, and Katya imposed herself in the space between him and her "employer." She, however, readily obeyed the princess's backward wave. Just like any good bodyguard.

The man, a port official, wore Magistrate blue and a sour expression, as if someone had pissed in his cereal. His fingers hammered his slate's display. "Cargo?" he asked, tone clipped.

Kadri stepped forward. "We have none." She extended her slate before continuing with an almost flawless Magistrate accent. "My employer" — she extended her hand to the princess — "is investigating a business lead for confectionaries." Then she waved to Zakhar and Katya. "Our captain and our bodyguard. I am the only one who can speak Magistrate."

The port official quirked an eyebrow and scoffed. "I'm sure." He ran through the assistant's slate. "A former princess." He snorted, shaking his head. "Fools. All enraptured by old lackluster gems. I don't understand why they bend over backward ..." he grumbled more under his breath. "Obliviously, they're not stationed here." He hooked his slate into the other, downloading their papers. "All's in order. Enjoy Tausafira. I'm sure you'll find it nostalgic."

The princess asked something of her translator, who reclaimed her slate and presumably summarized the conversation. Zakhar added to the conversation, leaving Katya the odd one out. She gritted her teeth. She'd effectively been silenced.

Once free of the pod, Zakhar led them through the small port with its relatively quiet halls, which were attached to other private pods. Her role never breaking, Katya stuck close to the princess, maintaining an alertness that wasn't an act. She tracked security, sought blind spots in it, and tried to determine what traffic the lesser port drew. They passed two talking sentries. One rolled her eyes before popping a piece of chewing gum into her mouth. The pair only shot their group a brief glance before resuming their conversation. Fresh tyros, Katya deemed. Bored out of their minds at a post that brought no challenge.

"The hotel is connected," Zakhar whispered into her ear. "You will remain with princess and Miss Tamm while I meet a contact. Relax. Tomorrow will be hectic."

Katya nodded, eyes set on a series of closed pods, which displayed the Magistrate eagle on their doors. What were they using those for? She pressed her lips together. She almost stepped on Zakhar's heels when he paused before changing directions into a pale blue tiled corridor. She hesitated before following. However, her thoughts lingered behind. Operations would be based in Magistrate-constructed spaceports, not in some cramped, outdated holdover from a former regime. Could they run Elites through this one? The Magistrate often kept Elite species isolated for various reasons.

Zakhar turned around and beckoned to her, saying something in Moscanov. His onward wave gave his meaning, and she followed.

The man guided them into a multistory atrium, where they could peer down from the third floor. Plants grew around the atrium's metal skeleton, basking in the light the walls of glass provided. From their sheen, they'd been crafted from old-fashioned glass. Katya lifted a hand to block the light and halted after she'd walked past a wall of vines. A giant gold statue, surrounded by cascading towers of water, stood arms stretched to the side, palms up. From their level, they were even with the statue's exposed midriff. It, meanwhile, towered above them, almost reaching the atrium's glass ceiling. It'd been intricately engraved and detailed, hair flowing past the woman's breasts and along her thighs. Within it, delicate jeweled flowers had been dispersed.

"Don't stare. First queen." Zakhar nudged her. "Gods are to be ever present but never gazed upon. Come now."

Katya lowered her gaze, but it was hard not to cast sideways glances as the statue glimmered in the sun. Continuing to walk, she tugged at her shirt's collar with her free hand and undid its two top buttons. Even without her coat in tow, her top was better suited to Aleksandr's cold palace. The princess, with her heavy damask dress, collected moisture on her brow. Her granddaughter offered her arm for further support while rolling the suitcase.

Leaving the atrium only provided mild relief, since the new hallway's vents pumped out the barest amount of cooled air. The short-lived respite ended when Zakhar opened the door to an open pedestrian bridge.

On it, the wind whipped Katya's bangs against her brow. The breeze provided little heat relief, though the roof of dangling green blocked the sun.

The princess muttered something and pointed to where peacekeeper vehicles hovered and obstructed an intersection. It'd resulted in a backup of floating hovercars miles above the ground. In upper walkways, people clustered together and craned over the railing. A man hoisted a little girl, placing her above the rest. Even from a distance, Katya made out the little girl's hands waving with excitement.

"What's going on?" Katya asked,

Then, through the intersection, a motorcade passed. Flags and regalia fluttered from the black hovercars that formed it—all composed of Tausafira emblems featuring the planet's fruits. The cars were devoid of the Magistrate eagle or laurel.

Zakhar's shoulder brushed against hers. "The present queen."

Sure enough, a convertible hovercar emerged in the middle of the motorcade. A finely attired girl, younger than Mina, sat in its backseat. Her flowing gold silk gown shimmered in the sun, as did its mix of orange and aqua jewels. She wore a gemmed crown, featuring fruits and flowers encased in gold. Her stylists had worked it into the curls of her black hair. She made no grand gestures to the crowd, which had all lowered their heads as she passed.

The motorcade disappeared past the hotel, leaving cheering crowds in its wake. The little girl beamed down at the man, who returned it, before they carried on with their day, walking along the far walkway, her still perched on his shoulders. Katya swallowed, a certain hollowness sinking in to her chest.

She pushed away from the railing and asked Zakhar, "Why is Tausafira joining?"

"Like Mramor, they are a proud people." He shrugged. "Unlike Mramor, their near memory of life before Magistrate is filled with remembrances of wealth ... or at least in the memories of the sizeable former upper crust. To reclaim that former glory is motivator."

Katya tried to remember how Tausafira had come under Magistrate jurisdiction, but the answer was not there.

Zakhar walked away. The princess and Kadri had already entered the hotel and its air-conditioning.

"And those who weren't the elites of society?" She called to his back.

"Like Mramor, they fear the erasure of culture, of religion." He held the door open for her, and she drifted into the hotel. It'd probably cost a fortune with its connection to the spaceport. "The Magistrate cannot understand Tausafira's religion, and its attempts to assimilate the people were sloppy. Never underestimate the power of belief. And in this case, how embedded worship of the royal family is." He closed the door behind them.

"Does the queen support this movement?"

Zakhar exhaled, air gushing from his mouth. "I imagine she is aware, but in her position, she can do nothing. Neither support nor oppose." The corners of his lips turned downward. "A sixteen-year-old girl who has lived in cage for entirety of her life. That fact is not likely to change, no matter who holds key."

A figurehead for all her life. "A sad existence."

"Perhaps, perhaps not." He smiled. "One cannot predict future, and it can always be worse."

She considered the girl's age. "What happened to the previous queen?"

"Palace walls cannot stop death," Zakhar said. "With an influx of foreigners, diseases were introduced and spread. They showed no favoritism to the rich or, in her case, to a god. However, given the Magistrate's previous actions, conspiracy took root that they'd had her killed."

"Did they?"

"Hmm ..." Zakhar started toward where the princess and her attendant waited. "Perhaps with indifference, but I doubt by sword, firearm, or poison."

Using an enclosed elevator, they went up a floor where Zakhar guided them to room four hundred and twenty-five. He removed his slate and tapped his finger against its surface until the door opened, exposing a minty fragrance.

"Ladies, your room. I am right next door." He stepped aside, giving them full entrance into the rather expensive suite, which had two bedrooms, a shared bathroom, a common sitting room, and a kitchenette. "Make selves comfortable. I will connect with contact." He transitioned to Moscanov, addressing the princess before departing. To Katya, he added, "I'll be back shortly."

He closed the door, sealing her with two women, who were inspecting her with steady interest. The princess perched on the sitting area's plush sofa and kicked off her shoes before crossing her legs. With a long sigh, she accepted her attendant's offering of a glass of water from the kitchenette. As the princess drank, Miss Tamm took her shrug and placed it on their bags. The former noblewoman brushed the back of her hand against her brow as she discarded the empty glass on a side table.

Kadri shuffled their bags into one room. Shifting her bag, Katya escaped to the vacant room, feeling her moves followed by the princess; however, the old woman didn't stop her progress. As Katya passed the first room, she witnessed Kadri unload the suitcases' clothing into a small armoire.

Her own room was smaller and only had one bed, which could comfortably fit two people. The space was air-conditioned, but she still felt overheated. Shuffling through her bag, she removed a loose, airy short-sleeved blouse. As she held it up, she froze. Behind her, someone padded their way into the room. She turned to find the princess with her arms folded before her. She then spoke in Moscanov. Katya could only blink at her since there'd been no gesture to attach meaning to the words.

"Now the guardian dog is away; it is time we talked," the attendant translated, coming to stand at the princess's shoulder. She then corrected, "You and Madam Menshikova, that is." She paused as her elder continued to speak. "I do not know what Zakhar sees in you. I know nothing of you. Just like smoke, you appear. Your loyalties are untested, untried … all I can see is a liability. No matter what skills you might possess."

Katya, her muscles coiling, let the words hit, unsure how to respond. The princess's lips became downcast.

"Where do your loyalties lay, Ms. Cassius?" The attendant translated after another burst of Moscanov. "Why have you agreed to this?"

She mulled over her options, never straying from the princess's impassive face. Her command in the meeting room suggested Menshikova held a lot of sway that could either benefit Katya or drown her. Zakhar's promise of helping her navigate Mramor's treacherous politics filtered to the forefront. But wouldn't it be better to secure more allies? More walls between her and the others. Katya dropped the blouse on to the bed.

"I have no other options." Blunt, honest. It drew a smile to the old woman's face when her assistant translated the answer for her. "I can't go home. I couldn't stomach Plasovern."

The woman dusted off her left shoulder and spoke, her assistant translating, "Zakhar sees a woman with ingenuity. I see a rudderless ship with no loyalties. Who is to say our cause will hold your attention for long? We may have been your homeworld in some small fraction of your life, but that is meaningless. You know nothing of us; you have no stake in our cause. So, I ask again. Why have you accepted Zakhar's proposal?"

Katya swallowed, her cheeks heated. "You're wrong."

The princess's brows lifted after she received the translation, her head slanting.

"You've misjudged me." A smile spread across Katya's face. "I served the Magistrate since I was eighteen. I would still serve it despite my career stalling."

The princess started to say something further, but Katya wasn't ready to cede the conversation.

"It's ingrained in me, as my teenage charge would say." She stepped closer while not invading the other women's space. "As for Plasovern, I never respected their methods. If I hadn't been bleeding out, I never would've turned to them."

The princess spoke. Her attendant translated, "And us?"

Katya hid her hands behind her back, where she clenched them together. "My loyalty lies with the two kids I'm caring for. The girl who will undoubtedly embrace your cause with gusto, as she's still very much in pain from what the Magistrate did to her. And a little Oneiroi boy who had his family ripped from him and doesn't deserve to be turned into a weapon. I will do everything to ensure their well-being, and Mramor is in line with that."

"The olive branch?" the attendant asked without the prompting of the princess.

"Possibly." Her chest tightened. She knew too little about the Oneiroi to guarantee Zakhar's statement.

"And what of yourself?" the attendant asked for the princess. "Have you no ambitions?"

"They come first."

The princess snorted once Miss Tamm translated the message. Her gaze traveled up and down Katya, lines deepening. It twisted her internally as the moment stretched, and she nearly jumped when the princess spoke.

"There is something familiar about you," the attendant supplied. "But she can't quite place it. Do you remember anything of your childhood on Mramor?"

"Blood and snow."

The princess shook her head, a downcast expression. She moved closer to her granddaughter, muttering something into her ear before exiting to her own room.

Kadri bit her lip, giving her a younger appearance. "It is no help to her. Too many can remember blood and snow. Rich, poor … too common. Though, it may strike her eventually. The princess is still quite sharp with her memories."

Katya swallowed hard against the pressure in her throat. She only nodded.

CHAPTER TWENTY

Katya yawned, though she hid it behind her hand. Once again, she shifted on the uncomfortable wooden seat, which reeked of polish, and its sliver of padding while below politicians from several worlds droned. With her adjustment, she winced when the cushion, made of leather, squeaked. It'd collected her sweat, of which there was plenty since the musty lecture hall lacked air conditioning. Over-sized ceiling fans offered the only air circulation, barely any at all.

Beside her, Zakhar had folded a nonessential paper into a fan and batted it up and down in front of his face. Unlike her, he remained enraptured by the political intrigue unfolding, unaware of the sweat collecting in his beard. She shifted toward him to catch the breeze of his fan, a fleeting comfort.

She wasn't made for this type of heat.

Pressing her lips together, she sipped from the lukewarm swill that paraded as coffee. Her second cup. Zakhar had purchased the first from a machine as he'd ripped them from their rooms before the sun had even risen. There'd been a staggered arrival plan for the "conference," held at an old university in a more residential section of the city. Their group had drawn the short straw, forcing them to arrive at the lecture hall before most other groups. She'd then visited a similar machine on the lunch break. Even with a cold sandwich in her gut and more coffee, she struggled to keep her lids open.

Running her clammy hand against the side of her face, she shifted again. This time her knee clipped the edge of the wood desk in front of her, drawing a grimace.

Stay awake.

At the old lecture hall's center, a man with a shaved head except for his long, braided black mohawk continued his recital of a trade article. In the morning, he'd introduced delegates from forty planets, allowing each the floor for grandstanding and posturing. Once that task finished, he'd transitioned into business: a complete reading of the League of Fuusi's confederation articles. Line for line.

All proceedings occurred in Magistrate—the shared tongue between them all. A screen in the desk transcribed the words for all to read, even though the sound system carried them well from where they sat. Though glancing at the princess's screen, it seemed to offer translations for select members.

Katya tried to follow the negotiations but struggled to keep details straight. Unlike those present, she hadn't spent the better part of a year poring over them. Most dictated roles within the league, which were nebulous at best, primarily concerned with creating buffers and preventing any one planet or system from domineering the confederation. Currently, less wealthy worlds sought greater protection, noting their limited resources. Quite a few hard-line planets, meanwhile, questioned what they would offer in return.

The princess's assistant had her work cut out for her, monitoring the screen's translation and adding finer points it had missed. The poor girl had to be going hoarse.

Taking another sip, Katya scanned the delegates, who filled the lecture hall's seats from around the rim of her paper cup. A mix of humans and humanoid species. The bulk followed the dealings without a translator. Unlike the Mramor assembly, calmness surrounded this gathering. No outbursts. Debating, lobbying, disagreements over minute details, yes. But there was no yelling, cursing, or bitter retorts. It all held promise, but Mramor couldn't be the only fractured planet. Add the correct amount of pressure to the right fissure, and it could all topple.

She shifted and brushed her bangs to the side.

A long-suffering sigh emitted beside her. "Settle," Zakhar muttered under his breath, not even averting his attention from the screen. "Or go. Slip out, get some fresh air. Just stop."

"Are you sure?"

Zakhar pinched the bridge of his nose above his glasses. "Yes. Go. We are getting to amendments, and I cannot be distracted."

She opened her mouth, but Zakhar silenced her with one finger held up.

"I have already told you. Precautions have been made, and sometimes face-to-face meetings are necessary to convey full meanings, particularly in matters such as these." He scrolled on his slate. "And with such matters, allies want to see each other's mettle. To know they are as committed and will put all on the line."

Katya tapped against her leg. She still thought it a foolhardy measuring stick that endangered the league's cause before it could solidly move against the Magistrate.

But the planets gathered didn't have long-standing histories compelling this alliance. Ironically, the Magistrate was the only tether between them. Not only had it provided the league with its parliamentary language, but it'd also installed a relay system that had spanned the light-years between member planets.

"Go."

Not needing further prodding, Katya crept along the aisle to the staircase, which she climbed to the third-floor door. She paused on the landing, scrutinizing the room's occupants longer. From the new angle, she estimated close to three hundred in the lecture hall. Despite Zakhar's assurances, her doubts remained. The Magistrate was neither blind nor ignorant.

Pushing open the door, she walked to the railing that presented an uninterrupted view of the ground floor. Below, Tausafiraians kept watch, chatting on coms. She assumed spotters monitored various parts of the city. They'd better be because even cloaked under the guise of academia, people from this many planets would attract attention.

She tossed her unfinished coffee into a trash canister and continued along the deserted hall. From this morning, she knew the floor connected with one of Tausafira's suspended walkways, and she wanted air.

When she opened the door to it, she discovered a Tausafiraian guard. She wore an airy blouse that blended as a civilian, excluding the military service arm at her hip and the assault rifle in her hand.

"Are they taking a break?" she asked.

"No, just me. They're diving into the amendments now." She put forth her most charming smile. Be memorable enough to make it back in without too much hassle because she was getting fresh air. "I'm just muscle for the Mramorian delegates."

She beamed at that. "Oh?"

"Don't be so quick to judge," she chided, tone light, untouched. "I'll be back around in a few minutes. I just need to stretch my legs."

"Enjoy."

She wished. The heat didn't decrease outside, though the mugginess became less oppressive. She inhaled deeply and experienced immediate regret. Sneezes ripped through her body. Pollen of some variety hung in the air around the campus. Through tears and the vines, she spotted many flowering trees below her. The culprit was probably the pink variety, which was dropping its blossoms.

She couldn't believe it, but she actually missed the chill of Old Imperiya and Aleksandr's dead garden.

Swallowing drainage, she strolled along the walkway. She staked out the campus below, which was smaller than some she'd visited in her father's orbit. Some of those were cities all their own. Amid a break, it was quiet with most of the students away. She would spot one or two meandering on the sidewalk below. The vines grew tighter together as she crossed over a hovercar lane, further blotting out the sun with the aid of Tausafira's towering buildings. On the other side, she looped around another building. She was unsure if it belonged to the university or not, but it didn't seem to be in use, at least not on this level.

As she approached the buildings' east face, she found herself in the dark, as the vines had grown so thick. A gap somewhere farther down allowed a swift breeze, which rustled her bangs and brought comfort. She discovered its source later: an observation deck. She lingered there, resting on the railing and soaking in the unrestricted view of the city to the east and its darkening sky. Soft lights came and went in the sky. Spaceships, she realized. Meanwhile, planetary traffic still moved at a steady clip, but only in the distance.

Pinpricks formed along her exposed neck, and she craned over the railing to take in her near surroundings. The traffic ways around the campus lay vacant. This realization sped her heart.

On Reznic, military security teams like hers would divert traffic from target areas before raids. Just a slight deviation from the norm. Enough to go unnoticed by most parties except for the hyper-vigilant. This academic, more residential area, naturally had less traffic. But—her brow furrowed—it shouldn't be nearly this dead. It hadn't even been this quiet in the morning.

Covering her mouth, Katya slowed her rushing thoughts and doubled back, rather than trusting the loop to connect with the lecture hall's platform. Despite the enduring heat, she ran. Her mind remained consumed with traffic patterns. There'd been ways to exploit Reznic's traffic control to get off-world; its glut of vessels served as a screen, but that was lacking on Tausafira. The prospect of running with Zakhar's freighter ... She dug her nails into her palm, an ache blossoming in her side. She only envisioned a ball of fire careening into the ground.

She grounded herself. It could be paranoia. She'd only been on Tausafira for a day and a half—it could just be a fluke, some event on-world she was unaware of slowing traffic in this area. But every fiber in her body screamed that a Magistrate operation waited to unfold.

As she neared an intersection near the south face turn, a man stepped into her path. Black jumpsuit. Eagle encircled by five stars. Her steps faltered before she yanked her firearm from its holster.

"Don't move!" she barked. Her hands didn't shake when she trained the AVI on him.

As his hands went up, the dark-haired man turned in small degrees to face her. When he did, Katya flinched and dropped her gaze. Black hair, pale skin with an almost translucent quality, a visor over his eyes ... All it would take was one look from the Oneiroi to incapacitate her, and she didn't have her little protector with her. Her jaw ached. The special ops jumpsuit would have built-in ballistic material. Shoot. Knock him on his ass. Ask questions—

"I trust you still have my nephew."

A jolt shot up her spine. The elusive uncle. The one she'd poked around for but could never uncover where he'd gone after the Jar'rask ship. She reexamined his appearance. It'd been too long ago, and there'd been a sizeable distance between them. Could she be sure it was actually him?

She didn't lower the firearm. She warred with what to do: torn between leveling the playing field and accepting him at his word. He could have used his ability the moment he'd met her eyes. And he hadn't. Her finger traced the trigger. He still wore his special ops uniform, all insignias in place. But there would be no return after what his crew had done—just like there'd been none for her. The intact uniform, however, provided excellent cover. Who was going to approach an Elite Oneiroi team and ask for their credentials? She swallowed hard. He was Sotiris's remaining family. His way home. Her jaw creaked.

"Did you go to the seeing room?"

"Yes."

A muscle in her neck twitched. "The boy?"

"With us." He lowered one index finger, directing it toward her. "My nephew?"

"He's safe off-world."

His lips narrowed at this. "And once again, you're my path to him," he ground out. Without her approval, he returned his hands to his side, but away from his firearm. "We need to leave now."

She stiffened. "I'm not—"

"A Magistrate incursion is impending on-world."

He glanced back the way he'd come and held up a hand. Thanks to the dense vines, Katya couldn't see what was behind him, but she assumed a team member.

"They've caught the whiffs of a separatist plot and have decided to entrap its heads here." He didn't approach her, but his body seemed coiled for action. "Given both of our standings with the Magistrate, it is inadvisable to dawdle."

The traffic patterns. She lowered the firearm. "What do you know?"

"It's *imminent*." He stepped toward her, unperturbed by Katya partially lifting her firearm. "You're coming with us and taking me to my nephew."

A rustling signaled the arrival of a female Oneiroi, who stayed at the intersection. Katya didn't know if it was because of her gun or—her eyes flew open, realizing the uncle in her distraction had closed the gap between them. He could quickly disarm and incapacitate her.

"We're wasting time we don't have," the uncle—Sarris, according to his nameplate—said with a hard edge. "My team has been hounded. We're not about to be taken in now, and I'm not letting you disappear with my nephew again."

The situation teetered on the edge of escalation. Exhaling through her teeth, Katya attempted to de-escalate it by holstering her firearm. Their posture grew less rigid with the gesture. But now what? She couldn't let him yank her from the planet without Zakhar.

Unable to help herself, Katya swiped sweat from her brow. Her shirt, by this point, clung to her frame. The Oneiroi's suits, meanwhile, seemed to make Tausafira tolerable for them. Deprived of such protection, Sotiris would wilt. She tilted her head toward Sarris, probably his surname. They may bear a homogeneous appearance, but she saw a family resemblance, similar facial qualities. The shape. The chin. With the visor, she couldn't tell if they shared the same eye shape. He was Sotiris's uncle.

She would reunite the pair, but how could she make him believe her? The Oneiroi before her were on edge, the impending Magistrate operations adding another layer of stress. Then, like a match being struck, an idea flared to life. The Oneiroi had a special ops craft. Much faster than the freighter. It would also blend amongst other Magistrate ships.

"We'll come with you."

He quirked his head. "We?"

"Sotiris is currently with a scientist who's refined a drug for the defect." She met his gaze. "This scientist is very close to one of my travel companions, Zakhar. If I return without him, I don't know what said scientist might do. More than likely, he'll turn his home defenses on your ship. He's amassed an impressive arsenal."

His jaw tightened, a muscle along it trembling. Swiveling from her, he rubbed his hand against his mouth and muttered something under his breath. "So we pick up this man."

"And my other travel companions." She smiled, not withering under his concealed glower, which his steeply down-turned lips gave away.

"And do tell, how did *you* become embroiled in revolutionary politics so quickly?" he asked.

"We're on borrowed time, aren't we?" She brushed past him toward the south face, her mind fixed on reaching the lecture hall's platform on the west face. "Let's get off-world."

Katya stiffened when she caught a third Oneiroi emerge from the connection. Her pulse jumped. Three special ops Oneiroi. Swallowing, she loosened her fists. They needed her, and she needed their interceptor. She continued her path forward, and the uncle matched her pace, always keeping her in reach. Until they had Sotiris in hand, they would comply to a certain extent; she couldn't push them too far. No, that would only ask for trouble, a breaking point. Cooperation was in all of their best interests.

They were fast approaching the west face corner when Katya stopped. "You and your team" — she gestured to the woman and man who had been a commander and lieutenant respectively — "will meet us here."

"That's—"

"You said it yourself. They're revolutionaries," Katya said. "What do you think their reaction will be to seeing Oneiroi?" She rested her hands against her hips. "We're traveling in an old freighter. We've no chance of breaking through a blockade or evading more nimble ships. You still have your Boita, correct?"

Silence. A tight nod. "But how do we know you won't slip away with another one of your revolutionary friends?"

"Trust me. They're hardly friends." She directly met his eyes. "You may not believe it, but I tried to track your team's movements. I got nowhere, but I did try." An acidic flavor scorched her throat. "I've wanted to get Sotiris home. Mina and I … we've done our best in the meantime. Maybe inept, but our best." Her throat tightened. "He needs you."

The Oneiroi traded some sort of silent conversation. Slight facial tics betrayed its apparently odious nature. They didn't like the thought of letting her out of their sight, but Katya needed them to let her go alone. It would be a mess if they didn't.

"I'm not lying about Aleksandr Lomonosov, the scientist. He's paranoid and suffers from PTSD. He'll react poorly if Zakhar's not there to soothe his nerves. There are also many factions on Mramor that don't get along. Zakhar's the only way past them."

The uncle's brow crinkled at that. "Why Mramor? Why did you take him there?" He stepped forward. "If you knew, the trouble—"

"I knew its troubled past, not its current political happenings." Her gaze dropped to the walkway before returning to him. "Like a lot of my decisions lately, it was a necessity. Sotiris needed help that was far beyond me. The name I was given was Lomonosov, and it was on the money. He's an acquired taste of a human being, but his work has been impeccable."

At that, the Oneiroi's posture shifted. Cautious but excited. Good. There was more value now to meet Aleksandr on a good footing.

A wisp of a solid buzz pushed aside that thought, stirring memories of Reznic. She went to the railing and pushed aside the vines. A metallic glint caught the setting sun. A Rapid Response Service Craft. For the rest of her life, she would never forget the slight buzz of a RRSC. It set her blood on fire, a rush of adrenaline born from past missions that entailed jumping from the crafts. The one still off in the distance was an older model, likely the same used when she'd first been posted on Reznic before the Magistrate had rolled out even quieter models.

"We're out of time," she said. "Wait here. I'll be back."

The uncle swept forward and grabbed her upper arm, fingers digging in. "Know this" — his breath beat hot against her face even with the planet's heat — "if you betray us, nothing will stop me from finding you."

Katya's breath hitched. She did not doubt for a moment he wouldn't be able to achieve that threat. Somehow, he'd been able to trace her to Tausafira. Against all odds and a massive galaxy.

"I'll be back."

He held on for a moment longer before releasing her. She didn't wait, scurrying away as fast as her shaking legs would allow. His threat brought memories of Strom's. How long would it be until she tried to make good on it?

Focus on the task at hand.

Her brain already composed plans with a new tool in her kit: the fear garnered by the Oneiroi. They could exploit it for escape. If the military brass had buried her desertion, they would have even more reason to hide an Elite special ops team going AWOL. It would be privileged knowledge that the average soldier would not be privy to. As "captives," the Oneiroi crew could shepherd them off-world with no one being the wiser.

As she approached the door, Katya collected herself, straightening her shirt, which had crept up during her running. Nothing, however, could stop the way it clung to her frame, plastered by perspiration.

The sentry from before whipped her assault weapon toward her, then recognition dawned on her face. "Oh, it's you."

"We need to evacuate," Katya said. "Carefully." The last thing they needed was to start a panic. "The Magistrate is diverting traffic, and I spotted an incoming RRSC."

"Our spotters warned us," she said. "The college's hidden tunnels are already in use."

Had Zakhar gone ahead? Katya rushed inside, ignoring the sentry's words. She retraced her steps to the lecture hall, where she sank with ragged breaths against the overlook's rail. A good chunk of delegates remained within, though the lower portion had been cleared. Tension fled her body when she spied Zakhar's bulky form standing in their row. He spoke with the still-seated princess. Something passed from the woman's hands to his, and her attendant followed the motion with a dour expression on her face.

Avoiding bumping into a group of delegates milling in the stairway waiting their turn to enter the tunnels, Katya rejoined them.

"There you are! Had they sent someone to bring you back?"

"No, I came back on my own."

Zakhar's face darkened at this, but Katya had no time to inquire further.

She nudged her head to the stairs. "Come on. We can't wait, and I've found a new ride."

"What?" Zakhar didn't budge.

Katya leaned closer. "Sotiris's uncle caught up to me. They have a fast vessel and clout that should let us pass through the net the Magistrate is tightening." She pointed to where the next delegation disappeared into a hallway, probably connected to the tunnel system. "That is going to work for the early leavers, but eventually, the Magistrate will catch on, especially if the pace quickens, becoming more noticeable. We need to take a lesser-traveled path."

Zakhar adjusted his shirt's collar, his Adam's apple bobbing. "Is he trustworthy?"

"Until he gets his hands on Sotiris, yes," Katya said honestly. "With what Aleksandr offers, maybe even past that."

Zakhar scratched his beard, then muttered something in Moscanov. The princess hesitated but, with the help of her assistant, rose. Her eyes lingered on Katya.

In broken Magistrate, the princess decreed, "We go."

CHAPTER TWENTY-ONE

Katya ushered her party upstairs, ignoring shouts for them to exit through the tunnels. They reached the observation deck unimpeded. Rather than feel relief, a weight settled between Katya's shoulders. What did she know about the Oneiroi? She thought she could trust them, but what if their ties to the Magistrate weren't severed? She glanced at Zakhar from the corner of her eye as they rushed from the hall itself. No signs of stress emitted from his placid expression.

Facing forward, Katya's lips formed a thin line. Let the rest think they were insane. The Messertev would never break the atmosphere in the impending firestorm. Though, the Oneiroi interceptor had its own pitfall: the Tausafiraians. The interceptor provided cover with the Magistrate, but their hosts would mark it as an enemy. Her chest tightened.

"Do the Tausafiraians have Aleksandr's designs?" She asked while the four of them bolted into the planet's heat.

Zakhar wiped his sweat-drenched face. "No. But they have their own."

"Do you—"

"No." He glanced at the princess and her granddaughter, who had fallen behind; the former clutched her cane while accepting support from her granddaughter. "But they are clever people with technological head start to us."

"It could be a slight hiccup for us."

Zakhar bobbed his head, still keeping up with her. "We're already investing in risk. What is one more component?"

"You're putting a lot of trust in me."

He laughed. "Why not go all in? Really test my investment: Was it correct or ill-conceived?"

A true madman. Though who was madder? Him or the woman who'd saddled herself to him? An answer never formed. Instead, the steady hum of RRSCs consumed all her thoughts. She considered entry points she would've chosen on the building. The small, dated windows too risky. She clenched her fists. However, the miles of suspended passages on each level with foliage as cover … It was ideal and offered multiple entry points. Any commanding officer would take advantage of it to tighten the net.

The humming dimmed when they reached the south face, the building blocking it. The unrestricted viewing platform would serve as a perfect landing site.

Swiveling but not stopping, she barked, "Pick it up! We need to move now!"

She didn't know what the north face's walkway offered, but if a RRSC team selected to take the south … Her heart thudded in her ears as she propelled her flagging team forward. She could imagine Sarris's face when they arrived. Their state would dismay anyone with a mind for strategy. Liabilities. But with any mission, one adapted. She would force them to.

Throat burning, Katya took the princess's other arm and slid under it. The older woman's eyebrows shot up, and she muttered something in Moscanov — likely "unhand me." But Katya didn't.

"On three, we lift."

"What?!" Kadri sputtered.

"A RRSC crew's coming. We need our special ops captors."

The young woman hesitated and looked at the princess, who gave Katya a hard stare. Her eyes widened, something flickering in her blue eyes. With a single nod from the princess, both women complied. The princess uttered no complaint when they hefted her off the ground and plowed forward. She maintained her impassive expression as if their manhandling were simply a waltz across the dance floor. Zakhar hovered behind, a protective guardian.

Ignoring her burning lungs, Katya strained her ears. A faint rustling. She shifted the princess's weight and grappled for her AVI-14, grimacing as it caught in the holster. She yanked harder and swung it upward when a dark shape separated from the murky shadows. Then she froze.

Sarris's posture relaxed, but his expression soured, taking in the elderly woman currently suspended off the ground. Behind him, additional Oneiroi emerged from the gloom. The number went from three to five: two women and three men. The female commander stepped beside him and also gave the impression she'd sucked a lemon. The silence hung, though, from the Oneiroi team's minute facial tics, she doubted their experience was the same.

The male ensign, who boasted a sturdy build, gave a full-arm shrug, earning a sharp elbow stab from a female ensign. The lieutenant in back laughed at the exchange, and Katya noted his quick grasping of his abdomen. An injury?

"How many of you are there?" Katya asked.

"Enough to compose a special ops team," Sarris answered with dry sarcasm. A muscle in his neck twitched. "So much for speed."

"It's all of us or none of us." She clenched her firearm. "Where's your ship?"

"A complex two platforms over." He scratched his chin. "We convinced a merchant to lend it."

Bullied more like. She stiffened; the thought had come so fast. Could he read that? Was he reading her every thought, even now? Before Sotiris's drugs, when the headaches had been constant, she'd wondered if that was what he'd been doing: surfing her mind. But since the rogue thought triggered no reaction, she decided he required the visual connection. She pressed her lips together. No one knew. Only the Oneiroi themselves. Even after a year with Sotiris, an outlier himself, she had no better insight.

Sarris waved the larger Oneiroi forward with two fingers, and he wordlessly approached them, hands stretching to the princess. He jerked away when the elderly woman slapped them.

"Our ruse only works if it looks like truth." Annoyance bristled in Sarris's tone. "We're running out of time. Another team's coming."

Kadri repeated this in Moscanov.

"Now." It exited clipped. Sarris looked behind before extending his open hand to Katya.

She surrendered her firearm to him, though her mind screamed when he added it to his uniform belt after checking its safety. Their lives were now bound in the Oneiroi's hands. When he seized her arm, Katya grimaced. Around her, the other Oneiroi took custody of the

Mramorians, with the bulky Oneiroi suspending the princess on his shoulder.

"Say nothing. Just move," Sarris hissed.

Without warning, he tugged her the way the Oneiroi had come from at a brisk pace. The others filed in behind, their footsteps punctuating the silence. The hum of the RRSCs was vacant, suggesting they'd dropped their loads and retreated.

She winced when Sarris's fingers pinched skin. The man didn't notice, his gaze never breaking from their path. A grim determination had settled on his pale face. While his body posture emitted calm collection, the tension layered beneath—surfacing at odd noises—said something else. As if he expected a trap to be sprung. His words struck her. *"Our standing with the Magistrate."* Despite the overbearing heat, she shivered.

A loud boom echoed deeper in the city, to the southwest. She craned toward it, but the vines concealed everything. *Boom, Boom, Boom!* Flashes of orange peeked through the barrier.

"Our friends will try to take relay and other key infrastructure," Zakhar said.

"Good." The uncle removed his firearm.

Katya could follow his thoughts: Embrace the chaos to slip out. The seizure of the relay would further enable that mission while preventing intel from coming in about a rogue special ops team. She resisted the urge to wipe sweat from her brow, even as a stray drop dipped into one eye.

How closely had the Oneiroi been followed? The irony almost brought a chuckle. This very team had tracked her crew at every step, and they'd been nobodies. The Oneiroi … they represented a genuine threat: to the Magistrate's partnership with their people and its pipeline of unseen weapons.

The shuffling steps ahead caused her chest to clench. In seconds, darker forms distinguished themselves from the walkway's shadows. Bulky, weighed with equipment. Katya's muscles pulled tight, anticipating the collision. The figures fanned out, their specialized headsets distinguishing their small group from the darkness. As they did, Sarris's fingers dug into her arm. His sunglasses probably marked the opposing team's movements.

Then the floodgates burst.

"Get down! Get down!" The RRSC team boomed.

Despite herself, Katya bent her knees, only prevented from complying by Sarris's uncompromising grip.

"Stand down," the Oneiroi thundered in response. He didn't even flinch under the line of assault rifles, all concentrated on them. "You will stand down!"

Katya expected a hailstorm at any moment, but Sarris continued to trade shouts with the other officer, attempting to bend him to his will. As he did, he dragged Katya forward with him.

"You will stand down, Captain," Sarris continued. "Our mission supersedes yours."

When he—and by default Katya—took another step, realization dawned. The opposing captain backpedaled, physically recoiling, face pivoting from the Oneiroi as if slapped.

"Whose orders?" The iron had left the man's voice.

"Admiral Spurius."

The name, like a key, cleared their path; in fact, the captain didn't seem capable of ordering his men back fast enough. Sarris said no more, taking the cleared path. As they passed the armored troops, a chill passed along Katya's back as she exposed it. Any moment she expected the tide to turn, but with distance, the noose loosened.

Their pace quickened, and they reached the eastern face with its sky bridge to another walkway segment. Its unrestricted view exposed a looming orange hue to the distant southwest. Around Zakhar's raspy breaths, pops echoed off the city's tall structures, which distorted them and made their location impossible to tell. Then the steady buzz of aircraft drowned them.

Their group reached the skyway's other side when another explosion billowed from the northeast, signaling a two-pronged attack.

Katya dipped when tracers cast an eerie light against the night. The sky grew more contested with planetary aircraft darting through it. A telltale whiz sounded nearby, almost like fingernails against a chalkboard. Sarris plastered her into the wall as it drew nearer. His body burned hot over hers, blocking her sight. The sound encompassed them, shaking their surroundings. Her breaths caught in her throat when a fighter slammed into a building too close for comfort.

Whipping her from the wall, the uncle lugged her forward like a doll, ignoring her unsure footing. "We need to move."

The commander overtook them along the walkway and signaled to another skywalk. Like before, the Oneiroi cut them from the plan with their silent communications. More explosions followed by the time they reached it, and with them, the power cut to the streetlights. Only the foreboding orange licks of flame, blossoming and expanding behind them, provided any guidance while promising utter destruction.

Katya swallowed. An unpredictable element, fire could jump neighborhoods. All it needed, the right wind.

From walkway to sky bridge, they wove a pattern that stretched miles. Zakhar and his minder, the lieutenant, trailed. From time to time, the lieutenant would guard his side while timing each of his steps to prevent jostling. Meanwhile, the Mramorian man could barely stand straight, and his face—when under the tracer's light—had become a blotchy red.

How much farther could they go? The question burned at her tongue. Two platforms over. Grinding her teeth together, she wondered what constituted a platform in the city.

The commander circled back to them from her scouting ahead.

"Captain," the woman said, her voice deeper than Katya would've expected. "There's a barricade established ahead."

It'd been said for their benefit. A courtesy, a warning. The captain—Sarris—didn't show the same consideration. He kept his response to their latest roadblock restricted to his team.

Ahead, flickering lights—fixed to helmets—marked the barricade.

Katya stumbled on the sky bridge's lip, but her captor righted her. Shaking her head to dislodge her bangs from her eyes, Katya conjured a dazed, terrified expression for show as they drew closer to the concrete barricades.

Soldiers' large AARs rested along their tops, gleaming when tracers blazed. The Oneiroi commander approached and bellowed for them to hold fire.

"Hold!" A frazzled lieutenant, the sides of his head shaved in a wave pattern, abandoned his crouched position. "This area's restricted. What's your mission?"

"Above your grade," Sarris belted back, his fingers sinking deeper into Katya's arm; she would have bruises for sure. "Stand aside."

The lieutenant, either brave or stupid, bristled at this. "No one's passing. Those are my orders from Admiral Spurius."

Sarris hissed, and with his free hand, he ripped a slate from its leather container and foisted it under the man's nose. "Mine come from *the* highest command."

The man's eyes widened. He dropped the AAR for his neck strap to catch and leaned toward the slate. Whatever he'd seen on it drew a whistle. He swiveled on the balls of his feet and waved them through.

As they crossed the threshold, the uncle returned the slate to its confines with one smooth action. Too quickly.

Katya swallowed and averted her eyes from the lieutenant. Whatever credentials, while impressive, were dated or forged.

"Are these agitators?" the lieutenant pressed. "I have—"

A soldier beside him screamed, grabbing at his face while his knees buckled. Katya flinched. She swung her head toward the man as he hit the ground. Hard. The female Oneiroi commander smiled, and it chilled Katya. Every scrap of hearsay bristled in her mind—well-earned fearmongering circulated after brushes with the Oneiroi.

Katya couldn't see the woman's eyes as she stood tall over the fallen man. Was she still looking at her victim, or had she already moved on?

"It doesn't concern you," Sarris ground out.

Katya's heart rattled when the commander took a step, her sway resembling a cat on the hunt, preparing to pounce. The commander kicked the man over while his comrades cowered, even forgetting their weapons—such was the Oneiroi's reputation. The other Oneiroi watched, amused. The specific way Valens had pronounced "human" when talking about the Oneiroi now spiked the small hairs on her neck. They weren't human. Humanoid, yes. But never human. They carried themselves apart. Even disdained humans.

With a coy smile, the Oneiroi commander circled toward the lieutenant. He yanked his face away and stumbled back, a twisted yelp catching in his throat.

"Lieutenant, we're taking them per orders." Sarris drenched each word in politeness. "Don't interfere, or else even Admiral Spurius won't know what hit him."

The man blanched, all further questions abandoned. "Let them through."

"Wise decision, Lieutenant." A smirk accompanied Sarris's words.

Their group continued along their route, and as they did, Katya caught Zakhar's gaze out of the corner of her eye. Edged concern resided there, asking what she'd landed them in. A sinking sensation hit her stomach. She refused to give in to doubt. For now, there was common ground with the Oneiroi, and from that, perhaps they could build understanding. At least, when they reached Mramor, the numbers wouldn't be stacked against them. Sotiris's small face rose in her mind. She hoped it didn't come to that.

Katya waited until they were a reasonable distance from the barricade before clearing her throat. "How outdated is it?"

"Over a year," Sarris replied. "Our original search warrant for your crew."

It must have had an impressive marker or name attached to it to distract from a date over a year old.

"Technically, we're still on that mission."

She couldn't help it—she snorted. "So you are."

She caught the ghost of a smile. Yes, common ground existed, but to forget their differences would be disastrous. Before forming any partnership, the Oneiroi would first have to see them as equals, not insects to be stomped on.

A short distance from the barricade, they met more civilians running from the ominous glow to the south. Their cries and screams coated distant pops. They fell over themselves to avoid the Oneiroi, though the commander, now in the lead again, avoided them too. Katya eyed the masses. All Tausafiraians. Among them had to be some rebels.

"Akakios," the commander called, circling back to them. "There's a cleared path."

"Take it," Akakios answered. "Stay alert, everyone."

From behind, Zakhar spoke, "I would like to point out the Tausafiraians are our allies."

Akakios nodded his head. "And I hope to avoid them all."

The commander shifted their path into a small passageway that cut between two residential buildings. It had a tidy courtyard with lush planters, empty benches, and silent fountains. A haunting setting when paired with the opened residential doors.

Katya wiped the sweat from her brow, though the humidity was breaking. Behind, Zakhar's breaths came in ragged waves, accompanied by little sputters. The Mramorian women were quieter, though Katya noted Miss Tamm appeared equally winded.

The commander guided them from the courtyard to a suspended sidewalk with a protective overhang. An explosion vibrated the walk, drawing a cry from Kadri.

"Move," Akakios called.

A few feet down, the commander kicked in a side door and waved them through with two fingers. The questions bristling on Katya's tongue went unvoiced as she and Akakios stumbled into a private parking lot. Akakios guided her through the rows of vehicles. From the way her Oneiroi escort's arm muscles twitched, she assumed the fact the rest fell behind weighed on him. Like it did her. Her teeth became set on edge with raging combat, the peppered weapons fire never breaking now. The window of escape was closing.

A shot scudded off the top of a car. With precision, Akakios shoved her head down but kept their forward momentum, the vehicles providing ample cover. She heard his breath hitch as he rose to trade fire with their attackers.

Katya pressed her hands against her ears. Additional clattering, like a violent hail-filled storm, struck vehicles and the concrete support beams.

"Don't kill them," Zakhar bellowed. "They're Tausafiraian."

Katya tilted toward him, dreading that he might expose himself.

"If it comes between them and us, I'll choose us," Akakios ground out before prodding Katya forward.

"Give me my weapon," she said. "I'll help."

"Too risky."

Katya winced when he twisted his fingers into her forearm, halting her grab.

"Prisoners don't keep weapons. All it will take is one person, and our cover's blown."

Biting back a retort, she followed him to the next car. Her skin itched, needing the firearm in her hand. Together, they crossed a gap between two sets of vehicles, and Akakios shoved her down and against a pillar, eliciting a yelp. Above her, Akakios hissed. He leaned into the beam, teeth bared. The shot had grazed his upper arm, damaging his suit and drawing blood.

"What were you thinking?"

He swung his firearm around the pillar and laid out a burst. Gritting his teeth, he returned to cover, avoiding enemy fire. "You're the only way to him. I'm not letting you check out."

"Giving me mobility could have prevented getting shot."

A thread in his neck twitched. "Or simply delayed it."

He hoisted her, but then rocked her into the pillar, knocking the air from her. An explosion deafened her. She stumbled when Akakios pushed her to continue. As she staggered to the nearest exit, she noted a burned-out hovercar. The source of the explosion.

The commander bumped into Katya when she rushed past. Without a word, she threw open the door, cleared the area beyond, and waved them through.

The ominous murky orange consumed more of the sky, and the air tasted of smoke and chemicals. Katya hated to think about what she was inhaling. She gagged, the concoction in the air choking her and reducing her eyes to tears.

"This way," Akakios said around a coughing fit.

Katya wiped at her eyes, still struggling against the fumes. What had they hit? A refinery? She staggered into Akakios, who slipped an arm around her, supporting more of her weight.

Behind, Zakhar coughed up a storm. The lieutenant with him muttered, "Almost there."

She heard nothing from the princess, Kadri, or their other escorts, except for the odd cough or throat clearing. She couldn't will herself turn. Her head was a jumbled mess, and movement would only throw it into further disarray. Dabbing her eyes again, she caught a brief glint of light.

Akakios's skin met hers when he leaned in. "Remember your part."

Prisoner. Now fumigated and manhandled, she looked the part.

"Special ops," the commander bellowed, her voice cracking. She coughed before repeating herself. It barely cut over the steady rat-tat-tat punctuated by explosions. "Don't fire! Don't fire!"

Katya and Akakios cleared the corner and entered a square behind the commander. Where their arms connected, Katya felt the Oneiroi's muscles constrict. It didn't take long to know why. At the square's far edge, military transports formed a tight wall. Gun barrels rested on their hoods, leveled at them.

Flexing her clenched fist, Katya steadied her breathing. Before her, she couldn't make out the faces of the soldiers manning the rifles; augmented visors obscured them. From this distance, even their uniforms proved unclear. Or maybe the fumes and damage to her eardrums had distorted her vision.

One soldier, AAR in hand, cleared a transport's hood and rushed to the commander. They traded words. Akakios's lips twitched. His commander likely passed whatever they said back to him.

"Our prisoners are our own," Akakios cut in, packing his voice with authority. "We're under specific orders to take them to Meracus Domus. Move aside." Akakios repeated the same trick with the slate.

Once again, the seal on it distracted the lieutenant, probably because of his young age. Katya imagined this was his first major engagement, given how he twitched with each new explosion resounding elsewhere in the city. The previous contingents had been equally green, and Katya could only assume the Magistrate had viewed Tausafira as tame. Though discounting Ereago, a gap in combat experience had formed across Magistrate ranks.

The Magistrate lieutenant glanced around, then back at the slate as Akakios lowered it.

"We have our orders, Lieutenant," Akakios pressed. He, however, didn't use his ability.

Katya swallowed against the chemical taste in her mouth. This wasn't like the other roadblock, which hadn't been fully mobilized. While the lieutenant stumbled, the rest maintained a steady bead on them.

She hoped Akakios knew flexing his muscle here would be a fatal mistake.

The lieutenant tapped against his weapon as he inspected every inch of them, seeing exactly what they wanted him to. Finally, he nodded and brought them around the string of transports.

"They really need to alert us about special ops missions in the area," the man griped. "It's already a clusterfuck."

Neither Akakios nor any of his Oneiroi team members gave the man air to continue his grievances, keeping an eerie silence that, if Katya were in the lieutenant's shoes, would've made her skin crawl, especially knowing what they were capable of.

"Thank you, Lieutenant. Your services are no longer needed." Akakios continued along a vacant pedestrian way, which led to a commercial port cluster.

Troops moved around them, their equipment clanking. Even against the fumes, body odor was prevalent. The heat had to be torture for them. Their presence, though, hung over Katya.

"One night awaits everyone." Some ancient emperor had spoken those words shortly before his own ministers had stabbed him.

Katya walked, her back tender. Sweat still trailed its length, and her shirt had long become more liquid than cotton. Dampness pooled on Akakios's brow, and he panted softly. Had the tear mucked up whatever embedded system mitigated external temperatures? How far could he push himself before he reached his species' limit?

He picked up their pace.

Behind, the Oneiroi lieutenant with Zakhar hissed, a high-pitch, pinched type of sound. It brought Akakios to a stop and loosened his jaw. Then, without warning, he broke into a run, diverting from the straight path and cutting through a drive-through warehouse, cleared of everything but the stench of oil and fuel.

Within, Akakios finally spoke. "Our tail caught up."

Katya blinked. "Tail?"

"A Magistrate speaker." He ground his teeth together, hard enough for Katya to wince. "We thought we'd lost her in the Mezzo."

It dredged up questions that Katya's tired, fume-addled brain struggled to separate. The how, the why, and the Oneiroi's movements mattered little. A speaker was on-world and now stood as a problem.

Around her ragged breaths, Katya commented, "How do you know they're on-world?"

"She found our ship."

Krezk.

Not stopping, he added, "It's still ours. Just no longer in the port."

"Will we be able to rendezvous?"

"That's the plan."

Katya swallowed. No other alternative existed. Their Messertev was well out of reach. Stealing another vessel, dicey. She eyed Akakios in the dim light. She trusted the Oneiroi to pull through. There was a reason the Magistrate leaned on them. They got results. They had proven it in blood, theirs and their foes'.

They left the warehouse, and Akakios redirected them farther from the spaceport, weaving in and out the alleys created by warehouses. They reached a fourth when Akakios broke their pace. Unlike the previous areas, functioning security lights lined it, probably powered by a generator. Magistrate soldiers had cleared the proximity except for a couple of parked skid steers. Likely, it'd become a major artery for moving equipment and other supplies.

An abrasive roar skirted through the sky above them before veering off its path, chased by the lighter *churr* of the planetary fighters. Through the inky darkness, Katya caught the outline of a B-Class Boita interceptor.

Footsteps approached, and Katya turned toward them. She hadn't realized the others had fallen so far behind, but from Zakhar's hunched, shaking frame, it became understandable. Even Miss Tamm's Oneiroi escort had hefted her on to a shoulder so they could maintain speed. The Oneiroi ensign lowered the Mramorian to her feet before resting her hands on her upper thighs to catch her own breath.

"Chrys" — the Oneiroi lieutenant said between gulps of air, shaking hand now pressed into his side, definitely the site of an injury — "is good and all, but —"

"I know," Akakios cut him off. "It's not ideal, but we'll have to trust he can lose them and double back without picking up anymore."

"So we wait here?" Katya asked.

"No." Even so, Akakios didn't move. "We'll need to get on the boardwalk on the other side … board from there." He lifted his head to the sky. "But for now, catch your breath. The armor's good on the Boreas, but it's at a disadvantage in the atmosphere. I don't want it picked apart while we board."

Not when there was a planetary blockade to overcome, Katya mentally added.

A click caused all to stiffen. The Oneiroi swung up their firearms, turning their backs to each other as they scanned their surroundings and the rooftops above. The Mramor delegates shuffled into the center between all the Oneiroi, except for the princess, who remained on the tall Oneiroi's shoulder. She'd been quiet through the entire ordeal, and Katya hoped she hadn't been wounded in the firefight.

The Oneiroi shifted toward a cross-section between warehouses, their sunglasses seemingly detecting something. Akakios steeled his grip and hissed through his teeth. Around him, Katya angled herself for a better look.

Two massive figures, carrying bulky Vitellius submachine guns, emerged, no fear even when faced with Oneiroi. Katya's throat constricted. Breks. Their pinched faces with teeth jutting out at odd angles sometimes infiltrated her nightmares. As they moved, unconcerned for the firearms aimed at them, their frames' long hair swayed unimpeded by armor. Just how thick were their hides?

A clambering on the warehouse roofs caused Katya to lift her gaze. Then realization sank in, chilling her face. Their enemy had corralled them.

Her focus shifted, drawn once again cross-section by a series of mechanical clicks. She remembered well the clicking that had echoed off *The Maelstrom*'s metal walls after she'd tapped into an Elite channel. These Breks had a handler.

"Sarris," an unseen voice called in pristine Magistrate. "Finally, we talk face-to-face. No more hiding. No more running."

Katya stiffened. That voice. It had taken to haunting her at night, blaming her for Anaïs's death. She couldn't recall the last time she'd heard it in person. She'd never really communicated with Zhihao, nor had her sister reached out to her—but she knew it to belong to her. Katya angled to see around Akakios's shoulder, just as Zhihao stepped into the opening.

In her hand, Zhihao held the clicker like some prize while her thumb emitted a series of commands.

"Drop your weapons," she said. "You may be skilled, but against Breks, I'm afraid you'll find your team overwhelmed. They're denser than us mere humanoids, in more ways than one."

The Oneiroi held on to their weapons. This drew an exasperated sigh from Zhihao, but her clicker remained silent and the Breks held their weapons on the Oneiroi.

Zhihao's flats sounded against the pavement on her approach. When she slipped out from between the two Breks, Katya's chest tightened. Her sister, as always, served as the very image of tailored perfection—hair spun into a bun and dressed in a knee-length skirt suit. It had Anaïs's fingerprints on each stitch and contoured her body while allowing movement since it flared around her legs. Made from a dark fabric, the suit blended with the night, its true color never revealed, even when under the security lights.

What was she doing here? Katya dug her nails into her sweaty palms. Her mind raced for an answer, only to meet blankness. She knew nothing about Zhihao's life, especially removed from her father's updates. Anaïs sprung to life with her comment about their sister working closely with their uncle.

Zhihao's painted lips pulled into a smile, and she tilted her head. "But to cross paths with you here in this den of sedition, I never expected it." She took another step, though Katya noted she avoided direct eye contact with the Oneiroi. "Why are you here?"

The light caught something metal on Zhihao's collar. Katya squinted before her eyes widened. A speaker's pin. Zhihao wasn't a cog. She'd transcended the system, circumvented it to its peak. Heat blossomed in Katya's chest. She swallowed against the burn, her nails digging in further.

Piles of transfer request forms, all denied ...

"Who did you manage to piss off, Cassius?" Valens had asked at one point when it'd reached ridiculous levels. Any posting that held potential—any worth—slipped through her fingers until Valens had stepped in with his own name and favors to secure *The Maelstrom.*

If Zhihao wore the speaker pin, then dear Uncle Pontius could be nothing other than a magistrate. Katya's jaw clenched. He'd been the wall her career had hit headfirst. Why had he meddled?

Akakios clung to sullen silence, ignoring Zhihao's question. "Did you kill him?"

Katya's eyebrows rose. Who? She glanced around him to her sister, whose expression remained neutral. Akakios mirrored it, though the same muscle in his neck twitched.

"Who?" Zhihao asked.

"Agoranomi member Anagnos."

Zhihao frowned, tilting her head in the other direction. "How about an answer for an answer?"

Katya heard Akakios's teeth grind together. Tension lined his entire frame. One wrong move and he would snap. With her knowledge of Zhihao, Katya expected her to trigger it. She weighed options to defuse the situation, exposing herself would at least dislodge her sister's focus. *"... You failed, Kat'ee."* Her throat constricted.

"Answer it," Akakios pressed.

Zhihao rolled her eyes. "I truly don't know what you're implying, Sarris. The esteemed councilor was quite elderly and under a great deal of strain." The cinnamon-hued lips quirked. "I doubt your visit helped."

Akakios's finger shifted on the trigger, and without thinking, Katya's hand gripped his elbow, pulling it to throw his aim.

"*... Watch over each other ... isn't that what sisters are supposed to do? ... You failed ... you failed.*"

Akakios grunted and angled toward her, his expression a mixture of irritation and surprise. He'd never fired, his finger slipping from the trigger as she pulled. Or perhaps he'd never intended on launching a firefight. His raised eyebrows lowered to a severe angle. She could almost hear his question of why.

Zhihao cackled, dislodging his intense inspection from her to their captor.

"And it all clicks together." Zhihao pointed to the ground. "Before anything unfortunate happens, I insist you drop your weapons. Now." Then, her voice adopted feigned cheerfulness as the Oneiroi complied, for a moment fully exposing Katya to her sister. "Ah, little Kat'ee! Imagine meeting you here as well." With a closed-eye smile, she added to Akakios, "Congrats, Sarris, you completed your mission. If only you'd done so earlier before racking up so much collateral damage."

A deep scowl covered Akakios's face, and as he rose from putting his gun and hers on the ground, he stated full of accusation, "You know each other."

"She's my sister."

CHAPTER TWENTY-TWO

The words hung between them. Akakios straightened and focused on Zhihao, not her. Katya wished she could see his eyes to better read him. She imagined his mind dissecting this new information—its meaning and its potential subterfuge. From the clenched muscles in his neck, she gauged his distaste for this revelation. Over it all, one question likely guided him: How did this impact his ultimate mission? Much like her life over the past months, everything centered on Sotiris.

Zhihao clicked additional instructions, which brought Breks circling in and taking them all in hand ... except for

Katya and the princess, who the Breks allowed the Oneiroi ensign to still carry. A strategic move on her sister's part. Separate her from the rest, give them reason to doubt her, and ultimately gain control of her through that alienation. Katya bit into her lower lip. Who wouldn't consider some elaborate ruse? Though she trusted that Zakhar would know better. She would've been the worst double agent, having caused massive collateral damage along the way. He, of all those gathered, knew how far she'd gone.

"Oh, yes," Zhihao said. "We never gave you the roster, did we, Sarris? Well, let me introduce you to Katya Cassius, human wrecking ball and former captain of *The Maelstrom*—that part you've found out yourself. Well done."

Zhihao smirked at Katya. "We should've just given the roster to you, knowing you would never fully appreciate that surname. It's the downside of your people. Beyond your governing body, you've never integrated or even learned the internal politics of the Magistrate. As long as you're left to your own, what need is there?" She rolled her eyes, the gesture over-exaggerated to be seen in reduced light. "In the Core and Mezzo, the name Cassius carries quite a bit of weight." Her sister fully faced her now. "But sharing that name, I wanted to protect it, but I sorely underestimated what my dear sister was capable of."

Katya's face burned, and she clenched her jaw.

Zhihao sighed. "Perhaps you share something in common with the Oneiroi, Kat'ee."

"What did you expect me to do?" Katya asked, voice pitchy as she tried to contain a torrent of emotion.

"To stop and think!" Zhihao didn't bother to control hers. "All you've ever had to do was use that name."

If not for the Breks, Katya would've stepped back. Her sister balled her fists, hot emotion brimming in her eyes. During their shared childhood, Zhihao had remained guarded and aloof. Katya had felt her annoyance at her slow integration into Magistrate life but never her anger. An unsteady breath left Katya.

"How was I to know that!" Her fingernails dug into her palm. "The Breks were going fire on my ship!"

"Yes, run from the Breks. But then, contact Uncle. Surely, you aren't so dense to not have noticed he carries sway." Zhihao's nostrils flared. "But you've always had to make things harder. Separate yourself. You've never appreciated your good fortune. No, you'd rather have your CO act for you than use the name given to you."

Speckles dotted Katya's vision. So many words battled in her mouth and would have poured out in a jumbled mess — the type Zhihao had mocked her for, especially as the Magistrate tongue supplanted her native one.

"We had a vested interest to smooth this over," Zhihao continued. "It would've been forgotten."

"And Sotiris would've been lost."

"He would've been cared for."

The muscle in Akakios's jawline twitched again, but he said nothing.

"I wouldn't call that cared for," Katya said, likely voicing his thoughts.

"We'll talk later. For now, I have a situation to contain." Her lips twisted into a smile. "And then you and I are having a very detailed conversation, breaking down each and every step you've taken. Why you are here, where you vanished to after the *Gershna* ... until you resurfaced on Trides. On the *Pollux*!" She snorted. "Did you bring something back with you?"

Katya withered under Zhihao's knowing gaze. Guilt, warranted or not, clawed at her innards. Anaïs stood between them, just as she'd always done. Their glue. Forever gone, yet never. Katya sucked in her quivering lower lip.

"We're bringing Anaïs home." Zhihao lifted her nose. "Is it still your home, Kat'ee? I recognize this man with you." She pointed to Zakhar. "Old Mramorian stock. Though we underestimated the depth of his dissidence."

"What can I say? I prefer keeping people guessing," Zakhar said from behind Katya. "And why should she not return to her home? Especially when the other discarded her for knowing its little secret. Would you not as well?"

A derisive snort followed. "Meracus Domus is my only home. It was my family's for generations before I became Cassius." The words flowed from her painted mouth as her chin raised. When her eyes flicked back to Katya, she asked, "Is Mramor your home now, Kat'ee? Do you feel it in your bones? Strong enough to turn against everything you *do* remember?"

Hollowness grew in Katya's body. "Is it still my home? What would it hold for me after everything."

"We kept your name clean, didn't we? We would've rehabilitated you back into the military if you'd chosen to be." Zhihao's bangs dipped into her face.

Rehabilitated? The word soured her stomach.

She glanced at Zakhar, who wore the same void mask he'd worn when they'd left the lecture hall. What was going through his mind at this moment?

Zhihao's hand went to her ear's com unit. A transmission. In response to a person on the other side, she said, "I'm wrapping up here. Use any measures to down the interceptor."

The Oneiroi lieutenant clicked his tongue against his teeth, and Katya caught the Brek twist his arm at the slight movement.

"We'll sort through uncomfortable truths when we're no longer on a burning planet." Zhihao extended a hand to Katya and gestured her forward with a flick of her fingers.

She, however, remained rooted. "One more uncomfortable truth. You and Uncle sent the Oneiroi. Did you send the Jar'rask?"

"You did," her sister threw back. "You stretched the search out too long, and others became involved. Now let's not make more of a scene."

Katya glowered at Zhihao and didn't move. She wondered who "others" entailed. Ultimately, she settled on other magistrates.

Zhihao rolled her eyes at her inaction, though the telltale buzz of an interceptor sweeping past arrested the motion.

"Tell your friends to surrender, Sarris. It's only a matter of time before they're brought down either by us or the rabble."

Akakios smirked and shifted in his Brek's grasp. "You were right back then, Speaker Cassius. I should thank the Magistrate." Akakios gave a sharp nod.

Eyes wide, Zhihao jerked up the clicker, but no message followed as she, like a discarded doll, collapsed to the ground.

Katya winced at the thud and odd angle that Zhihao's body landed in. It chilled her blood. Was she still breathing? Her body ached to step forward, even with the remaining threat of the Breks, to straighten her sister's form, ensure she was still breathing. Like she hadn't been able to for Anaïs.

A shot skidded into a warehouse facade, disrupting that thought. Katya grabbed her AVI. When she rotated toward the Brek holding Akakios, she froze. The burly creature released its captive and stumbled. Its gun thudded against the ground. Panic lit its eyes as it resisted the siren's call to sleep—as Katya recognized it now—but within seconds, it succumbed, crashing alongside its firearm. The siren could only have been the boy liberated from the Jar'rask ship.

As the other Breks dropped around them. Katya refocused on her sister.

"Zhihao!" She stepped forward and sought any telltale signs of life, but in the poor lighting, she found only stillness.

Anaïs dominated her mind, the concern she'd recently shown to Katya redirected to Zhihao. If the Oneiroi's attack had killed Zhihao or damaged her mind beyond repair, their father would effectively lose all of his daughters. While she'd never been close to Zhihao, Katya didn't want either to happen. Zhihao had meant a great deal to Anaïs, to their father. Despite petty conflict and differences in personalities—or perhaps they'd been too similar—Zhihao was very much her sister too.

A hand seized her and pulled her back.

Into her ear, Akakios hissed, "We're going."

She dug her feet in when he tugged her back. "Is she all right? I need to know if she's going to be all right."

"Once we're out of range, she'll be fine," he answered glibly.

She winced when his grip rubbed flesh and nerves against bone.

He jerked her again. "We're leaving now, and later we're untangling where exactly your allegiances lie."

"With Mramor," Zakhar said with a level of certainty that astounded Katya. He now stood next to Akakios with his Oneiroi handler. He met Akakios's gaze, not even blinking. "Where your nephew currently is. That should be our focus."

Katya cast one last look at her sister and nodded. "You're right. We need to move." Ignoring her father's voice in her mind, she turned from her sister and allowed Akakios to take the lead.

"Are you lying?" she asked while they ran toward the rendezvous point.

"She should be fine."

"Should isn't very concrete."

"Neither is our control of the boy."

Katya blinked. "So we could be floating dead in space then."

Akakios gave no response, which spoke louder than words.

Trust. Katya pressed her lips together. They had used the Oneiroi boy's mutation to target their enemies precisely.

That feat suggested some level of control, more than she'd ever achieved with Sotiris. It only became a matter of whether they could maintain that control until they reached Mramor and Aleksandr's drug.

Their feet carried them to a platform that overlooked one of the city's air lanes. It was wider than the ones near the college campus to accommodate larger vessels and their cargo. The Oneiroi's interceptor was nowhere.

Akakios turned to the injured lieutenant. "Anything?"

The other shook his head. "I can't reach Chrys, and Zin is … Zin."

Katya faced the direction they'd come from, half expecting to be greeted by Breks. They'd gone down with more resistance. If the boy's hold slipped even for a second, she imagined they would recover faster than she had. She'd lost hours to this Zin since she doubted the Jar'rasks had bothered with drugs afterward. The kid had packed a wallop.

A distant roar redirected her thoughts. Their escape was coming.

"Move quickly," Akakios said and waved the slower Zakhar forward. "You first. Are you fine, Pelagia?"

The Oneiroi female with the shaved head nodded while bending over to return the princess's attendant to the ground. Pelagia appeared as winded as her charge. The elderly woman remained quiet while the well-muscled Oneiroi adjusted her into a more comfortable bridal carry. Even in the dark, she appeared ashen, unwell. Her hand twisted into her dress.

Swallowing, Katya tilted her head, straining her eyes. The interceptor grew louder but blended with the sky. Closing her eyes, she couldn't discern the lighter buzz of planetary fighters. Perhaps the Oneiroi interceptor had broken free.

"There's the *Boreas*," the larger Oneiroi said. "Out of—"

The lieutenant elbowed him. "Don't say it."

"What?" the larger man sputtered.

"You know what."

"Both of you knock it off," Akakios said, attention not wavering from the interceptor.

The ship stirred the air, kicking Katya's bangs against her forehead as it came to hover alongside the platform. As soon as its back hatch lowered, Akakios pushed Zakhar forward and started to grab her arm, but she rushed past him, hopping over the slight gap between the platform and ramp. She relished the solid thud of her feet striking metal.

Zakhar settled his hand on her lower back as she continued up the ramp to give the others room to move. "Tell them nothing," he said in her ear, so close the heat of his breath tickled her skin. "Nothing of Plasovern. That can wait until we are firmly on Mramor's soil."

He pulled away as the Oneiroi who'd been his minder raced past them, hand pressed into his side. To the cockpit. He was the pilot, Katya discerned. She and Zakhar ambled to the side while the others boarded. The moment their boots hit the hold, the Oneiroi crew members flung into action, racing to their regular duties. The one carrying the princess settled her on the floor. Sweat layered her brow even in the chilled environment of the interceptor, and her breaths came as wheezes.

Zakhar kneeled beside her and spoke in hushed Moscanov. Her lips moved, a fluttering action. Her attendant shook and twisted her hands together while tears pooled in her eyes. Then with more strength, the woman clasped Zakhar's shirt, beckoning him closer. Whatever the woman said lifted Zakhar's eyebrows.

Katya rounded on Akakios. "She ..."

"Elpis," he said over her almost inaudible utterance. "We require your services."

A new Oneiroi, her hair in a coiled bun, traveled down on a lift. When she exited and approached, she glowered at the captain, eyes pointedly going to his injured arn, before she crouched beside the elderly woman.

"Your medic," Katya said fecklessly. She then regrouped her thoughts into something more useful. "Is she trained on human anatomy?"

"Of course," the woman said, her tone clipped. "The Magistrate trained me." She snapped her fingers together. "Pelagius, help me get her to the medical bay."

Akakios gestured to Katya and Zakhar. "You two are with me."

He took them, along with the commander, to the darkened cockpit, where two Oneiroi crew members already sent them hurtling upward. The viewscreen provided a portal to the exterior while its bulk comprised strands of information and reading. In stark contrast to any ship Katya had been on, they worked in silence … in a situation that would try even the most seasoned crew.

The Oneiroi at the helm, who didn't wear sunglasses and wore a mechanics attire, tilted them sideways between two tall skyscrapers that were an icy black in the darkness, devoid of electricity. Once he'd cleared them, the pilot took over, fingers gliding over the helm with practiced ease that relaxed Katya.

Meanwhile, the female commander eased into the weapons station, pushing aside the Oneiroi who'd been operating the console. No word passed between them; the male, with clipped hair, without an order went to the communications console and put on a headset to monitor. If their ruse had held to some extent, they could use the communications console to slip past any blockade by relaying false credentials.

Katya, however, didn't doubt Zhihao's efficiency in spreading information about a rogue interceptor. There'd been that com call.

A planetary fighter scrapped the *Boreas*'s exterior, triggering a series of flashing purple alarms and mechanical shrills. The pilot, lips pulled tight, whipped the vessel to the side and dipped down to use Tausafira's buildings as cover.

Katya's blood thrummed as they wove between one structure after another. Amidst hairpin turns, built-in gravity held the cockpit's occupants in place. Tapping a finger against her leg, Katya tracked the small gray, unclaimed dots—which had to be Tausafiraian fighters—and the blue Magistrate ones. The blue showed no interest in them, while the gray, like predators, worked to ensnare the interceptor, a prize they didn't know was no longer Magistrate.

The commander tilted to Akakios, who nodded. The weapons went live.

Zakhar clenched his hands. "I must insist on limited damage. Much like your people's hopes rest in a solution to a genetic defect, my people's hopes, including the person who has cracked your species' conundrum, need this alliance to continue. Mass destruction of property will not allow that."

Akakios pulled off his sunglasses, his milky, relatively pupil-less icy blue eyes meeting the Mramorian man's own. "Be restrained, Charis."

"Yes, sir!"

Katya witnessed one fighter spiral from the sensor. Her neck ached, muscles constricting. Ereago and the blockade run were so close in her memory. She curled her hand into a fist to stop the tapping. Every muscle ached for the helm. For complete control. She'd always been an active party, never a spectator. To be so powerless now grated on her.

Vice admiral.

Her heart's palpitation grew uneven. She wouldn't have the helm in that position. She'd be ceding some control but gaining more—more than she had in this circumstance, a guest on an alien vessel.

Distance burgeoned between them and fighters, and the Oneiroi pilot exploited it. The *Boreas* climbed steeply; the pilot pressed the atmospheric thrusters to an extent they really shouldn't have been. Katya clenched her jaw while the sky outside the viewscreen changed color and the sensor relay became peppered with warring dots, which included among their number several A-Class destroyers. There were other unknown readings, likely destroyers constructed by the Tausafiraians. Amid that were noncombatants caught in the crossfire. Some freighters, pleasure crafts, and transports had to belong to other delegates, but not all of them.

The pilot swerved around a split open freighter, and Katya winced. Its shielding hadn't activated.

"Slip the net, Ambrosios," Akakios said, breaking the silence. "We can't afford to be bogged down in this skirmish."

The pilot, Ambrosios, obliged using the chaos to maneuver wide and take advantage of a defensive gap.

Katya exhaled slowly and folded her hands behind her back. Even if Zhihao had gotten the word out, the battle's confusion would prevent complete focus from being dedicated to one lone interceptor.

A few Magistrate fighters diverged to intercept them, but the commander, Charis, had a deft hand on the weapons console and eliminated the threat they posed.

Ambrosios brought them into the range of a destroyer, which turned weapons on them. Their shielding flared even as the Oneiroi engaged in evasive maneuvers. The interceptor's nimbleness kept them ahead of the blasts; however, some shook the ship. Katya flinched when one collided with shielding and jostled them.

But they were so close. Beyond this destroyer, nothing but open space lay. As the interceptor's speed picked up, Katya widened her stance for more balance. Zakhar mumbled in Moscanov and waved his arms to stay upright.

Come on.

Ambrosios hit the thrusters for an extra boost. A massive vessel popped on to the screen a distance from them, approaching from the port side.

It'd broken out of FTL, Katya realized.

The Oneiroi pilot took the only option and jumped. With shielding damaged, an overwhelming nausea hit Katya and dropped her to her knees. Next to her, Zakhar did likewise, only he retched around curses. But they were away and clear of the blockade.

She glanced at Akakios, who leaned over in his seat. He straightened, but it was a gradual movement, one revealing the Oneiroi had been as affected.

Zakhar wiped at his mouth, mumbling under his breath. The other Oneiroi continued with their routines. No words, though she swore she heard the pilot snort.

"They are talking about us," Zakhar muttered.

Before Katya could reply, Ambrosios swiveled from the helm, a smile plastered on his face. "We really are."

"Get us underway to Mramor," Akakios said after rising from his seat. "You can clean up the mess later."

"That's not fair at all, boss," Ambrosios returned. "Should get Kyrillos to; he's got nothing of importance to do."

The Oneiroi at the communications station rolled his eyes. "Hey, I kept the ship in one piece."

"Set course to Mramor," Akakios repeated.

"Old Imperiya," Zakhar piped in. "I can give specific coordinates."

Akakios nodded consent, and Zakhar stepped beside the pilot, giving him the information.

From his seat, Akakios asked, "What can we expect?"

"In the week it will take to reach home, I am certain Magistrate's space-faring navy will have been expelled from our space," Zakhar said, turning from the helm, his hand resting on his stomach as if he were still queasy. "On planet itself, pockets of resistance are likely, but without control of space, they will have no choice but to capitulate."

"That doesn't concern me." Akakios stood, bringing himself a good head taller than Zakhar. "Is the location where Sotiris is secure?"

"Very. The securest place on Mramor."

Akakios mulled over this.

"I will need to contact my people," Zakhar continued. "To ascertain situation before we arrive."

"That'll be impossible if the relay blows like it did on Tausafira," Kyrillos said.

"We had steps in place to ensure it would be saved no matter when we were forced to move. Meticulous preparations. I have no doubt about our people."

The corner of Akakios's lips dipped in the silence that followed the elder statesman's statements. "I hope so. For now, you can use my quarters. Your companion will have to stay in the medic bay for now."

"Your hospitality is too great."

"Not at all." Akakios waved them to follow him.

The man's quarters were a few steps away from the cockpit. When he opened its door, he said, "Make yourself comfortable. You can visit your companion by taking the lift to the hold level. Please note you are being watched closely."

"There will be no need," Zakhar said, peeking his head into the Oneiroi's quarters. "We could have beneficial partnership, your people and mine. Until an accord is reached, no bridge should be burned."

Katya eyed the other man for a reaction, but he gave none. No hint of interest or distaste. She would expect nothing less from someone trained for special ops.

"We'll see." Akakios turned to leave them. "I'll share what information you wish to give my people, but in the end, I am just one, no matter how I'm viewed." The same muscle in his neck twitched. "Make use of my quarters."

"Wait," Katya said. She'd crossed her arms as a barrier against the cold. While escaping the blockade, it'd been easy to ignore the chill, but without adrenaline, it sank its teeth in. "We aren't prepared for this low of a temperature. Our cold weather clothes are back on Tausafira. Does your team have anything we could use?"

He pushed into the room and messed with its environmental controls. Warmth crept into the space, marginal at first, but over time, it would do. "Off Demos Oneiroi, we're reliant on our suits, so most don't pack many civvies. And those that are packed are lighter weight since this"—he gestured about the ship's interior—"is our normal."

He stepped from the display and returned to the exterior hallway, not paying them much mind. "You can also adjust the light to your liking." With that, he departed, the cockpit calling alongside more silent conversations.

Zakhar rushed into the room, rubbing his hands and muttering under his breath, and Katya joined him. The door closed, encapsulating them in the growing warmth. Still, she swore her sweaty shirt, which reeked of smoke and toxic fumes, had frozen to her frame. She adjusted the lighting, brightening the space and shifting its tone from the purplish-hued light preferred by Oneiroi.

Plopping on to the bed, Zakhar scoffed at her glower. "What? He said to make use of his quarters. I am." He sighed and ran his hands through his grayed hair. "I am not young man anymore. This has been proven to me tonight."

"Yet you're taking on a revolution."

That drew a smile. "I won't have to run." He flopped backward on the bed and closed his eyes.

Katya, meanwhile, swept the room, more from habit than any suspicion. The space reminded her of her own quarters on *The Maelstrom*: sparse, with very few personal effects. Everything in the room, from drinking glasses, a stray plate, piles of slates, and a few wayward weights, had a purpose.

She paused by a built-in nightstand next to the bed with a few photos—old-fashioned, holographic, and motion capture alike. In a few, she recognized their host with a man who had to be Sotiris's father. Tilting one back, she smiled at what had to be Sotiris as an infant—so small, but still with a shock of curly black hair. Her eyes drifted, and she faltered. Straightening the baby photo, she moved on to an all-too-familiar motion picture. It was identical to the one she'd saved from the *Aletheia.*

Was it the same or a duplicate? Had they liberated it from the Jar'rask ship?

She scrutinized the frame for any tell that it was the same, but found none. Made from basic materials, it and its copies would appear the same. If it were the same, they must have successfully commandeered the Jar'rask ship. Undoubtedly, their items had been stowed somewhere onboard. They wouldn't have left them on Jordah. She hadn't bothered to check, too blinded by her mission: save the kids. Then the Oneiroi teen had also done a number on her mind.

The picture frame marked one fragment missing from the story.

Katya pressed her lips together. Where had the Oneiroi gone afterward? How had they tracked her to Tausafira when the trail should've gone very cold? Those were some questions she would like answered. The special ops team would've been devoid of the resources they'd had while officially on the hunt. It should have been impossible, especially after Katya's slip into Medzeci space.

Katya returned the frame. While the room was sparse, it told her a lot. Family was the most crucial element. Anything else tied to their homeworld had been presumably left behind, guarded by the black-zone world. Zhihao's words about the Oneiroi's failure to assimilate echoed in her mind. Were the others' quarters as bare of such touches?

She stood over the frames. Even so, Akakios had bared this intimate part of himself in a way she'd never allowed herself. She'd rarely displayed photos prominently; instead, she hoarded them for private consumption. There'd only been the vase. An enigmatic piece.

What did that say of her?

Settling on the bed's foot, Katya freed her hair from the bun and tight braids, brushing the tangled mess with her fingers. It buffeted fumes and sweat to assault her nose.

The bed shifted when she started rebraiding.

"I no longer doubt my investment."

Katya's fingers stopped, and she faced Zakhar.

Eyes still closed, Zakhar added, "In heat of moment, no fear, no shake." His steel-blue eyes batted open, meeting hers. "It disappeared, cast off. You may well compartmentalize it. Put in box to focus on mission. Is that healthy? No. But you do as required, and that will serve our cause. Demons can be chased later."

She snorted. Hardly healthy. One day, she would have to face it, all the emotions, the trauma, that she'd boxed away. She resumed tying the braids into her bun. Without a change of clothes, she didn't plan to shower, no matter how badly she wanted one. It would be pointless.

"Besides, given chance to return to fold, you still came with us."

Tightness swelled in her chest. Thoughts of home burned her. "That doesn't say much. My kids were still on Mramor."

Pushing against the bed, Zakhar rocked to his feet. "Heh! I think it says a lot to your character. If we can earn that same loyalty, we will be quite blessed." He opened the electronic door. "I'll check in with the princess. Get rest."

Cold air struck Katya when Zakhar left, though the door's closing quickly cut off the draft. The adrenaline dissipating, she freed the thin sheet on the bed and lowered the lights using the smaller display next to the bed. She didn't want to think of the galaxy's current status—or what the following days, weeks, or years held for her. There would be no avoiding it when she woke up, but for now, she was amongst untroubled stars.

Zakhar hadn't returned by the time Katya woke. She fumbled with the display to find she'd gotten eight hours. A rarity anymore. She yawned and cringed after tasting her breath. She hoped the Oneiroi kept spare toothbrushes because she couldn't stand the taste. Rolling from the bed, Katya stretched as she stood. A quick survey of the room showed no signs of disturbance. They had all left her in peace. Buffering her nerve, she vacated the room. On the other side, she crossed her arms against the instant chill that gnawed at her frame.

Whereas most ships would shift their lighting to sync with planetary life, the Oneiroi ship didn't. It was as dark as it'd been when they'd boarded. Still cast in the same purplish hue. Katya stood in it, allowing her eyes to adjust before taking the lift to the medical bay's level.

Along the way, she spooked the Oneiroi mechanic, distinguished from the rest by his uniform. He frowned at her, stepped from her path, but tracked her as she continued with his milky eyes. She noted dark circles under his eyes; they clashed against his pale skin.

She said nothing to him and slipped into the med bay. She winced—the lights within a stark contrast to the space she'd come from. But at least the room was warmer. Marginally.

Zakhar straightened in a chair next to the princess's hospital-style bed with its built-in monitoring devices. They revealed a weak heartbeat. The princess was ashen, blending with the sheets. Her eyes also appeared sunken, and darkness muddled the skin under them. All combined, it didn't paint a pleasant picture.

Katya stepped farther into the space, but stopped. She was an intruder here. The attendant had fallen asleep on a foldable cot while Zakhar held the princess's hand in both of his. The medic wasn't present.

She wiped at her nose when she uncovered the Oneiroi teen resting at the clinic's back. The response was instinctive. Still, there was no blood, no assault on her mind. The machinery she'd last seen attached to the kid had been removed. Only two mechanisms remained on his forehead.

Zakhar's sigh drew her away from the teen.

"I fear we will lose our princess before we even reach Mramor." Zakhar squeezed the woman's hand. "We, she and I, didn't see eye to eye on all, but there was always respect there. Our paths in life were very different, but I dare say, we struck an odd friendship."

"I'm sorry."

Zakhar dipped his head. "As am I. But it is fact of life. You will lose those you care for along the way. Some for a time. Some … some for much, much longer." His shoulders sank. "But this was vital task. Its potential costs known."

"Nothing can be done?"

"No. The medic did what she could, and our differing anatomy played no part. The damage was already too late." His gaze drifted to the attendant. "Poor child. To lose her grandmother in such a way."

He shook his head. "Old Imperiya's gems cut. And I'm afraid some old ways refuse to die. It will not be easy for her from now on without an employer … with her background."

The concept remained foreign to Katya. The Magistrate family unit often had been stitched together, not confined by blood. If the head saw fit, they brought any person in. Their circumstances held no bearing. But perhaps they hadn't to the princess either. She recalled Militsa's words about the princess's past. "She knew how to achieve her happiness."

Zakhar smiled. "A royal rebel. Not one to let conventions stop her. And for it, she will be remembered well."

She swallowed, hating the uncouthness of what she would ask next. "Will her death impact proceedings?"

"We will lose an elder stateswoman, but it shouldn't give our uncertain allies grounds to move against us," Zakhar said. "I will need to contact Militsa. Ensure our situation. I tell our hosts one thing, but I fear the stroke from the Magistrate might have come too quickly. Though I trust our people to have made just enough gains to take planet, except for a few pockets."

"The sections without delegates."

"The belligerents," Zakhar retorted. "Once I've spoken with Militsa, I will contact Kuznetsov so he doesn't fire on our Magistrate interceptor."

"He's guarding the planet?" She thought of the mouse-faced man, the air of disdain, his role in the purges. It made her skin itch.

"Sobol has combat experience in space." Zakhar freed one hand to scratch his beard. "He is one to chase Magistrate out of our space, not Kuznetsov. He is also one to take out Kuznetsov if he uses his position to gain upper hand for his own ambitions."

"And who takes out Sobol if he pushes his own?"

"Aleksandr."

A pinched "heh" passed through Katya's lips. Her suspicions of a fail-safe layered into the new warship's design had been confirmed. Icy dread, however, permeated from her core. If discovered, it would shatter the alliance. Even as an outsider, she speculated the discoverer would discreetly nullify it and then use it to their advantage. It fit Old Imperiya's history.

"But we are hoping for best-case scenario." Zakhar returned his hand to the top of the princess's. "Everyone plays their role and puts personal ambitions aside." His gaze lingered on the princess's face, the breathing mask over her nose and mouth. "And Mramor can realize a much better future.

"One that we" — tears crept into his eyes — "could only have dreamed of for decades."

The words filled Katya's chest with something she couldn't pin. It tightened her throat. She stood, gawking, a dullard before two individuals who'd built lives around a better future for their homeworld, one that was indeed its own. She was an outsider here, still without a tether to the planet that'd birthed her. Any such ties or bonds had been shredded long ago, and she didn't tie herself to places quickly. Yet here she was, wholly enmeshed in the strands of a historic event that would reshape her homeworld. Still an outsider, but now with a pivotal role.

"Take it easy, Miss Cassius," Zakhar said. "I will stay with the princess for now. Everything else can wait."

CHAPTER
TWENTY-THREE

The princess passed that evening after never regaining consciousness. An Oneiroi crewmember informed Katya of this since she hadn't been in the room. But she didn't join them, leaving Zakhar and the elder stateswoman's granddaughter to mourn her death privately. They'd also begun working with the Oneiroi medic to preserve the princess's body until they could return home, using the small morgue space in the med bay.

She haunted the Oneiroi captain's quarters, mostly lounging on the bed, staring aimlessly at the ceiling. She hadn't really known the woman. *"There is something familiar about you."* The words sent chills along her spine upon reflection. One potential thread to her past had slipped beyond her grasp. Rubbing her forehead, she couldn't decide how she felt about that. Still, a dullness enveloped her heart.

When her stomach growled around two in the afternoon, she pried herself from the bed. She should have liberated enough rations from the Oneiroi's mess hall the last time she'd ventured out. The Oneiroi had refused to turn it into a neutral ground climate-wise, keeping it as cold and dark as any other corner of the ship. But she extended the benefit of a doubt to them. After all, the room had a wall dedicated to cultivating a type of fungi. Tubes surrounded it, which spectral fish traversed. Both organisms appeared to thrive in the dark atmosphere and purple light. Too much yellow light might kill them. One of the crew members—the pilot—had offered her a taste, with a smile she'd deemed too large. She'd passed. Having never been a fan of the edible fungi cultivated on Meracus Domus, she wasn't about to try alien fungi. Instead, she ate bland ration bars. Her stomach tolerated them, though they tasted off. She had decided not to ask.

Bracing for the cold, Katya stepped out and snaked past the other crew quarters to the larger door that opened to mess. She fell short of entering when she found the space occupied. Akakios and his commander—Charis—faced her, their gazes unnerving. Then, without a word, the woman rose from her seat at the small table and left her and Sotiris's uncle alone in the confined space.

Great.

Even absent, Zakhar's warning about mentioning her turn with Plasovern remained omnipresent. An excuse to avoid an uncomfortable topic, even knowing she would have to face such a conversation head-on in the near future. Staring at the man, sitting relaxed at a small metal table, she could well imagine his response. No matter her desperation, no matter the positive results for controlling the mutation, he would not like Plasovern's involvement. Neither would his people.

"So, I take it you didn't find the freighter business very lucrative," he said, breaking the silence. He stirred his soup, the type obscured in the dim light. "How's the mercenary business treating you?"

An overwhelming desire to cram the bowl in his face swelled, but she resisted. "Why? Interested in pursuing it yourself."

A smile tugged at his lips. "I suppose it's wise to keep options open." He winced a bit and straightened in his seat. "But such a pursuit is unlikely."

Katya folded her hands behind her back and twisted them. "I would've said the same. Survival takes odd turns." She rummaged through the cabinets, taking the ration bars. "I've sacrificed many things since rescuing your nephew. My position, my home, my family."

Behind her, the spoon clacked against ceramic. "I apologize. I didn't intend to insult you. I figured I might as well poke fun at our surreal circumstances." The spoon once again clattered off the bowl, followed by an almost inaudible slurp. "It's odd they would welcome you so thoroughly, so quickly. You couldn't have been on Mramor for too long."

The ration bars' wrappers crinkled in Katya's hand. "I'm originally from Mramor." It dripped off her tongue slowly, quietly. "I barely remember it. And no, I don't speak the language. But here I am. Zakhar's convinced I can be of use to him and his allies. And while I might have insight into Magistrate tactics and the military experience, he's largely blinded by sentimentality. That Mramor's war orphans can come home." After pocketing a few bars, she worked one's wrapper down and took a bite. After chewing and swallowing, she added, "But I'm out of places to go. So you could say I'm betting everything on this foolhardy endeavor."

"You expect failure."

"I try to deny it, but at my core, I'm still very much a Magistrate soldier, at least in mindset." She brushed her bangs aside. "I compare them to the Magistrate's military might, and I can't help but see failure. But it's ego. Look at what Plasovern has managed."

"Yes, forcing lost ground in Fringe. Decimating a Mezzo world while taking out a magistrate. It's rather impressive."

Katya blinked. A magistrate. Something akin to an electric shock shot through her. No wonder the military had been rampaging through the Fringe and clamping down any sign of malcontent.

"How did you hear that?" She fully faced him. Like their identities, the state concealed the magistrates' movements to the point some questioned their very existence.

He shrugged and drawled, "But you're right. We're all the sums of our parts. It's hard to move past one's own conceptions."

"Speaking from experience?" Katya asked, allowing the conversation to slip away from the anonymous source.

That actually drew a full smile. "Everyone's the other to us. We've always held ourselves apart. From other beings, from the Magistrate itself." He pushed his bowl aside. "My people never fully assimilated into the Magistrate, have never thought of ourselves as Magistrate. These uniforms are merely roles we step into for our own securities. Our inclusion, a mere partnership." He snorted. "And we've seen the fruit that's born."

"Do your people know?"

He clammed up, his mouth forming a stubborn line. His milky blue eyes bore into her.

"Surely, you've uncovered some means of communications by now," Katya pressed.

He shrugged. "Perhaps."

"I've placed a measure of trust in you."

He rose from the table, his chair scraping against the metal as he did so. "And how about your communications with Strom?" He leaned into her space. "How did those go?"

She clenched her hand. The wrapper crinkled further. How did he know?

He tilted his head and then rolled his eyes, picking up his bowl and taking it to the sink. "While we were pursuing you and your crew, we tapped into the cameras on R-20. I know she met with you there. You seemed agitated by her, but given how things went on the *Gershna*, her offer had to be more appetizing. As you've admitted, you've run out of places to turn to. I take it things didn't end well."

Katya swallowed. The man still needed them. But Zakhar was right: Some details were best discussed on terra firma, where they could display positive results while divulging the bad news.

"It didn't," she said. "Let's just say, I don't want to be near Strom soon." She discarded the halfway-eaten bar, her appetite gone.

The door opened, and Zakhar entered, quite haggard with rings under his eyes. "If my calculations are correct, now would be an opportune time to contact Militsa on Mramor. I need you to take us out of FTL for the call. I will make it from your quarters."

"I insist from the bridge—"

Zakhar rigidly shook his head. "This is Mramorian business. If the tables were turned, you would keep us from Oneiroi business. Allow us this."

Through the metal, Katya felt the shift from FTL to impulse. Despite knowing the Oneiroi's ability, it unnerved her.

"If you can even get through." Akakios's voice cast doubts about that prospect. "If the right relays were taken down, it's likely Mramor is experiencing a galactic communications blackout."

Zakhar shifted from the doorway, allowing Akakios to exit. "Time will tell," he whispered under his breath, though the Oneiroi was no longer present. "Come now." He waved to Katya. "You can listen in."

They sequestered themselves in Akakios's quarters: Zakhar front and center in front of the small communications console. Katya hung back, though kept in view out of courtesy to Militsa, who would answer if all had gone according to plan. She shifted behind him as he put in all the relevant contact information. Then they waited. The call appeared to be connecting, but there was no answer.

"Come on, come on," Zakhar whispered. The call died.

"Maybe she can't answer at the moment."

"We'll give it another try." He reestablished the connection.

Katya took to pacing in the background when the connection timed out again. Perhaps a relay had been taken down, or maybe …

She wrung her hands as Zakhar restarted the call. She fought to keep her breath steady, even as a cold sweat slithered along her spine. When a dizzy spell hit, she halted her pacing. Mina. Sotiris. What if … it'd failed. Suffocating pressure built in her chest. She ran a clammy hand through her bangs, pressing herself to breathe. She jumped when the screen went live.

Zakhar uttered something in Moscanov. "Militsa, it is good to see your face."

"Ditto. I feared the worst after hearing snippets about Tausafira." The woman's face was out of focus on the screen, which had a cascade of lines. "I apologize. I'd just stepped out to deal with politics in your stead. We have secured a large portion of planet and the relay. Our spies and plants served well."

"Very good. But I notice connection is not so good."

"Somewhere along the way, a relay was damaged either by the Magistrate itself or by one of our allies. I'm working with some of our allies to repair those within our space." A smile split her face as she spoke the last two words. "For now, it's a lower priority. The regions we anticipated providing the most resistance proved correct. Our ground forces have them contained. I'm informed they are unlikely to hold out for too long."

"They are predictable, at least." Zakhar stroked his beard. "Aleksandr's trap worked effectively?"

"Like charm. The net caught Magistrate completely off-guard but created debris that will need clearing. Some will probably break up in atmosphere." She pushed her braid to her other shoulder. "But because of it, we also have a sizeable number of prisoners of war to deal with. Once net was activated, they were trapped."

"They will make good bargaining chips when we eventually bring Magistrate to table."

Mramor just might do it. Katya's pulse thrummed. They had control of the planet. Seemingly a sizeable amount of space. Whether they could maintain their territory remained another matter. But they would only have to hold out long enough to dissuade the Magistrate from pursuing the conflict further. Zakhar's crazy plan could work.

"Sobol has chased them to Netchzi Nebula. My understanding is he will pull back shortly and set patrols."

"Excellent."

Militsa frowned, her brow forming several ridges as the screen flickered. "We caught them by surprise. They weren't expecting the firepower and organized effort, the sabotage. We will not be so lucky again."

"It would be too easy," Zakhar muttered. "We should arrive back on-world in another two or three days. We are coming on a Magistrate interceptor, called the *Boreas*, with its Oneiroi crew." He raised his hand as Militsa's eyebrows shot up. "Refer to them as diplomats. I feel a lucrative partnership could be had."

Katya nearly choked on her own spit. A bald-faced lie if there ever was one, but she held her tongue.

"Be careful on your approach home," Militsa said. "Expect action in space and on-world. Avoid our *old friends'* airspace. And be alert to debris fields. Send me your ship's information, and I will send alert to our navy, so maybe you make it home in one piece with your—what did you call them?—diplomats."

"Yes—" The screen went black, and Zakhar lurched forward to the controls, only to be rocked back when the ship quaked. "What the—"

A tug pulled at Katya's stomach, and her balance threatened to buckle. They'd jumped. She stumbled to the door and rushed for the cockpit, using the wall for balance. Her inner ears still throbbed from the sudden shift. It wasn't as bad as if she'd been on *The Maelstrom* without an RMP. She would've been immobile without the interceptor's updated jump system.

Pressing into the cockpit, Katya didn't stray far from the doorway, so she would be out of the way. Something had triggered the crew. The three present—Akakios, the female commander, and the pilot—operated their stations intensely. The commander had settled at the weapons station, where she peeled her eyes to the screen, seeking targets.

Finding her tongue, Katya asked, "What happened?"

Akakios's eyes flickered in her direction but returned to the viewscreen and its data. "A Magistrate vessel. We've lost it."

"We hope we lost it," the commander corrected. "Remember the last tail we had."

"This one was a freighter, not a new class of interceptor," the pilot, Ambrosios, said.

"We'll proceed with caution." Akakios tapped his fingers against his seat. "Anticipate coming across more."

The pilot worked the helm and got them back to FTL and on course. The stars blurred together. Katya, however, lingered on the navigations. They were still two days out from Mramor and would cross through populated systems. The screen would be lit up then with a jumbled mess of Magistrate and League vessels.

"We successfully reached our contact," Katya said. "Mramor is in hand. The jump disrupted the call, though. But Mramor has secured its own space. One of its newly christened admirals is pursuing Magistrate signatures within the system. If all goes according to plan, they'll know we're coming."

"And if they don't?"

"Evasive moves to the surface."

The uncle sighed and muttered something under his breath. A chuckle left the pilot, but they didn't let her in on the joke.

The cockpit door reopened, and Zakhar waddled in, stroking his upper arms for warmth while his breaths erupted in puffy bursts. "What has happened?"

"A Magistrate signal," Katya said. "We've evaded it."

Zakhar rubbed his hands together. "Good, good. I suggest avoiding all signals. Get us within an hour of Mramor, and I will contact"—he chuckled—"Admiral Kuznetsov."

"Why do you laugh?" Akakios asked, leaning over his chair's armrest toward the Mramorian.

"Inside joke."

"Not good enough," Akakios bit out.

"He is not, how do I say, military cloth." Zakhar waved a hand in the air. "It is hard to see him as admiral. Comical, really."

Akakios shifted to her, seeking further guidance.

She shrugged. "I don't know Admiral Kuznetsov."

Though Aleksandr's tale lingered: a little boy hiding while Kuznetsov and men like him gunned his parents down. Having sidled beside her, Zakhar remained cocksure, a smile plastered to his face. There was even a twinkle in his eyes.

Katya ran her tongue against her teeth. She felt none of Zakhar's supposed levity. He had to be raked by as many doubts as she harbored currently. He knew the man far better than she did. With that limited knowledge, she couldn't fathom why Kuznetsov had been allowed his position. Yes, the factions had to be given some trust, some power, but to trust him at the gates? She held her tongue, though some misgiving must have bled through her facial expression because Akakios's lips dipped.

Zakhar rubbed his hands together faster, louder, ultimately clapping them together. "It is far too cold in here. Let's return to our quarters and leave our gracious hosts to their tasks." He waved to Akakios, drawing an even grumpier expression. "Alert us an hour or so out."

"If you're concealing—"

"Kuznetsov will follow his commands," Zakhar said, not stopping in his strides to the door. "He will let us through. Come now, dear."

Katya felt Akakios's gaze burning into her back, but she didn't hesitate to leave. Her lips had gone numb, and her fingers were so stiff. The cold had seeped into her bones, causing her teeth to chatter. She followed Zakhar to the room, noting the tightness of the muscles in his neck—a crack in the cheery exterior.

Once they cloistered in their temporary home with its patch of warmth, Katya grabbed the thin blanket from the bed and draped it over her shoulders before pulling it close. Shivers coursed through her frame. Zakhar, meanwhile, paced, pumping his arms as he did.

"I still think it was unwise to place Kuznetsov in charge of planetary defense."

Zakhar paused his deluge of motion, his lips parting as he faced her.

"Especially knowing him as you do," she prodded.

Bowing his head, Zakhar pressed his lips together, his eyes half-lidded. "If we hold every sin"—the words passed off his tongue like syrup—"every wrong too tightly, there will be no one left."

Katya exhaled through her teeth. Of course, Zakhar clung to his blank sheets. The man wasn't—couldn't be— that naïve. He couldn't be so blind as to—

"He is not same man as then." Zakhar rubbed the side of his face with one hand, massaging his fingers in as if warding away a migraine. "People are not finite things. From day to day, hour to hour, we change. If we do not allow that understanding, that humans are capable of betterment, we sell ourselves and others short." He dropped his hand and thrust it into his pocket, resuming his pacing. "I am not same man I was then either—I'm not the same man as a few hours ago. Many of us have our regrets from that time; we'd gone insane. I do not deny he has done horrible things. But who am I to say he has not repented of them.

"And if he hasn't"—Zakhar grinned broadly—"I will thwart the knife before it reaches my back. Because no matter what, there can be no extremism, no wandering down the roadways of the past. Those ways cannot be revisited."

"Some would say you're inviting it by giving him this chance."

For a time, the only sound was Zakhar's steady plod from one side of the room to the other without pause. With each pass, Katya grew confident he would never respond.

"Behind him is a faction," he said, not stopping in the fluid motion of his walk. "They need a place. We cannot disenfranchise or divorce them from ourselves. Time has passed, and hopefully, with it, their radical leanings have mellowed, keeping principles and leaving bloody fervor. At their heart, they care for the common people. They can help us shape new laws, governance with their unique perspectives." He drew himself up, all movement ceasing. "And I fear if we cut them off, they will resort to bombs again. As long as they are at table working toward common ends, there is hope to avoid that. And they aren't Alyypriliv, even if only by hair."

He crossed over and clasped her shoulder. "I know it is risk, but work with them. But—"

"Don't get stabbed in the back."

"Precisely." He dropped his hand, leaving a warm imprint on her shoulder where it'd been. "But that will be another day."

That last bit drew a ghost of a smile from her. "And hopefully not when we arrive back."

A cross between a snort and chuckle rippled from Zakhar's throat. He shook his head and waved her away before entering the quarter's bathroom. Katya tightened her grip on the blanket and flopped on to her side. Her stomach growled again, but the thought of the odd-tasting ration bars crammed in her pockets held no charm. Soon, they would be back on Mramor and actual food.

Throughout the night, Katya would stir as shifts from FTL to jumps occurred. She'd considered going to the cockpit but stayed huddled in the blanket, embracing ignorance. There was nothing she could do, and if they were fleeing an enemy ship, she might as well die comfortably warm. Since there were no sudden impacts against the hull, she assumed the Oneiroi were engaging in avoidance or shortening their travel time. As soon as the ship settled into FTL for an extended period, she drifted firmly to sleep.

At some point, Zakhar nudged her awake. "They've shaved our time," he said as she rose. "Come, we are going to contact with Kuznetsov."

Katya undid her hair, which was already out of its bun, and left it to dangle. She straightened it to the best of her ability, hating the sensation of its greasy unkemptness as it passed between her fingers, snagging tangles along the way. She felt disgusting, like a layer of sweat, dirt, and skin particles had solidified. Temptation stirred to accept a change of clothes from the Oneiroi's limited wardrobes just to shower.

When they entered the cockpit, four Oneiroi greeted them: Akakios, Charis, Ambrosios, and Kyrillos. The names were sticking in her mind with the help of prominent features. Akakios shared characteristics with Sotiris. Charis was taller than the other women on the crew; she'd also worked in creative braids to her buns. Meanwhile, Kyrillos was stouter than Ambrosios, who reminded Katya of an imp with his amiable smile that hinted at a devious sense of humor.

Zakhar approached Kyrillos at the communications station.

"We're ready."

The Oneiroi backed away from the station, allowing Zakhar to reach over and key in whatever sequence would connect him with Kuznetsov. Before he patched them through, he cleared his throat.

"I will conduct this in Magistrate; I simply ask you hold your tongue or agree with me. Play this role: You are diplomats seeking to explore a relationship with the newly independent Mramor and League." Zakhar's finger hovered over the console. "Say nothing of your nephew. He doesn't know about the boy, nor should he. We will talk on Mramor, and who knows, maybe we will find common ground. We know a thing or two about lost children. But if nothing comes of our talks, take your nephew and leave."

"As I've said" — Akakios wove his fingers together — "we're only a tiny part of the whole. And we'll move with the whole."

Zakhar chuckled at that. "If only my people were so ... accommodating."

"Proceed with your call."

Zakhar activated the call, and it didn't go unanswered for long.

"Admiral Kuznetsov." The tenor voice rang over the speaker.

Zakhar's lips twitched. "It's Kozlov. We are en route to be in Mramorian space within the hour."

"Ah. I had heard such rumors of your survival." It came across as sardonic, and Katya could picture his mouse-like face puckering as if consuming something bitter.

"You know me. I am survivor." Zakhar settled into the chair at the communications station. "We will arrive in a Magistrate interceptor, *Boreas*, with a delegation of Oneiroi diplomats."

The pilot covered his mouth at the last bit, a gleam in his eyes.

Kuznetsov's line went quiet. On the other end, the microphone caught an audible swallow. "What are you playing at, Kozlov?"

"Is it not in our best interest to expand our allies if presented with opportunity? I saw one; I seized it." Zakhar typed something more into the communications console. "So you don't mistake us for the enemy, here is our signal."

"Proceed with caution." Kuznetsov cleared his throat. "There are considerable debris fields. It would be shame if you collided with any of them."

"Your concern touches me. We will be wary of them." He then cut the connection. "You heard the man. Watch for debris."

"He seems disappointed you're alive." Akakios leaned into his seat, crossing his arms as he inspected Zakhar.

"But he did warn us of debris fields." Zakhar stood and beckoned Kyrillos to retake his seat. "He can at least play the role of ally."

Ambrosios whistled. "There's a gutted destroyer up ahead. I'm betting everything from fine particles to chunks are spread throughout the area."

Katya leaned forward, taking in the navigations, catching the blink of a League vessel, which simply showed as foreign on the Magistrate-built console. Within seconds, it'd moved out of range.

"Avoid the field," Akakios said.

Their speed slowed as the Oneiroi pilot navigated past it. Katya stepped closer to the navigation screen. It was littered with debris warnings, which stretched well beyond this initial wreck. To see the screen so marked up brought tingles cascading over her back. It would tack time on to their journey. She'd seen nothing like it beyond photos taken during the Fringe Campaigns. Through the viewscreen, the skeletal remains hung suspended in an eerie scene. Her stomach hardened. It stirred memories of the *Aletheia*. Her gaze slipped behind her to Akakios, and she wondered if he was thinking the same.

Fine particles momentarily obscured the section of viewscreen broadcasting space.

There was a high possibility Elites had crewed the vessel. Had there been Oneiroi involved in the battles that roared through the area? She hadn't heard of them being in the Fuusi Arm before.

"Cut the screen," Akakios said, still poised in his seat. "Just the data and navigations."

Ambrosios switched the viewscreen's mode so it became consumed by data and a map of their surroundings, of the debris that wasn't too small to be picked up.

"Would other Oneiroi be out here?" Katya asked.

Out of the corner of her eye, she caught motion, a shake of the head.

"Not likely, except maybe a child with the defect," Akakios said. "Mostly, the Magistrate has stationed us in the Fringe near Medzeci when not performing interrogations or special ops missions in the Core or Mezzo. We largely serve as a reminder to Medzeci."

Small blessings, Katya decided. The way Akakios spoke of the whole suggested a strong pack mentality in the Oneiroi. If faced with brethren, they'd likely lay their arms down, which would place the Mramorian delegates in a bind if the "whole" couldn't be moved into helping or letting them pass.

Behind her, Akakios's jumpsuit rustled. Now leaning forward, his eyes roved the navigation screen while his hands formed a steeple and pressed against his mouth. Lines stretched across his forehead, and beneath his eyes, black rungs had set in, leaving her to wonder if he'd slept since they'd commandeered his quarters.

She brushed greasy hair behind her ear and returned her attention to the graveyard they had to traverse. For most, the display didn't share names or designations, simply wreckage of a man-made construction before detailing their elements—steel, traces of radiation, silicon, copper, proxizeeum, caeliset, and so on. Sucking in the side of her mouth, it further sank in: This would be her life. She could only hope whatever vessel she called her own didn't end up scattered across space. Part of her feared she'd been confined to ground posts for too long.

As they inched toward Mramor, she dusted off her academy years and ran scenarios in her head. She also dissected the scenes before them. These mind exercises blocked unwanted thoughts of what would happen when they arrived on Mramor. Still, in the background, they threatened to consume her brain whole.

CHAPTER TWENTY-FOUR

After forewarning Aleksandr of their impending arrival, Zakhar plotted a path to the palace for the Oneiroi pilot to follow. It skirted Old Imperiya's capital and whatever chance-medley reigned there. Puffs of dark smoke spun upward across the planet, a testament to the turmoil that had reigned. A debris field orbited the planet. It curdled Katya's stomach. What had she expected? A peaceful exchange of power was never happening, but — she clenched her hands — she had been naïve enough to hope for something less than this so her conscience could easily be assuaged.

She shifted from the viewscreen and inspected the Oneiroi, trying to glean their reaction. Their sunglasses, once again in place, concealed a good portion of their emotions. Their rigid postures and tight lips hinted at some apprehension. She could only imagine the conversations they were having behind their backs. Sotiris's uncle crossed his arms before relaxing them on the chair's armrests.

Her throat tightened. He would reclaim Sotiris and bolt. Though Zakhar's baited hook might tether them for a while.

Absently, she rubbed her breastbone. The realness now faced with Mramor sunk in. She would never see Sotiris again. He wasn't hers. He really wasn't. But yet, after everything, a part had claimed him.

"Where should I land?" Ambrosios asked while maneuvering the interceptor into the atmosphere with no interference from patrolling vessels.

"There is cleared space in garden. Can't miss it. Given size of your ship, you might set on some shrubbery, but it is no bother," Zakhar said. "Aleksandr will not care."

The pilot followed instructions, making a loop as he slowed the interceptor and brought it to Aleksandr's property. When he parked in the space, initially cleared for the *Pollux*, he took out some shrubs.

Zakhar straightened in his shirt. "Ah, happy returns. Open hatch, and I will soothe Aleksandr's nerves." He didn't wait to see if his instructions were obeyed, darting from the cockpit.

"This Aleksandr, has he had experiences with Oneiroi before?" Akakios asked while Katya stood, keeping her arms embraced around her.

"Just Sotiris. And beyond him depleting his caviar supply, he hasn't had any terrible experiences with your people." She shrugged. "It's more an unknown entity landing in his backyard. In his mind, everything is a potential threat."

"A wise assumption given the planet's current climate."

"You haven't met Aleksandr yet." She shot him a closed-mouth smile before following Zakhar.

Akakios closed the gap forming between them until he trailed a fraction of a foot to her side. Together, they stepped on to the unenclosed lift, and he activated it.

"Come now," Zakhar shouted from below, already at the ramp, ready to disembark. "Open the—oh!"

The hatch, unprompted, lowered. Katya glanced at Akakios at her side, who shrugged. By the time the lift rooted itself in the main hold, Zakhar had lumbered along the ramp, gesturing with his hands to some unseen person while speaking in Moscanov. Akakios shifted toward her as they stepped from the lift.

"I don't understand a word," she said, pushing forward while he lingered behind.

At the mouth of the ship's exit, Katya witnessed Aleksandr embrace Zakhar in the swirling snow. The poor man, like her, lacked a coat and shook like a leaf. Off to the side, Mina held Sotiris in place. The teen waved at them but stiffened when Akakios burst past Katya, hastening to close the distance between himself and his nephew. Katya slashed her hand through the air and called for Mina to let go of the toddler.

Sotiris didn't hesitate. Stumbling in the thick snow, he rushed to meet his uncle, the pair meeting in the middle with the boy melting into the man's arms as he dipped knee deep in the snow. There they huddled, simply embracing. As Katya drew nearer, she spotted tears tracking along the former special ops agent's cheeks as he bit down on his lower lip.

Katya clenched her arms around her, her chest a tangled knot of conflict—Mramor's air biting into her. Her lips and nose grew numb.

He was no longer hers. No claim could be made on this child she'd raised for more than a year. She rubbed her eyes before burying her hands into her pockets, fingers stiffening.

Close to the reunion, Mina stood mouth hanging as if someone had unscrewed a hinge. Even with a distance between her and the adult Oneiroi, the teen stepped back, her frame shaking despite her thick fur coat. The teen glanced at Katya, eyes wet. In response, she could only shake her head.

Sotiris remained burrowed in his uncle, some part just knowing. He was home.

Swallowing hurt. Her face's every movement hurt. She stiffened when a hand landed on her shoulder. Turning, she found Zakhar next to her. His arm draped around her shoulder and squeezed her before he tugged her toward the palace.

"Come now, there's no need for us to freeze to death." His fingers had to be turning to ice, exposed on her shoulder as they were.

She glanced back at Sotiris and Akakios.

"A selfless deed can be painful, but it is only thankless if one makes it so," Zakhar said, bringing her attention back to him. He smiled warmly. "Never doubt its worth. What you did for that boy, no matter where he goes, he will never forget."

Katya nodded, unable to speak. Her teeth clattered, and she stumbled a bit, feeling fleeing her extremities. Zakhar ushered her to his room, where he draped two thick blankets around her. He threw on a thick sweater before fishing out a decanter of amber liquid and two small sipping glasses. With trembling hands still stiffened from the cold, he poured one for her, then for himself.

"You did right by him." Zakhar sipped from his glass. He sighed deeply before sputtering around a cough. "That'll warm the body."

She followed his example. The liquor warmed and added an extra layer of numbness to her body. "It'll sink in eventually," she muttered.

He nodded. "Time is what we all need."

The words carried a dual meaning, even to Katya. The phantom promise that rang in them belonged to a Mramor that would exist once thoroughly forged together, all animus buried. She pulled the blankets closer, her joints aching, fingers still ice. The alcohol loosened the chill's hold, but it hadn't entirely removed its clasp.

"Will the price be worth it?" Her chest tightened as she inhaled, filling her lungs. Releasing it, she took another sip.

He closed his eyes and pondered that. "There will always be a price for change. We saw it before. Are we any better? Only time and history will judge." He chuckled when her jaw clenched. "You have been fed too many Magistrate fairy tales of rightness and justice. There is no grand, perfect cause. There never will be. There will only be winners and losers, imperfect people fashioned as heroes or villains while being neither. Imperfect people effecting change." His knuckles whitened around the glass. "And sadly, there will always be victims who are drowned in change. There will always be a price, and it will never be palatable."

Katya drained her glass, her mind a steady buzz of nothingness. Zakhar stirred and fetched them each a coat from his stored collection, muttering that since they were now thawed, they shouldn't leave their guests alone.

She took the offering and let the blankets slip from her frame as she tugged on the coat.

Zakhar, shrugging a coat on, cracked open the door and paused. "There was only one way for this to end on Mramor. Old wounds still run so deep and have become gangrenous. They will inflict the same pain on Alyypriliv; I can only hope it will stop there. That we can cauterize the other wounds and move forward."

She glanced aside. *"Everyone in Old Imperiya has ghosts."* She clenched the fur that lined the coat's sleeves. And now, those ghosts stirred and demanded vengeance. They'd never left, not for the planet, not for her. Her fingers twisted the fur coat's wool-lined pockets. The soldier's outline haunted her thoughts' peripheries, ever the murky phantom. Had he meant something to her? She pictured Akakios and Sotiris, their embrace, the promise of a home.

A faint hope, no matter what her heart told her, flickered. "I want to know."

"Know?"

"My ghosts."

Zakhar blinked, hand stuck to the doorknob. "As long as all lines remain to be traced, I can do so. Aleksandr will handle DNA, and I will pursue all leads."

Lurching from the bed, coat pressed close to her body, Katya joined him at the door. The good, the bad of it—at least, that nagging thought, which had dogged her, would be closed. "Thank you."

"We all deserve answers." He opened the door and allowed her to exit first. "Now, our guests."

Together, they retraced their steps and found Aleksandr, Mina, and the Oneiroi in the foyer. The adult Oneiroi surveyed the room. A couple paced along the far perimeter while the rest craned their necks at the dangling chandelier. The younger ensigns gaped at it, seemingly having seen nothing like it before. The others remained guarded. Katya noted the medic, pilot, mechanic, and Kadri were all absent. She wondered if they were working to move the princess's body.

Sotiris peeked at her from over his uncle's shoulder and smiled. She returned it, even if she felt no warmth.

"Pelagia and Pelagius," Akakios said, pointing two fingers toward Katya.

She stiffened next to Zakhar as the two Oneiroi former special ops agents approached her with two black duffle bags. They extended them to her, but she hesitated, keeping her hands hidden in the coat's too-long sleeves.

"We liberated them from the Jar'rasks," Akakios said.

Her lips parted, and she took them, arms sagging under their weight. She set them on the floor, where she unzipped them and sorted through their contents. Clothes that she and Mina had kept after they had sold the *Minerva*, toiletries, the remains of Mina's hair dye collection, and odd slates filled the bags.

Trembling fingers—thankfully concealed by the bag itself and her coat's voluminous sleeves—caught between them a paltry few photographs. On top, a family portrait. Anaïs. She pressed her lips together to silence the tremble. So bright, so happy. She flipped to the next photo. It featured her and her father at her academy graduation; in it, he draped his arm around her. She looked like a child with him dwarfing her. Then, Valens. The only photo she had of him. She drank in his face, chest constricting. Swallowing, she slid them back amongst her clothes, careful not to bend any of them. They remained the only images she had of these special people—the only ones she would have going forward besides the moments marked in her mind.

She pulled back Mina's bright pink sweater and discovered her AVI-13. Hello, old friend.

Leaving everything in the bags, Katya zipped them, her stomach hollow, realizing Sotiris's belongings had been separated from them. She lifted her gaze to Akakios.

"Thank you."

He shrugged, the action jostling Sotiris, who per his habit dug in his chin, earning a grimace. "A gesture returned."

She recalled the items removed from the *Aletheia*: the photo and the journal. Not wavering on eye contact, despite knowing what he could do if he so chose, she recognized a common link: grief. He understood the need for mementos. They may be different species, but this they shared.

Zakhar cleared his throat. "I did not want to say over com, but Mikhailovna is no longer with us. Miss Tamm and the other Oneiroi crew are caring for the body. Might you send Boris to assist them? Later, we will make arrangements to see the princess home."

Aleksandr stood, not even blinking for a moment, and then jerked his hand to the com pinned to his shirt's folded collar. He spoke to Boris in Moscanov for a minute or two, his voice somber.

Zakhar squeezed the other man's shoulder. "Thank you. Now, why don't we show our guests your laboratory? I hope you've cleaned."

"Militsa's warning gave time to tidy," Aleksandr said.

Mina snorted next to Katya and whispered just loud enough to be overheard, "One of us tidied."

Aleksandr shot the teen a dirty look, but wrapped in his polished demeanor for the dignitaries, he didn't offer a verbal retort. Instead, with exuberance, he directed them up the expansive staircase.

In his room, the taiga fiend watched them—intruders—with heavily lidded eyes from its nest in a pile of Aleksandr's clothes. The amber orbs tracked their movements, but closed again when left alone. But beyond that pile, the room was far cleaner than when Katya had last seen it. She wondered where the bulk of the clutter had gone.

"Don't look under the cot or behind the curtains," Mina said into her ear. The teen's ear-to-ear smile was refreshing after the past days, especially since it seemed tied to her return. A sign that their rift was closing.

"We have made much progress, as one can see." Aleksandr gestured to Sotiris. Then, from a table, he took a slate and, with both hands, presented it to Akakios. "A gift to you and the Oneiroi people, freely given by the Mramorian people and me. No strings attached. All of my research and findings from time with boy."

Akakios accepted it around Sotiris and flipped through its contents with one hand, his eyebrows rising as he did. "All of this? In how long?"

Aleksandr peeked at Zakhar, who gave a minute headshake.

"You had a head start, didn't you?" Akakios cut in. His years as an interrogator probably caught the movement and the delay. He lowered the slate, settling his attention on Katya. "Plasovern?"

"The drug manufacturer, Usha, laid the groundwork," Katya supplied. There was no need for subterfuge. Not now, not when trying to build an alliance. She clenched the sleeves' interior. "Before abandoning Plasovern, I tried to destroy all the information they'd compiled, but there were likely backups."

The Oneiroi seemed unperturbed by this information. "They'd approached our ruling council with many promises. They made assumptions Plasovern had gotten its hands on Sotiris." His fingers tightened around the slate. "But this … it's more than we've hoped for in years. We have another on our ship. How much of this drug have you produced?"

Aleksandr perked at the mention of another. "Oh! And how old is this one?"

Akakios hesitated before fishing a slate from a pouch attached to his waist; he set the other in its place. "Fifteen."

He gave the device to the scientist, who resembled a child receiving a wrapped birthday present, a smile plastered to his face while shaking in excitement. His eyes devoured the slate's contents.

"Ah, you used mechanical means to address mutation." He glared and nudged his head at Katya. "She forbade me from it."

"We were focusing on what was already working," she bit back.

He rolled his eyes and turned the slate, examining whatever was on the screen more closely. "It's crude—"

"Aleksandr," Zakhar chided.

He lifted his hand. "I was going to say I'm sure time and resources were lacking, not skill of one who performed this. This is quite excellent. Imperfect, but given time, I'm sure it would have been much improved."

"Our ship's medic," Akakios supplied. "She's with us."

"Good, good." Aleksandr's finger tapped absently against the slate's edge while his eyes scanned. He fell silent, but Katya could see the gears turning in his head. "I would like to examine this and boy in more detail, perhaps when paired ..." He shifted into a string of Moscanov, his thoughts likely spiraling quicker in his native tongue.

"Aleksandr," Zakhar pressed again.

The scientist quieted, though his narrowed gaze and puckered lower lip made him appear quite mulish about it. Katya would've almost thought the two Mramorians were Oneiroi from the silent exchange they were engaging in.

Aleksandr sighed. "It would have to be side project. I have ... other demands."

Katya smirked, noting he didn't relinquish the slate.

Akakios tightened his hold on Sotiris and glowered at Zakhar. "No strings, huh?"

Ever the savvy politician, Katya decided. He'd exposed the Oneiroi to Aleksandr, put the man's intelligence on display—a carrot. Then withdrew it. Go it alone, or come to our table and take a shortcut.

The politician didn't budge under the daggers being metaphorically cast his way. "We have achieved great deal for you. Now we must focus on war with opponent who has us outgunned." He pointed to the slate. "Surely, you have scientists who can expand on that."

"And find additional dosages," Aleksandr added. "That"—he waved to Akakios's pouch—"is tailored to him." He lifted his finger to Sotiris. "It will likely be too little for the fifteen-year-old. There is poundage to consider. Maybe variations in the mutation. A larger study pool would tell. Continual studies will be necessary, of course. To determine drug's long-term use. It may prove less effective over time."

The commander, Charis, squeezed Akakios's upper arm, where his suit had been repaired using tape. Katya could see some silent exchange happening, even through their shades. In the end, Akakios nodded.

"We'll reach out to our contacts. The councilor"—his voice dipped—"I trusted ... he's passed. Some of the other councilors are complicit, but if enough demand it, they will capitulate." His hand skimmed the pouch, his mouth forming a tight line. "It won't be easy."

Katya recalled Akakios's statement about the Oneiroi being stationed on the Fringe. A lot of space between them and home ... on Magistrate ships. She wondered what percentage of Oneiroi were currently serving aboard. A sizeable portion. Any rift with the Magistrate would be messy, perhaps even disastrous as a species.

"Change seldom is," Zakhar said. "Stay. Contact your people. Aleksandr can do more examinations in between." The man extended his hand. "Should they desire partnership, I will gladly speak with them." He swallowed. "Perhaps together we can liberate your children. Mramor knows thing or two about lost children."

Katya waited for the Oneiroi to do anything as Zakhar's hand remained suspended, waiting. The uncle's arm tightened around Sotiris, then with his free hand grasped Zakhar's. The two men shook, and Katya allowed herself to hope.

ACKNOWLEDGEMENTS

I cannot thank Amanda and Kylie enough for sticking with me through this process. Not only did they offer great insights and propel me forward, but they also served as my biggest cheerleaders whenever I hit my nadirs. Their genuine enthusiasm kept me going forward through *Descent* and continues to be a great blessing moving forward on the Heritage Lost Series.

Once again, I give a great big shout-out to my cover artist Maria Freed aka MissChibiArtist! She returns with another stellar cover. If you haven't checked out the rest of her artwork, you are missing out. Visit her at misschibiartist.com. You won't regret it!

I'm also grateful to my local writing group, The Workshop, at the Syracuse Public Library. Their support and encouragement offers a monthly pick-me-up and often gives me a creativity boost.

I also need to thank Dad and H for peddling *Heritage Lost* in local farmers markets. It is much appreciated!

Join The League

Subscribe to S.M. Wright's author newsletter to receive the latest Heritage Verse news, freebies, and more. Subscribers receive a free copy of The Promise, a Heritage Lost Series prequel novella.

Scan The QR Code

ABOUT THE AUTHOR

A lifelong resident of northern Indiana, S.M. Wright is an author of speculative fiction with the occasional jaunt into historical fiction. She has been writing since grade school and harbors fond memories of her mother taking her to Young Authors Conferences, which further encouraged her to pursue writing.

She published two works of short fiction—*Acceptance* and *A Long Way Down*—before launching her ongoing *Heritage Lost Series*. Even when writing speculative fiction, she loves working her love of history into each story.

Wright works full-time at her local library as a communications specialist and also serves as a magazine editor for a local publishing company. When not working or writing, she enjoys spending time with her clowder, geocaching, knitting, rocking to Sabaton, and reading.

Connect with her on . . .

Website: smwrightauthor.com
Email: info@smwrightauthor.com
Newsletter: http://eepurl.com/hvAsX1
Facebook: www.facebook.com/smwrightauthor/
Twitter: @smwright04
Instagram: @smwrightauthor

www.ingramcontent.com/pod-product-compliance
Lightning Source LLC
Chambersburg PA
CBHW011146190726
48288CB00010B/3202